# SHADOW MAGUS

## Journals of Natta Magus | Book 2

## Rob Steiner

Quarkfolio Books

October 2016. Published by Quarkfolio Books.

Cover illustration by Tom Edwards. Editing by David Drazul.

Sign up for my newsletter at www.robsteinerauthor.com to get a **FREE** compilation of Natta Magus short stories, along with news and previews of upcoming books.
Never miss a new release, and you can unsubscribe at any time.

*For Sarah and Amelia, always.*

# ONE

Stop me if you've heard this one: A time traveling magus from twenty-first century Detroit walks into a bar in ancient Rome—

No? Oh this is a good one.

*I* was that time traveling magus—stuck in Rome going on two years now—walking into the seediest tavern along the Tiber riverfront during the reign of Caesar Augustus looking for the scion of an equestrian family whose *paterfamilias* claimed the teenage boy had been "bewitched" into joining an acting troupe. And just so you know, prostitutes in Roman society were looked upon with one tick more respect than actors.

Told you it was a good one.

Like most Roman taverns, it was in the garden level of a rickety tenement that was ancient when the Republic was founded. I walked down five worn, brick steps, left the blue skies and bright sunshine of a fine Roman afternoon and entered the open doorway into the dark tavern.

The stench hit me first: spilled wine, stale *posca*, and human body odor. Pretty much what you'd expect from a Roman tavern. And it was so dark I might as well have been walking into the underworld. When my eyes adjusted, I saw long tables with benches, each holding a couple of lit candle stubs. Two large men almost my height sat at one table across from each other, their heads in their arms on the tables with wooden cups next to them. I couldn't tell if they were sleeping, passed out, or dead. Three plebeians sat at a table to my right taking turns rolling dice from a tin cup, alternating between cheers and groans depending on the rolls.

One of the sleeping men suddenly belched and then threw up on the stone floor next to him. I grimaced and looked away. *That* guy was still alive.

"Oy!" came a voice to my left. A man with large forearms shuffled out of a room in the back carrying two huge clay jugs with sloshing liquid and set them down behind a stone counter. I figured him to be the owner, since he wore a solid black tunica, and not the drab gray of a slave. He glowered at the nauseous drunk. "I told you to use the bucket at your feet next time, you *cac* stain!"

The drunk grumbled something and then went back to sleep.

The owner was about to say something else, but then noticed me standing in the doorway. He gave my black Wolverines baseball cap a long look, and then said, "Fancy a drink, *dominus*?"

I was about to ask for my runaway actor when I heard a burst of laughter come from a hallway in the back. The opening was covered by a thick red curtain, and sunlight peeked around the edges. The finder spell that I'd cast back at my shop to locate the actor wannabe made my feet want to walk toward the curtained doorway.

"Actually," I said, "I'm here to see the show."

"Two denarii, *dominus*."

I fetched two coins from the money pouch on my spell components belt and put them on the counter as I walked past the owner toward the curtained door. I pulled the heavy curtain aside and headed down a short corridor toward a sunlit courtyard at the end. I passed one room on the right that was filled with jugs and sacks. Another room on the left must've been the owner's residence: a woman sat in a chair next to a bed breastfeeding her infant child. She gave me a tired glare, and I felt my ears heat up. I quickly averted my eyes toward the courtyard.

The courtyard was about forty feet square with tenement balconies on all four sides of the three-story wood buildings. A small stage was set up at the far end where maybe a dozen plebeian citizens sat on stools laughing raucously at a bawdy comedy act that...well, let's just say that the Romans can't get enough of large, fake penises being used to humiliate their enemies. In this particular demonstration of quality drama, an actor playing a young Octavian was using his large penis to smack around Marc Antony and his Egyptian lover, Cleopatra, who had apparently persuaded Antony to do himself up with Eastern eye liner and clownish makeup. The actors playing Antony and Cleopatra—both men—ran around the stage trying to flee Octavian's raging manhood.

Apparently not even the thirty years since Antony's defeat at Actium was enough to diminish the humor from that bit.

My finder spell told me that "Cleopatra" was Septimius Naevius Balbus, the equestrian kid that I was looking for.

I sat on a stool in the back to watch the comedy unfold. Once Octavian finally stabbed Antony with his, um, weapon, the show took an even stranger turn. Octavian strode off the stage, proud of his victory, while Cleopatra wept over Antony's body. A troupe of musicians stationed behind the stage began a haunting tune with their horns and lyres. Then "she" began an equally haunting, yet beautiful dirge that literally gave me chills. The kid's voice went up and down in the tradition of ancient music that I'd become used to over the last two and a half years. I'm no musical genius, but to my untrained ears, he seemed to hit every note. The kid had talent and obviously loved what he did.

Which made me wonder about ratting him out to his father.

I admired many things about ancient Rome. My Praetorian friend, Gaius Aurelius Vitulus, was one. He was the epitome of ancient Rome's virtues: honor, bravery, and a righteous sense of justice. He didn't hesitate to protect the innocent, but if you crossed him, he wouldn't hesitate to kill you dead. Vitulus's wife, Claudia, was another. She knew my weird history, knew the danger I occasionally put Vitulus in during the "delicate" cases for which the Praetorians called on me—the *only* practicing magus in Rome—for help. Yet she never hesitated in opening her family's resources to me if I needed help. Even with a newborn son, she found time to send baskets of food to my shop on the Aventine Hill whenever she'd hear that business was slow for me.

But there were many things about ancient Rome that made me cringe. As a man of the twenty-first century, slavery, of course, was at the top of the list. A close second was the almost religious preoccupation with social status that was practically written into every Roman law. I grew up in Detroit, a city in the mid-western American Union, where even the poorest people had a decent shot at being successful if they worked hard and persevered. In Rome, it was also possible to rise up the ranks, though freedmen and citizens usually did it by "marrying up" to the next social rung, or distinguishing themselves in the legions, or becoming talented orators in the Forum (this, of course, only applied to the guys; the gals could only pray to Juno that daddy married them off to one of the above).

One of the things that annoyed me about the social system here, though, was that once your family *did* scratch and crawl its way to the top of the ladder, it was the height of scandal if anyone in the family wanted to descend a few rungs. Like the kid Balbus singing his heart out on stage. Balbus's father, the senior Septimius Naevius, had hired me to find Balbus and report back on the kid's location. I assumed so that the Naevius goons could drag the kid back home kicking and screaming and force him to be a good future paterfamilias. I took the job because, well, business *had* been slow lately, and while I appreciated Claudia's gift baskets, I was tired of feeling like one of her *clientela*. Vitulus and

Claudia were my Roman family, not my patrons, and I wanted to keep it that way.

But this case was bringing back memories of when I struggled to tell my parents that I wanted to study the Finder arcanum, not Energy like they had. It certainly wasn't the dire situation Balbus was in, but I had an inkling as to how he felt. My parents had just assumed that I shared their passion for developing magical batteries, routing magic via the Aether to power homes in Detroit, or just tinkering with magic-powered devices to make them more efficient. They were surprised when I told them that wasn't my thing, and I had seen the disappointment in their eyes. But they understood that my passions just didn't match theirs, so they went on to support my endeavors.

I couldn't imagine living in a place where my parents could've *forced* me to study Energy rather than Finder.

So once again, my conscience wanted to overrule my stomach.

I hadn't realized how transfixed the rest of the audience was with Balbus until he finished singing. The small crowd erupted in appreciative applause. The rest of the troupe joined Balbus on stage, all of them smiling as they bowed. I waited until the troupe had exited to the small, curtained backstage before getting up and making my way toward them.

I found the actors joined by the three hidden musicians. All six performers held a cup of wine in their hands and were drinking to a well performed show. They seemed filled with post-performance energy, laughing and joking about different parts. They still wore the garish makeup, and metal costume jewelry dangled from their ears, around their necks, and on their wrists.

When they finally noticed me standing there, I nodded to Balbus and said, "You're a good singer. I haven't heard a performance like that in years."

"My thanks, citizen," Balbus said, nodding back to me with a grin. "You can show your appreciation by telling your friends about us. We play here every evening just before sundown."

"Your father hired me to find you," I said.

Balbus froze, the grin on his face turning into a rictus and his eyes widening. His friends also stared at me with the same shocked expression.

"Look, I just wanted to let you know before your father sends..."

Balbus's eyes flickered to something behind me. He gave a quick nod.

I turned in time to see a fist the size of Mount Vesuvius heading toward my face before all went black.

# TWO

I awoke to find my jaw feeling two sizes too big, and the back of my head—where I presumably fell upon meeting the giant's fist—had a knot that sent waves of white agony through my entire body.

At first I thought I was draped over the saddle of a horse. Only natural since whatever was carrying me was big as a horse and smelled like one too. I opened my eyes just a crack and found I was actually being carried by the largest man I'd ever seen outside a mirror drama in Detroit. He had to have been seven feet tall and about four feet wide. He carried my lanky, six-foot two-inch body as if I were coil of rope. If his muscled calves were any indication of the size of his arms, I doubted I'd have the strength to squirm out of his grasp. Through my cracked eyelids, I saw sandaled feet following him, but all I could tell was that they belonged to a man. I heard more footsteps behind him and in front of me, along with the jingling of metal costume jewelry; my addled brain estimated five men, including the giant. It was dark, and the fishy sewer stench of the Tiber River hung beneath the giant's *eau de* horse.

I mostly felt angry at myself rather than fearful. Angry that I stupidly told the kid that his controlling father hired me to find him. That I thought the kid would clap and say, "Gee, thanks, mister," and we'd all share a drink to freedom. Of course he didn't want to be found. Of course he'd fight to keep doing what he loved. Of course he wouldn't trust me to keep my mouth shut.

The question was, what were the little punk and his friends going to do with me?

I played possum on the giant's back while I assessed my cell magic stores. Fortunately they hadn't knocked my Wolverines ball cap off my head, which helps me focus my magic. I would certainly need that focus, because the obvious concussion from the knot on my head made my grip on magic tenuous at best. I could barely focus my half-open eyes on the ground without seeing star bursts or seeing two grounds. Casting spells in that condition was risky to say the least. My spells might do anything from simply fizzling to backfiring on me.

But there was no way I could physically overpower Horse Man and his four companions in my condition either. I'd been practicing with Vitulus a lot over the last year, learning rudimentary gladius thrusts and parries, along with some hand-to-hand fighting, but that was more for exercise than serious combat training. Magic was my strength.

And magic was what I'd have to rely on to get out of this mess. Because if I didn't do something in the next minute, I might end up just another floater in the Tiber with his throat cut.

The group stopped, and then Horse Man let me drop to the muddy ground. I tried not to wince from the excruciating pain in my head and jaw, as even the slightest movement made them both flare.

"So who's going to do it," said a young man's voice to my left. It sounded like Balbus, but then the entire troupe was made up of young men, and the concussion had made me loopy.

There was silence to Balbus's question.

"I ain't never killed a man before," said a nervous sounding kid to my right.

"Me neither," said another.

"Well you're all a bunch of old women," snarled Balbus.

"Then you do it!" said someone next to Balbus. "He's your problem, anyway. Why do we have to do your blood work?"

"Because I'm paying for this whole troupe, Argyros, that's why!"

"We could throw him in the river," said a deep voice above me, who must've been the giant. "Let the gods decide."

"And what if the gods let him live, fool?" said Balbus. "We have to kill him so there's no chance he'll talk. If I go back to my father's house, then this troupe will have no patron. You'll all be starving in a week. So who's going to do it?"

There was silence and the shuffling of feet. The group dynamics gave my concussion-addled brain an idea on how to get out of this mess.

Balbus heaved an aggravated sigh. "Fine," he said. "I have to do everything else around here..."

I heard a dagger come out of a sheath, and I saw him kneel down next to me through my slitted eyes. When he slowly brought the knife to my throat, I struck.

I'd been working on my spellcraft a lot lately, especially spells that enabled me to cast them without components or trigger words. Lares, my shop's house spirit, was a tremendous help with that. When she wasn't constantly professing her love for me with Greek poetry, she was happy to give me her ancient knowledge and any nuggets of arcanum she got from the nearby house spirits. Between Lares and my own experimentation, I'd gotten pretty proficient at casting a few spells that used to require time wasting rituals.

Like my freeze spell.

When Balbus's knife neared my neck, I grabbed his wrist, siphoned the magical energy coursing through my body's cells, and willed Balbus to *stop*. Balbus yelped in surprise and tried to pull back from me, but I held his wrist tight for the single moment it took for my cell magic to burst from my body and into his.

Balbus's arm went slack and he dropped the knife, but he didn't freeze. It appeared that my freeze spell had only put his arm to sleep. *Damnation, my concussion warped the spell.* My idea had been to make Balbus freeze and then hope that the rest of his troupe—who didn't seem comfortable at all with violence—would be so shocked and awed by my terrible powers that they let me slip away. I know, it wasn't the greatest plan, but to be fair I *was* suffering from a concussion.

Before I could come up with another spell to throw at Balbus, the kid recovered from his surprise and punched me in my already swollen jaw with his left fist. It wasn't a hard hit—I'd received harder from Vitulus during practice—but its location couldn't have been in a worse spot. I saw stars again from the pain. It stunned me enough so that Balbus's minions had time to get over their own shock and hold me down. The big guy put all his weight on my shoulders with his meaty hands, while the rest jumped on my legs.

Balbus scrambled to pick up his dagger with his left hand and then stood above me. He tried moving his right arm, but all he could get it to do was sway uselessly with his shoulder.

"What did you do to me?" he cried, glancing from his sleeping arm to me with wide eyes. He raised his dagger above me and snarled, "Well you're going to die screaming for that."

No spells came to my mind that I could use to stop Balbus. Even if they had, I doubted my stunned brain could've mustered the concentration to focus my cell magic to light a spark globe. All I could think of at that moment was that I'd survived time travel, daemon attacks, and the darkest magus to come around since the Dark Wars in my home timeline...and I was about to be done in by a rich kid actor with a stage prop dagger.

So much for being the "chosen one".

I figured the cold blast of wind that suddenly blew over my body was the feeling of imminent death. But then the screams around me dispelled that theory.

Balbus's dagger hand began to sizzle and smoke, along with the hooped rings in his ears and the bracelets along his wrists. He screamed in agony as the dagger in his hand glowed as white as metal freshly pulled from a smithy's hearth. He dropped the dagger, but his blackened hand continued to sizzle. He desperately tried pulling the metal jewelry off his body, which were also glowing and smoking wherever they touched his skin.

Then I was free as the actors holding me down let go. They, too, screamed and grasped at their own glowing white jewelry that was burning holes into their bodies.

This turn of events stunned me about as much as the actors, but I'd been in enough scrapes during my two and a half years in ancient Rome to know when to take advantage of lucky break. I jumped to my feet, trying to ignore the vertigo from my knotted head, and ran. It didn't matter in which direction, so long as it was away from the shrieking actors behind me.

But when I got a couple dozen paces away, I skidded to a stop. Rome during the reign of Augustus had no street lanterns or torches, which made it terribly treacherous to be out at night. Not only could you get lost in Rome's maze-like alleys, but you never knew when you'd run into cutthroats lurking in the dark. Or actors.

That's why the magical aura coming from an alley to my right caught my eye. Auras are only emitted by magi casting spells and can only be seen by other magi. The aura on this magus was the color of desert sand with undulating blue streamers. It was dark, and I couldn't make out the magus's physical features, but he was clearly directing the spell that was causing all sorts of hell to my would-be assassins.

Then magus noticed me noticing him. He ceased his spell, whipped around, and ran back up the alley in which he'd been hiding.

Damnation. So I *wasn't* the only practicing magus in ancient Rome.

Double damnation. That magus just saved my life.

# THREE

For a brief, heart stopping moment, I thought that William Pingree Ford had somehow returned from the dead, but I just as quickly dismissed that idea. Every magus had a unique aura, and William's aura had been misty green with black and silver sparks. The sandy, blue streaming aura of this magus was definitely not William's.

I knew that other magi existed in the ancient world, but they were so rare that I'd only found one other during my two and a half years here. Magic wouldn't truly become a universal talent among humans until the Great Awakening three hundred years from now. Any magus who had the talent now would have wild talent; it would be unfocused and would usually end up killing the inexperienced magus more often than not.

Not like the magus who just saved my life. This magus was disciplined, knew how to focus, and could cast spells with accuracy.

And the cold blast I'd felt before the spell fired off was one of the markers of soul magic. I hadn't felt the wave of nausea that also accompanied it, but that could just mean that I was used to it after using soul magic in a desperate situation last year. Which only disturbed me more since I didn't *want* to get used to it.

Sad fact about soul magic: It's easy and powerful, but only Dark magi are crazy enough to use it because of its dangerous and corrupting nature. Whereas cell magi like me fueled our magic from the natural energy stored in our body's cells, Dark magi fueled their magic by either consuming their own souls or the souls of other people or animals. If they consumed their *own* souls, they would eventually lose all empathy, go mad, and kill themselves with their magic (and typically everyone around them). If they consumed the souls of *other* living beings, the guilt would ravage their minds and bodies to the point of madness.

I'd seen William Pingree Ford do the latter, and it was not pretty. It took a series of devastating wars in the early twentieth century to defeat the Dark magi and establish the atmospheric Aether, which made all soul magic fizzle.

So a Dark magus, whom I didn't know, just saved my life.

Or did he? Maybe his spell was meant for me as well as the murderous actors? It was only by Fortuna's grace that I wasn't wearing metal that night, or the spell would've had me howling with pain right along with the actors. How could he have known that? If I chased after him in my weakened condition, I'd likely have no way of defending against his magic. If I first didn't trip and crack my skull on Rome's dark streets, that is.

All of this flashed through my addled mind in seconds. I knew the wise course of action was to stagger back to my shop and heal myself. Instead, I chose to stagger after the mysterious Dark magus down a pitch-black alley.

It's a wonder I'd survived so long in Rome.

I turned my black Wolverines baseball cap around and took some fleece from my components belt. I waved the fleece over my head three times and murmured the bastardized Dutch incantation, *"Stilte voor mij."*

My cell magic rose like waves of summer heat from my skin and then ballooned outward. It was another one of my re-crafted spells, which had the affect of silencing everything within a ten-foot diameter sphere centered on me, yet I could still hear sounds from outside the sphere. At least the magus wouldn't hear me following him in the dark alley. I plunged into the darkness as fast as my pained body would allow.

Unfortunately the magus had stopped casting, so I could no longer find his aura amidst the darkness. All I could go on was the sound of running feet slowly getting farther away from me.

But then after running twenty paces, I saw the magus's aura flare about fifty paces ahead and then rise into the air. At first I thought he'd taken flight, but the aura only went up about ten feet before coming down again and disappearing. I was too far away to detect whether he'd used cell or soul magic, but it didn't really matter at that point.

This magus had skills.

I arrived at the point where the magus had leaped only to find the alley blocked by a seven-foot high gate with metal bars. It had a padlock on the door that I could barely see, but there was enough ambient starlight for me to focus a Rigney channeling on the lock. I focused my cell magic into my right index finger, touched the padlock, and it popped open. I opened the gate without a sound—which was in my silence sphere—and sped after the magus.

I rounded a corner to arrive at a stone dock at the Tiber's edge. Triremes and barges were lashed to the piers around me, and stacks of barrels and grain sacks lined the dock in front of silos and warehouses.

In the meager light coming from the opposite riverbank, I saw the magus skid to a stop at the dock's edge. His back was to me, but I could see that he was around five feet tall, had short black hair, wore a black tunica, and had a black scarf wrapped loosely around his neck and over his shoulders. I was about to yell out to him, but he dove off the dock, with a splash coming a moment later.

I rushed over to the edge and saw the waves rippling outward from his leap into the dark river water. It was a good ten feet down to the water from the dock. I waited for about a minute, looking for any sign of him surfacing, but he didn't come up. I scanned the docked boats nearby, thinking maybe he had come up silently near one of them, but I saw no movement, nor heard any splashing or gasps for air.

I glanced back to where the magus had dove in and noticed something floating among the ripples: his black scarf. I quickly searched the docks and found a long, hooked pole that sailors used to gather docking ropes leaning on a silo. I rushed over, took the pole, and then went back to the edge of the dock, where I used it to retrieve the soaked black scarf.

Still holding the scarf and pole, I scanned the waters around the dock one last time, searching for any sign of the magus or sounds of splashing. I saw and heard nothing.

This magus's simple existence implied that the history I knew was wrong—that disciplined magi *did* exist before the Great Awakening. Or it could mean that my arrival in ancient Rome, and my mucking around with my magic, had changed this timeline to enable disciplined magic use. The gods or the Fates or the Unknowable Will or whatever had decided last year that I had to live out the rest of my days in ancient Rome if humanity were to survive beyond the twenty-first century. I didn't know why it had to be me or what exactly I was supposed to do here, but I had a feeling that this magus was part of that answer.

I held up his dripping black scarf. I hoped he hadn't drowned trying to get away from me because I really wanted those answers.

# FOUR

Like I mentioned before, I tried to avoid Rome's labyrinthine alleys at night due to their complete lack of street lighting (and lurking cutthroats). If it was a moonless or cloudy night, you could find yourself stepping off the Capitoline's Tarpeian Rock when you meant to go home to the lower Suburba.

But wise ole me had planned for this possibility by setting finder beacons on my shop. All I had to do was reach out with a bit of my cell magic, and my feet would take me home.

The "reaching out with my cell magic" bit was the challenging part since my head screamed and vertigo threatened to knock me down at any moment. It took me an hour of stumbling and getting lost twice, despite my beacons, before I finally got to my garden level shop on the Aventine Hill.

The alley I lived on was about as gentrified middle-class as you could get in ancient Rome. On the right side of my shop lived a Canaanite scribe who wrote letters for the mostly illiterate Roman citizenry, and on the left was a lawyer who specialized in contracts and suing the bejesus out of anyone you aimed him at. It was late, so both shops were dark, as were the living quarters above them.

I descended the five, grooved concrete steps to my wooden door—I had engraved "NATTA MAGUS" on it just a few weeks ago—and opened the latch. I had plenty of enchantments on the door which made locks redundant; if anyone tried to enter while I was gone, they would simply find themselves walking in a different direction without remembering why they'd turned away.

I might have to update those enchantments now that another magus was running around Rome.

As soon as I opened the door, I was assaulted with the verbal equivalent of kisses and hugs.

"My honey fig, my sweet, I was so worried," cried a disembodied female voice. I glanced at the six-inch statue of a cherubic young woman that represented Lares, my shop's house spirit. It glowed with an ethereal white mist that only a magus could see. A small offering bowl sat in front of the statue with a bit of the Pompeian sweet wine she loved.

"I told you I might be late, Lares," I said.

My shop was dark despite Lares' glowing statue, so I lit the lamp in a small alcove on the left side of the door with a spark from my cell magicked finger. The oil-soaked wick brightened and then held a steady flame. I picked it up and brought it to the plank table a few paces from the door. Besides the table and Lares' shrine, the front portion of my shop was about ten feet long and six feet wide and pretty sparse. Secondhand curtains, which I'd bought off of Vitulus, separated the waiting room from my actual workshop/living quarters in the back. The curtains had gaudy geometric shapes stitched into them, but they were trendy by Roman standards and served to keep my working area private.

Before I moved in, this shop was once some kind of boutique, but my magical experiments and components were quickly masking the underlying flowery scents from the former occupants. I had hung an air freshener—an enchanted magical ring made of wood and feathers—above the door, which helped a little, but was far better at sucking in the street stench that tried to make its way into my shop. I probably had the best smelling home in Rome.

I sat down at the table in my waiting area and spread the still wet scarf across the pockmarked surface.

"Well it's been an eternity for me since I last beheld your presence, oh love of my lives," Lares said. "You forget how time does not flow for me as it does for you. I can watch the Republic rise and fall, and it would feel like the blink of one of your exquisite green eyes. But awaiting your return each time you leave feels—"

"Okay, Lares, I appreciate it. You missed me. Now I need to concentrate on this scarf for a minute."

I was a bit harsher with Lares than I'd meant to be, and I chalked it up to the painful lump on my head and my swollen jaw. Which apparently she did as well.

"My sweet, you are not your normal, kind self. Are you injured?" Her plump statue turned a fiery red with orange sparks leaping from it. "By all the gods, I will find this person who hurt you and make him suffer! Who was it? Where does he live?"

"Lares!" I said. But I took a deep breath, and then calmed myself before saying, "I appreciate your concern as always, but I really need to concentrate right now. There's another magus in Rome and this is his scarf. I need to find him."

She was quiet for several moments, and I cringed thinking that I may have hurt her feelings. The colors swirling around her statue switched from angry red to a metallic glow that felt like steely resolve to me.

"How can I help, my purring kitten?"

I relaxed. I always tried to keep in mind that she was a house spirit who was used to inhabiting a home where nobody could hear her. As a magus, I was tuned into the spirit world where it intersected with the mundane world. Very few house spirits were that lucky. Having someone live in her house who could hear *and* speak to her was the highlight of her millennium, so she tended to get way too overexcited around me. But after almost two years of living in this shop, she was slowly figuring out when it was appropriate to shower me with pet names or recite Greek love poems, and when it was time to get to work.

"I'm going to try a finder spell on this scarf first. Once I'm done, I'm sure I'll have some questions for you. Deal?"

"My spirit trembles in anticipation, love." And she wasn't being sarcastic.

I turned my ball cap around, put my palms on the black scarf, and gathered my cell magic. It's icy heat rose to the surface of my skin and created goose flesh over my entire body. I released the magic into the scarf by saying, *"Vinden magus."*

At this point in the spell, faces, images, emotions, and locations that were important to the most recent owner of the item would explode before my mind's eye. I was once a doctoral candidate in the Finder Arcanum back at Wayne State University in Detroit, so I had lots of experience with this. That experience would help me sift through the images and catalog them in my brain for future reference. Then the spell would give me a bearing and general distance to the person for whom I was looking.

But in this scarf's case, I felt nothing. Even if the last owner was dead, I should've felt at least a dim imprint of him. Hell, even if he just bought the scarf minutes before, I should've picked up a faint impression of the scarf's maker.

But I got zip, zero, nothing. It was like casting a finder spell on a tree.

Perhaps it was the pain in my jaw and my probable concussion that were interfering with my magic. It was possible, but if that were the case, I wouldn't have felt my cell magic rise to my skin at all.

*"Vinden magus,"* I tried again.

Once again my cell magic jumped to the surface of my skin, and I directed it into the scarf. And once again, I got nothing.

I leaned back, folded my arms over my chest, and stared at the scarf. This shouldn't have been possible. At some point, human hands had touched this scarf, and I should've been able to detect their imprints. It's not like this was the twenty-first century, where mechanical golems in a factory pumped hundreds of these things out per day. This was ancient Rome, where *everything* was made by human hands.

So why couldn't I find one pair on this scarf?

"Lares," I said.

"My sweet?" she said immediately, like a cat pouncing on a toy. Her statue pulsed various shades of anticipatory green.

"Do you know of any contemporary spells that enable a magus to cleanse imprints from artificial items?"

"Heart of my soul, you know the magic of this time is rare and nothing compared to your fair Detroit. There are shaman in the upper Nile region who can mask their auras from other shaman or supernatural creatures. But a spell such as you describe, where an artificial item is cleansed of *all* human imprints, is not known among the honored dead."

I wanted to ask her how big of a pool the "honored dead" was—Just Roman dead? All humans from the beginning of time?—but I knew I'd just end up more frustrated. She was ready, willing, and able to give me anything she could...except information about the afterlife or the "honored dead." I didn't know if it was some celestial edict by the Unknowable Will that metaphysically prevented her from answering those basic questions, but she would either go silent or change the subject to love poems if I tried asking her anything about it.

"Then there has to be some kind of new magic at work here," I mumbled, staring at the scarf. "It's impressive, really, to cleanse something so completely. We couldn't even do that in the twenty-first century."

"Perhaps, pudding cake, the bad men who attacked you hit you so hard that you imagined this magus? The memories of the honored dead are full of incidents where injuries to the head have created illusions."

"No," I said, shaking my head and then wincing from the pain in it. "*Someone* cast the spell that saved me. And an illusion doesn't explain why this scarf has not one human imprint."

Lares was silent a moment, and then said, "Oh, I have the answer, Natta Magus!"

"What? What is it?" She sounded so excited that I couldn't help getting excited in return.

"Perhaps your magus was not a human at all. Perhaps he's a supernatural construct...perhaps a daemon?"

I thought about this. If the magus was a supernatural being or a daemon, that would explain why his clothing did not contain a human imprint. Hell, if he was a daemon, his aura might have scoured his clothing of *all* human imprints from the makers on.

But then I'd never heard of daemons casting spells. They were usually strong and scary, and had magical abilities like ultra-fast healing, but they couldn't *wield* magic like I'd seen the magus do.

Still it was as good a theory as any. I'd start there.

"Not bad, Lares," I said. Her statue blushed red.

However, I looked back down at the scarf with a frown. "The only problem, though, is that I don't know how to detect a daemon imprint."

I drummed my fingers on the table. Damnation, it was hard to concentrate with this swollen jaw and fuzzy head.

"Perhaps, love of my lives, you could call on your friend Paetus."

I fought through the haze of my pain and fatigue, and then said, "Lares, you're a genius."

Her statue glowed pink. "Oh Natta Magus, nothing gives me more pleasure than to give you pleasure."

Verginius Paetus was a *flamen* of Jupiter who lived in the Suburba and the last of the Verginii, a once proud patrician gens. He was also a bit, um, eccentric even by the standards of a time traveling magus from twenty-first century Detroit. He performed his sacrifices to Jupiter during the local block festivals and weddings as a way to pay the bills, but his true passion was in daemon lore. He had the largest collection of scrolls, books, and tablets on daemons of anyone I knew in Rome. I met him over six months ago on a daemon case that Vitulus brought to me: a trickster daemon that looked like a puppy-sized spider with wings was devouring the togas of Roman senators. Paetus had been conducting his own secret investigation at the scene and helped me banish it back to the daemon realm.

I had paid him back by helping him set up a magical "safe spot" in his home, in case the often dangerous daemonology books he read and experimented with accidentally conjured up something nasty. All he had to do was rush to the circular spot on the floor that I'd drawn, utter an arcane word, and a donut-shaped barrier would drop down around him and within his home. He'd be safe in the hole, and the daemon would be contained within the donut so that it couldn't escape. Of course I had to explain to him what a donut was, and then he argued why it wasn't called a "do-ring" since the object was more like a ring than a nut. Fun guy.

But I may have burned a bridge with him after telling Vitulus all about him. I didn't stop to think that a flamen of Jupiter might have trouble getting religious gigs if it became known he also dabbled in daemon lore. The new morality laws that Caesar Augustus was pushing through the Senate also included laws that made it difficult for "practitioners of magic unsanctioned by the gods" to either get jobs or climb the social ladder. The laws applied to me, too, but fortunately I didn't care about climbing the Roman social ladder.

Paetus cared about jobs and the social ladder, though, especially as the last son of the Verginii. My telling a Praetorian Guardsman all about him (despite the fact that Vitulus swore never to tell anyone) made him pretty mad. I wasn't sure if he'd be all too happy to help me after that.

I was positive, though, that he would *not* help me if I showed up outside his door at midnight. And I was *definitely* positive that I'd kill myself stumbling through the dark alleys of Rome in my condition. I needed to heal myself before I went anywhere else, which meant I'd need a good night's sleep after expending the copious magical energy a self-healing required.

I got up from the table, pushed through the curtain, and entered my workshop and sleeping area. I sat on the cot and said, "I need to heal myself a little and then I'm going to sleep for eight hours. Can you wake me up then?"

"I shall watch you sleep and count the hours until you awaken, my plum cake."

I smiled, and, not for the first time, wondered when Lares would run out of desserts to call me.

# FIVE

I was dreaming that I stood on the floor the Senate House giving an important speech. Just outside the Curia doors, barbarian drums beat as Germanic warriors mustered for battle. But instead of senators, I was talking to a room full of cats wearing little white togas. And the cats kept jumping on each other, licking themselves, sleeping, and generally doing what cats do best—ignore their humans. I tried telling the "senators" that what I had to say was important, that they had to listen to me because the fate of Rome was at stake. They continued to ignore me. I had no idea what to do or how to get them to listen. The drums outside grew louder and more ferocious until the barred wooden doors to the Senate House burst open—

"Natta Magus, are you there?"

I awoke with my eyes closed and crusty, and it took great effort for me to open them. It was still dark in my shop. I remembered that I'd asked Lares to wake me in eight hours, which should have been well past dawn. I was about to grumpily remind her of this when I heard the voice again.

"Natta Magus, it's important!" It was accompanied by a hard knocking.

The voice was coming from my shop door and belonged to my friend Vitulus. Normally this would've had me jumping off my cot to find out what forced him to call at, well, whatever time it was. But I'd just healed myself, and the toll on a magus's body from a self-healing requires a good night's sleep to shake off. By the drunken way I felt, I'd probably only been asleep for a few hours.

I groaned and slowly sat up. The pain in my head and jaw were mostly gone, though a dull throbbing came from both locations. I didn't want to heal myself completely, for that would've put me out for at least a day. Trying to get out of bed after a partial self-healing was bad enough.

"Love of my lives," Lares said in huffing, insulted tones, "your friend Vitulus has absolutely no manners. To come pounding on your door at such a late hour? Why he's a—"

"Pain in the ass, I know," I said while slowly getting to my feet.

"Natta Magus!" Vitulus yelled while pounding on the door again.

"I'm coming," I yelled back. "And this had better be good..."

I shuffled through the curtain and went to my shop door. I siphoned a bit of cell magic to unlock the enchantments and then opened the door ready to growl at Vitulus.

But I stopped when I saw Vitulus and five hard-eyed Praetorians behind him, each with a torch in one hand and the other on their gladius hilts. And they all looked really serious.

*Ah, damnation, this is it,* I thought. Ever since Salvius Aper had sent Vitulus to me for my first job with the Praetorian Guard, I'd wondered if there would ever come a time when Roman authorities either: (a) forced me to come work for them exclusively or (b) saw me as too big a threat to Rome and simply killed me.

When it came to option A, I had already earned Salvius Aper's ire several months ago by refusing to magically assassinate a Germanic chieftain who was giving the Romans headaches, never mind that I continually turned down his offers of patronage. If I had sworn a *clientela* oath to him, I would've had no choice. But I didn't want to be tied down like that, even though Aper would've made me a wealthy man with his patronage.

As for option B...well, that's another reason why I tried to stay out of entangling patron-client relationships. In the snake pit of Roman politics, you never know when your patron will fall out of favor and be executed for treason, along with his most powerful clients.

So by the looks in the eyes of the men standing outside my door, they seemed ready to do one or the other. Even my friend Vitulus.

That woke me up.

I felt my cell magic rise to my skin in preparation to defend myself. I wasn't sure what I could do if they all rushed me at once, but I knew I'd make them pay—

"I apologize for the late hour, my friend," Vitulus said, "but something terrible has happened and we need your help right now."

I glanced between Vitulus and his Praetorian posse. I hadn't seen Vitulus this worked up in...well, never.

"I sense that I have no choice here," I said.

Vitulus gave me a grim stare, but said nothing.

"Can you tell me what this is about?"

"I'll tell you on the way," he said. Then his face seemed to shift from the hard-eyed Praetorian to the face of the friend whom I'd laughed with over dinner at his home. "Please, Natta Magus. Time is short. I give you my word, on my honor, that no one means you any harm."

I'd expressed my worries to Vitulus many times over options A and B, and he seemed to sense now that was the reason for my hesitation. Well, if I couldn't trust my best friend, then I was doomed anyway. I just hoped this wasn't one of those jobs that took days or weeks. I really wanted to find that mystery magus.

"Fine," I said. "Can I get my hat and belt?"

Vitulus nodded. "Quickly, though."

"My gladius?"

He got a pained expression. "No weapons."

That shot my paranoia meter up to eleven. Vitulus saw me tense and quickly added, "You won't need it. My word."

I grunted, then hurried back into my shop, grabbed my Wolverines ball cap from my cot, and picked up my belt filled with little pouches of my go-to spell components.

"I have a terrible feeling about this, love," Lares said, her statue taking on a black-gray tint. "Nothing good ever comes from a summons in the middle of the night."

"Don't I know it," I mumbled as I fastened my components belt around my waist. "Lock the enchantments behind me, will you? And keep thinking about our mystery magus. We'll talk about him when I get back."

A shade of pink flickered across Lares' statue, but the black-gray fear still dominated. "Be careful, Natta Magus. Your safety and happiness are all that sustain me."

I grinned despite my fatigue. It was kind of nice having someone waiting for me when I got home, even if it was the disembodied spirit of a long dead perfume merchant.

Vitulus and his men were already standing in the street, giving me impatient glares as I shut the door to my shop and climbed the concrete steps to the street level.

"Come," Vitulus said, and began to walk briskly up the narrow street. The other Praetorians surrounded me, waiting for me to follow Vitulus, so I hurried after my friend.

"So what in damnation is so important for you to wake me up in the middle of the night?" I asked him. "I do have a life outside these Praetorian jobs, you know. In fact I was on a very important finder job earlier this evening. I got into a fight."

Vitulus gave me a raised eyebrow. "Really? How did it turn out?"

"Well...actually they knocked me out, and I didn't do much fighting."

Vitulus returned his gaze to the dark streets before him, already bored with my lack of martial prowess. I guess I should've thought about that story before trying to impress him. Damned fatigue!

"Anyway," I said, "where are we going?"

"Salvius Aper's home."

I'd been to Aper's home many times, since that's where I was usually summoned when the Praetorians had a "delicate" situation that required my magical skills to deal with. He lived in a nice, walled home on the Palatine Hill, and we were definitely heading in that direction, so I allowed myself to relax a bit. But only a bit. The Praetorians beside me looked ready to behead anyone who stepped into their torchlight.

"What's this about?" I asked.

Vitulus's lips thinned, and he seemed to struggle with answering my question. "Salvius Aper will explain it all when we get there."

"Wait a second," I said, stopping in my tracks. The Praetorians almost ran into me, but they stopped as well, each one giving me the glare of a lifetime. Vitulus strode a few steps on, but then stopped and gave me the same glare as his men. *They must teach that in Praetorian school,* I thought. "You said you'd explain everything to me on the way there. Did you lie to me? And what's with the honor guard? You know I would've come with you if you'd shown up at my door alone. You're making me damned nervous, Vitulus."

Vitulus glanced once at the Praetorians surrounding me, an annoyed flicker crossing his face that I didn't think was directed at me. When he looked at me again, he said, "This is a matter of state security. I am under strict orders to bring you to Salvius Aper's home where you will be fully appraised of the situation. I cannot talk about it openly on the streets, Natta Magus. It is that important." Then he sighed. "And I swear to you again, on my honor as your friend, that you are in no danger from us."

I'd known Vitulus for over two years, and I knew he was a man who did not make oaths or promises lightly. If I had truly been in danger, he would not have made that oath.

But then again, he'd said "no danger from us." Did that mean he and his posse weren't going to harm me, but that others might? Back in the twenty-first century, we had to swear many Oaths with a capital "O" which had to be precisely worded or the swearer might find himself promising to do something he never intended; or, alternately, the swearer could leave a loophole that enabled him to get out around the Oath.

Damnation, but fatigue, a near-death experience, and a surprise magus made fertile ground for my paranoia.

"Natta Magus, please," Vitulus said, glancing again at the Praetorians around me. I felt like I was surrounded by marble statues for all the emotion they displayed. "We have our orders."

I exhaled slowly and began walking again toward him. "I trust you, and I trust your word." *Let him chew on that*, I thought. If I really was in danger by someone else and he knew it, those words would haunt him for the rest of his life.

But he visibly relaxed, gave the other Praetorians one more glance, and then we strode onward into the darkness, side by side and in silence.

# SIX

We arrived at Aper's home about a half hour later. Like most patrician homes on the Palatine, it was surrounded by stucco walls and had a large wooden gate at the front that was the only obvious entrance. I knew about his secret exit into the Cloaca Maxima, which Vitulus and I had the pleasure of taking last year. But Aper seemed to trust that I wouldn't blab its existence to everyone since he never asked me to swear an oath on it.

I tried not to think that he never made me swear an oath because he planned on killing me soon.

Vitulus knocked on the wooden door with his foot, and it only took a few moments for the barred porthole to open in the center of the door. It was Aper himself looking through the porthole, not his head slave Nicia, which told me that this situation was serious indeed. He inspected us all with his steady brown eyes, closed the porthole, and then I heard the bars lift from the gate on the other side. One side of the gate swung outward to allow us all to enter.

As soon as we all entered his courtyard, Aper shut the gates and barred them with the help of Nicia, who'd been standing on the other side of the gate.

"I apologize for the abrupt summoning, Natta Magus," Aper said, slamming the bar into place. He turned to me, and for the first time ever, I saw genuine nervousness in his eyes. Normally during the magical crises in which I helped him, he was either very focused and determined, or he maintained an aloof detachment that I'd come to associate with all Romans in command positions. I knew it had to be an act, but it did have a calming effect on the commanded to know their leader had everything under control.

First Vitulus, and now Aper. What could possibly scare the two bravest men I knew?

"What is going on?" I asked with far less respect than I normally used with Aper. "Vitulus hasn't told me a thing, and sending five goons with him to retrieve me sure didn't make me feel like coming."

Aper nodded impatiently. "I know, but things are a bit out of my control at the moment. If it were my choice..." He eyed the other Praetorians with the same annoyance that I'd seen Vitulus give them earlier. They all continued to stare at me as if none of them had heard what Aper said. He clicked his teeth once, and then said, "Come with me."

As if I had a choice, I followed Aper and tried to project his same aloof confidence. These Praetorians must've known my reputation, and I wanted my countenance to show them it was deserved. So I casually followed Aper—the Praetorians surrounding me—through his small courtyard, past a stable, and through the front door of his home.

Lamps and braziers illuminated the interior. Wax and marble busts of Aper's ancestors occupied the alcoves and tables near the front door. Beyond the entryway was an atrium about twenty feet square. Marble planters contained plants and flowers of various colors, while the center was occupied by a circular *impluvium* pool that gathered rainwater from the open ceiling above it. Cushioned couches were tastefully arranged around the atrium, and colorful frescoes of ancient battles and heroes adorned all the walls. Curtains were draped over doorways that led to other rooms in the home.

A toga-clad man in his mid-thirties paced the atrium in front of the impluvium pool. He was clean-shaven, and his hair was short and black with the bangs combed down in the "caesar" style of the day. When we entered, he stopped pacing and then stared at me as if I were a rat from the Cloaca Maxima.

"This is him?" he said to Aper while studying my face.

"Yes," Aper said, "this is Natta Magus."

The man's eyes narrowed, and he stared at me a couple more moments. "Perform a trick, then, magus. Prove to me you can do what your reputation says you can do."

"Trick," I said. "So what, juggling, acrobatics? I might need to stretch first, though."

The man scowled, Aper sighed, and Vitulus leaned forward. "This is serious, Natta," he said quietly. "Please."

"Well then somebody *caccing* tell me what's going on," I growled to them all. "You pull me out of bed in the middle of the night, march me through the streets of Rome with a goon squad, and now I'm being interrogated by Mr. Patrician Asshole from central casting. *What. Am. I. Doing. Here?*"

Fatigue from my healing and general lack of sleep, plus the lingering soreness in my head and jaw, plus my fear over what these guys wanted with me, equaled one grumpy magus.

The toga man scowled at me through my outburst and maintained his scowl for several moments as I awaited his response. "First," he said slowly, "the trick."

Their stubbornness wore me down. I exhaled sharply, held my right hand out, and siphoned a bit of cell magic into it. A spark globe the size of an apple popped into existence above my hand, illuminating the room in an ethereal white light. "I'm not juggling it," I said.

The man's eyes widened to my satisfaction as he stared at the spark globe. He swallowed once, and then gave me a quick nod. I let the spark globe wink out.

The man licked his lips. "I am Capito, chief adviser to Caesar Augustus. You will address him as either Augustus or Princeps, *not* Octavian or, if you value your head, Octavius. When you see him, do not bow; he is the First Citizen of the Republic, not a king. And if you even think of casting a spell while talking to him, you will have five swords in your heart before you can flutter your hands. Is that clear, magus?"

Now it was my turn to gape. "Hold on. I'm meeting *the* Caesar Augustus?"

Capito arched an eyebrow. "Do you understand my instructions?"

I swallowed the huge lump that had suddenly materialized in my throat and nodded absently.

"Good. Wait here." Capito turned on his heel and strode out of the atrium and through a curtained doorway behind him.

Vitulus leaned toward me and spoke quietly again, "I told you this was serious."

# SEVEN

*I'm about to meet Caesar Augustus. Cac on a sandal.*

My first instinct was to run. I was a huge Romanophile back home, before my former friend and mentor kidnapped me and dumped me in ancient Rome, so I knew that Augustus wasn't a psychotic tyrant like Nero or Caligula. But I also knew he wasn't someone you wanted to cross either. He could be quite ruthless to those who tried to thwart his will. He may have been far more subtle about it than his descendants—since he went out of his way to pretend the Republic was still a republic, and he was not its absolute ruler—but his enemies did tend to disappear or suffer tragic "accidents."

What if, so to speak, he tried to make me an offer I couldn't refuse?

"You could've told me," I whispered to Vitulus next to me. "A hint, a wink, something."

"Orders," he mumbled back.

I looked at him. "So what happens the next time your orders conflict with our friendship?"

He got a pained expression and opened and closed his mouth several times to say something. Fortunately for him, Caesar Augustus entered the atrium from the curtained room in which Capito had disappeared, and Vitulus snapped to attention.

Augustus didn't have the godlike aura that history tended to paint around him. He was in his sixties, a bit shorter than the average Roman male, and had short brown-gray hair that tended toward the curly side. He looked a little thin for someone in his tax bracket, but I attributed that to the multiple illnesses history said he suffered throughout his life. Dark circles surrounded his eyes, indicating either fatigue or one of those aforementioned illnesses.

But the eyes themselves were bright, clear, and zeroed in on me. They lingered on my black Wolverines ball cap.

His wife, Livia, accompanied him, looking every bit the proper Roman matron. Her long, black-gray hair was arranged in braids upon her head, and she wore a tastefully elegant sky-blue stola dress. Bracelets adorned her wrists and several necklaces hung around her neck, but none of the jewelry was gaudy or elaborate. She gave me the same evaluating look as her husband; she was Augustus's chief "unofficial" adviser, and they would be discussing me in length later on.

Augustus stopped on the other side of the impluvium pool and stared at me with those clear eyes, while Capito whispered something into his ear. Livia glided around the pool with a warm smile and then actually *bowed* her head to me.

"Thank you for coming so abruptly," she said with a motherly tone. "I cannot imagine how startling it must have been to be awoken at this hour."

Well that threw me. All I could do was return her bow and reply lamely, "Um. No problem, my lady."

"Whom do you serve?" Augustus asked abruptly. I looked back at him as he studied me. Capito stood a pace away with his hands clasped behind his back and studied me the same way as Augustus.

*Oh, boy. Trick question, trick question*, my mind screamed. Did I tell him what he wanted to hear, that I "served" Rome? If I did that, I'd acknowledge that he had the power to order me around. If I told him I *don't* serve Rome, then he could I say that I have no rights as a citizen and could have me thrown out of the Republic or executed.

But if he was going to do the latter, he would've done it already. He brought me here to meet me and to ask for my help. So I gambled and went with the honest answer.

"I serve no one, Princeps." And then I tried not to wince.

But the right side of his mouth curled up in amusement. "We all serve someone or something. I serve the gods and the Roman state. Salvius Aper serves the state and me. Young Vitulus next to you serves Salvius Aper." His gaze became even more penetrating, if that was possible. "Whom do *you* serve?"

It appeared that he wouldn't let me leave this room without giving him an answer, so I tried to think up something. For the last eleven months, ever since my final showdown with my old friend William Ford, I'd been struggling with the fact that the gods, the Fates, the Unknowable Will, or something had decreed that *I* had to live out the rest of my days in ancient Rome if humanity were to survive past the twenty-first century. I still had no idea why it had to be me, and I tried not to get a "chosen one" complex over it. In fact, since last year, nothing world-changing had happened to put proof to the notion that I was integral to humanity's survival. I'd taken regular finder jobs from regular Roman citizens, along with a few daemon banishments for Vitulus and the Praetorians. Nothing too taxing.

So why me?

Until I found that celestial answer, all I could do was keep on doing what I'd been doing: using my talents to help people.

I gave Augustus a steady look—as steady as I could—and said, "I serve...a future where humanity lives forever."

Capito gave a derisive snort, but Augustus nodded slowly, considering my answer. "I suppose I, too, serve such a future," Augustus said. "A future where all humanity prospers under a lawful and moral ethos. Rome is the beacon for such a future, and I am her caretaker." His gaze took on a faraway look as he seemed to think on the ways he had guided Rome and what he had yet to do. I suddenly wished that my life's purpose was as clear to me as his was to him.

"With respect, Princeps," I said, "why am I here?"

Augustus blinked, turned back to me, and said, "Yes, to the point. I've heard that about you."

His eyes shifted to Livia, who now stood between Augustus and me on one side of the impluvium pool. She gave him a barely imperceptible nod, and he turned back to me. He put his hands behind his back, and his posture seemed to shift from curiosity and wariness to that of the Princeps addressing a subordinate.

"As I said, I serve the gods and the state," Augustus explained, "but I'm also a practical man. I know of what you did in Germania Superior last year. I also know where you come from."

I shot Vitulus a quick glance, and he shook his head once. Aper then. Hell, I never asked Aper to keep my origins quiet. But I figured I was his secret little weapon that he pulled out whenever keeping the peace in Rome got to be too, um, strange. Because of Augustus's morality laws, I never thought he'd tell Augustus that he was flouting those laws by using me, a non-religiously sanctioned magus.

"And I would be a fool," Augustus continued, "not to use you when the situation requires it."

*Here we go,* I thought. I opened my mouth to tell him in the most respectful way possible that there was no way in all the Hells that I'd be a weapon for Rome.

But he said, "Earlier today, valuable property of the Roman state was stolen. I need your help to find and retrieve it."

# EIGHT

I'd been ready to tell him where to stick it if he asked me to assassinate some Persian or Germanic king, that his request for my help in finding something didn't register at first. Once it did, I blurted out, "So this is just a finder job?"

Augustus raised an eyebrow. "Oh this is far more than 'just a job', young man. Before I explain, I must have your solemn vow that you will not repeat what I'm about to tell you to anyone outside this room. For if this news were to get out, there could be chaos in the streets and across the Republic. Do I have your vow?"

Even though I wasn't swearing an Oath that would bind me and my aura to whatever I promised, I still hated making promises before I knew the details of what I was promising. He wasn't asking me to do something, though, just not to repeat what I heard here. I supposed that was harmless enough...

"Sure, my lips are sealed," I said. When Augustus stared at me as if I was speaking a foreign language, I translated, "You have my vow."

He nodded once. "Romans, as you are aware by now, agree on very little. The things they do agree on, however, are so existential to Roman identity that if anything were to happen to one of them, the Roman people would likely panic. As I said, there would be chaos in the streets, and every enemy of Rome might see that chaos as a signal that Rome was weak and open for plundering. I do not want that to happen, thus the secrecy tonight."

Augustus stared into the impluvium pool as if seeing foreign invasions in the water's reflection.

"What was stolen, Princeps?" I prodded.

He looked back up at me with the same faraway gaze. "You are not from Rome or even this time, so I do not know the depth of your knowledge. Have you heard of the Sibylline Books?"

I thought back on my early Roman history and shrugged, "A little. I think they were prophecies given to a Roman king by a witch before the founding of the Republic."

Augustus smiled once, and then said, "Not prophecies. More like instructions on how to navigate catastrophes that should befall Rome. During the reign of the last Roman king, Tarquinius Superbus, a priestess of Apollo from Cumae came to Rome with these instructions written in nine books and offered them to the king for a fairly exorbitant price. When Tarquinius refused, the priestess burned three of the books and then offered him the remaining six for the same high price. Once again, he refused, so she burned three more and then offered him the final three for the same price. Tarquinius finally relented and bought the three books for the full original price, whereupon the priestess disappeared and was never seen again. The three books, however, were kept under tight control by the Senate on the Capitoline Hill for hundreds of years until I moved them to the Temple of Apollo Palatinus eight years ago."

Bits and pieces of what Augustus told me were coming back as he explained the origin of the Sibylline Books. There wasn't much evidence in the history that I knew to indicate they were actual magical artifacts. I did remember that the books were consulted during Hannibal's invasion of Italy and after he crushed the Roman Legions at the Battle of Cannae. Supposedly the priests of the day consulted the books and learned that in order to avert Rome's destruction, they needed to bury alive two Greeks and two Gauls in the Forum. That wasn't a magic ritual that I'd ever heard of; not even soul magic rituals would call for such a thing, since they mostly thrived on *seeing* the actual moment of death.

I'd need a study date with Lares to get the real story on the books.

"Since then," Augustus continued, "the books have been consulted on everything that threatens Rome, from earthquakes to plagues. Their instructions on placating the gods were followed, and though Rome may have endured temporary suffering, she always prevailed. Every Roman child has been taught from birth that the books are Rome's divine shield against calamity. That if something should happen to the books, an unimaginable doom would befall Rome. So if the citizenry ever learned of they were stolen..."

I nodded. "Mass hysteria, dogs and cats living together. Got it. So when did you notice they were gone?"

Augustus glanced at Capito, who stepped forward. He still looked like he'd rather eat a live eel than speak to me, but he followed his boss's nonverbal order. "I was in the Temple of Apollo Palatinus in the late afternoon speaking with the chief flamen about the Ludi Apollinares, which begin tomorrow."

"The what?" I asked.

He frowned at my interruption, but said, "The holiday in honor of Apollo. It is an annual festival with games and sacrifices. It is a large event that must be coordinated between the religious obligations and the accompanying entertainment. Is that clarity enough for you?"

"Yes," I said, "proceed." He scowled again at my orders, and I knew I had annoyed him, but I couldn't help myself. I really hate officious people. Vitulus shifted next to me, which was his subtle way of telling me to be careful. I supposed I shouldn't have poked at the Princeps' chief adviser who likely had the power of life and death over me, so I quickly added, "With respect, sir."

It didn't mollify him, but he continued, "As I was speaking with the flamen in the outer portico, we heard a loud crash from the temple's inner *cella*. We both raced inside to find..." Capito took a deep breath, as if stealing himself to remember a memory that he'd rather forget. "We saw a man dressed in a black tunica, with black hair and a beard where both sides reached down to his clean-shaven chin. The statue of Apollo had been cast aside, and he was reaching into the pedestal where the Sibylline Books were stored. He picked out the three scrolls and then looked at us as if seeing us for the first time. He smiled and said, 'Tell Natta Magus that I await his move.' And then he just disappeared through a...window in the air."

"Whoa, wait a second," I said, holding up a hand. "Another *magus* stole the Sibylline Books?"

Capito gave me a contemptuous look. "If that is what you call yourselves..."

I glanced at Vitulus, who simply stared at his sandaled feet. *You knew*, I thought to him. *You knew, and you all wondered if I was in league with this guy.* It all made sense now: the "honor guard," the silence, the way Capito had studied my face when I first entered. They had to make sure it wasn't *me* who stole the books.

And did this make *two* other magi in Rome, or was it the same mystery magus who rescued me earlier? Whoever he/she/they were, they obviously knew me.

"Damnation, Rome is getting crowded," I muttered.

Augustus took a step toward me and held my gaze with his clear, haunted eyes. "Will you help us find the books?"

A deep, deep weariness seemed to suck the energy out of me, which had nothing to do with my post-healing fatigue. After Germania Superior last year, I'd sworn to myself that I'd never again take another "national security" job. I was going to stick to the personal finder jobs. I liked those jobs. I like helping individuals: The money keeps me fed, and they're relatively low-stress (the case of Naevius Balbus, notwithstanding). They kept me somewhat under the notice of Rome's major players. Salvius Aper was my only patrician client, but I was his "black ops" guy—he only called on me when things got too weird and they needed quiet, unofficial help. It was about as good of a life as I could ask for, considering my circumstances.

Or at least it used to be. Now I had Caesar *caccing* Augustus, who knew he was in over his head, asking me to find the stolen Sibylline Books. Retrieving them from another magus, no less. And if he was right about Roman super-stitions—and judging by my experiences among them, he was spot on—then how could I live with myself if the city of Rome descended into paranoia-fu-eled anarchy when the people learned that the books were gone? How many innocent people would be hurt or killed in panicked, religious riots, all because I refused to help and chose to return to my little magus shop on the Aventine (if I was even allowed to go back, at this point)?

It was that same damned feeling of responsibility and guilt that drove me to sacrifice my twenty-first century life to stay in Rome in the first place.

*So much for the quiet life.*

"I'll help," I said to Augustus. You didn't have to be a magus to feel the tension release in the room with my answer. "Now about my fee—"

Capito exploded. "You dare try to profit from this crime?"

"Look, I'm a *professional* magus. Taking on a job like this means I have put other paying jobs on the back burner. If I do that, I'm losing money, and I certainly don't have huge tracts of ancestral farmland to supplement my income."

All that was true, but I mostly asked for the fee to establish that this was *busi-ness* and not an honor-bound *patron/client* job. If I did this for free, it would imply that a patron/client relationship existed between me and Augustus, and thus make it much harder for me to say no to future requests. In a business relationship, however, it was much easier for me to say no to the crass and undignified—to patricians, at least—exchange of money for services. It was the same tactic I used with Aper, so I sure as hell wasn't going to let Augustus off the hook.

Capito was about to have a stroke again, but Augustus raised a calming hand to him and then said to me, "You will be compensated for your time, Natta Magus. I will double your normal rates so that you may concentrate solely on this task."

"Thank you, Princeps." Then I grinned at the red-faced Capito. "Take me to the scene of the crime."

# NINE

With my services secured, Augustus gave me a detailed description of what the Sibylline Books looked like: They were actually three papyrus scrolls about two feet long, each with the seal of the Roman Republic (the letters "SPQR" surrounded by laurels) in the top right corner of each unfurled scroll. Afterward, Augustus and Livia left Aper's place and went back to their own home about six blocks away. The "honor guard" that accompanied me went with them, which confirmed to me that, while Aper was the official prefect of the Praetorian Guard, those Praetorians were *Augustus's* men.

Dawn was approaching, which made Capito worry about curious citizens seeing me walk into the Temple of Apollo Palatinus. I guess my lanky six-foot, two-inch height was a bit distinctive compared to the five-foot, six-inch Roman male. Not to mention that I can honestly say there was nothing like my black Wolverines ball cap in the ancient world. So Capito wanted me to take my cap off and wear a flamen's white, purple-banded toga. I said yes to the toga, but hell no to removing my cap. Under normal circumstances it would've been a polite no, but with one or two mystery magi running around Rome, I felt the "hell no" was more appropriate. I'd need all the magical *umph* I could get if I ran into them, and removing my cap would be like tying one arm behind my back just before a battle. Capito argued, I refused, and to break the impasse, the annoyed Aper suggested I ride in his wife's covered palanquin. This satisfied everyone, so off we went. Vitulus marched beside the palanquin while Aper stayed behind to attend to day-to-day Praetorian business.

I'd never ridden in a palanquin before, as they were mostly used by patrician women or men who were too old, sickly, or fat to walk the streets of Rome. I gotta say it was pretty nice despite having to sit cross-legged all the way, since my long legs would've dangled over the sides. The silk cushions were cozy.

Although the fact that four burly slaves were forced to carry me dulled my enthusiasm considerably.

We arrived at the Temple of Apollo Palatinus just as the sun was breaking over the eastern horizon. I pulled back the curtains on the palanquin enough to peek at the temple. It was connected to Augustus's expanded and renovated private home on the Palatine Hill by a columned corridor. The temple itself was pretty much what you'd expect of a Roman temple: a rectangular building with columned porticoes surrounding the interior, windowless rooms. The columns were all painted yellow, and reliefs were painted upon all the walls depicting various mythological scenes. Black marble statues of women carrying jugs upon their shoulders stood between each column. One thing I never realized back in the twenty-first century was just how colorful all the Roman temples originally were since all we had left were the weathered ruins. The Temple of Apollo Palatinus was a fine example of Roman artistry lost to my time.

The slaves had to carry my palanquin up the steps, and I felt guilty once again as I heard them grunting with the effort. I'd never met Aper's wife, but I had seen her and knew she was about half my weight. *Sorry guys.* Once we arrived within the shadows of the temple's columned porticoes, the slaves lowered the palanquin, and I stepped out with as much dignity as I could muster.

Vitulus gave me a half-smile and said, "Have a nice ride?"

"It was a blast."

We stood in front of the open, ivory doors to the temple's interior rooms. Capito stood outside the entrance along with Augustus's five Praetorians.

"In here," Capito said, then turned on his heel without waiting to see if I followed. I glanced at Vitulus, who shrugged. We followed Capito inside.

The room was dark except for the lit oil braziers in each corner. It was about fifty paces long and twenty wide, with wood benches arranged before an altar at the front, and more marble statues of minor gods and goddesses standing sentinel along the walls. Frescoes and bas-reliefs adorned each wall, and I felt like I should be whispering inside such a beautifully decorated place of worship. The faint smell of incense from previous rituals still hung in the air, slightly masking the ever present miasma of Rome.

The marble altar at the front covered, in dark red blood stains from animal sacrifices, brought back the reality of most Roman religious rituals.

Capito stood at the front of the temple behind the altar and beside a large pedestal. As I approached, I noticed the pedestal had recently been the home of the ten-foot tall marble statue of Apollo that lay to my right, mostly smashed to pieces. The pedestal itself was rough from where the statue was once attached, and a rectangular hole about two feet square was carved into the center. It was empty. I noticed a metal door with a lock along the side of the pedestal which priests would normally open to retrieve the Sibylline Books. It was still locked. The magus could've easily ripped that little door off its hinges, but he instead decided to toss the one-ton Apollo around like a toy. He was showing off. He was making a statement.

"What did this guy look like again?" I asked, inspecting the statue and pedestal without touching anything.

"As I said earlier," Capito explained with a suffering sigh, "he had short dark hair, with a half-beard down to a clean-shaven chin. He looked Greek or Syrian. He wore a black tunica. There was some kind of head dress or scarf wrapped around his neck—"

"A scarf?" I said, my eyes snapping to Capito. "About this long, this wide."

"I could not discern its dimensions, for he was wearing it."

If the magus had been here at dusk, that left plenty of time for him to come down to the Aventine to rescue me and then lose his scarf in the Tiber. I still couldn't rule out that my magus and the book thief were different people.

I turned my Wolverines ball cap around, siphoned a bit of cell magic, blinked once, and then studied the broken statue of Apollo. Normally a magus leaves his or her magical imprint, or "fingerprints," behind when they cast a spell with the power that it obviously took to wreck the statue. But as with the scarf, I saw nothing but broken marble. Not even the pedestal or the surrounding area had so much as a twinkle of aura. Damnation, this magus wanted me to know he existed, but didn't want to give me any clues as to his identity. What the hell was he playing at?

"Is everything exactly the way you found it?" I asked Capito. "You didn't move anything or take anything away after the magus left?"

Capito raised an eyebrow, reached into a fold of his toga, and took out a small black item. "I did find this on one of the benches behind you."

I tried not to groan too loudly, or scream for that matter. "And why are you just telling me this now?"

Capito frowned and drew his chin up at my tone. "Because I didn't deem it important. People leave items behind all the time in the benches. It's just a *fascinus* token."

Ancient Romans had a fascination with flying penises. I kid you not. You could find the winged fascinus on necklaces, bracelets, sculptures, and painted on walls in almost every home. I'd even seen fascinus lamps being sold in the Forum where the flames came out of the, um, business end. From what

I gathered, Romans used them as wards against evil and for protecting crops from disease.

But what Capito held in his hand was not a fascinus. It looked like a black pawn from the game of chess.

A game that wouldn't be invented for another thousand years.

# TEN

At this point, I felt that if I got one more world-upending surprise today, my head would explode into fairy dust.

A chess piece? What in damnation was a chess piece doing in ancient Rome? It was obviously a chess pawn, and a well crafted one at that: It was about two inches tall, had a smooth spherical head at the top, a halo supporting the head, and a swooped column down to a round base.

Just who was this mystery magus? As I well knew, time travel was possible, so the only explanation I could come up with was that he came from the future. How else could he have a chess piece?

Then another disturbing explanation came to mind: Did the magus once know William Ford? The man who wrought supernatural havoc across the Republic before I killed him last year? The odds of finding another human being with magical talent before the Great Awakening were sky high to say the least. Possible, but I had a better chance at becoming Augustus's heir. Never mind the fact that soul magi like William trusted each other about as much as they trusted cell magi. They rarely ever worked together or took apprentices because they were always more focused on their own personal power and/or insane goals.

But even more disturbing: What if I *hadn't* killed William? What if he'd somehow survived the cave-in beneath the Aventicum garrison? I had no idea what sort of soul magic he'd learned and acquired before our final meeting. What if he'd learned something that faked his own death?

I had trouble swallowing the huge lump that had formed in my throat.

"Where," I said slowly, staring at the chess piece, "did you find that?"

"I told you, it was on the—"

"Which bench?"

Capito pointed at a bench in the second row near the edge of the aisle. He went over and set the pawn down on the edge of the bench.

"I found it just like that," he said. He frowned at me, but it wasn't his usual holier-than-thou frown. It was a genuine worry frown. He must've seen the worry in my face and heard it in my voice. "Why, is this important?"

"I'll tell you in a minute," I said. Then I took a deep breath, released it, and siphoned my cell magic for a First Scan on the pawn.

First Scan is more about getting a general sense of the magics enchanting an object or area: Was it cell magic? Was it soul magic? Did it have wards? There were six levels of Scans, and I'd only learned the first three before William dumped me in Rome.

I walked around the bench twice, keeping my gaze on the pawn. My Scan spell enabled me to see the pawn's magical aura: It was alight with an orange glow, and green sparks flitted about it like jumping aphids. I breathed a minor sigh of relief: It wasn't William's aura. If he had cast the enchantment on the pawn, it would've been a green glow with black sparks. I'd never seen this aura before.

Beneath the aura, I got a sense of...stickiness. As if I'd put my hand in half-dried glue. I could even smell it. And then I felt like I'd touched the glue on a door frame while walking through it to...

A roiling black fog where nothing good could ever exist.

The thing about First Scan is that it only gives you vague images on the nature of the enchanted object. The nature of this enchantment certainly wasn't cell magic. Which meant it was Dark. Someone had used soul magic to create it.

And the fact that Capito had touched it was not a good thing for Capito.

"Well?" he said.

I didn't want to scare him when I didn't know exactly whether he should be scared. "I need to perform a more in-depth scanning spell. It requires a simple ritual. Is that okay here?"

Capito looked uncomfortable—regarding the pawn or my request, I couldn't tell—but finally nodded. "Just do not mention this to anyone," he said sourly, glancing toward the temple entry. "The flamens of Apollo would have us burned for using magic here."

Vitulus, who had stood quietly behind me this whole time, said to Capito, "I will have my father slaughter another pig in your name during our Ludi Apollinares feast tomorrow."

Capito gave Vitulus a grateful, yet nervous nod.

With Capito's religious conscience appeased, I reached into my components belt and pulled out a vial of quartz powder. I poured a small circle around the pawn, then siphoned my cell magic and tapped the circle with my right finger. The quartz flared with an ethereal white light, and then a small dome with the same light appeared over the chess piece.

I had learned from my experiences last year that you never do a Second Scan unless you build a containment between you and the object you're scanning. If my poking at the object set off a ward, then the ward's magic would be contained within the circle.

Safety first.

With the pawn contained, I began Second Scan. I walked around the bench twice in the opposite direction as First Scan and then stopped. I gathered my courage and cell magic, then touched the pawn with my right finger.

It was definitely not cell magic. It was suffocating, like I imagined how it would feel to be buried alive. I wanted to run out of the temple and into the open air so that I could breathe again. *Just when I thought soul magic couldn't make me feel worse...*

I had to focus my will on simply continuing the Scan without pulling my finger away from the smothered feelings the pawn sent through me. But I pushed through it and delved into the functionality of the wards covering the pawn. At first I was confused, because the wards didn't make sense to me, but then I realized what they did. It was like reading words that were jumbled at first glance, but then realizing the letters were spelled backwards. Once I figured out the pattern, I could easily read the spell.

It was a kind of reverse finder spell. A rather ingenious one, despite the fact it was cast with soul magic. Rather than the item telling me where its owner was located, the item imprinted itself on the person who touched it to find out where *their* home was located, or at least the place where that person thought of as home. The impressions currently imprinted on the pawn showed me a vineyard on rolling hills, surrounding a red-tiled stucco villa complex behind tall brick walls. Slaves picked grapes or tended to the vines while goats, pigs, and cattle milled about the enclosed pastures near the walled complex. I also saw children, two young boys who looked like twins and one girl who looked about ten years old, running about the fields with nanny slaves chasing after them and a well dressed Roman woman watching the scene with amusement as she sat beneath the shade of an umbrella pine just outside the walls. It looked like a scene right out of a Roman patrician's ideal life.

It was Capito's home, and now the magus knew where to find it.

But what disturbed me even more was the gate spell that was also enchanted onto the pawn. Again, it was ingenious because it combined a *reizen* spell—which transported the caster to a place where he'd already been—with the reverse finder. In other words, a magus could use the memories obtained from the reverse finder to gate to the home imprinted on the pawn.

I pulled out of the Second Scan too quickly, which made me woozy and forced me to plop down onto the bench next to the pawn.

"Natta?" Vitulus asked beside me.

"I'm fine," I said, taking several deep breaths to clear my head.

I looked up at Capito, who also stared at me. I saw concern on his face, but I knew his concern was whatever curse the pawn may have laid upon him. Even for an officious schmuck like Capito, I really hated to tell him what kind of trouble his family was in.

"Where is your home?" I asked him.

He blinked. "I live in the Princeps' residence. Why?"

"No, I mean your home. Where is the place you consider *home*?"

"My family home is in Pompeii. Why?"

"Do you own a vineyard? Do you have twin boys and an older girl about ten—"

"Yes, yes! Why are you asking these things, magus?" He was growing angrier and more frightened by the moment.

"This item is not a harmless token," I said, "but an enchanted piece from a game. When you touched it, it imprinted your family home's location onto it. Another magus can use that imprint to travel there."

He stared at me several moments, trying to process what I was saying. He then shook his head and asked, "Why would—? What does this magus want with *my* family?"

"I don't know, but I don't think it's anything good."

He bared his teeth in a frustrated growl. "Then I will have men sent there to protect them. It will take three days of hard riding, but they should arrive before this—"

"They won't get there in time," I said, shaking my head. "He can travel there *instantly*. With magic."

His face paled. His lips moved but he didn't speak. I really did feel sorry for the man. "What can I do?" he whispered.

I looked back down at the pawn and thought, *Well I know what the magus wants us to do*. He put the gate spell on the pawn for a reason. He wanted me to go to Capito's vineyard. This was a trap, and the magus knew it was one that I'd walk into voluntarily. I didn't think he wanted to kill me. Judging by the asphyxiating power of the soul magic on the piece, he could've killed me easily by waiting for me at this temple. No, he was playing a game of chess with me for some reason. And he was using Capito's family as pawns.

"We can use the gate spell on this pawn to go to your home," I said. "But it's likely a trap."

"I don't care," Capito growled. "I must protect my family. Do what you have to do to get me back to my family, magus."

I nodded, and then looked at Vitulus. "Ready for another *reizen* spell?"

He drew his worn, pearl-handled gladius from the sheath at his belt and said, "Always."

# ELEVEN

I smudged the powder circle surrounding the pawn to break the containment, then I ordered Vitulus, Capito, and the five Praetorian Guardsmen that Capito wanted to bring with him to stand next to the pawn.

I looked at them all and said, "This is going to feel strange, and you may have some disorientation as soon as we arrive."

"It will pass quickly, though," Vitulus assured them. He'd been on the receiving end of a *reizen* spell last year. "Once you arrive, close your eyes a moment and then open them. It helped me."

For the first time since they arrived at my door in the middle of the night, every one of the stoic Praetorians looked nervous. None of them wore fearful expressions, but they shuffled their feet, and their hands tightened on the hilts of the swords at their sides. They were trained to face mundane human threats. Given all the supernatural threats over the last couple of years, I wondered if Vitulus and Aper would need to begin a crack training regimen for everyone. Or maybe a dedicated "supernatural" squad. I'd mention it later.

If we survived this.

Capito, however, wasn't as good at hiding his fear as the Praetorians, which was understandable considering his family was involved. "Fine, we understand. Cast your spell, magus."

One of the Praetorians had given him an extra gladius, which he gripped with the insecurity of someone not used to holding one. I hoped he wouldn't hurt any of us with it.

"Okay, then," I said, "but before we go, I'm going to cast a minor shield spell on all of us that should keep us safe from any magical booby traps on the other side."

They all stared at me a moment before Vitulus asked the question they were all thinking. "How is a 'booby-trap' different than an ordinary trap?"

"I just meant trap. Sorry. Anyway, I'm going to throw some dust on you now."

With my ball cap already turned around, I took the pouch from my belt that was filled with a mixture of iron, quartz, and talc dust, poured some into my hand, and then threw it above the heads of everyone while saying in my bastardized Dutch, "*Shild, shild, shild.*"

The dust sparkled as my words and cell magic activated it. Most of the men blinked as the dust settled around them. One of the Praetorians sneezed. A part of me cringed at using so much of the expensive dust, but better to use it and not need it than risk getting fried by an inferno spell when we popped into Capito's vineyard.

"That'll give us a few minutes of protection," I said, tying the pouch back to my belt, "so we need to go now. Hang on, everyone."

The mystery magus made it easy for me. All I had to do was siphon some of my cell magic into the pawn to activate the *reizen* spell. I stepped up to the pawn, drew the magic from my body's cells, and then channeled it into my right index finger. I tapped the pawn's head and said, "*Reizen.*"

I'd only used the *reizen* spell once before, and the way this spell fired off was very similar. A blue light flared before my eyes, and I felt a powerful tugging at the base of my spine toward the pawn as if it were pulling me into it. There was a tremendous sense of tunnel vision as I flew toward the pawn...then the pawn pushed me backward as fast as it had pulled me in.

And then I stood in a sunlit courtyard. The earthy smells of a farm—tilled soil, hay, animals—made me feel like I'd stepped into another world after the miasmic stenches of downtown Rome. My fellow Romans had come through the *reizen* spell all right, though Capito and a few of the Praetorians staggered a bit as they regained their equilibrium. Vitulus, who stood next to me, was already scanning the courtyard with wide eyes as if he'd just walked into the next room rather than magically traveled 150 miles in an instant. The pawn stood upright on the courtyard's dirt and straw.

No magical booby traps had fired off, so that was a good thing.

"Decima!" Capito yelled out, and then he rushed toward the main entrance into the home.

"Capito, wait!" I cried. But he either didn't hear me over his own yelling or didn't care, and he disappeared into the house. The five Praetorians hurried in after Capito. Vitulus and I exchanged annoyed glances and then followed the party inside.

I cast a spark globe as soon as we entered the dark atrium and ordered it to hang near the ceiling in the center of the room. The interior of Capito's country home looked like almost every other Roman home I'd seen. Or would have if it hadn't been trashed. Statues, pottery, and furniture were broken and strewn around the atrium. Flowers and plants had been trampled on the tiled floor and floated in the impluvium pool in the center of the room.

I noticed small pools of blood the further I went into the atrium. One of the Praetorians ahead of me grunted, and said grimly, "There's a body here."

I hurried over and then had to look away. The glimpse I did get was the upper torso of a man who'd been torn in half. His right hand still clutched a gladius, while his left arm appeared to have been chewed off.

Vitulus studied the body with cold assessment, and I tried my best to look at something—anything—else. He then looked at me and asked, "Daemon?"

"Probably. Though there are Dark spells that could—"

"Decima!" Capito continued to yell from the other side of the house as he ran from room to room.

"Damnation, he's going to kill himself and the rest of us," I said.

The Praetorian who'd found the torso said, "Habitus, Fronto, and Cotta are with him."

"No offense to your men, but I doubt they'll do much against whatever did that," I said pointing at the body without looking at it.

I pulled the spark globe that I'd sent to the ceiling and directed it in front of me as I hurried toward where Capito was yelling. Vitulus and the other two Praetorians followed. No sooner did I reach the hallway through which Capito had disappeared when I heard new voices, screams, and crying. I sprinted toward the sounds, around one corner, and then stopped.

Capito was holding his wife and three children, who all clung to him crying with fear and relief. Three other people stood behind them, a young man and two women, who I assumed were among the estate's slaves. They also cried tears of relief. All three held a gladius at their sides.

I stopped just in front of them and scanned the dark hallway and rooms for any signs of danger. I figured I'd let them have their moment of reunion before giving them the harsh truth that we weren't safe yet. The house seemed to be crawling with soul magic; it was an indistinct feeling, like catching something scurrying out of the corner of your eye, but never finding that something when you look in that direction. It was giving me the creeps, and I wanted to get out of here as soon as possible.

"How are you here?" Decima cried, hugging Capito. "You weren't supposed to come home until the fall, and we received no messages about your travel."

"It's a...complicated story," Capito replied. "What happened here?"

I could see Decima's shoulders visibly shudder in the soft light of my spark globe. Her long, black hair hung down her back in frayed braids, and her red eyes furtively looked up and down the hallway. In her terror, she had not noticed the spark globe floating nearby, but her three children stared at it with wide, curious eyes.

"Are those things still out there?" she asked in a shaky whisper.

"What things?" Capito asked. "We didn't see any *things*. Gods, woman, tell me what happened!"

After scanning the hallway to ensure no *things* would jump out at her, she said, "A man arrived in the early evening. He told us to hide in the house and lock our doors for the rest of the day. Canto told him to leave, but he only smiled. It was a wicked smile. Then he pointed to one of the goats and it...changed. Right before our eyes. It screamed and cried during the change. It grew long claws, limbs like a person, scales, terrible teeth."

*Corruptions*, I thought, as Decima took several deep breaths to calm herself. Technically they weren't daemons, because they weren't conjured wholesale from the daemon realm. They were corrupted living things, but they were just as nasty and dangerous as daemons, as the torso in the atrium could attest. The good news was that they could be killed with mundane weapons like swords, and I could use my cell magic to end the corruption which would unfortunately kill them in the process. The bad news was that they were likely lurking around the house, not to mention the Dark magus who created them. That itchy, creepy feeling intensified.

"We all ran into the house, and Canto barred the door," Decima continued. "We could hear more animal screams outside. And then all was quiet for a few hours. When Canto unbarred the door to go investigate..." Her voice broke as she said, "It must've been waiting by the door. It got Canto. We ran here and barricaded the door. We could hear them scratching at the door and pacing back and forth. Their claws clicking on the tiles. It was maddening. We've been here all night."

During Decima's story, I noticed the Praetorians repositioning themselves on either side of us, staring into the darkness in their battle stances. Vitulus still stood by my side, but he too scanned the darkness while Decima spoke.

"My lady," I said as gently as I could, "what did the man look like?" I already suspected the answer, but I had to be sure.

"Black hair. A strange half-beard. He wore a dark gray tunica."

I exchanged glances with Capito, who nodded.

"Did he also wear a black scarf or head dress?" I asked.

She blinked several times, trying to think through the haze of fear that was gripping her, and then nodded. "I believe so. Do you know this man? Why did he come here? Why did he do this to us?"

Her voice was taking on a panicked edge that told me she was about to lose what little control she had left. I looked at Capito and said, "Sir, why don't you stay with your family. We'll check the rest of the house. You should be fine as long as you keep this door locked."

"Can you kill them?" he asked.

I glanced at Vitulus, who gave me a grim nod. I gave Capito what I hoped was a confident grin. "Yeah. We've done this before."

# TWELVE

With Capito, his family, and the remaining slaves locked away in their safe room, I turned to the five other Praetorians in the hallway. I didn't need to tell Vitulus what we had to do, because like I mentioned to Capito, we'd done this kind of thing before. So I needed to give the boys a primer in Magical Battles 101. I knew their names were Habitus, Fronto, Vibius, Scribeo, and Cotta, but I had no idea who was who. All five had the same dark hair and steely eyes of Roman veterans who'd seen plenty of fights, so it was easy to consider them one mass of legionary muscle. Besides, I had this thing about learning the names of people who were likely to get killed soon. I tried not to.

"Okay, these things are called 'corruptions'," I explained, "and I do know magic that can kill them, but I need to get close enough to touch them. It'll be up to you guys to keep them off me while I cast my spells. Corruptions can be killed by weapons, but it might take more hacking then with a normal animal. They are fast, they are strong, and they love to jump out of the shadows when you least expect it. So open the eyes on the back of your heads."

All five narrowed their eyes at me, and then one by one, glanced at Vitulus. He said, "Square the magus. I'll take point."

They all nodded as if that cleared everything up. They formed a protective box around me with Vitulus at the front. "That's basically what *I* said," I muttered, and then moved forward as Vitulus and my Praetorian box headed back toward the atrium.

I directed my spark globe to shine the way ahead of our party. When we got to the atrium, I motioned Vitulus toward the torn body of Canto where we stopped. I took several deep breaths and tried to put on my dispassionate academe's mask, and then I stooped next to the bloody, gory mess that used to be a human being. I took a dried rose petal from my component belt, wadded into a little ball, and then rubbed the ball in a gaping hole in the man's left shoulder from which his arm had been chewed off. The wound would contain a bit of the corruption's saliva, which I would use to locate the monster. Then I took the little ball of bloody rose petal, grimaced, and put into one of my nostrils.

I siphoned some cell magic—noticing that my reserves were getting very low—into the rose petal and said in my bastardized Dutch, "*Spoor.*"

The scent from the rose was not exactly pleasant while soaked in blood, but it was like a meadow in spring compared to the scent of corruptions now filling my nostrils. Take the most vile portions of the Cloaca Maxima beneath the public latrines and cross them with the alleys behind the butcher shops after slaughter day, and you'd have maybe fifty percent of the stench now filling my nostrils. I'd been prepared for the awful, awful smell, so I only gagged once without vomiting.

Once I regained a measure of control, I blinked my eyes once and looked around the atrium. Daylight came down through the atrium's open ceiling, but I didn't need the sun or my spark globe to see the glowing black paw, talon, and hoof prints covering the atrium's tile floors. The prints would only show for me if the creatures still existed, so while I was satisfied that my spell worked, the growing knot of fear in my chest worried about the numbers of corruptions that we were dealing with.

"What do you see?" Vitulus asked, his eyes still scanning the shadows around us.

"Judging by the prints around us, I'd say at least five corruptions."

"Where are they now?"

I saw trails go off into the kitchen area, toward the hallway where Capito and his family were holed up, and out the front door. The things managed to get into everything. I took a vial from my belt, uncorked it, and poured a bit of the oily mixture onto my right palm. I put away the vial and rubbed the mixture all over my hands as if I were washing them.

"They're everywhere," I said, once my hands were good and oily. "Pick your poison." When he gave me an annoyed look, I said, "Let's try the kitchen first."

He nodded and stepped forward slowly toward the kitchen entrance, his gladius raised. I could see up ahead of him that a small fire still burned in the hearth, which cast Vitulus's back in a dark—

A mass of screeching white feathers dropped from the ceiling onto Vitulus's back. The corruption looked like it had once been a chicken, but turned into something with taloned hands at the ends of its wings. Its feet looked more like a monkey's fingers, but with sharp claws. It dug those claws into Vitulus's back, he screamed, and the corruption used its elongated beak to peck at his shoulders.

My five Praetorian bodyguards were frozen in that moment of shock that grips all people when they encounter something supernatural for the first time. I really couldn't fault them for it because even the bravest person in the world gets flummoxed at *something*.

So I shoved two of them out of the way, placed my oily hands on the thrashing, corrupted chicken's back, and yelled, *"Schoon!"*

The corruption stopped attacking Vitulus. It immediately began to shrivel, and I could feel its cracking bones and writhing organs in my hands. It issued one last high-pitched cluck and then was still.

But that wasn't even the nasty part. I'd drawn the corruption energy out of the chicken, but that energy had to go somewhere. Before I could disperse it into the magical ether, I could feel it inside me. It was soul magic, taken forcefully from another life, and it made the stench of my *spoor* spell seem like that spring time meadow. That act of violation turns the beautiful force of life into something wretched and ugly. It was vile; it was nauseating.

And, oh, so tempting to keep. For it was also power that I could store in my own body and use for later. I wouldn't need spell components or even to say an arcane word. I would just will the soul magic forth, and it would do whatever I wanted. Of course, it would also corrupt my soul to the point where I'd no longer be capable of love or empathy or even qualify for a peaceful afterlife. But, hey, that was years down the road. I'd have time to mend my evil ways, atone for anything I might have done. I'd do it later. Right now, this power was something I could use to wipe out all the corruptions in this estate, rescue the innocent people trapped here. Maybe find that mystery magus and force him, screaming if necessary, to tell me who he was and what he was up to...

Fortunately I'd been tempted with soul magic before and I'd learned to recognize those same thoughts and feelings. But even with that recognition, the temptation was so *strong*.

Without thinking too much on it, I released the corrupted soul magic into the ether. It fled from my body, and I felt like I'd just stepped out of a bath after a week of shoveling manure.

By this time, the five Praetorians had charged into the kitchen and set up a protective perimeter Vitulus and me. My friend was on his knees, cursing through clenched teeth as he held the open, bloody wounds that the corruption had torn. I inspected his wounds, and in my terribly non-medical opinion, they didn't look life-threatening. Looked painful as hell, though.

"I don't have the reserves to heal you right now," I said. "Will you be okay?"

He cursed again before saying, "Yes." Then he stood up with a grunt, brought his sword up again, and scanned the kitchen. It had small rectangular windows near the ceiling through which the light of dawn was gradually increasing. "Love to jump out of shadows, eh?"

"Told you."

He grunted again and then returned to his point position. We continued on.

My *spoor* spell showed me where the corruptions had been, but it wasn't doing much to tell me where they were. We searched all over the house for the creatures, cautiously searching every room and closet besides Capito's locked room, before I pronounced the home free of corruptions. Besides, the sun was up, which greatly reduced the number of shadows in which the creatures could hide. It's not like the sun hurt them—they could certainly run around in broad daylight—but they just preferred to hunt in the dark. The open atrium and the small rectangular windows in each room were flooding the home with light and banishing the shadows.

So where would creatures that loved darkness hide out until sundown?

I directed our party to the courtyard where, sure enough, the *spoor* trail led to the cellar entry beneath a separate building on the other side of the courtyard straight ahead. Judging by the wooden wine barrels nearby, I figured this was where they stored their wine while it fermented. The heavy doors to the cellar looked to have been torn off their hinges, and lay on either side of the entrance. I could see a stone ramp descending into darkness. The cellar was about as inviting as a torture chamber.

But it was our first lucky break. I saw *spoor* trails all over the courtyard, some of them coming from the animal barn to my right. I didn't think there were any corruptions in there because the barn had a lot of windows and looked too well lit from the sun now. No, they were all in that cellar, waiting until night. All bunched up in one place.

Capito would not be happy with what I was about to do to his wine cellar.

# THIRTEEN

"They're in there," I told the party, pointing toward the wine cellar. Vitulus, still bleeding from his neck and back and wincing, frowned at the cellar opening. I knew exactly what he was thinking, so I said, "We're not going in. We just have to keep them from coming out."

He gave me a curious glance, and I told him my idea. He simply shrugged—as he was now beyond doubting my magical talents—while the five Praetorian seemed dubious. They'd come around. I told one of them—Fronto, I believe his name was—to go light a torch from the kitchen hearth fire and bring it back. He got a confirmation nod from his squad leader and then ran back into the house.

We went to the open cellar door and stopped at the threshold. I stooped down at the start of the stone ramp that angled down into the darkness. I smelled the terrible *spoor* rot coming from the cellar, and a chill breeze seemed to waft up at me, though I knew it was more my magical senses than a physical breeze. Vitulus and the other four Praetorians took up a position just in front of me, facing the darkness with white-knuckled hands on their sword hilts.

I took some chalk from my belt pouch and began drawing a line on the stone around the entrance, all the while chanting under my breath, *"Niemand zal passeren...niemand zal passeren...niemand zal passeren..."*

The warmth of my cell magic passed through my fingers, into the chalk stem, and then onto the line. My legs got a little wobbly, and I felt my hands shaking as I drew; I was getting dangerously low on magical reserves and would need some food and rest soon. I pushed on, though, drawing the line along the brick walls near the entrance and then on the overhang just above the ramp. I made sure that the perimeter of the entire opening was surrounded by that chalk line without so much as a hair's width of a break.

By this time, Fronto had returned with a lit torch. "Okay, guys," I said to Vitulus and the four other Praetorians, "back up behind the chalk line. And cover your eyes."

They backed up, eager to get back into the light of the sun. I took the torch from Fronto, siphoned some of my dwindling cell magic into the fire, and said, *"Verbruiken."* Then I threw the torch as far as I could into the darkened cellar.

At first nothing happened as the torch rolled down the ramp, issuing sparks as it went. It finally stopped at the bottom of the ramp...and then flared when it began to consume all the oxygen in the air around it. But it didn't stop there. It leaped to everything else that was flammable in the cellar: wooden barrels and tools, wheelbarrows, clothing and woolen sacks, lamp oil.

Not to mention the flesh of the corruptions hiding out down there.

Once the fire really got going, it expanded within the blink of an eye and raced up toward the cellar entrance with a blinding explosive force, ready to consume even the air outside. But fire crashed against the invisible wall of the *passern* spell that I'd drawn around the entrance. The *passern* wall flared with blue and red swirling lights—which I've been told are the colors of my magical aura—that glowed like sunlit oil film on the surface of calm water. Neither the fire nor heat could escape that wall, but it was bright as hell to look at. I stood my ground in front of the cellar entrance, squinting at the flames, while Vitulus and the Praetorians flinched away from it. I knew that magic and physical material could go in, but nothing—not even fire—could come out.

I was about to get all cocky over standing my ground, when several corruptions slammed their blackened, burning, and screaming bodies against the *passern* wall. I yelped and jumped backward to join my equally startled Praetorian pals. Two of the chicken things flung themselves against the wall over and over again, while two more creatures that I assumed were once goats did the same with their large, tusked heads. All of the corruptions were on fire, all of them were issuing teeth rattling shrieks of pain. And while it may sound ridiculous to be afraid of barnyard animals, their burning, corrupted bodies with their unnatural claws and tusks and bulges would be my nightmare fodder for weeks to come.

One of the Praetorians muttered something under his breath and made a warding gesture. I had no idea what god or goddess he was calling upon, but I understood the impulse.

It took several minutes for the corruptions to finally die. Once I was sure their fire ravaged bodies were no longer moving, I raised my hand toward the fire and said, *"Blussen."*

Through the *blussen* spell, I explained to the fire that it was time to stop feeding and go to sleep. Since the fire was from a non-magical source in the kitchen hearth—magical fires are stubborn as hell—it quickly acquiesced and went out with a pop. The corruptions were nothing more than blackened, smoking skeletons. I saw no other flames on them or further down the cellar. Once I was sure the fires were out, I disenchanted the *passern* wall by touching it with my right hand.

Smoke billowed from the cellar entrance, finally released from its confinement. And with it came the terrible stench of burned flesh mingled with burned wood and a myriad other burned odors, blasting out of the cellar like its own acrid fire.

But the foul odors from the *spoor* spell were gone. I scanned the courtyard and the animal barn entrance and saw that the corrupted prints had disappeared. I immediately plugged one nostril and snorted the bloody rose petal out of the one in which I'd shoved it. Then I glanced at my Praetorian friends and snarled, "*That's* how it's done, gentlemen."

Fatigue and adrenaline make me do loopy things, like show off my manliness to a bunch of manly Praetorians.

"Are they dead?" Vitulus asked, staring at the skeletons.

"Oh yeah." I turned to the Praetorian squad leader and said, "It's safe for the citizens to come out. Bring them back here, and we'll take the pawn back to Rome." The enchanted pawn still stood in the middle of the courtyard looking all innocent and mundane, yet anachronistically out of place in an ancient Roman villa.

The Praetorian nodded to me as if I were Salvius Aper and then led his men back into the house. I was amazed at how much respect a little magic could earn me.

Vitulus still stared at the corruption skeletons only ten feet away. "They're not going to...rise up again or something? Attack us when we turn our backs?"

Over the past two years, Vitulus and I had fought many nasty supernatural things, and he had learned by now to expect the unexpected. He'd come so far from the disbelieving, scoffing Praetorian who had walked into my first shop so long ago.

"No, not these." Then I put a hand on his shoulder and said, "And I'm proud of you for asking, buddy."

Vitulus winced; I'd accidentally placed my hand on one of his wounds. I quickly removed it and muttered, "Sorry." And then I grinned at him. "Wait till I tell Claudia you were roughed up by a chicken."

He glared at me. "A *daemon* chicken." Then he winced again, and said, "Are you going to insult me or heal me?"

"I think I want to insult you a while longer." I returned his glare. "You did scare the *cac* out of me when you dragged me into this without an explanation."

"I told you," he growled, "I was under orders not to give you the details outside of Aper's home. Besides, if it wasn't for me and Aper, Augustus would've had you killed just for being mentioned by the thief. *We* talked him down from that. *We* told him you were an ally and our best hope to find the books. I am your friend, Natta Magus, and I think that I've proven before that I would rather die by your side than betray you. Have I not proven that?"

I clicked my teeth together a couple of times. I knew that he had proven many times over that he was my friend, and he had stood at my side when the supernatural *cac* had hit the oscillating wind machine. But knowing all that didn't make me any less angry at him at the moment.

Fatigue plus adrenaline equals loopy.

I glanced at the animal barn to the right and saw a bench beneath the roof overhang, which provided some shade from the dawn sun.

"Go sit over there," I told him.

"Why?"

"So I can heal you. Bad ass Praetorian can't handle a few chicken scratches."

He began walking to the barn. "Well you would've fainted by now."

He eased down onto the bench and then laid on his chest. I pulled down his shredded tunic from around his neck to inspect the wounds. Damnation, he was right. I *would've* fainted with these wounds. His back was soaked in blood and looked like it had taken five or six knife wounds around his shoulders. A three-inch long flap of skin dangled from the base of his neck, exposing blood and muscle underneath. He was *caccing* lucky the corruption hadn't raked his jugular with its hand claws. I couldn't believe he'd been able to stand much less run around searching for the corruptions.

Healing spells aren't terribly difficult, especially minor traumatic injuries (diseases and poisonings and such are whole different beasts that are far beyond my skill level). But they require a lot of magic, and I was pretty much down to my last few drops before I'd need a quality meal and a good night's sleep to recharge. Vitulus was pale, trembling, and had lost a lot of blood. Now that his own adrenaline rush had subsided, I didn't think he'd be able rise up off the bench again without some healing.

I grabbed his forearm, siphoned what magic I had left in my cells, and directed my aura into his body. My mundane senses faded to a gray nothingness as my magical sight entered his body and sought out the wounds. The spell enabled me to see the destruction at a cellular level, so I directed my magic to repair each torn nerve, muscle fiber, and skin cell just enough to stop the bleeding and ease his pain. I'd basically just sped up his body's natural healing schedule by two weeks.

With Vitulus healed enough so he wouldn't bleed all over everyone, I pulled out of the healing spell, back to my weak body in the mundane world. I dropped to one knee and panted as if I'd just ran from Rome. Vitulus immediately sat up on the bench. While he still looked pale, he looked a lot less ready to die. He moved his shoulders around and slowly turned his neck from left to right. He grinned slightly as he found them working much better and far less painful than a moment earlier.

"Just when I think your powers cannot surprise me anymore," he said.

I realized this was the first time I'd ever healed Vitulus. He'd seen me heal others, but he'd never experienced it. "You're welcome," I said through heavy breaths. "We need to go now. Gotta rest."

"Right," he said. He stood, but winced a little at his still healing wounds. He extended a hand to me, I took it, and he helped me stand.

By the time we were finished, the Praetorians had gathered Capito, his family, and the remaining slaves into the center of the courtyard where the pawn still stood. The morning sun showed the fatigue and fear still resident on all their faces. Even the Praetorians looked ragged from their new experiences: All five of them continued to cast wary glances at the wine cellar and the burned corruptions still smoking near the entrance.

Capito stared at the smoke billowing from the cellar and turned to me. "What did you...?"

His voice trailed off when he found me glaring at him. Something on my face must've told him that now was not the time to give me any lip on just *how* I had saved his family from being ripped to pieces. He stopped saying whatever he was about to say and turned his eyes back to his family.

I ensured everyone was within the pawn's gate range and then shuffled toward the pawn. I didn't have the energy to tell everyone to hang on again, or to give Capito's family and slaves a head's up on what to expect, so I simply tapped the pawn head and said, "*Reizen.*"

I felt the same pulling in the pit of my stomach toward the pawn...and then I was suddenly encased in terrible, bone-chilling cold. The cold pulled me back from the pawn's *reizen* spell, and I fell backward onto the courtyard. The fall knocked the breath out of me, and it took me a few moments of gasping before

I had the wits to look around me. Vitulus also lay on the ground beside me, looking just as stunned as I felt. But Capito, his family, and the Praetorians were gone.

The mystery magus. He was here. And he didn't want me to leave just yet.

Vitulus and I scrambled to our feet at the same time. I siphoned my dwindling cell magic, ready to cast in an instant, and held my hands up on either side of me. Though I doubted I could do much good against this guy. Whoever he was, he far outclassed me if he could pull two people out of a *reizen* spell.

I glanced to where the pawn should be on the ground. It was gone, along with everyone else. Vitulus and I were alone with no way back to Rome besides a 150-mile walk.

Vitulus held his gladius up, scanning the courtyard with wide, predatory eyes. "Was that—?"

"Yes."

"Where is—?"

"I don't know."

I knew he could see us, because a spell like that required line of sight. He was hiding, somewhere, in the courtyard. We'd searched the house earlier and found nothing. The barn? It had lots of the small rectangular windows, just like the house that faced the courtyard. The tool sheds to my left? They didn't have windows, but the doors were open and he could be hiding in the shadows. Damnation, there were tall hills not too far from the villa where he could see us through an oculus spell.

He could be anywhere.

"Ideas?" Vitulus asked through clenched teeth. He hated attacks that he couldn't see. Hell, I hated them just as much as he did.

"We need to get out of this courtyard. He can see us—"

And then one of my nightmares suddenly came true.

My limbs wouldn't move. I couldn't budge my arms from where I held them up on either side of me, like I was a traffic cop motioning both lanes to stop. I couldn't turn my head, shuffle my feet, or even blink. For a brief panicked moment, my lungs stopped pulling in air, but they expanded again so that I could breathe. At the same time, my eyes were released, too, and I could move them around. But that was it.

And the only thought that ran through the surface of my mind was that I did not *want* to move. This was all *my* idea. I had very good reasons for standing there, unmoving, and they were all *mine*.

But the panicked part of my mind screamed, *Gods above and below, I'm enthralled.*

# FOURTEEN

T he reason that magi in my home time first began wearing focus items was to prevent enthrallment. Very early after the Great Awakening, people developed spells to control the minds of other people about as quickly as spells to turn lead into gold. And just as quickly, anti-enthrallment wards were developed to block them. Ancient magi used focus items, worn on their bodies, to stop the enthrallments and any other form of mind control. Over the centuries, the focus items also turned into ways for magi to increase their magical talents and siphon *more* magic from their cells. My Wolverines ball cap was my focus item and had served me well throughout my life. So enthrallment was a rare event in my time due to the defenses that every magus had against it; and, of course, I didn't have to deal with it in ancient Rome since no magus existed who had the power to even consider an enthrallment, much less blast through my cap's wards.

Well what do you know? A magus like that did exist.

I turned my eyes to Vitulus, who also seemed frozen in place. Cac, *the magus has him too.*

But then Vitulus *un*froze. He took several deep breaths as if he'd just come up from underwater. At first, I was relieved. Then Vitulus looked at me, and my panic went into fifth gear.

His eyes didn't have the fear or surprise they should've had after such an experience. No, his eyes regarded me with blank non-recognition. Then he brought his gladius up and strode toward me with purpose. Killing purpose.

Panicked Me used my remaining cell magic to slam against the enthrallment spell, like someone slamming their shoulder against a locked door. I figuratively felt that door creak and crack, so I continued my assault. The superficial part of my mind, however, kept my limbs frozen as if it were the best idea in the world to just stand there and let my best friend stick a gladius in my heart.

*Come on, Vitulus,* Panicked Me screamed inside me as I battered against the enthrallment. *Fight the bastard!*

But I knew he had no chance of breaking the enthrallment. He had no wards on his mind like me, which were the only thing giving me the split personality I needed to resist. As far as he was concerned, the whispers in his mind were his thoughts.

He raised his gladius for a killing stab just as I broke my own enthrallment.

I dove to the ground beneath Vitulus's thrust. All he got was empty air. I somehow had the energy and wits to complete my evasive roll—the same kind of roll that Vitulus himself had taught me in our sparring sessions—and leaped to my feet just out of his swinging range. I reached for a pouch on my component belt, but Vitulus quickly recovered from his missed thrust, whirled around, and stabbed at me again. He missed me by inches. I flung myself out of the way. I found an empty bucket near the barn entrance, grabbed it, and tossed it at Vitulus's feet. I got lucky, for my bucket attack forced him to leap over it. His right foot got caught on the handle. It took him a moment to shake it off, which I took complete advantage of and leaped through the barn entrance. I had to put *something* between me and Vitulus. *Damnation, why did I have to heal him first?*

I raced inside and nearly tripped over the carcass of a dead cow. I jumped over it just in time, but came down next to another one. I quickly scanned the barn and found it littered with dead animals. There was no blood anywhere, however, which told me they could've only died by one thing: My mystery magus had stolen their souls to fuel his magic.

I found a ladder to a second level loft and scrambled up it as Vitulus entered the barn. He wasn't so nimble as me and actually tripped over the dead cow. I remembered that enthralled people were not the most dexterous; the body spends a fraction of a moment resisting the magic before the magic slams into place and forces the body to comply. It was why Dark magi rarely sent enthralled into battle, because they usually didn't stand a chance against an opponent in control of his own mind.

And it was the only reason Vitulus hadn't gutted me by now.

As soon as I got to second level, I moved away from the ladder and tried to stay as silent as possible. I heard Vitulus get up with a grunt and then stop. I made my heavy breathing as quiet as I could, but my heart pounded so hard that I thought all of Italy could hear it.

I used one hand to silently opened the pouch of dried Aegean sponge pieces on my components belt that I'd been trying to grab. I slipped two fingers through the cinched end and withdrew a couple. Now for the hard part: I had to come up with enough spit to saturate one of them so that it would stick to Vitulus when I threw it at him. But my mouth had never felt so dry in my life. I tried thinking of different foods that I missed from Detroit: that mouth-watering barbecue place in Corktown, the dueling coney dog diners downtown, chili-cheese fries.

That got the spit flowing.

Unfortunately my stomach also let loose with the loudest growl ever. I heard Vitulus rush toward the ladder.

I quickly spit as much as I could into the sponge piece as I heard Vitulus scramble up. Then I said in my bastardized Dutch, *"Vrij zijn!"*

My cell magic sparked, sputtered, but flowed into the spitty sponge. It flared once with the anti-enthrallment spell. When Vitulus's head poked up out of the ladder well, I dove forward and slapped the sponge on his forehead. But even with his enthrallment, he managed to bring his gladius up for one last stab at me. I felt the wind of the gladius pass by my cheek and eye. But I rolled out of the way in time and saw Vitulus collapse down the ladder as the anti-enthrallment spell hit him. I prayed he landed in one of the cushy straw piles beside the ladder and not the brick floor down the center of the barn. I had nothing left for another heal spell. In fact, I didn't have much left but to roll over and see if I'd killed Vitulus rather than free him.

His grunts and curses from below answered that question.

I turned over onto my back and lay there staring up at the ceiling as all the energy drained from my limbs. *This survival was brought to you by adrenaline, my favorite stress hormone.*

# FIFTEEN

"**I** swear by Invidia's vengeance that I will kill this magus," Vitulus growled.

He wrapped my spit-saturated sponge under a piece of torn cloth around his arm so that it stayed in contact with his skin. It *should* block any future enthrallment attempts. But then again, the magus had blasted through my supposedly impregnable ball cap wards. Still, it was better than nothing.

"Get in line, buddy," I replied weakly. I still sat cross-legged in the second level loft of the barn with my spell component belt spread out before me, trying to come up with ideas to find the magus. He definitely wasn't in the barn, and all the high-level windows only showed open sky, so I was reasonably sure he couldn't see us to cast another enthrallment spell. "This guy is confusing the hell out of me. Does he want to kill me or protect me?"

I then told Vitulus about my experience yesterday evening when a magus had rescued me from Balbus's goons.

"So yesterday he saved your life and today he tries to kill you?" Vitulus asked. "You're sure he's the same man?"

"Their descriptions match. Capito said the thief was dressed in black and had short black hair. That's pretty much the same description of my rescuer. But then I only saw the guy from the back. I didn't see if my guy had the half-beard that Capito described."

Vitulus shook his head. "So we could have *two* Dark magi running around?"

I shrugged. "Or just the one. I don't know at this point." I stared at my components and then muttered in frustration, "I didn't bring rabbit dung? Why didn't I bring rabbit dung?"

Vitulus stood. "This whole event seems like a waste of time. Did he bring us here to enthrall us? To kill Capito's family? If so, he failed miserably."

I eyed Vitulus. "If those were his goals, then yes. But maybe those weren't his goals."

"What do you mean?"

"He's playing a game with me. Calling me out when he stole the books, leaving a chess piece behind, putting Capito's family in danger because he knew I'd run here to help. He knows me well. But how? I don't know any magi from this time who have anywhere near his strength, much less who know a game that won't be invented for another thousand years."

"Could he be from your home time?"

I shrugged again. "I suppose it's possible. It's also possible he knew William. And it's also possible that he's just some guy who came along after our party at Aventicum last year. There were dozens of artifacts in that underground temple, and some of them could've been just as powerful as my Ring of Saturn. Maybe he got to one..."

Vitulus frowned. "The legions did return to Aventicum in force and rebuilt the fort there, but that wasn't for another two months. That was indeed plenty of time for someone to pick through the ruins." He sighed as he watched me pick through my spell components. "Regardless, we're no closer to finding the thief of the Sibylline Books than we were hours ago."

I looked up at him. "How hard do you think it would be to convince Augustus to submit to my finder spell?"

Vitulus shook his head. "He already told you—"

"I know what he told me. Yes, legally and publicly, 'the state' owns the books. But if Augustus believes in his heart that *he* is the state, then he owns the books as far as my magic is concerned. He may be the only link I have to using my finder magic to locate the books."

"Augustus is not the state," Vitulus said through tight lips. "He is simply the First Citizen of the Roman Republic." Vitulus paused, and then said, "I grant you, he has far more power and prestige than any Roman since the Tarquin kings, but he has never claimed kingship and he never will, for he knows there would be revolution in the streets. The Republic is still a republic. The Senate still passes laws, two consuls are still elected each year—"

"All with Augustus's approval," I muttered.

"Yes, because *someone* needs to ensure it all runs smoothly!"

I gave a soft chuckle at Vitulus's positive spin on the current Roman government. He was either very naïve or in heavy denial. Either way, I couldn't fault him for supporting Augustus. Octavian Caesar Augustus may have been the man who destroyed the republic and ushered in the age of emperors, but he *had* ended the generations of civil wars that had ravaged Rome. Most Roman citizens felt the Republic was dysfunctional anyway and were happy to have someone at the top who could blast through all the corruption and roadblocks to Get Stuff Done.

Too bad they couldn't see into the future like me. I knew all about the psychotic emperors to come. And even if Romans could see the future, would their opinions of Augustus change? It was human nature to seek prosperity now at the expense of the future, especially after enduring a long period of suffering. *We* deserve a break; let our great-grandchildren fix our mistakes.

"Look, I don't mean to argue politics right now," I said, "but I'm saying that it would really help our mission if Augustus would—"

A cold breeze tickled the back of my neck, obviously out of place in the warming barn. The hairs raised on my neck, and gooseflesh ran over my entire body.

Then the real shock wave hit. I got that smothering feeling again, as if I were choking on dirt while it was slowly piled on top of my head. I jumped to my feet, adrenaline giving my limbs a surge, and I rushed to the ladder.

Startled by my actions, Vitulus asked, "What is it?"

"The magus, he's casting," I said as I scrambled down the ladder. "Come on!"

Vitulus came down the ladder almost on top of me. We both leaped over the dead barn animals and skidded to a stop at the barn entrance.

A glowing blue oval hung in the air in the middle of the courtyard. I caught a glimpse of a foot going through it—tan, hairy leg, black sandal—and a brick wall on the other side, before the gate imploded with a crack like two stones smacking together.

Directly beneath the gate was another object. I approached it carefully. Vitulus went with me, his gladius drawn. We both stooped down next to it.

It was another black chess piece. This time the smoothly carved horse head of a knight.

# SIXTEEN

"**D**amnation," I swore aloud in English, staring at the knight. I rarely spoke English anymore other than to swear, so Vitulus had heard me say that particular word many times and didn't need a translation.

He stooped down next to the chess piece.

"Don't touch it!" I cried.

He glared at me as if to say, *What, is this my first day?* Then he nodded to the piece. "A continuation of the game?"

"Yeah. But I hate how he's forcing me to make the moves he wants me to make." I didn't need to do First Scan to sense the smothering soul magic emanating from the knight. "I'd bet my shop that this thing is enchanted with whatever move he wants me to make next."

"Can you see what that move is?"

I pulled the talc and quartz powder pouches from my belt and said, "I will in a moment."

I poured the powder around the knight like I had with the pawn back in the Temple of Apollo Palatinus. I was so exhausted that I felt dizzy just contemplating magic; that brief rest in the barn had done barely anything to recharge my cells. But I had to figure out the enchantment on this thing because it was my only clue. Which, again, was another move my opponent was forcing me to make. It was either this or we leave the knight here and begin walking back to Rome.

With the knight encircled, I walked around it twice and then tapped the powdered circle with my right finger, sending a small burst of cell magic into the containment shell.

And that's when I realized my mistake.

I hadn't performed First Scan on the knight because I had sensed the soul magic. I knew the basics that First Scan would've given me. But if I *had* performed First Scan, I would've noticed the *reizen* spell primed to go off as soon as I tried a Second Scan.

It was one of those horrible realizations that happen simultaneously: *I'm casting the spell* combined with *Oh,* cac, *for the love of Juno, don't cast the spell!*

Too late. I felt the familiar *reizen* tug at the base of my spine, a rush toward the knight piece and a whoosh of air filling my ears, and then a sudden rush backward. All I could do was pray the magus hadn't sent us to the bottom of the Mediterranean.

But I fell backward onto a brick road, skinning my elbows but fortunately keeping my head from colliding with the ground. I took a moment to ensure I was all in one piece then scrambled to my feet as fast as I could, ready for whatever else the magus threw at me. Vitulus was next to me, and he had beaten me to his feet by a fraction of a second. We nodded to each other, signaling we were okay, and then scanned our new surroundings.

We were certainly in a city, for the miasmic stench hit me as hard as I'd hit the brick road. Most ancient cities at that time had the same kind of smells, so I couldn't immediately tell which city we were—

"No!" Vitulus cried, and then sprinted off to our left.

Again, he'd been a fraction of a second ahead of me to recognize that we were back in Rome. And that we were standing a block away from his house on the Caelian Hill.

I ran after Vitulus. A fear had suddenly gripped me that I'd rarely known since I'd arrived in Rome. It wasn't the bowl-loosening fear for my own life that I got every time I was about to fight something supernatural or mundane. No, this was a deeper, helpless fear for the safety of someone I cared about. I was suddenly terrified beyond all reason that the mystery magus had hurt Claudia and Lucius. This was no longer a game or a fight between me and the magus. It had become viscerally personal. Vitulus and Claudia were not just my friends; they were my only family in Rome. The magus had struck at my heart. A burning rage welled up inside me as I ran, supplanting the fear. I no longer cared about the Sibylline Books or the magus's identity. If he had hurt Claudia or Lucius, he was going to die screaming.

We arrived at the heavy wooden door to the home, where Vitulus stopped and pounded on it with both fists.

"Claudia!" he yelled. "Open the doors!"

People walking past us stared curiously at Vitulus. It was morning in Rome, and her citizens were out and about. There were several shops nearby, too, where customers and shopkeepers alike glanced at Vitulus with frowns.

He noticed one of the shopkeepers, a clothier judging by the reams of cloth displayed outside his door, and cried out, "Vindex, have you seen anyone enter my home in the last few moments?"

Vindex shook his balding head and said, "No, *dominus*. Well, I did see Calla come back from an errand about an hour ago."

Calla was Claudia's nursery slave, so Vitulus shook his head in irritation and then began pounding on the door again. "Claudia!"

A moment later I heard the bar slide back from the door and watched it open. Ambio, Vitulus's house slave, opened the door, his pale Gallic face alarmed.

"Dominus?" he said

"Ambio, is all well?" Vitulus asked, pushing his way through.

His eyes scanned the vestibule, as did mine. Like most Roman homes, marble and wax busts of Vitulus's ancestors lined the alcoves at the entryway on either side. The vestibule opened up to the atrium six feet away where sunlight poured down from the open ceiling and onto the impluvium pool. Though not has large as Aper's, or as impressively decorated with murals and plants, it was still a tastefully stylish for a wealthy equestrian family.

"Yes, dominus," Ambio said, confusion plain on his face.

"Claudia!" Vitulus yelled again, rushing into the home. He shot like a loosed arrow toward the nursery, and I followed close on his heels. I opened my magical senses, trying to see with what little strength I had left, but I felt no magic at work in the house. That didn't mean the magus wasn't hiding in here though.

"Vitulus?" came Claudia's voice from the nursery. "Why are you yelling?" Her tone was curious, with a hint of annoyance, and not fearful at all. I felt my legs suddenly weaken with relief.

Claudia met us at the door to the nursery, holding up her hands as if to shush us. Her dark hair was braided and hung down around her shoulders, and she wore a tunica dress that was obviously made for a nursing mother; her left shoulder was bare and the upper part of her left breast was exposed. I stopped in the hallway and turned away to give them both a little privacy.

"Lucius just fell asleep," she said in whispered tones. "What's—?"

I glanced behind me and saw Vitulus sweep Claudia into his arms in a tight embrace. His face was pressed into her hair when he said, "I was so scared..."

"Vitulus," Claudia said, fear beginning to creep into her voice, "what's happening? Why were you scared?"

Before he could explain, I said, "I'm going to check the house."

Vitulus glanced from me to Claudia with what looked like conflicting loyalties.

"Buddy, this isn't even a choice," I growled. "Stay with your family. I'll yell if I find anything, all right?"

He gave me a quick nod and then said to Ambio, who was sanding behind me, "Go with him."

Vitulus reached down around his calf and handed Ambio the dagger he had sheathed there. Ambio took it with a grim nod. I got the feeling that Vitulus's Gallic slave, who only looked a few years older than me, had seen his share of fights. I felt marginally better that I wasn't doing this on my own.

⋙⋙⋙ ⋘⋘⋘

Ambio and I searched every nook, cranny, and loose floor tile in the house, but found nothing. We even searched outside around the house and a block in every direction, but found no sign of the magus or the taint of soul magic.

Which worried me even more than if we had found something. The magus had already proven he was good at hiding things in plain sight; had he somehow entered Vitulus's home and left a sick trap designed to spring later when we least suspected it? Just a few hours ago the bastard had me strung up like a puppet and moving to his will. I was still his puppet, but now it was my own paranoia pulling the strings.

It was almost noon by the time we returned to the house and went back to the nursery.

"Vitulus, it's me," I said as we approached the curtained entry. He pulled the curtain aside with one hand, while his pearl-handled gladius was clutched in the other. Claudia stood up from a *XII scripta* board, a kind of early precursor to backgammon that she and Vitulus loved to play while watching their son sleep. They both gave me questioning looks.

I shook my head. "Nothing. He's not in the home, and there's no sign that he used magic to try to enter. Or that he cast any spells from the street."

Vitulus gave me a penetrating stare. "But you can't be sure."

I sighed. He knew enough about magic to know that virtually anything you can imagine is possible. "No, I can't."

He seemed to deflate, which for Vitulus meant a slight slumping of his shoulders and an almost imperceptible lowering of his chin. The man was a rock, someone who I'd depended on to keep my courage in the dicey situations we'd encountered over the last two years. For him to give even a hint of despair meant that the magus had hit him hard. And the magus hadn't even taken a real swing.

"Look," I said, "if this magus really wanted to hurt your family, he would've done so. This was just another one of his mind games. Hell, I don't even think he wanted to hurt Capito's family. He told them to hide *before* he released the corruptions."

"Maybe not now," Vitulus growled in a low tone, glancing at his sleeping infant son, "but he just told us that he knows where my family lives. He could come back any time he wants!"

"I can put wards on your home. They'll stop anyone from casting magic within it."

He snorted. "What, like the wards on your cap? The ones that were supposed to keep other magi out of your mind? How did those work for you?"

"Damnation, Vitulus, I'm doing my best—"

"Your best is not good enough!"

Young Lucius began to stir in his crib from Vitulus's raised voice. Claudia hurried over and calmed him, rubbing his head and whispering something soothing to the boy. He went back to sleep.

But the whole time I stared at Vitulus. I whispered, "Don't you think I know that?"

I think Vitulus regretted his outburst, because he wouldn't meet my eyes. But he stood defiantly before me, his posture maintaining the accusation that my magic sucked compared to the mystery magus.

Claudia put a gentle hand on Vitulus's muscled sword arm, where his grip on the hilt made his hand look as white as the pearl handle. "Gaius," she said, using his more personal *praenomen*, "Natta Magus is trying to help. Let him."

Claudia was only eighteen years old—still kind of a kid to me—but I always felt she was an old soul. She had the grace and wisdom of an elderly Roman matron, and always knew how to calm Vitulus when his inner savage beast started roaring. With a simple touch and a quiet word, I'd seen her persuade Vitulus to do things that were unheard of for Roman men, like holding his son while he cried or changing a soiled diaper (which was my fault since I told her that's what dads did in my time). This time was no exception.

And it was all because their marriage was a peculiarity in ancient Rome: They actually loved each other. In an age where marriages were arranged for economic and social reasons, and never, ever love, they'd gotten lucky when all three aligned. Very lucky.

Vitulus took several deep breaths and then sheathed his gladius. He finally looked me in the eyes, but his face was still a hard mask. "I apologize, Natta Magus. I did not mean to impugn your skills. I know you're trying to help. I'm just..."

He seemed to struggle for the word, so I finished his sentence for him. "Scared?"

He glanced at Lucius and Claudia, and then gave me a jerky nod.

"Me too, buddy." I looked at them both. "We're going to find this guy. And I won't let him hurt any of you."

I wasn't sure who I was trying to reassure, them or me.

# SEVENTEEN

Warding a home like I had done with my shop takes a pretty hefty chunk of magic, and I was too exhausted to flick on a spark globe much less take the time and energy needed to do a ward right. So Vitulus and Ambio took first watch in the nursery with Claudia and Calla while I slept for a couple of hours in the guest room that I had used numerous times while sleeping off the mass quantities of wine I'd consumed at one of Vitulus's dinner parties.

After my two-hour nap, I still felt exhausted, but at least my cell magic had recharged to the point where I'd have enough to get that ward up and running. I always kept a stash of valuable spell components at Vitulus's home, ever since my first shop was destroyed by a mad imprint daemon a year and a half ago. Eggs in one basket, and all that. I used some of the components to set up a rudimentary anti-magic ward around the home, even though I knew that mystery magus could blow through it as if it were fog. But at least the ward would let us know he was coming and we could prepare to do...something.

After setting up the ward, I told Vitulus that I'd run back to my shop for components to build more powerful wards. I also wanted to retrieve that scarf and take it to Paetus for analysis. It was the only physical clue we had regarding the mystery magus or magi. I needed to figure out whether or not the mystery magus who saved me last night was the same one that tried to kill me this morning. I was a little worried about leaving Vitulus and his family alone since he looked as exhausted as I'd felt before my nap. But I think daddy adrenaline was keeping him going, which, judging by his pacing and snarly tone of voice, I figured would keep him awake until the twenty-first century. Once I returned, he would hurry over to Salvius Aper's home to brief him and inquire about what happened to Capito and his family. After asking Vitulus for a skin full of his finest Pompeian wine for Lares—he rolled his eyes and gave it to me—I left his Caelian home.

I jogged back to my shop on the Aventine, the wine sloshing inside the skin strapped over my shoulder, which thanks to all my exercising wasn't as arduous a trip as it sounded. It was mid afternoon and the day was sunny and hot, and I was sweating by the time I was halfway home. All the while I kept thinking, *Will these wards even do any good?* The mystery magus had shaken my confidence badly. Vitulus was right about my ball cap. Nobody should've been able to blast through those wards. Damnation, personal wards were perfected so much that by my time, they were the only "impenetrable" magic known. This guy had blown through them like they weren't there. And the worst part was that I could still hear the echoes of the enthrallment's foul, alien whispers in my mind. I needed to sit in a hot bath for a week.

I was so lost in planning for what I wanted to do about the mystery magus that I didn't even notice the fancy palanquin parked just outside my shop door until I tried to walk past it to get inside. I stared at it a moment, noticed the four large men standing nearby wearing matching yellow tunicas and daggers at their belts, and then groaned inwardly. *Aw, damnation, I don't have time for this.*

"Natta Magus," came an elderly male voice from inside the palanquin, "I would speak with you."

Two of the goons strolled around the palanquin behind me, while the other two stood in front of me with their meaty forearms folded over their chests. I had no idea ancient Rome could produce four men who looked as juiced as pro-wrestlers in my home time, but there they were. I suppose money can buy or find anything.

One of the goons in front of me opened the silk curtain on the palanquin to reveal an obviously sick old man who was so thin that he probably weighed less than Lares. He was propped up against several cushions at the back of the palanquin, and he was covered in thick, finely embroidered blankets despite the hot day. His face was gaunt and had a yellowish tint to it. Perfume wafted out of the palanquin's interior, but underneath I caught the faint odor of *cac*. Pretty much the only healthy thing about this man were his brown eyes. Despite the dark circles around them, they regarded me as if he were assessing whether or not to slaughter a prized pig.

I gave a quick bow with my head and tried to calm my heavy breathing from my jog. "Marcus Naevius, sir, how are you this fine—"

"Have you found my son, Natta Magus? You promised me his location by noon today. It is well past noon, and yet I do not have his location. Why is that, Natta Magus?" Like most wealthy equestrians who wished they were patricians, Marcus Naevius had a way of pronouncing each word precisely and deliberately. I'd never seen a session of the Senate, but I guessed that's how they talk there, too. If I had to sit through a session where hundreds of men were talking like that, I'd probably claw my ears out.

"Well, sir, I did find your son last night." I paused, waiting for the good news to at least get me a smile of approval, or maybe a sigh of relief, or something. He just stared at me as if I'd said nothing. I supposed you don't build your gens into the largest distributor of cattle in the city without a good business face. "Unfortunately, he and his friends tried to kill me." I glanced at Naevius's wrestlers and thought, *Which seems to run in the family...*

This actually brought a quick smile to Naevius's bloodless lips. "Ah, that boy. He is a born leader. He will make a fine *paterfamilias* for the Naevii. So you know where he is, Natta Magus?"

"I know where he *was*. But he's probably gone into hiding again because he correctly guessed that I was working for you."

His eyes narrowed. "How did he know you were working for me?"

*Because I was trying to be a nice guy*, I thought. But I shrugged and said, "Lucky guess. Anyway, I can still find him. The spell I cast will lead me—"

"People I respect tell me you are the best in the city, Natta Magus. So I am paying you well to find my son and bring him home before tomorrow night. Have I told you why my son must return before tomorrow night?"

"Um, yes, sir, you explained everything when you—"

"Then let me remind you, since you do not seem to be giving this matter the attention it deserves. I have well-paid augers who tell me that tomorrow night is the most auspicious night we will have for another two months. My son Balbus *must* take the oaths to become paterfamilias tomorrow night because, as you can see, I do not have another two months to wait. He is headstrong and independent, but deep inside he knows his duty is to his gens. This is the last matter that I must resolve before my imminent passing— Tallium, rat."

I never would've suspected the big goon in front of me to move so fast. Literally, within the blink of an eye, he pulled out his dagger and stabbed a rat that had been lurking in the refuse pile against the lawyer's shop next door to mine. He held the dying animal up to Naevius, its mouth opening and closing, and its limbs spasming. It gave a few more twitches and then was still. Naevius inspected the rat for several moments until he was satisfied that it was dead, and then he gave Tallium a quick nod. Tallium flung the dead rat into the refuse pile and then wiped its blood off his dagger with some dirty cloth in the same pile. He sheathed his dagger, returned to his folded-arm stance, and resumed aiming his stony glare at me.

"I despise rats," Naevius said with a delicate shudder in his chin. "Filthy little scavengers. Always digging through the garbage or taking what is not theirs. I always have my men kill them whenever I see them." His face turned all business again, and his eyes held mine. "As I was saying, this matter must be resolved in a timely fashion, Natta Magus. So I will pay you triple the fee we agreed upon yesterday morning...if you find my son by noon tomorrow."

"Triple?" I blurted. Damnation, he'd already paid me a pretty hefty "motivation" bonus yesterday. If he tripled that, I could live comfortably for months without taking another job. Hell, I could buy up all the spell components that I'd only dreamed of getting because I couldn't afford to buy them *and* food *and* pay rent.

"Yes, triple, Natta Magus," he said. "But with great reward comes great risk. I have already given you a respectable sum as a deposit to locate my son. If you do not bring my son home by noon tomorrow, then, well, it would be like you had taken money from me that was not yours." His voice got quieter, and its sickly tone made it seem even more ominous. "You are not a rat, are you, Natta Magus?"

"No, sir, I'm not—"

"Wonderful," Naevius said, as if I'd just pulled his son out my pocket. "You may bring him back to your shop here or bring him to my home, whichever is more convenient for you. I will have Tallium meet you here if you choose your shop. Do we have a deal, Natta Magus?"

Tallium continued to stare at me as he flexed his folded forearms, the muscles in them shifting and the veins popping.

I briefly flirted with the idea of telling Naevius that I had bigger things going on right now, but I got the feeling that wouldn't fly with a man like this. He was dying and desperate and I seemed to be his last option. Which made things mighty dangerous for little old me. I wasn't too worried about facing Naevius's goons in a head on fight—my magic could at least delay them enough for me to run—but I couldn't spend the rest of my life looking over my shoulder whenever I stepped out of my warded shop's front door. I don't care how skilled of a magus you are, there isn't any magic in the world that will stop a well-timed, sneaky dagger in the back.

But I have to be honest, all those extra sesterces were already clinking around in my brain, pushing the Cautious Me into the back of the room. The things I could do with all that money! I knew I could find Balbus—my feet wanted to start walking toward him just thinking about him—but it would take time and planning. I wasn't going to just walk up to him again, all merciful and understanding. That punk and his goons had knocked me out and tried to kill me. Him and his gangster dad deserved each other.

All I had to do was go into my shop, get the components I needed for Vitulus's wards, grab the mystery magus's scarf, drop it off with Paetus for analysis, run back to Vitulus's, place the wards, and then I'd have a few hours before sundown to track down Balbus. I'd sleep him before he even knew I was there, drag him back to his dad's home, and dump him on the front stoop with a big bow on his head (I didn't want Tallium the Rat Killer anywhere near my shop again). Easy money.

Well it sounded easy at the time.

I nodded to Naevius and said, "Yes, sir, we have a deal. I will deliver your son to you by noon tomorrow." I planned on that evening, but I knew the best way to delight my customers was to under promise and over deliver.

Naevius gave me a rictus smile, as if he were baring his teeth at me rather than expressing any joy. "I look forward to it," he said.

He tapped twice on the palanquin. Tallium closed the drapes and then all four men picked up the palanquin's hand rails with as much effort as picking up a dead rat. They strolled back down the crowded Aventine ally in front of my shop, rounded a bend, and were gone from sight.

I glanced at my shop's wooden door and the *Natta Magus* plaque in the middle.

*There's no* way *I'm telling Lares about this.*

# EIGHTEEN

I managed to get through my front door and into my shop without Lares spiritually tackling me to the ground and kissing me to death. She was understandably worried about my abrupt departure last night, so I told her everything that happened. I left out Naevius's little visit since I knew she was close to blowing her mind with worry over the magical threats I faced. No use throwing mundane threats of impalement into the mix.

She took it all in with far more calm than I expected, never interrupting me or flying into a panicked fit like she always did when I was in a dangerous fix.

"So," she said slowly once I had finished, "in one night you've faced one, perhaps two Dark magi, with the power to enthrall you; a pod of corruptions; you've personally met Caesar Augustus; and you've taken on a job to search for the stolen Sibylline Books. Am I missing anything, my honey fig?"

I chewed the inside of my lip as I searched my component shelves for the ward ingredients that I needed for Vitulus's house. I'd already gathered a couple of vials and pouches on my worktable. "Um, no, that about covers it. I did have a few questions about—"

"You're a terrible liar, Natta Magus."

I glanced at her cherubic statue through the open doorway into my shop's front room. Its glow shifted back and forth from an angry red to a melancholy blue. I sighed inwardly because I knew what was coming next.

"And I know why you lie to me sometimes," she said, her voice catching. "I know I can be very protective of you, my love, my sweet pudding. It is only because I care for you so much. It wounds me, *wounds me*, dear Natta Magus, that you do not trust me enough to tell me the truth about the threats you—"

"Vitulus gave me some of his Pompeian sweet wine," I said, picking up the skin that I'd brought home with me. "Want some?"

I walked over to the small offering bowl in front of her glowing statue, uncorked the skin, and poured about a tablespoon into the dry bowl.

"Oh," she said, "oh my. That is superb." Her statue turned from its shifting red-to-blue glow to a more stable and content magenta. "Vitulus truly knows his...Wait, you cannot silence me with a fine wine, Natta Magus!" Her statue pulsed red again. "I may be a spirit, but I have emotions that must be expressed every bit as much as a corporeal human, or I will simply explode."

"I get that, Lares, but I need to leave soon, and I was hoping your wisdom would help me right now. You have the greatest, most beautiful intellect I've ever known, and you are one of the people who's kept me alive in Rome. Now I need the real story on the Sibylline Books, and you're the only one I trust who can give it to me. Will you help me, Lares?"

I watched her statue continue to pulse red a few moments, and then, as if she threw her hands in the air in surrender, the statue turned a loving pink.

"Oh, Natta Magus, my cheese puff, I cannot resist your sweet, silver tongue, even though I know you are using it to manipulate me. I don't care! If only I had a physical body, I could show you other ways to use—"

"Please don't go there, Lares," I muttered, rubbing the bridge of my nose.

She issued a suffering sigh. "Very well, pudding. What do you wish to know about the Sibylline Books?"

"For starters, are they magical?"

"They're not enchanted, if that's what you mean."

"Ah, so that priestess who sold them to Tarquin wasn't really a magus?"

Lares' statue pulsed orange with her amusement. "Oh, that story always tickles me in ways I wish you could, love. The real story is that Tarquin's men stole the books from a traveling priestesses in Magna Graeca outside Cumae. The whole story about the priestess selling the books to Tarquin was made up later to make the hated tyrant king look foolish."

I snorted. "I'm not sure how the original story wouldn't do the same. Stealing the Books strikes me as pretty dishonorable."

"Natta Magus, sometimes your ignorance of the Roman mind is so endearing that I just want to gobble you up." The statue shifted back and forth from pink love to a lustful red. "You confuse honor with foolishness. A Roman man who is bested by a woman in a business deal looks far more foolish—and is far more emasculated—than a Roman man who steals from a woman by force."

"Er, right. So if the books aren't enchanted then they're just...books?"

"Oh no, sweet buns, they're not 'just books'. They contain magical knowledge that someone with your talents could use to great effect."

"What kind of magical knowledge?"

"How to channel the power of belief."

"Okay..."

"Your intelligence is also beautiful, my plum, but I fear that I'm not making myself clear. You're able to cast spells mostly because you have the talent, but also because you *believe* you can. Without talent and belief, you could not wield magic. Most people in this time do not have that talent, so they cannot cast magic no matter how strongly they believe they can. What they *can* do, however, is believe together. If they do that, it draws attention from the spirit world, and sometimes their desires are realized."

I tried to keep my voice even, and asked, "What kind of spirits?" Lares had always been vague about the afterlife no matter how much I probed her, and I wondered if she had just given me an opening. My hopes were quickly dashed, though.

"Ah, love of my millennia, you are so precious. You know I cannot give those answers while you are this side of the veil. Suffice to say, strong beliefs shared by hundreds or thousands of people within a narrow location—like the city of Rome, for example—have the possibility of working their own magic. The Sibylline Books give magi knowledge on how to channel that."

The effects of belief on the spirit world, especially from a lot of people who believed the same thing, was known in my time, too, but it was also not well understood since the spirits that we communicated with were just as vague as Lares. My twenty-first century had almost as many faiths and religions as the Romans, but when you came right down to it, we knew about as much about the real spirit world as ancient Roman priests. Personally, my favorite was the Unknowable Will concept: the belief that God or gods/goddesses created it all, made up the rules, and intervened whenever the whim struck Him/Her/It/Them. Unfortunately there was no way to know the nature of that Will unless it chose to reveal itself. Or once you died, which I had no desire to hasten.

"So then...this mystery magus doesn't want any other magi to channel the belief magic of Romans? Why?"

"That is, as you say, the mystery, love."

"Do you know what's in the books?"

She gave me an uncharacteristic silence. I glanced at her statue, and it seemed to have frozen between pink and red.

"Lares?"

After a few moments, the colors seemed to shudder, and then they blinked out altogether.

Now I was worried. "Lares, are you all right?"

I stared at her statue, willing her to talk to me, to flicker, to do something. I prayed that I hadn't gotten her into trouble with my questions about the books. If they had something to do with belief magic and the spirit world, then I was treading awfully close to topics that she wasn't allowed to reveal.

I hesitantly let down my ball cap's wards to see if I could still sense her presence, which I could normally do when she was around. But I got nothing.

"Damnation," I muttered, my frown deepening. "Lares, if you can hear me, I need to go place those wards on Vitulus's home and then drop this scarf off at Paetus's. After I do that, I'll come right back and...figure something out. Okay?"

Still the unnerving silence and non-glowing statue. I gave a frustrated sigh and then left my shop.

I really hoped my roommate was okay.

# NINETEEN

I 'd just warded my shop door when I turned around and almost *cacced* in my linen breeches. The sun was high and in my eyes when I looked up, which cast the black figure standing on the street above me in shadows.

"Natta Magus, forgive me, I did not mean to startle you," said Tanith, the wife of the Canaanite scribe, Balnor, who lived next door to me. She had a thick Semitic accent, but she spoke Latin fluently. She wore a black tunica dress and black headscarf over her graying dark hair. She once told me that all the black helped when she inevitably got black ink on her clothes. She had a kind smile and always brought me water and "medicine" whenever my once-per-month food poisoning hit.

"It's alright, Tanith," I said, climbing the five steps up to the street. "I'm just a little jumpy. Busy day," I said, trying to edge my way down the street.

"Yes, you are always running to and fro," she said, her eyes crinkling with a smile. "Could you spare a moment? I wanted to point out something regarding the scrolls you ordered last week."

"Oh, I—"

"Helva!" she yelled past me. "Bring me those parchment sheets I asked you to gather!" She smiled at me again and said, "This won't take long, Natta Magus. So...is everything well?"

"Um, can't complain." I eyed my closed door, still worried about Lares. Romans and non-Romans alike believed in the spirit world and some iteration of house spirits who protected their homes, but most of them didn't really *believe*. That is to say, if they actually heard one talking to them, they'd probably run from their home screaming. So I wasn't ready tell Tanith that I might've finally broken my house spirit with too many questions.

"Really?" she said, one eyebrow raising. "Because I heard several armed men outside your shop last night..."

"Oh *that*," I said, then waved it off. "It was just Vitulus. Brought some of his friends and took me out for a night of, um, drinking."

"Vitulus. Your Praetorian friend? The clean-shaven one who never smiles...whose tunics and togas are impeccably white. He took you out *drinking*?"

"Yeah," I said, "he surprises me, too, sometimes. Listen, I really have to—"

"Helva!" she yelled again. "Where is that girl?"

I heard activity behind me, turned, and saw Tanith's niece, Helva, hurrying out of the shop carrying a stack of parchment. She also wore a black tunica dress and head scarf, similar to Tanith's, and had the Canaanite light brown skin with dark eyebrows and brown eyes. She was around nineteen years old and had come to live with Tanith and Balnor several months ago after her family was killed by bandits outside of Jerusalem.

I knew all this because Tanith tried to marry us every *caccing* time she saw me walk out my door.

Helva momentarily paused in her stride when she saw me, a look of exasperation tightening her lips, and then she continued toward us. From her expression, I got the feeling she was just as annoyed with Tanith's matchmaking attempts as I was. She certainly was a pretty girl, but I ached over losing Brianna. Even though it was eleven months ago.

"Tell Natta Magus how you acquired these sheets," Tanith said, practically pushing Helva toward me.

Helva gave me a quick, respectful nod, and then said, "Salve, Natta Magus. I know you ordered papyrus, but I...um, was able to procure parchment at the same price. My aunt suggested that I might offer you this as, um, an alternative since parchment is far more durable than papyrus." She gave her aunt a quick glare that Tanith didn't see since she was smiling at me and gauging my reaction to Helva's bargaining skills.

Parchment was indeed far more durable than the papyrus I usually ordered from Balnor and Tanith, but also far more expensive. "Thank you, Helva. I'm impressed. Same price, eh?"

She clenched her teeth and nodded once.

I had to at least act like I was considering the offer, even though I knew I'd take it. Most Canaanites were consummate traders, and it was a bit insulting to them if I didn't try to haggle a little. But what Helva was offering was such an obviously good deal that it was practically a gift. Should I haggle for a gift? I'd been writing all my spell experiments on papyrus since I arrived in Rome two years ago, and the first scrolls were already brown around the edges. It wouldn't be long before I had to re-copy everything onto new papyrus. This parchment, however, would keep for decades.

"This is a very generous offer," I said, rubbing my chin.

Tanith gave me a dismissive wave. "Consider it a gift as our way of thanking you for all of your orders over the last two years, Natta Magus. Right, Helva?"

"Yes," she muttered, "a gift."

"However, if your conscience needs to be assuaged," Tanith said, her eyes twinkling. *Ah, here's the real price,* I thought. "Perhaps you'd like to have dinner with us tomorrow evening? Helva knows many exotic recipes from Egypt, and my own Syrian recipes will only compliment hers. You won't find a better meal outside the Near East."

I glanced at Helva, who continued to stare at the parchment sheets in her hands, a pink flush showing on her brown cheeks. I couldn't tell if she was more embarrassed or angry with her aunt.

"Oh, um, I'm working a case with the Praetorians right now, so I'm not sure I'll be around tomorrow night. But that dinner sounds great, and I'd love to try out those recipes. Maybe another day?"

Helva looked a little relieved, Tanith looked a little disappointed, and I was a little impatient to get moving. Before Tanith could say anything, I said, "I really need to get on with that case, so maybe you can hang onto the parchment, and I'll pick it up when I return?"

Tanith nodded, her smile widening again at the prospect of another excuse to have me interact with her niece. "Of course we will, Natta Magus. We look forward to your return and that dinner."

"Me too," I said as I walked a few paces backward, gave them both a wave, and then merged into the foot traffic along the alley.

It's not that I don't want to get married someday. I do. Every time I see Vitulus and Claudia and little Lucius, I think that he's the luckiest guy in the world. It's just that...

Well, eleven months after losing Brianna, and it still felt like I last held her yesterday. Not a day went by that I didn't wonder what she was doing in the twenty-first century. How she was moving on with her life. And how it was likely with another man.

Damnation, it still brought a huge lump in the back of my throat when I thought about it. It wouldn't be fair to another woman if I jumped into a marriage while I was still in love with someone else.

Not to mention the crazy-huge cultural differences between me and any woman in this century. Brianna and I had deep personal *and* cultural connections. How would I find the same thing here?

So between my worry over Lares, my brooding over my love life and lack thereof, and the fact that the fate of the Republic seemed to rest on my shoulders, I was one grumpy magus by the time I arrived at Paetus's home in the Suburba. The Suburba, if you don't already know, is the vast maze of haphazard tenements and shops that lay in the valleys between Rome's Seven Hills. Paetus was technically a patrician, but you wouldn't know it by his home: it was about the size of my shop and wedged between a brothel and a gambling den. While Paetus's home was made of brick, the buildings around him were mostly wood and seemed to either collapse or burn down on a yearly basis. I had no idea what Paetus's financial situation was, but he never seemed to have trouble feeding himself or obtaining the scrolls and/or books he wanted for his daemonology library. Paetus wasn't happy unless he was in his home reading and writing.

I tapped on the heavy wooden door, trying to ignore the half-naked women standing outside the brothel next door promising me all sorts of ways to distract me from my worries. One of them actually had the same hair color as Brianna, and about the same height, same figure—

I shook my head and started pounding on the door with my open hand. "Paetus, open up, it's Natta."

I heard the bar on the other side slowly retract, and then the door inched open with the sound of wood scraping on stone. "Were you napping...?" I asked, and then my words trailed off and were forgotten.

A tall woman with long, straggly black hair stood before me. She was completely naked and her entire body was a sickly gray pale. She slowly raised her head, and the black hair fell away from her face. Her eyes were completely white. She had no mouth. A nauseous feeling hit me that I had come to know all too well whenever I encountered her kind.

I had time to think, *A* caccing *daemon*, before she lunged at me.

# TWENTY

When the naked daemon woman lunged at me, I had a horrible flashback to the strix daemons that I'd fought last year. They were also preternaturally fast, had absurdly long nails on absurdly long fingers, and could rip a man to pieces in seconds. I still had nightmares of them at least once a week. So seeing this nightmare come true leaping for my throat made my limbs freeze. This creature was going to gut me, and there was nothing I could do about it.

And then it hit an invisible barrier just inches from my nose. The barrier expanded from where the daemon's claws touched it, like it was pushing out the film of a bubble. But the barrier held and the daemon bounced backward.

I fell backward away from the door and scrambled on my bottom into the middle of the alley. The daemon tried to break through again, but this time I noticed the multicolored streaks that its claws made on contact with the barrier, which promptly disappeared. The daemon swiped at the barrier several more times within a fraction of a second, but then abruptly stopped and moved back into the shadows of the doorway where I could barely see it, as still as a marble statue.

The whole attack had taken maybe five seconds and had been soundless.

I must've stopped breathing, because I was suddenly gasping for air as if I'd just been underwater. I stared at the daemon, which stared back at me with its milky white eyes beneath the greasy black hair hanging over its mouthless face. Its pale, naked body was, um, anatomically correct for a twenty-something female. I suppose the better to distract you while the thing tore you to pieces.

"Damnation," I sputtered, finally able to form words. Men and women walked around me as I still sat in the alley leaning on my elbows. Most just ignored me, while some grumbled curses about "filthy beggars." The ladies next door kindly offered to "take care" of me right there since I was already in position.

None of them seemed to noticed the *caccing* daemon in Paetus's doorway.

I finally stood and brushed the dirt off my hands. "Okay," I muttered under my heavy breathing, "okay. Daemon. Right. What the hell did you summon, Paetus?"

"Natta, is that you?" came Paetus's voice from inside. "Help me!"

Apparently the magical "donut" that I had helped him set up had worked as designed—the daemon was trapped within the donut's anti-magic ring, while Paetus was still alive in the donut's hole in the center of his home. I'd enchanted a piece of chalk for him and told him to draw a circle in the middle of his home for this possibility.

Of course, the anti-magic properties in the barrier prevented me, someone with magic in his cells, from crossing it, too. I did have the components on me to bring the barrier down, though, and I did have spells that would banish the daemon back to its realm. The problem was that the banishment spell would take several seconds of casting; once the barrier came down, that thing would be on me in a *fraction* of a second.

I walked slowly toward the door and stopped at the point where I'd stood just out of the daemon's reach, which was basically the border between the building's shadow and the bright sunlight. The creature didn't move from its shadowy position. It just continued to stare at me with its milky eyes.

"Paetus," I yelled inside, "are you hurt?"

I heard a groan and immediately thought the worst. But then he said, "I'm so hungry, Natta!"

"How long have you been in there?"

"The whole night! There are grapes on my desk but they're in the do-ring." Paetus couldn't wrap his mind around the term donut. *It looks like a ring,* he'd said, *so it should be called a do-ring.*

"But are you hurt, Paetus?"

"No," he said sullenly, "just hungry and thirsty and feeling foolish."

"Okay, what am I dealing with here?" The daemon's milky eyes watched me as I yelled at Paetus, so I tried desperately not to look at it. It didn't even seem to be breathing, and I was stealing glances at its chest to be sure...

Damnation, I really hoped it had some kind of succubus mojo clouding my mind. Otherwise I *really* needed a girlfriend.

"I don't know what it is. I could tell you if I could get to my books."

"Then how did you summon it?"

"I didn't! It came out of a—"

At that moment, the daemon took a swipe at me again. I was wary enough not to *cac* my breeches, but I did cry an unmanly yelp and jumped back. This time, however, the daemon's claws broke through the filmy barrier with multicolored sparks. It took several more swipes within the blink of an eye, but it couldn't get more than its claws through the barrier. It settled back into the shadows again and stood still, watching me as if it hadn't moved.

"Aw, damnation," I muttered. *The barrier is fading and I know why.* "Paetus, you didn't happen to cross the barrier during the night, did you?"

"Well," he said, "I did reach for the water jug on my shelf when the daemon wasn't looking. Only my arm crossed that time. Then I had to piss, but I aimed it outside the barrier. I guess that counts as a crossing. I mean, I wasn't going to sit in my own—"

"Okay, Paetus, the barrier is going to fade pretty soon. We need to figure out how to banish this thing before it gets to you or escapes into the city."

I didn't want to get into the fact that his crossing the barrier several times had accelerated its expiration date, which should've been more like a month if it was left alone. Yeah, it was a design flaw, but the barrier was only meant to be a temporary sanctuary to keep him safe if any of his dabbling went awry. In that respect, it had worked beautifully.

"Great, I am covered in ears," he yelled.

I had to grin despite the circumstances. He loved to use my twenty-first century Detroit metaphors (like "I'm all ears"), but rarely ever got them right.

"I'm going to drop the donut barrier—"

"That thing will attack me, you have no idea how fast it is!"

"No, it's going to attack *me*." I gave it one more glance. It seemed to know that I was up to something, for its head had leaned forward almost imperceptibly as if it were preparing another lunge. Its white eyes stayed on me through the greasy black hair over its face. "And yes, I know how fast it is."

I stepped back several steps, into the sunlight and onto the alley's brick road and the foot traffic of oblivious Romans. I turned my Wolverines ball cap around so that the bill faced backwards and pointed my right hand, palm out, toward the barrier. I siphoned some cell magic, felt its warmth caress every inch of my skin, and then released it with, *"Omlaag brengen van de barrière."*

The donut barrier winked out with a magical pop that only someone with arcane senses could feel. And at virtually the same instant, the daemon lunged toward me again. It got past the point where it had been stopped before and crossed from the shadows into the sunlight...and then stopped, writhing in obvious pain. It didn't make a sound, but it jumped back into the shadows. Its entire body shook so badly that I thought the thing was going to explode right there. But it held itself together. It really looked pissed now: It opened and closed its clawed fists and shifted from left to right on its bare feet. The daemon shook its head back and forth in jerky moves that would've broken a human being's neck.

"Yeah," I growled at the angry daemon, "figured you'd hate sunlight. The pasty skin gives it away, you know."

I heard several screams to my left and quickly glanced at the ladies who, a moment before, had been slinging propositions my way. They stared in horror at Paetus's doorway, where the daemon had slunk back into the shadows.

"You may want to go inside," I told them.

They simply looked from me to the doorway, frozen in shock a moment, and then they all rushed inside. I didn't think I'd have to worry about them getting in the way.

I didn't look around me to see if any other pedestrians had noticed the daemon, for I didn't want to lose my focus on it. I siphoned more cell magic for the banishment spell and cried, *"Dit alles hier worden bewaakt in de tijd, en er in de eeuwigheid!"*

I immediately knew something was wrong. The daemon should've started steaming and bubbling and melting into a pile of daemon goo with that spell, which severs the daemon's link to this world.

Instead, it started to shake even more. And then a second head popped out of its shoulders. Then another pair of shoulders, and arms, then a torso, until finally a second daemon had pulled itself out of the first. Now *two* daemons stared at me, shifting on their feet in obvious anger.

"You gotta be kidding!" I cried. This thing had an anti-banishment ward? Daemons, as a rule, cannot cast magic. Either this was a brand new daemon that could break those rules...or another magus had summoned it and cast the ward on it.

As the first daemon continued to watch me, the second one turned into the house.

That's when Paetus started screaming.

# TWENTY-ONE

So now I had two daemons with supernatural quickness and nasty black claws and shapely bodies to distract me. I couldn't banish them because they somehow had an anti-banishment ward that not only blocked the spell, but caused them to duplicate. And now, while the first one blocked my way in, the second was on its way to shred Paetus.

Sometimes being the "chosen one" sucks.

Since banishment didn't work—and I sure as hell didn't want to spawn another one by trying the spell again—I had to get creative. One thing I did know was that they didn't like sunlight. Could I lure the daemon out to me again? I doubted it. Since the thing kept to the shadows, it looked like it had learned its lesson.

And then it clicked. If I couldn't bring the daemon into the sunlight, maybe I could bring sunlight to the daemon.

I held my palm up, siphoned a bit of cell magic, and a spark globe popped into existence about two feet above my open hand. Its ethereal glow didn't shine as brightly in the daylight, but it was like its own little ball of sunshine. And I sent it zooming right toward the daemon in the entry.

The daemon immediately backed away from it and started trembling in the same unnatural way it had when actual sunlight had touched it. I pressed my attack, pushing the daemon back into Paetus's home as I stepped over his threshold. I backed the daemon into an alcove that must've once held a tall statue. The creature quivered so fast now, like a fly's wings, that I could only see it as a vague fuzzy shape. When I pushed the spark globe onto its skin, the daemon exploded into a yellow-white goo that looked like pus. I didn't have time to gloat as Paetus was screaming for my help.

I raced through the small atrium—empty planters surrounding a dry, circular impluvium pool—and charged into Paetus's small library, which seemed the only place in the house that looked lived in.

Paetus was hiding behind a workbench, with the second daemon on the other side taking the occasional swipe at him with its long black claws. The daemon quivered as fast as the one I banished, which I figured was symptom of the sunshine its twin had endured. It was probably weakened, and the only reason Paetus was still alive.

"Natta, help me!" Paetus cried from behind the workbench.

The daemon whirled around and faced me as soon as Paetus cried out. Without hesitating, the thing lunged toward me, all silent and naked, sharp claws ready to disembowel me.

I flung my spark globe at the daemon just as it got within three paces of me. As soon as the globe touched the daemon, it exploded into the same pus-like goo as its sibling.

Between the first daemon and the second, I realized that I was covered in the stuff from face to feet. I tried to find a clean spot on my tunica that I could use to wipe my mouth before I accidentally licked my lips. It wouldn't hurt me, but I had no desire to swallow daemon guts.

But as I was wiping the crud off, it began to steam and then evaporate before my eyes. It only took moments before my tunica and face were dry.

One good thing about daemons: Kill them right, and they clean up nicely.

Paetus stood still, his eyes wide, his back against some shelves, where he had knocked over several items. Or maybe they were already arranged haphazardly. I could never tell with brilliant, disorganized Paetus. He was short even for a Roman, had curly auburn hair and a beard to match. He actually looked more Gallic than Roman. He wore a dark blue tunica that symbolized his flamen social status. He was a portly fellow who reminded me more of the guys in Detroit who argued obscure hockey stats over the mirror nets, than the scion of an old Roman patrician family.

When he didn't move after several moments, I said, "You're welcome."

That seemed to break his shock. He lunged for the bowl of grapes on his workbench and began devouring them with as much gusto as the daemons would've likely devoured him. Or tore him to pieces, I suppose, since they had no mouths.

"Gods above and below," he said through mouthfuls of grapes, "I thought I was going to die. That thing just stood there and stared at me the whole night. The whole night, Natta Magus! I yelled and screamed, but nobody helped me!"

"In this neighborhood?" I said. "Strikes me as the kind of place where people yell and scream for help all the time. What in damnation was that thing?"

Paetus had somehow located a half loaf of bread and was adding it to the grapes already filling his mouth. "Don't know what it was," he mumbled through the food. "It came out of that thing." He waved a hand toward the edge of his reading table, but I didn't see anything there.

"Came out of what?"

"Floor," Paetus said.

I looked around the table to all the junk that had fallen on the floor during Paetus's flight from the daemon. More scrolls, wax tablets, an oil lamp that had somehow avoided burning down the house, and a—

My skin went cold and my hands started sweating.

It was a black bishop chess piece.

# TWENTY-TWO

As soon as Paetus stopped stuffing food in his mouth, I wanted to throw questions at him as fast as the daemons could move, but I knew I'd only confuse him and/or make him so nervous that he'd start eating again.

"Where did you get that?" I asked slowly. I didn't touch the bishop, nor did I try a First Scan on it. I had to think about what I wanted to do because the mystery magus was awfully good at getting me to nearly kill myself. I stared at the bishop and hoped that its secrets would just reveal themselves to me. No such luck.

Paetus came over next to me, and before I could stop him, he reached down and picked up the bishop.

"Paetus!" I yelped.

"What?" He looked around the room as if another daemon had jumped into existence.

"Don't touch that thing!"

He dropped the bishop and backed away. "Oh Juno, did I summon the daemon when I touched it?"

"When did you touch it?"

"Many times!" He was getting panicky now, staring at the bishop as it rolled back and forth on the floor where he dropped it. "Do you think more will come out?"

I immediately brought my spark globe to hover above it just in case something did come out, but nothing happened. It stopped rolling back and forth on the tile floor and came to a stop on its side. After several moments, I started breathing again.

I glared at Paetus. "Tell me *exactly* what happened: how you got that thing, how the daemon was summoned, everything. Do not leave out any details."

Paetus licked his lips, which still glistened with grape juice and bread crumbs. "A few weeks ago a man came in saying he was the slave of gens Furia and that his dominus had an interest in daemonology, and wanted to borrow some of my books for—"

"What did this man look like?"

He shrugged. "He looked Greek to me."

"Details, Paetus!"

"Oh, ah, short black hair, black eyebrows, spoke with a Greek accent. Had this silly half-beard that ran down the sides of his face, but stopped near his chin."

I frowned. *At least he's making it easy for me to identify him. Is that the point of his stupid half-beard?* I nodded for Paetus to continue.

"So he borrowed a few of my texts on the underworld pantheon. They were mostly just religious rituals to appease Pluto, nothing that actually summoned any of his servants. I figured they were harmless enough to give to a capped."

I once slipped in calling non-magical people "capped" in front of Paetus, and he had run with that description ever since, as if he was a magus, too. I know, I know. Some non-magical people find it insulting, but I came from a world where maybe 1% of the population was born without magical talent. Condescension toward them—intentional *and* unintentional—was so ingrained in my time that I sometimes didn't even think about it. It took my marooning in ancient Rome among the "capped"—to be the *real* odd one out—for me to actually think about it.

"And then yesterday morning he came back with the texts, thanked me for them, and then gave me that totem," Paetus said, pointing at the bishop. "He said it was a hand-carved fascinus that his master wanted to give me as a token of his appreciation. He set it down on my workbench. I told him I was honored, and then he left. Afterward, I"—Paetus swallowed—"picked it up and placed it on my totem shelf. It didn't match with the other totems, so I put it back on my work table so I could decide what to do with it later."

I glanced around at his, to my eyes, chaotically organized shelves and briefly wondered what his definition of "match" was. Shelves lined all four walls, from floor to ceiling, and each shelf was haphazardly packed with scrolls, proto-books, wax tablets, and various baubles and knick-knacks that had varying layers of dust.

"When did the daemon come out of it?" I asked.

"Just before dusk," Paetus said, and then groaned. "I was about to eat dinner."

Around the same time as the mystery magus was stealing the Sibylline Books. *Coincidence?*

"So you didn't do anything to summon it?" I asked. "You didn't touch the, um, fascinus or say arcane words? Maybe *look* at it?"

He shook his head miserably. "I was picking up a *caccing* grape! May Jupiter strike me if not so!"

"Okay, I believe you." I sighed, then asked, "What kind of daemon do you think it was?"

"Oh, I know exactly what it was: A Dea Tacita daemon."

He walked around behind me, so that he didn't have to step over the bishop, and then stopped at a shelf that looked just as disorganized as every other shelf in the dark, little library. He rummaged through a few wax tablets and scroll tubes until he found the tube he wanted. He pulled the scroll out and then spread it over his worktable. My spark globe still hung in the room, so I was easily able to see the scroll's Greek writing and the pictures.

"I copied this two years ago from a text I found in Ravenna," he said, sounding more like himself and less crazy with fear and hunger. "According to common tradition, Dea Tacita is one of the goddesses of the underworld, but that's not entirely accurate. The text that I copied was far older than the common rituals of today, so it must be *more* accurate."

I didn't want to argue with Paetus that just because the text was older that didn't make it "more accurate." Besides, further words melted away as I suddenly spied the image of the Dea Tacita that Paetus had copied near the middle of the scroll: a thin, naked woman without a mouth. Her black hair reached down to her feet, but other than that, the drawing was spot on with what I just banished, right down to the long claws on her fingers.

"In this text," Paetus continued, pointing to a few lines near the image, "the Dea Tacita has been called the 'silent goddess' for, well, obvious reasons. But in addition to the mouth thing, she's also a rather effective assassin."

"Assassin?" I said. Ah, damnation, was this another attempt on Augustus's life? Or maybe a senator? A patrician? Someone who accidentally stepped on the mystery magus's toes? Me? The target could be anyone.

And that was what turned my blood cold. The magus could put a chess piece, or any enchanted object, wherever he wanted, and out would pop a Dea Tacita at a certain time ready for murder.

I had to tell Vitulus right away.

But I also knew that Aper, not to mention Capito and Augustus, would want more information about this daemon and its capabilities. And I certainly didn't have the time or patience to learn Greek to read it myself, so...

"You have to come with me so we can explain this to Vitulus's boss," I said. "And before you turn me down, let me remind you that if it wasn't for me, you'd either be starving to death or there'd be little pieces of you all over your collections."

He suddenly remembered that he was supposed to be mad at me for outing his daemonology interests to Vitulus. "No. Sorry. Can't do it."

"Come on, Paetus, nobody's going to throw you in jail for your work."

"Maybe, maybe not. But I have a lucrative role performing religious rituals for my family's clients and patrons. Some of them are very much on the side of Augustus's morality laws. It's bad enough your Praetorian friend knows about me. If my patrons found out I'm into this stuff—"

"People already know you're into this stuff!"

"But not the people who pay me," Paetus said. "The people who know *me* and the people who know my *family* inhabit two different worlds. I thought you knew how that worked by now." He shook his head. "I'm sorry, Natta Magus. I'll help you as much as I can, but only from this room."

I shrugged. "Fine, I'll just leave this 'fascinus' here and be on my way." I walked toward his door.

"What?" he sputtered. "You can't just—Hey, what if it comes back!"

"Then you can study it in this room," I said over my shoulder. I continued out through the open door and into the alley. The ladies next door were still inside, but the alley was just as busy with oblivious citizens as it was before I banished the daemon in their midst.

Now there was no way I was going to just leave that bishop behind for Paetus or someone else to re-summon the Dea Tacita. If he hadn't stopped me within my next ten steps, I would've turned around and marched back into his home to put a containment dome over the bishop, whether he came with me or not. But Paetus didn't know that. I knew I was putting him in a difficult spot, and I felt pretty rotten about that. I didn't want to do anything to destroy his only source of income, but I also knew that my mystery magus was probably planning an assassination and that the Dea Tacita was the perfect weapon. Vitulus and Aper had to be warned now, and they would have a ton of reasonable questions that I couldn't answer alone. Paetus and his scrolls *had* to come with me.

And I also knew the mystery magus was still playing a game with me. What did the chess pieces mean? They were growing in value with each one I found:

first a pawn, then a knight, and now a bishop. Did that mean the danger would rise as well?

And how long had this guy been watching me to know that I was friends with Paetus? He must've known I would consult my daemonology guy at some point during this game, so did he set this trap for me? This guy was really scaring me with how much he knew about me and my methods. Not only was he was corrupted by soul magic, he was still brilliant enough to plan all this out.

It was William Ford level planning. Queue cold shiver.

"Fine, I'll come with you!" Paetus yelled from behind me.

I stopped and turned around. He stood in his doorway with the rolled up scroll in his hands, hugging it to his chest like a newborn. "But what are we going to do about..." He gave the passing citizens a worried glance, then made a sideways nod inside.

I walked back to him. "I'll take care of it," I said. "I know how difficult this is for you, so thank you."

He gave me a nervous scowl and said, "The fate of the Republic better be at stake here, because I'm risking an awful lot for this."

I sighed. *I sure hope Fortuna didn't hear that.*

# TWENTY-THREE

After I raised a small containment dome over the bishop—and put a "walk away" ward on Paetus's door—we both marched up the Caelius Hill toward Vitulus's home. Paetus seemed to turn a sickly shade of pale green the closer we got, and I wondered if he was going to vomit all the grapes and bread he ate on Vitulus's front door step. I also made sure that we walked side-by-side so that I could grab him if he decided to run off.

"You're going to be fine," I assured him during our walk. "Vitulus could care less about your daemonology interests. In fact, he's pretty glad I know someone who can give me all the knowledge you have. If you hadn't told me how to banish that toga-eating *vermis* daemon, there'd be a lot of naked senators debating in the Curia Julia right now. And *no one* wants to see that."

As if he didn't hear me, he mumbled under his breath, "I can't be banished. I have nowhere to go. And if they fine me, I can't pay. They'd have to flog me. Gods, I can't be flogged; my skin is too tender! I've had paper cuts that took days to heal!"

"Paetus, you're not going to be flogged."

"They might throw me into the Tullarium," he muttered miserably. "I've read the ghosts of past prisoners haunt that dungeon." He grabbed my arm as if he were a drowning man. "What if they execute me, Natta Magus?"

"I'm no lawyer, but I think executions are reserved for treason."

"But believing in beings that contradict the Roman pantheon could be construed as treason to Augustus's—"

"Paetus," I said, stopping in the street. "Look at me; I'm about as far away from the Roman pantheon as you can get, and yet nobody has fined me or flogged me or executed me." *Yet,* I thought, and then quickly banished that ever present fear. "And I've been working with the Praetorians for almost two years."

That seemed to calm him a little. He blinked several times and nodded. "Yes. Very true. They'd probably kill you before they killed me. Yes."

"Now can we get moving?" I asked.

He nodded, and we continued on to Vitulus's home. He still looked scared, but at least he wasn't about to run off screaming.

When we arrived, I tapped my foot on the heavy wooden door in the polite Roman fashion. We only had to wait a few moments before Calla opened the small porthole to peer out at us and then shut it to unbar the door. When she opened it, she nodded her head to me like I was a patrician and said, "Salve, Natta Magus."

I glanced past her and asked, "Is Vitulus around?"

"No, Natta Magus," she said, her eyes directed at my chest. "The *dominus* took his family to Salvius Aper's home. He was very adamant about telling the prefect what happened last night."

Paetus gave a small squeak and started to back away. I grabbed his forearm in what I hoped was a good Vitulus-style grip, but kept talking to Calla.

"When did he leave?"

"About an hour ago, Natta Magus."

"Thank you, Calla, we'll meet him there."

"Yes, Natta Magus," she said, and then shut the door and barred it again.

The door had barely clicked shut when Paetus said, "I am *not* going to the home of the prefect of the *caccing* Praetorian Guard!"

I put my hands on his shoulders. "Remember what I just said? I've been working with Vitulus and Aper for almost two years. They will not arrest you, because they haven't arrested me!"

*Yet*, Cynical Me repeated.

*Stop it*, yelled Trusting Me.

"That's because you're useful to them," he groaned. "I'm just a short flamen from a dying gens. I'm the kind of man they make examples of."

"Then *be* useful! You sit in your library all day studying your texts, but what do you *do* with all that knowledge? Do you try to make a difference to anybody? I know you don't, because every time I see you, you're either collecting and reading or reading and collecting." I sighed, and then gave him a penetrating stare. "A great oracle in my time named Tolkien once said that even the smallest person can change the course of history. That includes 'short flamens from a dying gens'. Do you want to resurrect your gens? Well helping me is a great way to start. I can't translate that text without you, Paetus, and I don't have your daemonology knowledge."

Paetus groaned again, never meeting my eyes. He lowered his head and then nodded.

"I'm not going to have to put a chain on you, am I?" I asked suspiciously. "I don't want to worry about you bolting in the crowds the first chance you get."

"I won't bolt," he said sullenly. "You'll just find me later anyway."

"Okay. I trust you then."

I had to pull on his arm to get his feet moving, but once they did, he followed without hesitation. I understood the instinct to want to keep your head down in a society where non-conformists were either ostracized or worse. It's what I had wanted to do when I first arrived in Rome, though I did a miserable job of it. But my experience at Aventicum showed me that I didn't have that option. I was in ancient Rome for a reason. Though I still had no idea what the reason was, my instincts told me that it wasn't to keep my head down. All I could do was use my magic to help out where I could. Maybe that also included using my persuasion skills to help Paetus do the same.

We arrived at Aper's home on the Palatine Hill about a half hour later, and I tapped on one of the large wooden double doors with my foot. Nicia, Aper's head slave, opened the door for us. He knew me well, and said, "Salve, Natta Magus, but my dominus is not here right now."

"Oh," I said, glancing past him into the small courtyard beyond the door. "Did Vitulus and his family show up?"

He nodded. "A few hours ago. And then they all went to the Circus Maximus. The Princeps himself invited them to watch the races in his personal box."

I didn't want to look at Paetus. I didn't sense him move at all, which I couldn't tell if it was a good thing or a bad thing.

But I was also annoyed with Vitulus for deviating from the plan we had discussed this morning. Not to mention that he was off watching chariot races in the midst of a national crisis, or what I assumed was a national crisis. And he had taken his family? I thought he was scared to death for them and wanted to keep them safe behind warded walls?

I still needed to tell him what was going on, and I didn't want to wait until the evening when he returned.

"Nicia, can you take us to the Circus and...the Princep's box? We *really* need to talk to Aper and Vitulus. It's state security stuff."

He nodded at once. "The Praetorians guarding the box know me, so we should get in without a problem. The crowds are rather large today, though, with the holiday, so it may take us some time to get through them."

"That's fine, but we need to leave now."

"Of course, Natta Magus. Let me inform the rest of the household first." He turned around and went into the house, leaving the door slightly ajar.

I turned to Paetus who was simply staring straight ahead with a blank, expressionless face.

"You doing okay?" I asked.

He nodded once.

"You heard what Nicia said, right?"

Another nod.

"You're not going to faint?"

He shook his head. At least he understood my words and had not gone completely catatonic at the thought of meeting Augustus. I only hoped he was able to speak by the time we got to the Circus.

"I'm betting we won't even see Augustus. Nicia will just send word to Aper, and then Aper and Vitulus will come out and meet us."

Paetus nodded. I decided to shut up lest I say something that would break his tenuous hold on his courage.

Nicia returned with another slave, who shut and barred the doors again behind us, and then we were on our way to the Circus.

And Nicia wasn't kidding about the crowds. We had only walked two blocks from Aper's home when we found the Circus foot traffic flowing through the narrow Roman alleys and streets. The Circus Maximus itself could hold around 150,000 people, but on holidays like Ludi Apollinares, the streets around it were usually packed with double that number: people gambling over the races, browsing the carts that sold food or wares, or just simply milling about trying to catch a glimpse of famous racers, gladiators, or senators.

The Circus Maximus itself wasn't as impressive as the Colosseum that would dominate the Roman skyline in about eighty years, but it was still a sight to behold. It was made mostly of wood timbers and brick archways. From the outside it looked like a 2,000-foot long rectangle with rounded ends on the short sides. Some of the bleachers, particularly in the middle, rose about fifty feet high, while the rounded sides were only about twenty feet. All around the Circus building were alcoves for shops and gambling dens, where merchants called out their wares and odds, only adding to the din of the crowds. It was easily the largest and most crowded structure in the entire empire.

Nicia led Paetus and me through the crush of people with the purposeful stride of a bloodhound. I was lucky since I was easily six inches taller than most of the people and could see where I was going. Paetus, however, was easily six inches shorter than everyone and had to endure virtual blindness and stale body odor. I had to push him ahead of me while holding tight to his shoulders as he hugged the Dea Tacita scroll to his chest. Not only did I keep an eye on Nicia, but I also glanced around the crowd for my mystery magus. Every time I caught a glimpse of a black tunica, or a man with short black hair and a beard, my heart would leap into my throat. Hell, I was so hyper-aware of everything that I was seeing almost everyone I knew in the crowds: the printer's wife, Tanith; her niece, Helva; Vitulus; Aper; Capito. I briefly lost Nicia at one point, but found him again after a few moments panic.

I really hate large crowds.

Nicia finally got us to the southeast end of the Circus and to an archway that faced the Palatine Hill and Augustus's palace. There were far fewer people here since the main Circus entrances were on the other side. Several Praetorians in blue tunicas and swords at their belts stood by an open stairway. This was where senators and other connected Romans entered.

Nicia stopped a dozen paces from the guards and said, "Let me speak to them first, Natta Magus. They know me, but I do not think they know you."

I nodded, and Nicia walked over to the guards.

I glanced at Paetus, who still wore the wide-eyed look of a man about to face the lions in the arena. "It's going to be all right, Paetus," I said. "You want anything to eat?" The smells from the nearby food stalls were making my stomach growl despite my ramped up nerves.

Surprisingly, Paetus shook his head, continuing to stare at nothing with those wide eyes. Then he licked his lips and said, "I'm not worried about that anymore."

"Well good, because you don't have to—"

"I am worried about that, though," he said, nodding to the spot where he'd been staring all along.

I followed his gaze to a spot on the floor near the brick arch. Right next to the arch column sat a black bishop chess piece.

"And that," Paetus said, pointing to a second bishop at the next archway. "And those..."

Next to every archway that I could see, going around the Circus, sat a black bishop chess piece.

*Damnation*, I thought. *His goal isn't to assassinate. It's to slaughter.*

# TWENTY-FOUR

I jogged a short way around the semi-circular end of the Circus. Every archway and entrance into the arena did indeed have a bishop piece. There had to be dozens of them. Hundreds, maybe. A few had been kicked around by the jostling crowds, but I didn't think the mystery magus cared. A lot of people would die no matter where the chess pieces lay. I saw it all in my imagination in grisly detail: Dea Tacitas disemboweling and dismembering thousands, panicked crowds stampeding the young and the weak.

Rome could literally fall today.

I ran back to Paetus just as Nicia came back with a questioning look. Before he could speak, I said, "We need to talk to Aper and Vitulus *now*!"

Startled by my sudden panic, Nicia said, "They want you to come up."

"Even better," I said.

I grabbed Paetus by the forearm and led him toward the stairwell and the Praetorians. Two of them led the way up the stairs, while another two fell in behind us. Paetus didn't even resist. I got the feeling that he'd rather be in the presence of Augustus than a hundred Dea Tacita daemons.

I had to physically restrain myself from running up those stairs, too. When was the magus going to release the daemons? Was it going to happen if I tried poking at one of them? Would it happen at a certain time? Was it happening *now*? I tried listening for terrified screams from the crowds but could hardly hear anything over my thundering heart.

The Praetorians led us from the stairwell to a long hallway where another contingent of three Praetorians stood. Responding to some hidden signal from the two in front of me, the three at the doorway opened the door and stepped aside to let us pass.

When I stepped onto Augustus's private Circus box, I first noticed the twenty or so benches and couches arranged overlooking the Circus. Augustus and

Livia sat near the front, their backs to me, while Aper and his wife, and then Vitulus and his family sat to Augustus's left. Some other senators that I didn't know sat to Augustus's right. Capito was noticeably absent.

After noticing the people in the box, I took a moment to stare at the spectacle beyond them. The last time I'd been in the Circus was when I woke up from William Ford's memory wipe spell two years ago, and it had been completely empty then. From this perch, with the 150,000 Romans spread out before me cheering on the thundering charioteers on the sand track below, it was a quite different place. I'd been to loud, raucous sporting events in my home time—nothing like playoff Wolverines baseball!—but those events were commonplace. What I saw from Augustus's perch was a spectacle that only Romans could enjoy, because it did not happen anywhere else in the ancient world.

Pennants of myriad colors hung from dozens of poles on the median on the track around which the charioteers raced. The other side of the Circus had sections reserved for senators, as almost everyone there was dressed in gleaming white togas. The sections behind them were full of plebeians and non-citizens dressed in drab gray and brown tunicas. The occasional colored pennant waved among the crowds, all in the plebeian sections. I noticed a blue chariot had broken down at the turn nearest to me, but the action didn't stop as racers careened around the median and tried their best to either avoid the accident or push their opponents into it. Multiple criers stood atop small towers in the dividing area using long cones to call out lead changes, or warning of accidents to spectators on the other side who couldn't see them. Above the Circus, long multicolored awnings stretched over the crowds along ropes that crisscrossed the arena, shielding all but the track from the hot sun.

Vitulus suddenly interrupted my gaping. "I apologize for not waiting, but I felt I had to—"

I waved him off. "Forget it. You need to evacuate these people from the Circus, and you need to do it now."

Vitulus stared at me, a smile creeping onto his lips, which then disappeared. "You're serious."

"Yeah," I said, as Aper joined us.

"What's wrong, Natta Magus?" he asked.

Paetus was still with me, looking nervous as ever, but I pulled him forward and then told Aper and Vitulus exactly what happened with the Dea Tacita daemon. And then I told them about all the bishop time bombs arranged throughout the Circus. The expressions of Aper and Vitulus turned from disbelief to fearful to stony resolve at almost the same pace. Both kept glancing at their families near Augustus as I explained the bloody violence that I suspected the Dea Tacitas would unleash.

"I have no idea how many there are down there," I said, "but if each one releases a daemon all at the same time..."

"Sir," Vitulus said to Aper, "if Natta Magus says there's a danger, I believe him."

"I believe him too," Aper said to Vitulus in low tones, "but I can guarantee the Princeps will *not* cancel the games and tell everyone to go home. This holiday has been planned for months. We'd have a riot on our hands."

"What is this talk of riots?"

We'd been so focused on our discussion that Augustus had approached us without any of us noticing. He had a mild, inquisitive expression, but he spoke in the same low tones that we were using. Paetus squeaked once beside me, but held his ground. Vitulus and Aper straightened, while I turned to Augustus and screwed up my courage.

"Sir, the people in the Circus are in danger, and I think...I think you should cancel the games and tell them to go home."

He raised an eyebrow, but at least he didn't laugh me out of the box. He glanced at Aper, who merely returned his look with a grim one of his own. Then Augustus said to me, "Does this have to do with what happened at Capito's farm in Pompeii and the...thief?"

Now it was my turn to raise an eyebrow. I wondered what *that* debriefing must've been like. "Yes, sir. I believe they're related. The thief has set up daemon traps throughout the Circus. If we don't get everyone out, the daemons will kill hundreds if not thousands of people."

Augustus turned to Aper again. "And you believe there will be riots if I cancel the games like Natta Magus is asking?"

Aper nodded grimly. "I do, Princeps. But I've also worked with Natta Magus long enough to believe him when he says there is a danger. The way I see it, we have to choose between a riot or a slaughter."

Augustus pursed his lips and then looked out among the cheering and screaming throngs below his box. "Most of these people," he said distractedly, "have very little to look forward to in their lives. I give them these games to distract them from that fact, even if it is for a day." He looked at me. "You would have me take that away from them?"

"To save their lives? Absolutely, sir."

He smiled. "Ah, yes, you serve a 'humanity that lives forever'. Just be careful not to confuse humanity with individual humans."

I just stared at him, not sure what he meant by that. But then he nodded once to indicate that he'd made a decision. "Very well. Magister Cocceius?"

An older man with balding white hair, who'd been sitting in the section to Augustus's right, looked up and then rose to approach us. "Yes, Princeps?"

"Tell the officials below to halt the race. Then tell your criers to announce that the games have been canceled for the day due to inauspicious signs from the gods. Everyone is to leave the Circus in an orderly fashion and return to their homes, lest the gods grow angry and bring doom upon Rome. I'll leave the details of that doom to you, magister."

Cocceius's face grew paler as Augustus relayed his orders. When Augustus finished, Cocceius sputtered, "But, Princeps, the people...they won't like it!"

Augustus smiled at Cocceius's understatement. "I'm aware of that, magister," he said mildly. "Carry out my orders nevertheless."

Cocceius gave Augustus a reluctant nod. "Yes, Princeps," he said, then hurried out of the box.

Augustus then turned to Aper and Vitulus. "Take whatever men you can gather to ensure the crowds disperse in an orderly fashion. I do not want any rioting, so use whatever force you deem necessary to deal with any malefactors."

I knew that he had nowhere near the amount of men it would take to put down a full-fledged riot with 150,000 people. The Praetorian Guard wasn't exactly a police force—in fact, Rome at that time didn't really *have* a police force—so they were not trained to enforce order. But I also understood that they were the only organized, armed body that had any hope of doing so. Aper and Vitulus exchanged grim looks, but Aper acknowledged Augustus's orders with clenched teeth. I knew they'd do their duty with what they had.

Aper then turned to me and asked, "If these creatures should appear, how do we kill them?"

"I know sunlight will do the trick if you can keep them out in it for a while. Paetus, anything else in your scroll?"

Paetus gave me a jerky nod, and said, "L-Let me read a m-moment." He unfurled his scroll with shaky hands and started reading through it.

As Paetus read, Aper turned to Augustus. "Sir, I apologize if this request is an imposition, but would you be kind enough to take our—"

Augustus raised a hand and said, "Your families will be cared for. Both of them. My personal guards will escort them to my home, where they will be safe. At least as safe as anyone can be if these daemons should appear."

Aper and Vitulus nodded gratefully. History said how gracious Augustus was to those who served him, yet ruthless to his enemies. I suppose he understood that as Rome's first *de facto* emperor—never mind what he called himself in public—he had to earn the loyalty of his subjects if he wanted to stay in power and not suffer the fate of his mentor, Julius Caesar. He reigned for forty years in my history, so he certainly did something right.

"H-Here it is, Natta," Paetus said in his nervous, squeaky voice. "The Dea Tacita can also be banished by striking it in the mouth—er, at least where its mouth should be."

"What sort of strike?" Vitulus asked. "Must it be with a sword, a fist, what?"

"Um," Paetus said, reading furiously. After several moments, he shook his head and gave Vitulus an apologetic look. "I'm sorry, the original text only said 'strike!'"

"The best thing," I said, "would be to lure them into the sunlight, or at least get the citizens into the sunlight. I can use a spark globe to banish individuals, but I can't do that to an army of them."

Vitulus said to Aper, "With your leave, sir, I will gather the men." Vitulus kept his eyes on his prefect, but I could see he had to restrain himself from glancing at his family behind Aper.

But Aper shook his head. "I know that is your duty as my second, but I want you to stay with Natta Magus. If his...talents are needed, then you are the best man here to guard his back."

Over the last two years, Vitulus and I had worked so many supernatural missions that we had grown into an actual team. So I was very happy to hear Aper's orders; Vitulus, however, looked disappointed. I knew it had nothing to do with working with me and everything to do with his Roman pride taking a hit. As Aper's second, it should've been *him* leading the Praetorians into battle. I was a bit proud of my understanding, since just a year ago I would've taken Vitulus's sour look as annoyance with me.

Yay, me.

Aper called over one of the Praetorians manning the door to the box, relayed Augustus's orders, and then the Praetorian hurried off to assemble their forces.

By this time, the cheering had died down considerably, and a confused murmur had arisen from the crowds. I glanced down at the Circus floor and saw that the charioteers had all proceeded to the staging area near the opposite end and disappeared through the archways. The criers on the towers in the median were yelling through their cones the order to disperse. I heard the one nearest the Princep's private box yelling, "By order of Caesar Augustus, these games have been canceled due to a loss of favor by the gods. You are to disperse and return to your homes. The games will resume once the auspices are more favorable. By order of Caesar Augustus, these games..."

Livia, Claudia, and the others in the box looked back toward Augustus questioningly. He gave them all reassuring smiles and said, "I regret that today's entertainment had to be canceled so abruptly, but I invite you all to my residence where my personal musicians and dancers will hopefully fill the time."

Livia gave Augustus a steady look as if she understood that something was up, but she played the gracious Roman matron and ushered the twenty or so people in the box toward the exit and Augustus's residence, which was conveniently attached to the Circus via a columned walkway. Claudia also gave Vitulus the same look as she passed him. Vitulus didn't try to reassure her or smile; he was telling her the seriousness of the situation without words. A steely resolve came over her, and she held the infant Lucius closer to her breast.

Once they were all gone, Augustus and Aper strode over to the balcony to monitor the Circus's evacuation. Leaving Paetus, Vitulus, and me in the back. Vitulus glanced at me and gave a bitter laugh. "And I thought they'd be safer here in public."

I wasn't sure what to say, so I nodded toward the balcony. "Let's see how it's going."

Vitulus gave the now empty exit one last glance and then nodded.

The criers continued to shout out their messages to the crowds, which, remarkably, seemed to be so confused and shocked by the sudden cancellation that they were actually doing what the criers ordered them to do. I could hear a few jeers and whistles of disappointment, but people were beginning to move toward the exits in a non-riotous fashion. I glanced at Augustus, Aper, and Vitulus, who all looked on the dispersing crowds with guarded relief.

I was beginning to share their relief when the mystery magus struck.

A sharp gust of wind blew into the box, whipping the togas of Augustus, Aper, and Vitulus. I had to shut my eyes momentarily from the dust that the wind whipped up. Though the wind felt hot upon my skin, a cold tingle raced across my body when it hit me: this was a magical wind.

The dust and sand on the Circus floor swirled into small eddies that raced across the track, leaving neat little grooves in their wakes. But then the eddies coalesced near our side of the track. The swirling dust and dirt slowly built up into a howling, fifty-foot vortex that looked like a brown and tan column. The vortex spun for several moments before consolidating into the shape of a giant man.

Though the giant sand man was still a swirling mass of dirt and sand, there was no mistaking the sideburns on his face.

The giant turned its head toward us and a triumphant smile spread across its brown face. "Octavian," it boomed, like the sound of boulders crashing together, "your murderous tyranny is at an end."

# TWENTY-FIVE

My first instinct at seeing this monstrous sand man was about the same as the instincts of the tens of thousands of people still exiting the Circus Maximus: Scream and run. A literal stampede was taking place in the stands as people struggled to get out of the arena and away from the gods-spawned giant that had suddenly materialized. I didn't even want to think of how many people were being crushed or trampled to death right now.

But I couldn't give into my first instinct. I didn't have that luxury because I was probably the only guy in Rome who had any idea what we were dealing with here. I had to stand fast and at least look like I knew what to do.

Vitulus, Aper, and to his credit, Augustus, stood their ground, but stared open-mouthed at the sand man. Paetus stood his ground, too, though his eyes blinked furiously. I couldn't tell if it was from the wind or if he was about to faint.

"Who are you?" Augustus shouted over the wind, his eyes squinting in the face of the sandstorm. His voice cracked a bit from the shouting and the wind, but I was surprised he even had the wits to speak.

"One who has come to balance the scales," the giant boomed. "One who has come to bring justice for your crimes as Rome's *First Citizen*."

As the sand man began to list Rome's crimes—its enslavement of nations, its gluttony—I fought through my paralyzing fear, focused my mind, and tried to analyze the spell the magus was using. First, his Latin was in the accent of a Roman aristocrat, which would've been normal coming from a patrician senator rather than a fifty-foot sand giant. Second, as soon as I focused on the magical currents flowing through the giant, I immediately recognized the monster as a simple avatar spell. A damned *powerful* avatar spell, but one that I could've generated myself if I had the components, energy, and practice. And the good thing about an avatar spell was that they were all bluster; it wouldn't go stomping through the stands crushing people. If it took a swipe at anyone, it would be like walking into a sandstorm—annoying and uncomfortable, yes, but not inherently life threatening.

And third, the spell was a line-of-sight spell, which meant that the magus needed to be looking at it while he cast it. The mystery magus was here, somewhere in the Circus Maximus. I could easily disenchant it with a disruption spell that didn't require any components, but I needed to keep him talking so I could find him. The avatar spell required concentration, which meant the magus would be standing absolutely still and staring at the sand giant. I scanned the Circus's upper bleachers, the stands where people were still fleeing, and the archways through which the charioteers had left earlier, but I didn't see anyone at all fitting the magus's description or standing still. All the people I saw were running for their lives or lying wounded in the stands.

*Where in damnation is he?*

"Therefore," the sand man said, finishing his list of crimes, "Rome needs an enlightened ruler, one who can abolish the absurd notions of elites ruling simply because they were born first. One who can reign in the Roman addiction to bloody entertainment and excess. One who can put Rome in its proper place in the eternal order of the universe."

"What gives you the right to attack us?" Augustus demanded. "By what authority do you judge?"

"Authority?" the sand man sneered. "*Power* is my authority, not noble birth. Tomorrow night, you and the Senate will gather on the Capitoline Hill and hail *me* as Rome's king. It will be a small change, eh, *Princeps*? If you and the Senate do not do this, then all firstborn Roman citizens will die."

I looked at Vitulus and saw his face pale. In the two years since I'd known him, I'd never seen him look so scared and angry.

"And to prove that I can do what I say," the sand man boomed, "here is a taste of what I will unleash if you do not comply."

*The Dea Tacitas,* I thought.

I whipped my ball cap around, wound up my right hand like I was about to throw a baseball, and hurled the disruption spell into the sand giant. A clear ball of energy expanded mid-flight into a comet-like missile with the swirling red and blue colors of my aura. It flew toward the sand avatar and plunged right into the forehead. The disrupter created a red and blue hole in the avatar's forehead, as if I'd thrown it through a dense fog, and then the entire monster collapsed into a shower of dust and sand.

I glanced at Vitulus, Aper, and Augustus and saw them all staring at me. I ignored their incredulity at basic magic and said, "We need to get as many people into the sunlight as possible. He's about to release the Dea Tacitas."

But more screams from beyond the Circus exits—screams of terror now mixed with screams of pain—told me the Dea Tacitas were already popping out of those damned chess pieces. I looked down into the stands and saw people stampeding *back* into the arena.

Then a Dea Tacita popped out of an exit fifty feet to the right of Augustus's box and landed amid the shoving lines of people. It had the same greasy black hair, sharp claws, and naked female body as the two I found at Paetus's place. Its body was already covered in bright red blood, even across its mouthless face. I could even see its milky white eyes from where I stood. Its victims, all men, seemed to pause a moment to stare at its body, which confirmed to me that it had some sort of succubus aura about it. That momentary pause was enough for the daemon to slash the throats of anyone caught in its aura.

I saw more Dea Tacitas emerging from the exits around the Circus doing the same thing as the one near me, slaughtering people in ones and twos. The same thing was likely happening at the archways beneath the stands.

But like at Paetus's home, the daemons all stayed within the shaded areas beneath the Circus awnings. I wasn't sure if the people streaming onto the Circus track realized that, or if they were simply running in a direction that didn't have a daemon blocking their way.

There was a commotion from the Praetorians behind us in the hallway just outside Augustus's box. Vitulus and Aper whipped around, their swords drawn. We couldn't see what was happening, but we heard cursing, grunts of pain, and then bodies thumping to the floor. I drew on my cell magic and produced a spark globe just as the first Dea Tacita daemon leaped into the room.

Aper and Vitulus were momentarily stopped by the creature's succubus aura, but now that I knew its powers, I was able to focus my attention toward its milky white eyes, even though my eyes desperately wanted to wander lower...

Damnation, it was strong!

Before I could lose my concentration, I flung the spark globe directly at its head. The thing's eyes widened in the globe's ethereal light, and then the globe struck it in the face. As before, the daemon shivered as fast as a hornet's wings until it exploded into a pus-like goo, coating the fancy couches and snack tables nearby.

Vitulus, Aper, Augustus, and Paetus all stared at the yellow-white goo that was quickly evaporating.

"I couldn't move," Vitulus said to me. "I was..."

"Distracted?" I said. He gave me an embarrassed nod, and Aper and Augustus looked equally uncomfortable. "It's one of their powers. Now that you know, it makes it easier to focus the next time you—"

A Dea Tacita jumped from the stands and into the box. I only had time to turn around and see it raise its claws at Augustus, who stood frozen and staring at his imminent death.

And then Paetus swung the end of his scroll rods at the daemon, hitting it where its mouth should be with the blunt knobby ends. It wasn't a very hard hit, and I probably could've hit it much harder with my fist, but it was enough. The daemon shivered violently and then burst into pus that coated us all.

I glanced at Paetus as I spit the tasteless, evaporating pus from my lips. His face couldn't have been more conflicted with emotions: fear, pride, embarrassment, triumph. Augustus was the first to gain back his wits back, and said, "It would appear that I am in your debt, Paetus Flamen."

Paetus gave Augustus a shaky nod and a mad grin.

I didn't have time to congratulate Paetus. Two more Dea Tacitas charged into the room from the hallway: I sent my spark globe at one while Vitulus charged at the second. The spark globe did its job with the first daemon. Vitulus dodged a swipe from the second daemon and then plunged his sword into its jaw. Both daemons shivered at the same time and exploded.

"We need to move you, Princeps," Aper said, hurrying toward the doorway. He peeked around the corner, grimaced at the Praetorian bodies on the floor just out of my sight, and then gave the all clear signal. A sound to Aper's left down the hall made him whip around, his sword raised, but he visibly relaxed.

"Just my men," he said. "Sir, we'll escort you to your residence."

I glanced at Paetus and then Aper. "Prefect, can Paetus go with you?"

Aper narrowed his eyes, but Augustus said, while striding toward the doorway, "Of course he can. I'd like to know more of the man who just saved my life."

Paetus gave me a fearful look. "Aren't you coming too?"

I shook my head. "The magus who's doing this is somewhere in the Circus. I need to find him. Go with them."

Paetus paused, seeming to consider which was more dangerous: being in the same room with Augustus or fighting Dea Tacitas with me. He swallowed once and then followed Augustus. Vitulus approached me as soon as they all left.

"Where do you want to look first?" he asked.

I scanned the Circus once again for anyone matching the magus's black hair and sideburns. Between the panicked crowds and the Dea Tacitas, it was complete, bloody chaos. The archway exits on the dirt track already had more panicked people streaming *from* them due to the daemons outside the arena. The awning scaffolds above the Circus looked clear of any people, but I couldn't see the scaffolding above Augustus's box. Was he above us?

But at that moment, my eye was drawn to the median and the small towers where the criers stood. There were six towers, each with a basket at the top for the crier to stand, spaced evenly along the median. Five of the criers were furtively looking around at the carnage below them, obviously judging their position to be the safest place to be.

But one crier stood still with his palms at his sides pointed down. I stared at him for several moments...and then glimpsed orange and green sparks flitting around him. He was masking his aura and doing a fine job of it; I wouldn't have noticed if I wasn't looking directly at him. He had black hair, but no sideburns...which he could've shaved off this morning after making us believe we were looking for a man with sideburns. Clever bastard.

"There!" I said, pointing him out to Vitulus.

Vitulus nodded once. "How do you want to play this?" Which was his way of asking, *What spells are you going to use so I can stay out of their way?*

"Just watch my back," I said. Vitulus grimaced, knowing that was my way of saying, *I have no idea, but follow me anyway.*

And then I jumped over the balcony railing.

# TWENTY-SIX

F ortunately, I didn't twist an ankle in the five-foot drop to the bleacher seats below the balcony. I landed rather smoothly in a crouch on the stone walkway then hurried down the stands by taking large strides on top of the bleacher seats. People still streamed out of the exits, but there were far fewer than before since most had already gathered in the sunlight on the Circus track. Dea Tacita daemons still attacked people in the sections to my right and left. I desperately wanted to help the people over there, but I feared that, if I took my eyes off the magus in the crier basket for one moment, he would send a magical attack my way, and I wouldn't see it in time. Or worse: He would disappear somehow, and my best chance at stopping him would be ruined. And if I didn't stop him now, it sounded like a much worse fate awaited all of Rome—including Vitulus's son, Lucius—tomorrow night.

The screams of the dying around me would just have to haunt my nightmares with all the others.

Which raised the question, just what *was* I going to do about him? He had enthralled me once, which meant that he was far more powerful than me. He had set up this elaborate game, which meant that he was probably smarter than me. Hell, he could even grow a fuller beard than me. How was I going to stop someone who seemed so much better than me in every way?

I finally reached the edge of the bleachers and jumped down another six feet to the soft dirt track of the Circus floor and out of the awning shadows. Vitulus landed beside me a second later, his sword drawn and his eyes scanning everywhere at once. I got a brief sense of déjà vu as I jogged across the track. The last time I was on the Circus floor, I had just arrived from the twenty-first century without an idea as to how or why. I shook away the sudden memories of lying there and watching William Ford walk away from me as I begged for his help. That was all in the past and distracting me from...

A distraction. Well then. Took me long enough to think of that.

The magus had not moved from his palms-down position, so I figured he was concentrating on a spell. I didn't need to be a dice player to bet that it somehow controlled the Dea Tacitas. They certainly weren't behaving like your average rampaging daemons—they had come out of the exits almost at the same time, methodically pushing the people down the bleachers, forcing them to escape onto the sunlit Circus track.

Thousands of panicked people all gathered upon the Circus track...I didn't like where this was going.

I had to distract the magus, which might break his hold on the Dea Tacitas. Of course, if he lost control of the Dea Tacitas, they might commence with mindless rampaging, but at least they wouldn't be herding people to where the magus wanted them to go. Some might break through the Dea Tacita blockade that was forming around the edges of the Circus.

I pointed at the magus and said to Vitulus, "We need to distract him."

"Can't you cast a lightning bolt or something?"

I grunted. "I'm a magus, not Jupiter. Besides, I think he's shielded himself from magic. Something more mundane might work better..." I saw four Praetorians jog from out of an archway in the middle of the Circus track, their blue tunicas torn and bloody. Three carried a gladius, while one carried a bow and had a quiver of arrows strapped to his back.

"Like that guy," I said, motioning to the archer.

Vitulus nodded once and then ran toward the four Praetorians with me following. He shouted orders for them to stop, which all four did when they noticed Vitulus.

"Can you reach that guy from here?" I asked the archer, pointing at the magus.

The archer stared at the magus about a hundred paces away, and asked, "You want me to shoot the crier?"

"He's not a crier; he's the one who's causing all this. Can you reach him or not?"

"I think so, sir," the archer said. Then he drew an arrow from his quiver, nocked it, aimed, and fired it at the magus.

Which he missed by a wide margin. At least he missed *behind* the magus, who didn't even flinch when the arrow went by.

"Sorry, sir," he said, drawing another arrow. "Think I got the range now." He aimed and fired again.

This time, the arrow struck the magus in the arm, almost knocking him out of the basket. The magus had stopped casting his spell and clutched at the arrow in his arm. I couldn't see his face clearly, but his body language sure indicated he was hurting and angry.

"Yes!" I shouted, and then slapped the archer on the back. He wore a satisfied grin as he stared at the wounded magus.

I scanned the Dea Tacitas gathering around the edges of the Circus just inside the awning shadows. But rather than taking up positions to keep the people on the track, they suddenly started roaming around the stands attacking victims that had not reached the track or were fleeing to the exits.

"Okay," I shouted to Vitulus over the screaming crowds, "start herding everyone toward the charioteer stables—"

A blast of hot air pushed me from behind and made the Praetorians in front of me grimace and take a step back. I turned to see a large fire explode in the middle of the stands. Sparks reached so high that they caught the fabric awnings on fire. The fire, seemingly of its own will, spread in opposite directions, gaining speed as it raced around the mid-section of the bleachers. I glanced toward the charioteer archways, but saw black smoke and orange sparks billowing from them. The fires effectively blocked all the exits in the stands and pushed the Dea Tacitas, and any humans unlucky enough to be on this side, toward the Circus track. I tried to ignore the horrible screams of people burning in the fires. I couldn't do anything for them.

I ground my teeth.

The fire seemed just as lethal to the Dea Tacitas as to humans, for the daemons fled the fire toward the edge of the awning shadows. They seemed struck between a fiery death and a solar one. They scrambled helplessly along the edges of the shadows, striking at anyone who tried getting past them to the track. At least we didn't have a daemon problem at the moment.

But we certainly had a big problem. The fire quickly surrounded the track, and the heat grew almost unbearable. Nobody had to tell the people on the track to move toward the center, as Vitulus, the four Praetorians, and I were pushed by the crowd toward the median to escape the heat.

Another one of the magus's traps. No fire could've spread that fast without some sort of magical or chemical propellant. I looked up at the crier basket. I was closer to him now and could see his face a little better. He indeed looked Greek, or perhaps Syrian, with black hair cut short. He was clean-shaven today, which made him look far younger than I thought he'd be—probably in his early twenties. His right hand was raised above his head, while the arrow still protruded from his left arm. His lips were shouting something, but I couldn't hear it over the screams of the crowd and the roar of the fires in the stands.

However, I didn't have to hear his words to know what he was doing.

The smoke from all the fires was rising in thick, black clouds above the Circus. The clouds should've shifted and swirled in the drafts generated by the heat or the natural Roman breezes. But they hung above the track and began to coalesce into an oval roof over the Circus and the surrounding city blocks.

A roof that blocked out all sunlight.

The Dea Tacitas surrounding us began leaping down onto the sunless track.

I turned back to the magus. A blue-rimmed, horizontal *reizen* gate had opened in the air like a silvery, rippling pool of water a few feet from his basket. He climbed over the lip of the basket, his arrow wound making it difficult, and disappeared through the gate. Once he was through, the gate vanished.

And then the Dea Tacitas attacked.

# TWENTY-SEVEN

I'd seen enough sudden death during my time in Rome to understand that nobody *really* expects it to happen to them. Right up until the moment where the eyes turn glassy, the people whom I've seen die believe that someone or something will come along to save them at the last moment.

And then they're gone.

That was pretty much my frame of mind when I saw the mystery magus leap through his *reizen* gate. With fires surrounding me and an army of Dea Tacitas mowing down the people around me, I still didn't quite believe that I was going to die. Hell, I'm sure every single one of the people murdered today by that bastard thought the same thing before their throats were torn out or they were consumed by flames. But I'm different. I'm the "chosen one," or something. The Ring of Saturn assured me that I had to stay in ancient Rome or else humanity would not live past the twenty-first century. I still had no idea why, but I felt it to the core of my being that it wasn't to die here in the Circus Maximus.

The magus was a mass murderer. He had killed hundreds, perhaps thousands, of people today. People who thought they would spend a holiday at the races, who assumed they'd go home to their families afterward, or to the temples to worship, or to the taverns to play dice, or whatever individuals did to bring joy to their lives. They were gone because of this guy.

No, it wasn't fear that I felt; it was anger. Red, boiling anger as bright as the flames surging around me.

So I decided to fight with the reckless abandon of one assured of his immortality. I should've thought up a way to stop the fires since that would've helped the most people. But that involved too much thinking. I wanted to act. I wanted to take out my anger on the magus, but since I couldn't do that at the moment, I went after the magus's creations.

I didn't even glance at Vitulus and his Praetorians before running toward the nearest Dea Tacita. I sensed my friend following me, though, even as I siphoned my cell magic for a spark globe. I held the white orb in my hand as I charged through the crowd flowing past me, away from the daemons and the fires until I finally came face to, um, face with a monster.

The creature's naked body and succubus aura startled me for a fraction of a second. The thing silently leaped at me, all claws, pale flesh, and milky white eyes. I willed my spark globe into the monster's chest, which stopped it in mid-leap, making it shiver violently, and then explode into pus-like goo.

I searched for another, found a daemon crouched atop a dead woman whose throat was gone. I willed my spark globe into the daemon's back, making that one explode as well. I searched for another target, found a daemon about to jump into a group of men who were trying to gang up on a second one; my spark globe destroyed the jumper, leaving the men to beat the second one into elemental pus. I glanced at Vitulus behind me as he drove his sword into the mouth of a Dea Tacita and watched it explode with satisfaction.

Unfortunately it seemed like every time we killed one, two more popped out of the crowd or the stands. Where in damnation did this magus get all the daemons? Did he have a chess piece factory set up somewhere? He must've conjured a few and then doubled them with magic like he had at Paetus's house. The daemons were everywhere. There were groups of men and a few women here and there putting up a valiant fight with nothing more than their fists, but the Dea Tacitas were too quick. Even if a large group of people ganged up on one, the daemon slashed the throats of a few before it was pummeled into pus beneath the weight of the group.

One of the Praetorians screamed in pain. I turned to see a Dea Tacita drive its claws into the man's belly and its arm all the way into his sternum. The Praetorian's eyes went wide, and his screams turned into a bloody gurgle. Vitulus yelled a curse and charged at the daemon, his sword raised to lop off its head. I instinctively brought my spark globe to hurl it at the daemon—

A cold, solid body rammed into me, knocking me onto my back. The blow had driven the wind out of me, and as I gasped for breath, a Dea Tacita jumped atop my chest, straddling me and pinning my arms to my sides with its thighs. Its white breasts hung inches from my face and the succubus aura had a hold of me, causing me to freeze even though I knew its claws were a fraction of a second from ripping out my throat.

My feeling of invincibility from earlier had fled, and the bleak realization that my death was at hand hit me as hard as the daemon. And with that realization came one absurd thought: *Damnation, I don't want the last thing I see to be daemon breasts.*

I somehow found the strength to shut my eyes.

And then the weight upon my chest disappeared, and I was showered in warm goo. I cautiously opened my eyes. The daemon was gone, and I was coated in its off-white guts. Hovering just three feet above my chest was the spark globe that had banished the daemon. I rose to my elbows, gaping at it in shock.

How had my spark globe killed the daemon without me directing it?

*That's not my spark globe.*

I looked beyond it and saw a young woman five paces away dressed in black and holding her hand, palm up. The spark globe flew toward her open palm and then hovered about a foot above it.

"Helva?" I sputtered.

She scowled at me. "I grow tired of saving your life, Natta Magus."

# TWENTY-EIGHT

I still lay on the ground, propped up on my elbows, the daemon pus evaporating off me. I stared at Helva, the shy niece of my Canaanite neighbors who certainly didn't look shy right now. She looked annoyed.

"How did...? You're a...?" My brain was still fuzzy from the succubus aura and near death experience, so I wasn't very articulate.

But my brain woke up when I noticed the Dea Tacita leaping toward Helva's back. I didn't know where my spark globe was, but I immediately willed it at the daemon. The globe hurled toward Helva from where it was hovering behind me. She saw it fly toward her and she ducked. The globe smacked right into the daemon just as it raised its claws. The daemon exploded.

I leaped to my feet and searched for other daemons that were about to attack. Helva also kept an eye out for daemons, but she said to me, "So this is your plan? Kill them one at a time? Not very efficient."

"If you have a better idea then I'm all ears, Helva," I said. "If that's your real name."

"We've no time for proper introductions," she said. "I need to get you out of here."

"What?"

She extinguished her spark globe and then reached into a pouch tied to her black waist belt. When she took her hand out, it was filled with white sand, which she threw into the air in front of her as she said some arcane words that sounded Middle Eastern to my untrained ears. The air shimmered and then a silvery oval about six feet high and four feet wide appeared in the air.

A *reizen* gate.

She pulled my arm and said, "Let's go."

"Wait!" I said, digging my feet into the sandy track. "I'm not leaving these people to die!"

"You can't stay here," she snarled. "Your death would be meaningless here."

I yanked my arm out of her grip and yelled over the din of the battle and the fires, "I don't know who you are or what you're talking about, but I'm not going anywhere until I've done something to help. Now you can either go or you can stay and help me."

At first she looked startled, as if she was used to having her commands obeyed. But then fire reflecting in her brown eyes matched the anger that spread across her face. I thought for a moment that she was going to leap through that gate, but she took a deep calming breath and closed the gate with an arcane word.

"Fine," she growled. Then she reached into another pouch and pulled out what, at first, I thought was piece of black rope. But when I got a better look at it, I noticed it was tightly woven hair. "I know how to destroy the daemons, but we'll have to link up to do it."

"That'll take too long," I said. "We don't know each other. Our auras will need at least an hour to negotiate through—"

"Not if we use this," she said, wrapping one end of the hair rope around her wrist. She handed the other end to me. "Tie this around your wrist."

I stared at the rope, all sorts of alarm bells going off in my mind. What she was suggesting—an instant link-up via this rope—was something unknown even in my time. Aura linking between magi provided a way for us to combine our strength to cast spells more powerful than we could on our own. But it required a necessary give and take process between both auras so that neither one could consume or enthrall the other. Even between two magi who trusted each other, a first-time link could take an hour or more. It got easier and quicker the more two magi did it; Brianna and I had reached the point where it only took seconds.

I had no idea who this magus was, so trust was impossible at this point. The linking that I knew how to do would take *hours*, if we could even link at all. And I especially had no idea what that black hair rope was. I could be handing her my soul for all I knew.

She rolled her eyes impatiently. "The longer you stand here not trusting me, the more people will die. And so you know, this rope does not link us the way you understand: It only takes the power that you freely give it. I will then use your power to cast the spell. And considering the daemon numbers, I will need as much as you can give me."

I stared at her, the screams from the citizens around me and the heat from the fires almost fading from my senses as I tried to open my magical senses to Scan her. As I suspected, her aura was blank to me, just like the headscarf she had presumably left behind in the Tiber River last night. I couldn't tell if she was a cell or soul magus, sane or mad, nothing. It would be crazy to simply tie myself to her based on her word that she wanted to help.

"Natta Magus!" Vitulus yelled from my right. I glanced at him as he hurried toward me, and noticed only two of the Praetorians were with him, both bloodied and in obvious pain. Vitulus looked warily from me to Helva. "Who is this woman?"

I glared at her. "Yeah. Who *are* you?"

She gave me a half-smile. "I'm your neighbor, Natta Magus. Now do you want to save these people, or will I have to push you through the gate myself?"

The screams of the dying and wounded came back to my senses, along with the terrible heat from the spreading fires. I had to take the chance that she could do what she claimed. Or everyone, including me, would be dead anyway.

"Vitulus," I said, still watching her, "I'm going to link up with her, kind of like I did with Brianna last year in Aventicum. Watch us. If she or I do anything that endangers these people...I want you to kill us both immediately." I looked at him. "Understand?"

His eyes narrowed, and he nodded to his two remaining Praetorians. They took up positions around me and Helva, their swords ready. Vitulus then stared coldly at Helva.

Helva's half-smile turned into a sneer. "A hero till the end, eh, Natta Magus? Are you going to use the rope or not?"

I took the other end of the rope and tied it around my right wrist. The rope was smooth against my skin, as if it were made of silk. Once I had securely tied it, I asked, "Now what?"

"Now will into it whatever magic you want to give me. Again, I suggest as much as you can give. Once I start casting, just follow my lead."

I caught Vitulus's gaze and said, "I'm serious."

"I know," he said, returning his eyes to Helva.

And then I willed my cell magic into the rope in one great surge of power. I didn't give her everything—I'm not crazy enough to empty my cells for her—but it was a lot. She took in a sudden breath and gave me an appreciative look. "You're stronger than you look, Natta Magus. The things you could do, if only you had the right priorities..."

"Cast the spell," I growled.

She nodded once, as if giving me a mocking slave-to-master salute. Her eyes glazed over, and she began to chant in the same language she'd used to open the *reizen* gate. She focused on the nearest Dea Tacita, which was locked in a battle with two other men with clubs who were trying to keep it from attacking another man who lay in the dirt bleeding from several claw wounds. While she chanted, she used her free hand to reach into a large pouch on her belt without taking her eyes off the Dea Tacita. She pulled out a handful of sawdust, but kept her fist closed tightly around it. Then she started walking toward the Dea Tacita with me in tow. Vitulus and the two Praetorians flanked us, as wary of us as they were of the daemon we were walking toward.

When we got within a few paces of the men clubbing the daemon, I yelled, "Back away!"

The men kept their clubs up, gave us one glance, and then moved away from the daemon. Once we were between them and the daemon, the men bent down and dragged their wounded comrade away from us. The Dea Tacita stared at us a moment with those milky eyes, its shapely feminine body straightening as it seemed more curious about us than afraid. I shook off the succubus aura and turned my eyes to Helva. She continued her chanting as her eyes focused on the Dea Tacita. And strangely, the daemon didn't move. If I didn't know any better, I would've said that Helva had enthralled it somehow. She walked up to the daemon, bringing us within just a few feet of the monster. I had to use up almost every ounce of courage just to stay near Helva. She then brought up her fist of sawdust, took in a deep breath, and blew the particles into the daemon's face. The daemon jerked its head to the side and then up, as if it were about to sneeze.

And then it exploded into pus.

All around us, I heard the pop and splatters of similar explosions. Everywhere I saw a daemon, they burst into sparkling droplets, much to the stunned surprise of the citizens who'd been either fighting them or fleeing from them. Most people were huddled against the median, trying to get as far away from the daemons and the fires in the stands as they could. Vitulus and the Praetorians scanned the dark, smoky track around us. My friend nodded in satisfaction, while the Praetorians—unaccustomed to magic—looked on the daemon explosions with wide eyes and growing smiles.

But now that the daemons were gone, the people looked up bleakly at the fires, desperately searching for an escape. There was none. The fires completely surrounded the track and were creeping closer down the stands. If we didn't burn to death, we'd all die from the black smoke that was swirling around us, turning the once bright day into a black, acrid nightmare.

I looked back at Helva. She blinked once, the glazed look disappearing from her eyes. She said, "Can we go now?"

"No! We need to put out these fires, too!"

"I cannot put out fires of this size. At least now these people won't have to fight their way through—"

"I can cast a *blussen* spell," I said.

She shook her head impatiently. "I do not know this spell."

"It tells the fires to extinguish themselves. I've done it before, but it requires a lot of power. If you send me power through this rope, I can at least put out fires on the archways over there." When she narrowed her eyes at me, I said, "Now it's time for you to trust me."

She growled what sounded like a curse in the same language she had used for her arcane words and then untied the end of the hair rope around her wrist. "Use this side and I'll use that side," she said. I got the feeling she wasn't doing this out of concern for the people around us, but simply because it was the only way I would leave this place.

I tied her end around my wrist and asked, "How do I work this?"

"Instead of siphoning your magic from your cells, take it from the rope. There you'll find the magic I give you."

I nodded and then focused on the rope. Rather than drawing from my cells, which had nowhere near the power I needed for the *blussen* spell, I visualized drawing magic from the rope.

And I almost recoiled from the magic Helva sent me. Her magic was nothing like the comforting warmth of my cell magic; her magic gave me the same smothering, buried alive feeling that I'd felt from the other magus. If this was soul magic, it was unlike the soul magic that I'd felt last year. That soul magic was an aggressive adrenaline rush that demanded immediate action. It was powerful, but hard to control. It brought ecstasy that cell magic couldn't match, but made it easy to lose myself in the magic and forget the spell that I wanted to cast. It stimulated every sense in my body and, as a result, was highly addictive. But it also made me want to throw up everything I'd eaten that day.

Helva's magic, however, was slow and cumbersome, but with the unstoppable power of a moving glacier. I also got the feeling that, if she chose, her magic could explode with the intensity and destruction of a volcano. And it didn't make me sick at all.

I drew in Helva's magic, suddenly feeling impassive about the chaos surrounding me, as if I were a mountain watching the generational comings and goings of the people who lived in the valleys below me. I had to wrestle with that indifference to keep from losing my focus on the *blussen* spell—it would've been so easy to just stand there and let everything pass me by as I had for millions of years—but my previous experience with different magic helped me take control. Once I had a firm grip on the magic, I released it at the same time that I called out the bastardized Dutch words for the *blussen* spell, *"Sator arepo tenet opera rotas!"*

I imagined a huge transparent box descending over the fiery, smoky sections around the archways through which the charioteers had escaped before all this chaos erupted. The walls of the box sliced through the fires, the bleachers, and then into the stables and archways at the bottom.

*Sleep*, I told the fires within the box.

The fires inside the box were non-magical, so they didn't talk back to me like a magical fire would have. I gave an internal sigh of relief. The *blussen* spell made them think that they had consumed all flammable material, so they immediately extinguished themselves. All that was left of the fires were wispy tendrils of black and gray smoke that swirled around in the heat wind generated by the remaining fires. With no fire to fuel it, the smoke that obscured the archways began to clear, and I could actually see daylight on the other side.

With the *blussen* in place, I threw in as much power as I could to keep it active. It would stand for the next several hours, certainly long enough for everyone trapped on the Circus track to flee.

Vitulus didn't need me to tell him what to do. He immediately started yelling, "The archways! Escape through the archways!"

His two bloodied Praetorians took up the call as well, running through the crowds and telling them to go to the archways. The crowd surged toward the now open archways, leaving behind bodies and wounded people. Some citizens helped a few of the wounded out, while most simply ran for it in their panic to get away from the fires and any lingering daemons.

Vitulus took a step toward his Praetorians, but stopped and gave me a questioning glance.

"Are you—?" he began.

"I'll be fine," I said. "Go, get everyone out."

He gave Helva one last warning glare before heading toward the groups of people who hadn't noticed the cleared archways. But she either didn't notice or didn't care. "Now can we—?"

"I'm not going anywhere with you until you tell me who you are and why you're trying to be my guardian angel."

"I will tell you everything," she said, looking up at me with the fire flickering in her brown eyes, "but I'd prefer to do it in a place where we won't be roasted like quails."

I glanced around at the fires and had to at least agree with her on that point. My skin felt like I'd been lying naked in the sun all day on a temple roof. We needed to follow the wisdom of the mob and get the hell out while we still could.

But I also knew this fire was too big for even the relatively well-organized Roman fire *vigiles*. They would attack it with water buckets, but they'd need hundreds of people and buckets to make a dent in this thing. The fire was consuming more and more of the Circus—I heard one section behind me collapse—and would consume the heart of Rome before it was put out. Not to mention the wounded people groaning and writhing on the ground who couldn't make it out on their own. Only Helva and I could contain it at this point.

"How much power do you have left?" I asked her.

She shook her head vehemently. "This building is lost, there is no way you can save it."

"I don't care about the building. I care about all these wounded people here, not to mention the city. The *vigiles* will never stop this fire before it burns down Rome. Only *we* can stop it."

"Why do you care about the Romans?" she asked, genuine confusion upon her face. "What have they done for you?"

"If I leave now without trying to help, then I will regret it for the rest of my life." I thought back to my experiences in the Ring of Saturn last year. "And I've felt that regret hundreds of times. I'd rather die than feel it again."

I was gambling hard on her mysterious desire to keep me alive. Just how badly did she want to keep me safe? Was she willing to risk her own life to do so?

Apparently she was. She bared her teeth in frustration and asked, "What do you want to do, oh Achilles-reborn?"

"Give me all the power you have left, and I mean everything," I said.

"I'm *not* giving you everything, Natta Magus. But you'll have enough."

I scanned the fires and hoped it was enough.

Once again, I siphoned magic from the hair rope rather than my cells, and once again I felt the smothering, impassive, unstoppable power from Helva's soul magic. I glanced at Helva, saw her eyes closed, her teeth clenched, and a large vein pulsing on her neck. I wasn't sure if she was giving me everything she had, but it looked like it was almost everything.

Because I would need it to change the weather.

Weather spells were complex, required lots of power, and never lasted very long. I'd once cast a small, localized ice storm to put out a house fire on the Aventine Hill around the time I first met Vitulus. But that had required some aurichalcum metal to power the spell. I never could've done it with my cell magic alone. Helva's magic—plodding, yet potentially volcanic—combined with my cell reserves should be enough to make it rain over the Circus.

I drew on all the power I possessed, focused the ice storm spell, and then yelled the arcane Dutch words, *"Vurige merk, stop je ritme; vurige merk, stop je zweet!"*

I cried the words over and over, my voice reverberating and growing loud in my ears. My entire body vibrated, from my toes to my bones to my organs to my recovering concussed head. My voice drew all the moisture left in the fiery air into a cold wet wind that whipped around me. The wind expanded as I continued my chant, now pulling in moisture from outside the Circus and the surrounding Seven Hills. I even sensed the spell drawing evaporating water from the Tiber River. It all swirled above me and the black smoky dome that the other magus had cast above the Circus.

Lightning flashed above us, and a tremendous explosion of thunder almost sent me sprawling to the ground with the force of the sound. The cold rain from the spell was mixing with the intense heat of the fires to create a towering, gray cumulonimbus cloud above the Circus. More lightning, another explosive crack of thunder...and then rain began to pour in sheets over me, Helva, and the wounded people on the track. Along with the fires raging around the Circus. The intense heat had transformed the ice into simple rain, which was fine with me. Wet was wet.

I raised my face up to the rain, feeling it wash away the dirt and heat that had covered me for what seemed like hours. Helva's magic had turned from indifferent plodding to volcanic ferocity—I howled in triumph at the storm I had created. Me, I had created this wonder of nature. I could create anything, destroy anything. I could be anything I wanted...

Wait. No. *No, no, no.*

With a groan of effort, I released Helva's magic and felt like a human being again. An exhausted, wet human being. Once I released the magic, the rain spell began to dissipate, but it had done its work. Fires still burned in small places around the blackened and charred Circus Maximus, but the now wet and soggy areas would keep them from spreading. The vigiles would make short work of them.

I looked at Helva. Her shoulders were slumped and chin lowered, but she stared at me with hooded, tired eyes. "Now can we leave?"

I turned my Wolverines ball cap back around so that the bill was facing forward again. "*Now* we can leave."

# TWENTY-NINE

Helva and I stumbled out of the Circus Maximus archway and onto the street outside. Hundreds of vigiles, citizens, and conscripted slaves had formed efficient bucket lines. There were almost as many wounded as there were healthy people. Most stumbled around and stared at the smoldering Circus, while others cried out for family or friends whom they'd lost in the chaos. Everyone was either bloodied, smoke-blackened, or in shock.

I guided Helva down the street away from most of the crowds toward the Tiber River bank. I made sure to keep her ahead of me and within arm's reach, for I still didn't trust that she would stick around for our chat. She simply walked through the crowds as if she were the one leading me. She frowned, and appeared to be thinking hard on something, for she didn't even glance at the wounded or wailing people as she stepped through or around them.

We reached the open plaza of the Forum Boarium, which was mercifully free of cattle. We headed toward the Great Altar of Hercules, where several flamens in black tunicas were preparing goats for sacrifice to the Greek and Roman hero. They had probably been planned already due to the holiday, but they seemed to take on extra meaning as the flamens kept glancing fearfully at the smoking Circus several blocks away. Helva and I found a quiet place next to the river, just above the Cloaca Maxima storm drain. The river was low, and there wasn't a whole lot coming out of the drain, so the smell wasn't any worse than any other place in the city.

We were both immeasurably exhausted from all the magic we'd just wielded, so we sat down on the concrete bank and dangled our feet above the river five feet below us. I glanced to my left and saw several long bucket lines ending in the river. I had no idea where they'd gotten so many buckets so quickly. Maybe there was a "bucket station" on every block. Barges moved up and down the river past us, propelled either by rowers, rudders, or sails. Most of the crews were staring at the smoke filled sky above the Circus.

"Ask me your questions, Natta Magus," Helva said, breaking the silence. To be honest, now that the excitement was over, my exhaustion had pushed all thoughts from my mind besides sleep. Not even my intense curiosity about Helva had broken through the numbness until she finally spoke.

"Is Helva even your real name?" I began.

"It is the name my Canaanite nurse gave me," she said, staring at the barges and boats on the river. "I do not know the name my parents gave me."

"Why are you following me?"

"I swore an Oath." By the way she said that, it sounded like an Oath with a capital "O." That made me shiver a bit, for it was how people in my home time referred to it.

"Did you know...William Pingree Ford?"

A tired smile spread across her lips. "I swore another Oath never to reveal that. Interpret that how you will."

*Gods,* I thought, *she was William's apprentice.* It had been eighteen months between the day that William had dumped me in ancient Rome and the day I found him again in Aventicum. We'd briefly crossed paths in Rome during that time, but they were fleeting encounters where Vitulus and I were typically running for our lives from whatever daemon or monster he had conjured for his dark schemes. I had no idea what he'd done during the times I lost track of him. He could certainly have found this young woman, seen her talent, and given her some quick training. Dark training.

"William was your mentor," I said.

The tired smile remained. "Is that a question or a statement of fact?" She looked at me. "You know how this works, Natta Magus."

"A statement of fact."

She nodded, then returned her gaze to the river. "Then I'm released from my Oath, since you now know the secret I swore to keep. William Pingree Ford was my mentor for about a year."

I studied her as she watched the river boats. She didn't look insane or have the sick look about her that would've marked her as either a Dark magus or someone who routinely took soul magic from living things. She looked pensive and brooding more than anything. And the fact that she cared about her Oaths made me all the more confused: Dark magi had no problem with breaking Oaths, since their auras were already tainted with the far more vile residues of soul magic.

"I haven't lost my wits, if that's what you're thinking," she said without looking at me.

"That remains to be seen," I said. "Did William make you swear an Oath to follow me?"

"Yes."

When she said no more, I asked, "Why? Come on, Helva, I want answers."

She turned to me and regarded me with disgust. "He said that about you. You always want to find answers, to fix things, to make everybody safe. You think you still live in your Detroit homeland. That is not how *this* world is. It is filled with many people who take what they want when they want it. There are no such things as heroes. The gods have given me power to protect those I love, and that is how I use it. No matter who gets in my way."

"So to the underworld with everybody else, then?"

"Yes," she said, as if it were the most self-evident thing in the world.

I sighed, not wanting to have this debate right now. "Tell me why William made you swear an Oath to follow me."

"He said you were important. He said you were meant for great things. That mankind's future depended on you." The sarcasm dripping from her tone could've flooded the Forum. That's pretty much what William told me just before I killed him in that temple beneath Aventicum. I certainly didn't believe him when he said it, but it took my experiences in the Ring of Saturn to convince me that some*one* wanted me to stay in Rome to do some*thing* that I hadn't yet figured out.

"So William wanted you to protect me while I 'fulfilled my destiny'," I said. "And you didn't believe him."

She continued to sneer. "Of course not. Did you not hear what I said about heroes?" She turned her eyes back to the river. "But William wished it, and I wanted to please him. He was the closest thing I had to a father since..." Her words trailed off, and her face twisted as if recalling a painful memory.

I felt an irrational twinge of jealousy. That was exactly how I once felt about William. When my parents died while I was an undergraduate, William had become a father figure to me, too. He was there during the funeral arrangements, helped me settle their estate, helped me through my grief, and still worked me harder than any of his other students. And then he betrayed me to save the future. Sure, if you go by numbers and the survival of the species and all that, it was the only logical choice. But it wasn't the fatherly choice.

"Yeah, I didn't believe him either when he tried explaining it to me." Her eyes narrowed as she stared at the river, but I continued. The too-much-information filter on my brain tends to break down with exhaustion. "The only reason I'm still in Rome is because I was given a choice within a magical artifact last year: Go home and watch my world and the people I love be destroyed, or stay in Rome and ensure their survival. Every day I wonder if I made the right choice. I wonder if it was all some hallucination that I fell for hook, line, and sinker. Sometimes I wonder if all this"—I waved my hand about—"is a hallucination, and that I'm really back home in bed about to wake up. And then there are times when I miss the woman I was going to marry so much that I can't even breathe. Sometimes I just want to go to the top of the Capitoline and scream at the gods or the Unknowable Will, *'What am I supposed to do?'* And then things like the Circus Maximus happen. Well, nothing that horrible, but little things. And I'm able to help people who never could've been helped without my powers. And that makes me wonder that maybe I am doing what I'm supposed to do. One person at a time."

She stared at me with genuine confusion. "I've watched you for many months, Natta Magus. You have power: I've seen it now. Yet you spend all your time finding lost baubles." She lowered her voice into a fierce whisper. "You could be *Princeps* if you wanted."

Now it was my turn to frown at her. "I'm pretty sure my destiny was not to take over the Roman Republic. And don't say things like that. They don't trust me as it is."

"Right, and they never will," she said. "Oh, they may use you, but they will never trust you. The Romans are many things, but they are not fools. They see your power and they wonder amongst themselves behind your back: *When will he use his power against us?* Tell me, what was your first thought when five Praetorians showed up at your shop door last night?"

I hesitated a fraction of a second, but it was enough for Helva to infer many things. "You thought they were finally moving against you," she said.

"No," I lied. "I was startled, yes, but Vitulus was with them. I knew he wouldn't let them hurt me."

"Well we agree on that, at least. Because when the Romans finally do move against you, they will not come knocking on your door with your best friend in the lead. I've seen Roman treachery up close. It will be quick, quiet, and you'll never know they were there until you lie bleeding to death in an alley."

I shook my head. "All right, enough of this. We need to find this other magus before tomorrow night. I'm guessing that since you knew how to banish those Dea Tacitas, you know something about him."

She looked away from me and toward the river again. She knew something, but was now hesitant. I opened my magical senses and was surprised to see her aura surrounding her, a brown desert glow with wispy blue streamers. I also saw the Oath she had sworn as a white point of light that floated in a stationary spot above her heart. It was a strong Oath, for the white color of the point meant that she intended to die herself to keep it. She must've really loved William to put that much strength into it.

"Helva, you're still Oath-bound to protect me, so you should know that I *am* going after this guy. Helping me will make it a lot easier to fulfill your Oath."

"But you want to save *Romans*," she said, staring at the river in disgust.

"I want to save human beings," I said, "who happen to be Romans. I'd do the same for anybody. Now what do you know of this magus?"

She stared at the river for a few more moments, and then exhaled sharply. "I know a lot. He's my brother."

# THIRTY

Now that she mentioned it, I could see the family resemblance. Helva and the magus were both in their mid-twenties, both had dark hair and the same sharp cheekbones. "Twins?" I asked.

"Yes," she said, still watching the river flow by. "His name is Silanus."

"How did William find you?"

"He found us in Syria," she said. "As to the 'how', he said it was the gods who guided him to us. We assumed it must be so, for the Romans had just killed..."

She glanced at me again, as if she said too much, and then continued, "Killed our Canaanite nurse."

"Why did the Romans kill your nurse?"

"Because they're evil," she said simply. "William found us soon after her murder. He sensed our power and decided to teach us."

"What made your brother turn all super villain?"

She frowned at me. "Your words are confusing like William's. With him, it was endearing. With you, it is annoying."

"Fine. Why is your brother attacking Rome? Why is he leaving cursed chess pieces for me to find? Why is it that you swore an Oath to protect me, yet he's doing his damnedest to kill me? Does that clear things up?"

Her frown only deepened, and for a moment I thought she was going to get up and leave. She seemed to have a pride streak a mile long and apparently I kept smudging it with my sarcasm and orders. I had just watched about a thousand people die horrible deaths, and maybe thousands more maimed for the rest of their short lives. I was in no mood to be polite.

But she took a deep breath, and said, "He does not want to kill you. At least not yet. You have to understand how it was for us. Our parents were killed when we were very young, but we both remember it. Vividly. Our nurse protected us from the assassins and then raised us. When she was murdered, though we were both in our late teens, our only family was taken from us. Sure we both had our magic, but we couldn't control it, and it manifested randomly. When William found us and told us how special we were...he became our spiritual father."

A smile replaced her frown as she fell into her memories. "He taught us so many things. I learned more from him on how to survive in that one year than in my whole life up until that point. He was so patient and encouraging. The day he helped me cast my first spell—one that *I* controlled—was the day I was truly born. I loved him very much."

"What about Silanus?" I asked.

Her smile melted, and she clicked her teeth together, watching the river barges. "Silanus felt the same as me, but perhaps more so. He loved our nurse, and she died to protect us, but a boy needs a father to teach him how to be a man. Add William's general wisdom on life with his knowledge of magic, and Silanus looked on William like commoners once did the pharaohs. William not only gave him knowledge, but taught him how to think. They played your chess game for hours, until Silanus eventually started beating William almost every time."

*Damnation,* I thought. *William had been considered a chess master in Detroit. Silanus was a quick learner.*

She turned to me and said, "The only problem was that William couldn't stop talking about you."

I nodded slowly. I could see where this was going. William kept impressing upon the twins my destiny, my importance to humanity's future. Silanus grew jealous with each reference and grew to hate a man he'd never met, but was being groomed to protect. A man who would always be more important to his new father than Silanus. Again, I got an inkling for what was motivating Silanus: William had abandoned me in ancient Rome to serve a greater good, which was far more important to him than I was.

But daddy issues didn't justify the suffering and terror that Silanus was inflicting on innocent people.

"Okay, so I get why he hates *me*," I said, "and I understand that he hates Romans for killing your nurse. But killing thousands of people? Trying to become Rome's king?" I shook my head. "Isn't that overkill?"

"For several weeks before William left Syria, Silanus was having trouble understanding William's goals. He constantly questioned William, tried to get him to abandon his 'greater good' quest and just become the divine ruler that his power enabled him to be. To forget about *your* destiny. But William rebuked him, gently at first, but more harshly as Silanus persisted. Until finally they...fought with magic. Neither really wanted to hurt the other, but the force of their spells almost destroyed the village we were living in at the time. Silanus wanted to leave William...but I chose to stay with him. It was the hardest decision I've ever made. Silanus didn't take it well, but he left anyway. Then William and I journeyed here, where he made me swear the Oath to protect you no matter what. I had my doubts, but I loved and trusted William, so I did it."

"Where did Silanus go after he left you?"

She shrugged. "I don't know. Today was the first day I'd seen him since he left."

"The Darkness has taken him, hasn't it?"

"Not in the way you mean," she said. "William taught us the difference between 'cell' and 'soul' energy to power your magic, but we can't use either. Silanus's madness is emotional, not magical."

I felt my brow furrow. "Wait. You're telling me you don't use cell *or* soul magic? Then what in damnation do you use?"

She smirked. "William had the same incredulity as you when he found out about Silanus and me. It is the earth that gives us the power we need."

"The earth?"

"This world lives," she said, gently placing her hands on the brick and concrete pier on which we sat. "Certainly not in the way you and I, or animals, or even plants live. Deep inside this world beats a vast heart that gives off energy that I and my brother can tap. That is what we use to power our magic."

"Wait, are you sure he can't use soul magic? I was just at a farm where Silanus had turned all the animals into corruptions. That was soul magic. I felt it." I shivered remembering the feeling of drawing in the soul magic from the corrupted chicken that I'd wrestled off Vitulus's back.

Helva pulled out the horsehair rope that we'd used in the Circus. "William made these for us so that we could link with him. It converts cell or soul energy into earth energy, or vice versa. Before Silanus left, he figured out how to use it to draw soul energy from animals and then corrupt them with it."

*Whoa.* She'd just told me something that upended centuries of established magical philosophy in my home time. Nobody, and I mean nobody, in my time knew of a way to tap into the earth's energy to power magic. We knew of geothermal energy and magnetic energy and elemental decay and the kinetic energy of the weather, but those were natural forces that had nothing to do with magic. Magic was all about tapping the divine spark in every living being, whether it be from the energy stored in a body's cells or its soul.

Helva had basically said that rocks can jump up and start dancing on their own. I couldn't believe it.

But it would make sense. I always knew there was something off about their magic because of the smothering, "earthy" feel it gave me when I encountered it, rather than the vile, nauseous cold of soul magic.

If she was right, then Helva and Silanus were a new branch in human-magical evolution.

*Whoa.*

And if that was true, then how the hell was I supposed to fight Silanus? William had apparently taught him all about cell and soul magic, but I knew nothing about this "earth" magic. I *really* needed Helva's help.

But would she help me destroy her own brother? Because at this point, that's probably what I was going to have to do.

"How can I find him?" I asked.

"He'll find you," she said quickly. "He's not done with you yet."

"I kind of got that, but I'd like to surprise him first. Not wait around for him to send me another cursed chess piece that might kill innocents."

She shook her head. "I don't know how to find him." I wasn't sure if she was telling me the truth or not. Regardless, she wasn't going to make this easy.

"Then where do his gates go? They have to be somewhere he's been to before. Is there any place where he feels safe?"

She smirked at me again. "My Oath is to keep you safe, Natta Magus. Not help you help the Romans, and certainly not help you kill my brother."

"I am going to find your brother...and he may try to kill me. What if it comes down to a choice between saving me or him?"

She was silent, and returned her contemplative gaze to the river and the low sun beyond. "I will fulfill my Oath. And make every effort to keep my brother safe."

"Look, I don't *want* to kill him. If there is a way to stop him without killing him, then I'll certainly take it. But I do have to stop him, and it'll likely involve less killing if you help me get to him *before* he attacks me or more innocents."

She didn't say anything.

"Okay," I said, after a long minute of silence, "why did he steal the Sibylline Books?"

I thought she was going to ignore me, but she said, "I honestly don't know." I stared at her for many moments until she finally sighed and met my stare. "I speak the truth, Natta Magus. I don't know why he wants those superstitious scrolls."

I frowned. Whether or not she was telling the truth, I was right back to speculating. In my time, history said that the Sibylline Books were burned in the third century by a Roman general who thought they would delegitimize his rule over the Western Empire. Nobody ever knew what was really in them. Could they have been written by one of the few rare magi to evolve before the Great Awakening? Could they contain information on how to stop Silanus from killing all of Rome's first born?

"How do you think he will kill every firstborn Roman? That's a mighty powerful and targeted goal, even for a soul magi. Can earth magic accomplish something like that?"

"No, nothing that big. It would require the linking of at least a dozen magi to make it even remotely possible, and this world certainly doesn't have magi in the numbers that William foretold in your future. I don't know how he's going to do it."

So back to the beginning: I needed to find the Sibylline Books, figure out the magic written in them that Silanus didn't want me to know, and then use it to stop a magical genocide. All by tomorrow night. Oh, and find a spoiled rich kid and return him to his life of horrid luxury before his dad's goons stuck me like a rat. *Lovely.*

"I need to tell Augustus about this," I said. "Will you come with me?"

She barked a laugh. "What do you think? They don't trust you, what makes you think they'll trust me?"

I opened my mouth to say that I would vouch for her and protect her. But could I really keep such a promise? Vitulus would certainly trust me, and maybe Aper, but Augustus? Capito? After what another magus had done today? She'd be lucky they didn't fill her full of arrows the moment she admitted who she was.

"I may still need your help, Helva."

She stood up. "I'll be around." She turned to go, but then stopped and looked back at me. "You have a good heart, Natta Magus. Do not let anyone use it against you."

Then she disappeared into the growing crowds of people heading to the river from the Circus to wash away their wounds and those of the people they helped carry. I was left to wonder how I would tell the Roman Emperor that I had no idea what to do next.

# THIRTY-ONE

The sun was almost below the horizon across the river by the time I'd gathered my wits and rested a bit. I stood and made my way through the crowds either bathing or milling about. My first thought was to get to Augustus's home on the Palatine Hill, right next to the smoldering and blackened Circus Maximus. Somehow his palace (which, like being emperor, he publicly denied was a "palace") had escaped any damage. I figured Salvius Aper, and maybe even Vitulus, would be there planning on what to do next.

But now the Princeps' home was besieged by crowds of citizens asking for help with their wounds, for his blessings in his role as pontifex maximus, or simply demanding that he attack one group or another whom they blamed for the Circus catastrophe: everyone from Germans to Persians to Hebrews. I even saw the red-striped togas of senators among the crowd leading one faction or another, confirming my bias that politicians of all eras and cultures never failed to milk political advantage from tragedies. There was no way I'd be able to make my way into the palace.

So I figured I'd have better luck heading to Aper's home, which was only a few blocks away down the Palatine. I had to fight the flow of the crowds, but I eventually got to Aper's far less crowded street. When I banged on the front door with my foot, Nicia was almost immediately there to open the barred porthole, nod once to me, and then unbar the door.

"They're expecting you, Natta Magus," he said, quickly shutting the door after I entered.

"Who's here?" I asked.

"The *dominus*, Aurelius Vitulus, and the portly flamen."

I had to grin at that, despite the circumstances. But I figured after spending time alone with Augustus, Paetus was more than happy to hang out with Aper and Vitulus.

All three of them met me at the door to the home, Vitulus in the lead. He looked harried, dirty, and still had blood all over his tunica, but he seemed relieved to see me. He grabbed me by both arms and then embraced me tightly. I was a bit stunned by his lack of decorum, but I patted him on the back uncomfortably and said, "Missed you too, buddy."

When he pulled back, he said, "We thought you had perished in the storm and lightning above the Circus. Reports conflicted. Witnesses said you were consumed by the lightning, or that you ascended into the clouds, or that Juno took you away in a shower of gold. None saw you actually leave the Circus."

I snorted. "Your witnesses weren't very observant. We just walked out like everyone else. Well, after we created the storm that put out the Circus fires. Got any food? I'm starving."

Aper stood behind Vitulus, and Paetus stood next to a column in the atrium behind Aper. Aper stared at me blankly for a moment, but then said, "Yes, I believe there's some bread and fruit in the kitchen. Nicia?"

Nicia stepped past us and hurried to the kitchen. Vitulus gave me a sideways grin and said, "Lightning storm, eh? And you said you weren't Jupiter."

"What happened to the woman who was with you?" Aper asked, glancing behind me. "Vitulus said she was another magus?"

On my way to Aper's, I'd thought about what I should tell him and what I should leave out. I'd need Helva's help before this was all over, so I didn't want to do anything that might make her skittish about working with me. But Vitulus had seen her and had already revealed to Aper that she was a magus. How would Aper take it that Helva was the sister of the monster who had caused the Circus massacre? When the time came, would he trust her when I needed her help to stop Silanus? Would Vitulus? I figured at this point, the least I could tell them, the better. And then, maybe in the future when she earned their trust, I'd reveal a little more.

It was a good idea at the time.

"Yes, she's a foreign magus. She happened to be in Rome for the holiday and wanted to help. She's not Dark, so you can trust her." *All true,* I thought. *I'm not lying to my friends...*

But Aper stared at me with the same blank expression I'd seen while he interrogated a suspected criminal. "How very...fortuitous."

Vitulus didn't look like he was buying it either, but he didn't say anything.

"Look, guys, she wants to help me stop the magus who's masterminding all this chaos. Isn't that enough? I trust her. Do you trust me?"

The silence hanging in the air was about as stifling as Helva's earth magic had felt. Vitulus at least looked conflicted as he frowned at me. Aper continued watching me with that blank look. Paetus looked like he was trying to melt into the column behind him.

Thankfully Nicia returned with a platter of breads, fruit, and wine cups and set it down on a table in the atrium. "Wonderful," I exclaimed, and then strode past Vitulus and Aper to the atrium. I took a little clay bowl from the platter and filled it with grapes, dates, and a small round loaf of emmer bread. I filled a cup with wine and sat down on a nearby couch with my feast in my lap and began to eat. I tried to ignore the doubtful silence coming from Aper and Vitulus.

"We estimate," Aper finally said, "that 2,300 people died today, between the daemons and the fire. Another 5,000 suffered wounds."

I'd been in mid-chew when Aper gave me the body count. And with those numbers, the food in my mouth seemed to turn to ash. I chewed it slowly, swallowed, and then set my clay bowl aside.

"Not to mention," Aper continued, walking into the atrium with his hands clasped behind his back, "we face a calamity tomorrow night that will make those numbers seem paltry. So forgive me for being a bit...skeptical of a new magus who appears out of the crowd at the exact same time as our daemon conjurer. I believe it is you who always claimed that magi are exceedingly rare in this age. One in a million, you've said. Now we have three in one city of about a million people. I believe in the gods, Natta Magus, but I do not believe in coincidence."

"She is *not* working with him," I said. I paused to swallow my tasteless food. "But she does know who he is. His name is Silanus, and apparently he wants revenge on Romans for killing his beloved nurse." I left out the little detail where he and Helva were both trained by William because then they'd *really* flip out. "And if you want to stop tomorrow night's calamity, then we all need to work together. Because this magus, the one who attacked us today, can and will do what he says. We need to figure out how he's going to use these Dea Tacita daemons to kill Rome's firstborn. Now he can point them in a certain direction, but he doesn't have the power to tell each one to target a particular person, much less figure out who's a firstborn."

"Natta Magus," Vitulus said slowly, "you do understand why we're skeptical, right?"

*Damnation,* I thought, *are these people even listening to me?* "I get it," I said a bit more forcefully than I'd intended. "You don't trust us because of our power. But when are you going to understand that magi are just human beings? Yeah, there are some bad ones, but there are also honorable ones. We just have talents that most people in this age don't have."

"Talents," Aper said, staring down at me, "that up until two years ago, we assumed belonged only to the gods."

I held Aper's evaluating gaze and said, "We are not gods."

Paetus sucked in a breath behind Aper and then unfurled the scroll he had brought with him.

"No you are not," Aper said, drawing my attention back to him, "but there are many today who assume so, especially after what they saw you three do." The blank expression on Aper's face finally broke, and I saw once again the respect he had for me. "I trust you, Natta Magus. You've earned that trust. But this woman magus has not. And with so much at stake right now, I must remain skeptical of her intentions."

"Okay, fine," I said, "you don't trust her. What can I do to make you trust *me* when I say that you can trust *her*?"

Aper shrugged. "To start, where is she? Why isn't she here with you now?"

"You really need to ask that? After the third degree you're giving me now? Because she knew this would happen, or worse."

Aper gave me a small smile. "Ah, so you don't trust *me* now?"

"Well it must be in the air with all the smoke from the Circus."

"Sir," Vitulus said to Aper, "Natta Magus is correct in that we must work together. The lives of thousands of Romans are at stake." He glanced at me. "I trust him. If he says we have nothing to fear from this woman, then I believe him."

*Bless you, Vitulus,* I thought. *I know you're really trying to believe me. But I still don't see it in your eyes, buddy.*

Aper and I stared at each other a few more moments, and then Aper began speaking as if the previous conversation had never taken place. "Finding the Sibylline Books now is more imperative than ever. The Senate and the people have already cried out to the Princeps to open the books to learn how Rome can escape this dire situation. As you can imagine, this puts the Princeps in the awkward position of denying that is necessary. So. Have you any leads on where the books are, Natta Magus?"

I sighed. "All I know is that Silanus is the one who stole the books. He believes there is a spell hidden in them that a magus can use to stop him tomorrow night. But I don't know what that spell could be, and I don't know how he's going to direct all those Dea Tacitas to find only firstborns."

"I know how," Paetus said quietly from behind Aper. When we all turned to look at him, I saw that he had his scroll unfurled on the tile floor and was reading it from his knees. When he looked up at us, his rotund face was paler than usual. "He's going to enthrall a god to do it for him."

# THIRTY-TWO

N ow I've had capped people ask me many times what I know of the divine, and all I can tell them is, "About the same as you."

You see, magic is just another force of nature to me. It doesn't tell me anything about the afterlife or the existence of divine beings. Yes, I can commune with spirits sometimes, but as with Lares, they are vague to the point of nonsense when questioned about the hereafter. I don't know where daemons come from. I don't know where the spirits of the living go upon death. All I know is that daemons come from one place and that spirits go to another place. If that answer frustrates you, then welcome to the club.

So when Paetus said that he thought Silanus wanted to enthrall a god, I took it with a huge grain of salt. The term "god" or "goddess" was thrown about in the ancient world as the power behind everything from a thunderstorm to a soft breeze. Hell, some people even referred to house spirits like Lares as "gods" (she can certainly act like one sometimes).

"Okay, take a deep breath, Paetus," I said. The poor guy looked like he was on the verge of fainting again. "Tell me exactly what the scroll says, word for word."

Paetus took a few shaky breaths while we crowded around him over the scroll. The Greek letters were simply scribbles to me, and I resolved that if I survived all this, I would learn to read and speak Greek. All the coolest scrolls these days seemed to be in Greek.

Paetus pointed to a block of text around the crude illustration of the Dea Tacita. "This block says that Dea Tacitas are quiet assassins, that they can be summoned to kill a particular person. But the summoning and direction require very elaborate magic. The way this Dark magus used the Dea Tacitas today was not very efficient based on their abilities."

Vitulus snorted. "They killed thousands of people. How is that not efficient?"

"Because it's like what Natta Magus said, individual Dea Tacitas can be directed to kill a specific person, but it's nearly impossible to direct a swarm of them toward specific individuals. According to this scroll, that level of control is not possible for a human being, even if he is a powerful magus." Then Paetus swallowed. "But it's not impossible for a god. Specifically, Invidia, the goddess of revenge."

He pointed to a block of text and recited:

*"Servants of the Cold Dark,*

*Obey the will of your goddess, She of the poisoned tongue.*

*Follow Her eye, become Her vengeance."*

"Invidia," Paetus said, "is known to have a poisoned tongue."

"So you think Invidia will direct the Dea Tacitas for Silanus? Okay. How will Silanus get her to do that? If he can actually summon and enthrall her to begin with." I doubted a mortal scroll might contain anything accurate about a divine being, but then the scroll was pretty spot on regarding the Dea Tacitas.

Paetus shook his head helplessly. "I don't know. Sacrifices, perhaps? Maybe with his magic, he can imbue his sacrifices with enough power to draw her attention."

I thought back to what Lares told me about the Sibylline Books and their wisdom on belief magic.

"Do you know anything about the role of belief on the spirit realm? I'm talking the mass belief of hundreds or thousands."

"Yes, it draws their attention. Belief in evil creates evil, just as belief in good creates good. It is why so many people wear a fascinum, because they believe it makes them invisible to evil."

"Maybe that's why he stole the books," I muttered. "He thinks I might be able to use that belief in the fascinum to make Roman firstborn invisible to Invidia."

Paetus nodded. "A good theory."

"My only theory," I grumbled.

"Then we're back to where we started," Vitulus said in frustration. "We have to find the Sibylline Books." Vitulus eyed me. "Can you contact your woman magus? She knew his name, so she must know how to find him."

"I already asked her. She's, um, thinking about it."

I could practically see the steam rising from Aper's ears. "She'd better think quickly," he growled, departing from his usual stoicism. "We don't have time for her to ponder where her loyalties lie."

"I'll talk to her," I said. "I think she wants to help, but it's going to take some persuasion."

"I have men who can persuade her," Aper said ominously. I couldn't tell if he was serious, or if it was his frustration and fatigue talking. But I had no doubt he was truthful about the "persuasive" talents of his men.

"I'll talk to her," I said again. "In the meantime, I have some ideas on how to locate Silanus. He's using a form of magic that I was unaware of when I tried my finder spells before. Now that I know what it is, I may be able to figure out a spell that can locate him. But I'll need Lares' help."

Then I suddenly remembered that Lares had gone silent earlier today when I was questioning her about the Sibylline Books. A lump of worry formed in my throat, and I hoped she had returned. And not just to help me with saving Rome.

"I'll come too," Paetus said quickly, nervously eying Aper and Vitulus. He rolled up his scroll and was at my side faster than I'd seen him move since the Dea Tacita was chasing him in his library.

Aper stared at me, his face turning blank once again. "Very well. Figure out your spell. I expect results by dawn, Natta Magus. Vitulus, I require your counsel."

"Yes, sir," Vitulus said. "May I first walk Natta Magus to the front gate."

Aper nodded once and then strode into his office room.

As soon as we stepped out the door and into the courtyard, Vitulus said to me in a low voice, "Today was the first day Salvius Aper ever saw a daemon. I've never seen him afraid before."

"Everyone gets afraid," I said in the same quiet voice. "Even Salvius Aper."

"True. But Aper knows how to hide it and perform his duty. Especially in front of his men. Today, though, was the first time I'd ever seen panic in his eyes. As if he were about to *run*. And this was in front of his men. He didn't, of course, but the thought was there. For him to be scared enough to show it..." Vitulus shook his head. "The internal security of Rome and that of the Princeps rests on his shoulders. So when he speaks of trust and loyalty and torture, it is because he will do whatever it takes to perform his duty." We had finally stopped in front of the gate, and he gave me a serious look. "Do you understand, my friend?"

*Yeah*, I thought. *I understand that maybe Helva was on to something...*

But instead I nodded and asked, "How are Claudia and Lucius?"

His face softened. "They are well. The Princeps and Livia were very kind to them. They all escaped the daemons and the fire unscathed. If you hadn't put out that fire when you did, it might have spread to Augustus's residence, and then they would've..." He took in a shaky breath. "But once again you saved us all. On behalf of a grateful Rome, I thank you."

It was funny how a simple "thank you" could disarm my pensive thoughts and remind me why I was doing all this. It wasn't for Augustus or Aper or even the idea of Rome. No, it was for Vitulus and Claudia and Lucius and all the nameless and faceless innocents who had no hope of fighting daemons and magi on their own. I was still angry and frustrated with not being trusted, especially after all I'd done, but at least I knew that distrust wasn't shared by every Roman.

I put a hand on his shoulder. "Thanks, buddy, I needed that."

He nodded and grinned. "Now go save us all again."

"Yeah, no pressure."

Once Aper's gate shut behind us, and Paetus and I were back on the street, he took a deep breath, and said, "Until we meet again, Natta Magus." Then he started walking in the opposite direction of my Aventine Hill shop.

"I thought you wanted to come with me?"

"Oh," he said over his shoulder, "I just said that to get out of there. And I will never forgive you for leaving me alone with Augustus."

"Hold on," I said, rushing over and grabbing his arm. "You have that scroll. I still need your help!"

When he turned to face me, I saw him grinning in the fading light of dusk. "Of course I'm going to help. I just wanted to give you a small measure of the panic you gave me today, you *caccing* fool." He barked a laugh, but I just stared at him with my best Aper glare. I obviously wasn't as intimidating as Aper because Paetus just kept grinning. I don't know how he could be so skittish at the mere thought of a Praetorian, but have no problem goading a magus.

"I may have some books and scrolls in my library that might shed further light on the Sibylline Books," Paetus said. "I'll look through my collection and bring any interesting materials to your shop by dawn."

I let go of his arm with a scowl. "You remember me saving your life today, right?"

He rolled his eyes, and then started walking away. "You're going to use that every time you need something from me, aren't you?"

"You better believe it," I called out to his back.

He just gave me a backward wave and disappeared around the corner.

Normally street traffic was pretty sparse after the sun went down. But tonight, the streets and alleys were filled with citizens with packed bags and wagons leaving Rome. News had apparently gotten out about Silanus's threat to kill all of Rome's firstborn. I certainly couldn't blame them after what had happened at the Circus, and I came to think that they were probably doing the wise thing. I didn't know if Silanus's firstborn spell had a range on it, but it was probably a good idea to get as far from the city as possible just in case.

I wondered if Balbus Naevius had skipped town since he was firstborn, thus saving me from having to find him by noon tomorrow. But my feet immediately wanted to take me into the Suburba at the thought of him. No, he was still around, judging by the power of the finder spell that I still had on him.

As if I didn't have enough to do.

When I arrived at my shop, I stopped at the steps that led down to the garden level door. The wards were still in place—the door glowed with swirling reds and blues in my magical sight—but I was worried that I would walk in and find that Lares was still gone. She was really my first friend in ancient Rome. When I moved into this shop, I had already met Vitulus, but I had only worked with him on one job. We certainly weren't friends by then.  Even though she was overprotective and said some pretty risqué things, the thought of her not being there made me as lonely as I'd felt last year after returning from Aventicum without Brianna.

Only one way to find out. I walked down the steps, canceled the wards with an arcane word, and then opened the door.

Silanus sat at the table in my front room with a lit candle and a setup chessboard. He gave me a friendly smile.

"Fancy a game, Natta Magus?"

# THIRTY-THREE

nother question I've been asked from time to time by the locals in Rome: What kind of weapons do people use in the twenty-first century? To which I half-jokingly respond, "Our bare hands."

And I say it half-jokingly because it's partially true. After the Dark Wars of the early twentieth century, the victorious Allies pumped the world's atmosphere with the Aether, a magical substance that not only stops Dark magi spells from materializing, but also gives all cell magi the ability to raise a defensive shield around themselves to stop any magical or physical attack. One of the first spells that magi in my time learn is how to draw on the Aether to raise that shield.

So if I were in the twenty-first century staring at Silanus, as he calmly sat at my shop's table, I'd have instantly drawn on the Aether to raise my defensive shield and confidently begun interrogating him. But I was in ancient Rome. There was no Aether. I had no defensive shield. All I could do was stare at him without looking like I was about to *cac* my trousers. I had my ball cap, so he theoretically shouldn't be able to enter my mind, but he had proven just how useful my ball cap was back at Capito's farm when he enthralled me.

I could've ran, but where would I have gone where he couldn't eventually catch me? And if I ran, I'd miss this golden opportunity to glean some sort of information from him on his plans. I tried to calm myself with the fact that if his goal was to kill me, he could've done it the moment I walked in. Or from one of the myriad dark alleys and alcoves that I'd passed on the way here.

He wanted to talk. So I would talk. Besides, this was my shop, and it had a few tricks of its own.

"Why are you here?" I managed to ask with more confidence than I felt.

He shrugged. "I told you, I want to play a game with you, Natta Magus." He gestured toward the chessboard. "White or black?"

His Latin was good, though tinged with an Eastern accent like Helva's. As I'd noticed in the Circus, he'd shaved the extra long sideburns. His black hair was wavy and thick and hung over his ears and around his neck. He also wore a black tunica with silvery trim, which displayed his muscular shoulders and arms. I noticed the place where the arrow had struck him earlier was completely healed without a scar to show that he'd been hit. He had the same deep-set eyes and sharp cheekbones as Helva. They both could've been runway models in a Canaanite fashion show.

"Seems to me you've already started the game," I said, slowly shutting the door behind me. I glanced at the plump little statue near the front door that normally would've been glowing per Lares' mood. The statue was still and I did not hear her voice. "Chess is for two players. If you want to play me, then play *me*. Leave the Romans out of this."

Silanus grinned. There was no madness behind that grin. If I didn't know what he was, I would've seen it as a good-natured, friendly smile. This was a guy I could have a *posca* with at the local tavern and talk about the latest chariot races. He seemed in complete control of his mind. It was disturbing as hell.

"Oh, there *are* only two players in this game," Silanus said. Then he looked wistfully down at the chessboard. The "board" had been drawn onto an unfurled papyrus scroll, while the pieces were carved out of light and dark wood. They were crude representations of the pieces I knew, but were recognizable enough to me. They didn't look as nice as the pieces he'd cursed.

"Chess is a fascinating game," Silanus said. "William taught it to me days after we first met. The goal is deceptively simple: Capture the king. The piece moves are simple as well. It only takes moments to learn. But the tactics, the strategies...those can take *years* to master. When to attack, when to defend..." He glanced up at me. "When to sacrifice."

"So, what, the Romans are just pieces on a board to you?"

Silanus chuckled. "Obviously. You and I, Natta Magus, are the only true players in this city. *We are gods.* We should be ruling them. And not just them, but all mundane humans. All they do is fight and drink and gamble. They waste their lives on watching chariot races or praying to their false gods. If we ruled them, we could direct them to a higher purpose."

"What higher purpose?"

He gave me an earnest look. "Peace." Then he glanced at the stool on the other side of the chessboard from him. "Please, sit down so we can talk like civilized gods."

"We're not gods. And I'd prefer to stand, thank you."

He slammed his open hand on the table, knocking over many of the chess pieces. *"I said sit!"*

His enthrallment spell came out of nowhere. It smashed through the wards on my ball cap like a sword through paper, grabbed all the muscles in my body, and forced them to move toward the table and stool. My mind panicked, just like at Capito's farm. I felt the desire to just submit to him, to do whatever he said, to bask in his approval, but my mind was aware of this symptom and could resist. But for how long?

*This isn't possible! He shouldn't be able to do this!*

But it *was* possible. He *was* doing it. And there wasn't a damned thing I could do about it.

I sat down.

"Now," he said, his joviality returning, "isn't this better? Two intelligent men playing a civilized game of strategy and wits?"

My panic had abruptly given way to rage. This man had killed thousands of people today, and he was implying that we were the same? That all those people were just pieces in his game? If I could've moved my mouth, I would've screamed at him.

"Oh," he said, "forgive me. I love to win, but I'd rather my opponent make his own moves. You may speak and you may move...but if you try touching your magic, I will kill you. Understand?"

The enthrallment suddenly ended. My muscles sagged with the release, and then I tensed them again as I brought them back under my own control. I fought to contain my anger at his violation. I wanted nothing more than to grab Lares' statue and smash his face in. But I knew I couldn't flinch without him slamming the enthrallment back into place. For now I had no choice but to play his game. I gave him a jerky nod to indicate my understanding.

"Grand," he said. "Well, seems I'm on the white side so I'll go first." He moved his king's pawn forward two squares.

"Why are you here?" I asked again, and then moved my black bishop's pawn forward two squares.

"Ah," he said, staring at my move, "William called this the Sicilian opening. I always found it odd that such an elegant set of opening moves could be named after an island full of gravel and barbarians." Silanus moved one of his knights.

"You've picked up William's annoying habit of avoiding my questions," I said, and then made my move. "Why are you in my shop, Silanus?"

He raised an eyebrow at me. "You know my name?" He suddenly looked hopeful. "Did William tell you about me before you murdered him?"

"I didn't murder William! He—" I exhaled sharply, brought my anger under control, and then thought for a second. If I told him that William never mentioned him at all, then he'd probably figure that I learned his name from Helva. But what if he didn't know that Helva was in Rome? She could be my ace in the hole, so to speak, if she truly decided to help me stop Silanus. And if I survived this chess game.

"Yeah, he mentioned you. Said you were his apprentice. Said you were awesome. Now, again, why are you here in my shop? And don't tell me it's to play a chess game."

His eyes grew wistful when I told him that William had mentioned him, but then he looked amused after I asked him again why he was here. He wagged his finger at me. "William talked about you a lot, too. He said you loved to get right to the point of things, that you hated...ah, what was that delightful metaphor he used? That you hated beating around the shrub."

"The bush, and yes, I hate that. Now if the next words out of your mouth are not an explanation as to why you're here, then I'm leaving. You can enthrall me or kill me, sure, but then you'll have no one to play your stupid games with."

A fire seemed to flash across Silanus's brown eyes that was not a reflection of the candle on the table. We stared at each other for several moments. When he finally blinked, I took some small satisfaction from the meager victory. It was the only victory that I'd had over him since this all started.

He relaxed, looked at the chessboard, and then made his move. "I told you why I'm here: to offer you a partnership in Rome's new order. And Rome is only the beginning. With our combined power, we can guide humanity to the glorious, peaceful future that William foresaw."

"For some reason I don't think you want me as a *partner*," I said, and made my move. The board, like this conversation, was getting more complex.

"Of course I do," Silanus said after castling his king and rook. "William had a vision for a peaceful humanity that survives into eternity, one that I share. One of which you were a vital component. I want to carry on William's vision *with* you." He shrugged sheepishly. "Now I admit, I'd be more the *senior* partner in our relationship, but that doesn't diminish your importance." He glanced down at the board. "Think of me as the king and you as the queen. I would rule, while it would be your role to protect me and to clear the board of threats to my reign. I'd say that's a rather important destiny for you to fulfill, yes?"

I made another move and then asked, "Why did you steal the Sibylline Books?"

Silanus laughed. "Right to the point, again. Well, I cannot reveal the answer to that question until I'm sure I can trust you, Natta Magus. Can I trust you? Will you join me and fulfill William's vision?"

I gave him a level stare. "What do you think?"

Silanus folded his arms. He stared at me with a frown, though I got the feeling my answer wasn't unexpected. "William always said you had, um, 'a moral streak about a mile wide.' He admired it. Counted on it, even. It was the whole basis of his Aventicum plans last year." He leaned forward. "But I find it insufferably tedious. By the way, how is my sister?"

*Damnation.* "Your sister?"

"Her headscarf is on your workbench," he said. "Either you took it from her, or she left it here on purpose. We have our differences, but I should be rather disappointed if you hurt her. Where is she?"

The enthrallment tickled my mind, and the only reason I noticed it was there was because I got the sudden desire to tell him everything I knew about Helva. Its subtlety terrified me the most. He was very good at it; someone unable to cast magic would've immediately answered his questions without a second thought. For now, however, it was not as all powerful as it had been when he forced me to sit.

"If that's your sister's scarf, then I had no idea," I said. "I found it yesterday in the Tiber."

He wagged his finger at me again. "You see, this is why I'm finding it hard to reveal too much to you. I can't trust you to be honest with me. I may not be revealing much about myself to you, but the things I am revealing are the truth. Can you say the same?"

"Then it seems we're at a stalemate," I said. "I won't join you, and you won't tell me what you're planning. What happens now?"

"Indeed," he said, looking over the chessboard. "I would like nothing better than to continue this game. The position is very complex. But alas, I cannot give you the chance to win."

I didn't like the sound of that, and I suddenly knew that I wouldn't get anything else out of Silanus. Not to mention he was about to enthrall me again.

So I muttered, "*Shaakmat.*"

As with Paetus's library, I had set up anti-magical domes in my shop just in case a spell went awry, or I summoned an angry spirit or daemon. And just like Paetus's library, the dome didn't require any magical talent to trip. I just had to say the word in the right way.

The dome slammed shut over the entire front room. My magical senses turned off as if I had just closed my eyes to sight. Silanus felt the dome as well, for he jumped up from his stool with a snarl. I stood and drew the gladius from my belt that I had used in my exercises with Vitulus.

"Now that you're stuck here," I said, pointing the gladius at him, "let's talk about this plan of yours."

# THIRTY-FOUR

S ilanus looked from me to the gladius in my hand, and then his eyes scanned the room. He smiled at me. "I knew you'd be a wonderful opponent," he said. "I thought I had disabled your wards. How did you hide this one?"

"It's not cell magic," I said, trying to hide the disgust in my voice.

He raised an eyebrow. "Soul magic? Well, you surprise me again. William said you'd never use it due to said moral streak."

"I'm a different man now. Where are the Sibylline Books?"

"And if I don't tell you, we fight like mortals?"

"If we must—"

"Natta Magus!" cried a disembodied female voice. "Thank the gods I've finally found you again, my honey love, my sweet!"

I glanced at the cherubic statue and saw its glow alternating white, red, and pink, the colors switching back and forth manically. Silanus grinned as he glanced from me to the statue. He seemed to hear Lares, too.

"Lares? Where have you been?"

"Where have *I* been? Where have you been? Your manly presence was hidden from me for an eternity, and I have been desperately searching the earth for you!"

"I think it's only been since this morning, but—"

"Why did you throw me out of our home, honey fig? I thought we were having a wonderful conversation and that you loved me! Though I know you do not love me in the same way that I would love you for every night of your life—"

"I didn't throw you out!" Then I noticed Silanus's smirk and said, "But I think I know who did."

"Oh, don't look at me," Silanus said.

"What did you do to her?" I asked, slowly walking around the table with the gladius pointed at him. "How did you cast her from this building? She's celestially tied to this dwelling; she cannot be cast out."

Silanus walked the other way, slowly, toward my door. "I give you my word that I did nothing to your house spirit. Now here is what's going to happen. You will release me from this ward, and I will leave through a gate. If you do not, then we will fight right now. But I warn you, I've been trained by Egypt's best swordsmen. You will not kill me that easily."

"Egypt's best—?"

Silanus grabbed the candle sitting on the table and threw it at me. As my eyes instinctively watched it come toward me, and my body instinctively tried avoid it, I didn't notice Silanus following right behind the candle. Before I could bring my sword up, he had knocked it out of my hand with one arm and punched me in the jaw with his other fist. I fell backward onto the floor. Silanus stood above me with the sword in his hand, the point under my chin. He wasn't even breathing hard, but his eyes were lit with anger.

*Well, damnation.*

Lares screamed, but Silanus ignored her. "It is fortunate for you that I do not consider our game finished," he growled. "I will beat you. I will show the world that *I* am its greatest magus. And in the end, when you meet William's spirit in the Duat, you will tell him that he was wrong about you. You will tell him that I was the one to bring peace to humanity, *not you.*"

"You can't leave here," I said, trying to keep the tender part of my throat away from my own *caccing* sword's point. "Your body contains magic. It cannot pass through the dome over this room."

He shrugged. "Then I will wait for a mortal to cross the threshold. If your dome follows magical principles, it will weaken, and then I will break out. Most likely by killing whomever crosses it first. Who do you think it will be? Your Praetorian friend? The fat flamen? Maybe some sorry plebeian child wanting you to find her lost cat?"

"I won't let you hurt anyone," I said. Though how I would stop him was beyond me.

He smiled. "I said I don't *want* to kill you. But then I cannot allow you to stop me either. Given that choice, I will kill you now if you wish." He pushed the sword point farther into my chin, and I felt a hot gash of pain as it pierced my skin and drew blood. "What will it be, Natta Magus? Let me go and live to play the game another day, or die right here and now?"

"If you hurt him," Lares screamed, "I will see to it that no house spirit in Rome lets you sleep a restful night again! I will call on the daemons to riddle your manhood with boils! I will—!"

"Lares," I grunted, "I think he gets it."

Silanus's expression didn't change; his gaze never wavered from mine despite Lares' insults and threats.

I've always been a "live to fight another day" kind of guy. But what would happen if I let him go and I couldn't find him again before he killed all of Rome's first born? Yeah, it was a risk, but if he killed me know, he'd eventually escape my magic dome when someone inevitably crossed the threshold.

He leaned closer toward me, the sword point still at my throat. "Now that I have your answer to my offer of partnership, all I want to do is leave. Make your decision now, Natta Magus."

"Fine," I growled. "Take your sword from my throat, and I'll release the dome."

Silanus removed the point from my throat, but kept the sword aimed at me. I slowly stood and then picked up the candle that he'd thrown at me. It was still lit, but fortunately it hadn't caught my wood floors on fire. I put the candle back on the table and then reached for a pouch on my component belt. I took a pinch of powdered lava rock and tossed it at the door to my shop.

"Natta, my love, are you all—?" Lares began, but her voice was immediately cut off as soon as the rock powder hit my door. A hole in the air rimmed with blue and red light suddenly appeared, flared around my entire front room, and then my ears popped. I could feel my cell magic again, but Lares had gone silent. Her statue no longer glowed.

I glared at Silanus. "What happened to Lares?"

He raised my sword high and drove its tip into the wooden floorboards about two inches. The sword hilt swung back and forth when he released it. He took a pouch from his black tunica, tossed in all the chess pieces from the table, and then rolled up the papyrus board. He strode around the table opposite from me and then put a hand on the door to my shop.

He turned to me and pointed his papyrus board at me. "I told you, Natta Magus, I am not responsible for your house spirit's problems." Then he sneered and said, "Why don't you ask Helva about it? I look forward to continuing our game."

He opened my door and strode off into the dark alley.

# THIRTY-FIVE

A few moments after Silanus left, I rushed outside and watched him stroll down the street as if it were broad daylight and he was shopping for new scarves in the Forum. Then an oval of blue light erupted in front of him—a *reizen* gate—and he stepped through. Once he did, the gate vanished.

I turned left toward the printer's shop where Helva lived. There were no lights on inside at this late hour, but I began pounding on the door nonetheless. "Helva, we need to talk!"

It didn't take long for Balnor to open the door. He held a candle and was dressed in a sleep tunic. The meager gray hair on his balding head floated in wispy disarray. He squinted at me in confusion.

"Natta Magus? What is wrong?"

"I need to speak to Helva," I said. "Is she here?"

"Well of course she's here. But why must you speak to her at such a late hour?"

"I apologize, Balnor, but it's very important that I speak to her now."

"Now?" Balnor glared at me. "It is highly improper for a young woman to speak to a man in the middle of the night. Do not misunderstand, though, that I would support a match between you two. But these things must be done properly—"

"Uncle," Helva said from behind him. She also wore a sleep tunic, though she had a thick linen blanket draped over her shoulders. "It is all right. I will speak to Natta Magus."

"But, my dear, you cannot—"

"Uncle," she said again in soothing tones while putting a gentle hand on his arm. "It is all right."

Balnor frowned at her, but then nodded once. "Very well. But do not go far." He gave me one last warning glare and then retreated into the shop.

Helva stepped outside and closed the door. "We'll talk in your shop," she said, then strode toward my door.

"What about your uncle's honor?" I asked.

"He'll be fine," she said, and then stopped in front of my door. She looked at me in the moonlight, her eyes in shadow. "Your wards?"

"They're down. Your brother was kind enough to destroy them."

She stiffened and then pointed her palms toward the ground. Her head swiveled around, searching the shadows. "He's here?"

"He was, but he gated out of here a few minutes ago. We need to talk."

She took a few moments to scan the street. Some wagons rumbled down an intersection a block away, but other than that the street was clear. After she seemed satisfied that Silanus was gone, she opened the door to my shop and entered without waiting to see if I followed.

When I went inside, she was standing before my table, her back to me. "He was here," she murmured. "I can see the work he did on your wards."

"Yeah," I said, closing my shop door. "And he tried to make me an offer I couldn't refuse."

She turned to me sharply. "What offer?"

"He wants me to help him rule Rome. As his number two, of course."

"Interesting," Helva said. "When we last spoke, he wanted to kill you."

"Yeah, well, I think he still does. After he finishes his game."

"Did he ask about me?" She looked worried as her eyes seemed to catalog every item in my shop. "Does he know I helped you?"

"He asked about you, but I don't know if he knows you helped me at the Circus."

She muttered something in that language I couldn't place and then looked lost in thought.

"Hey, I've got a question," I said. "Did you enthrall Balnor and Tanith?"

She glanced away from me for a moment, then her eyes returned to mine. "Yes."

"Now I know where your brother gets it from..."

"I needed to stay close to you. They were Canaanites, and I had a Canaanite nurse who taught me her language. It was as if the gods set this up. I have not forced them to do anything against their nature. I only planted a vague memory of Tanith's cousin in their minds so that my story would be believable. I simply expanded the kindness that was already in their hearts." Her face softened. "They are good people."

"But that's where it starts, Helva. With a desire to do good. That's what killed William."

Her eyes narrowed. "Do not lecture me on magical ethics, Natta Magus. How many Oaths have you broken since you've been here? How many times have you used *soul* magic? You think your cell magic is so pure, yet it can violate and kill just as easily as any other magic."

I know. I'm the last person to tell another magus to beware of Dark magi spells. To resist the temptation to use them in order to accomplish an honorable goal. She was right, I used cell magic to help kill William. I used soul magic last year to help stop the strix daemons rampaging through the Germanic forests. I even used it to set up shop's my anti-magic dome. These were things that I'd taken Oaths against, and yet I broke my Oaths to save lives and stop evil. Oaths and personal ethics were easy to follow when everyone around you played by the same rules. Not so much when you get thrown into an alien civilization and a whole new set of rules.

I didn't want to dwell on that or defend myself, so I asked, "Question number two: Are you blocking my house spirit?"

Helva sighed. "Yes."

"Why?"

"She annoys me with her *sickening* love talk. Our walls are thin, and I can hear her voice better than yours."

"Bring her back," I said. "She's my friend. And she knows how to help me find the Sibylline Books. She was about to say something about them yesterday when you..." Helva looked away from me again for just a moment, but then returned her steely eyes to mine. I was beginning to notice her little tells. She was guilty about something. "Which is why you silenced her, right? How?"

"It is a simple earth spell to block spirits. I could do it even before I met William." She held her chin up. "If your house spirit gave you any clues about the books, you would've gone after them, and I would've had to follow to keep you safe. And I do not want to confront and possibly...hurt my own brother to keep an Oath."

"Then stay out of it!" I said. "I'm not asking you to go anywhere with me. Just tell me how to find him and the books, and I'll take care of the rest."

She was shaking her head at me as if I were stupidest person she'd ever met. "I swore an Oath to the man I consider my true father. I will keep you safe until my last breath. Wherever you go, I go."

"Look. If you don't release Lares so that she can give me my answers, I will be forced to find them elsewhere. And when I do find those answers, I will confront Silanus. Unless you're prepared to enthrall me, you might as well make this easy on us all and *help me*. Because the more you help me, the less likely I'll be forced to do something stupid that will either result in my death or Silanus's." I stared at her with as much resolve as I could muster. "I'm not going to let him kill thousands of people just so he can prove he's better than me."

She was about a foot shorter than me, so she had to look up when she leaned closer. I caught a mild, flowery scent from the oils she used in her short black hair. "Where you go," she said slowly, "I go."

"But you won't help me."

She continued to lean close, and to be honest, it was quite distracting. After a few moments, she backed up and wrapped her linen blanket tighter around her body. "Do we understand each other, Natta Magus?"

"Yeah. Get out."

She gave me a tilted nod and then walked out my door.

I was so furious that I wanted to kick over every chair in my front room that wasn't already kicked over from my fight with Silanus. How could she say she wanted to keep me alive, but yet not help me? Okay, so it was her own brother that I was trying to stop, but what I said was true: If she helped me, it was less likely that I'd have to do something desperate. Why couldn't she see that? Why was she so worried about protecting me, but didn't give a damn about the possible slaughter of thousands of innocent people?

*Because she loved William and hates Romans*, I replied to my own question. It was that simple. Life was cheap in the ancient world. It was just a given that if your nation goes up against another nation, you did everything in your power to kill them. Romans had killed her parents, therefore they should all die. I could see killing the people who did it; hell, even striking at the Roman legions was fair. But targeting *innocent* Romans? Children? Yes, she wasn't the one doing the targeting. But she was going to let it happen, and that was just as bad to me.

An explosion shook the foundations of my shop. Components crashed to the tables and floor in my back workroom, dust rained down from the floorboards above me, and I heard surprised screams from the family that lived above my shop. I raced out the door and up the steps to the street.

The first thing I saw were legs. Legs the size of tree trunks. I followed them up to a naked pelvis, massive torso, muscled shoulders, and then the head...aw, damnation, the head looked like it was made of gray stone. The giant's hair and beard were carved in disheveled spikes. Its eyes glowed orange, and orange flame flickered from its wide open, sharp-toothed mouth. All told, the giant stood at least fifteen feet tall. It looked down at me, took in a deep breath, and roared a gout of flame right at me.

# THIRTY-SIX

Fortunately for me, I had already decided to leap out of the giant's line of sight before he vomited flames at me. I ran across the street and crashed through the thin plank door of a tenement building and into the small kitchen. I felt the heat of the flames on my back as they splashed up from the cobblestone road where I'd just been standing. Screams came from the back of the apartment. Children scrambled from behind a curtain to my right and rushed into the curtained section next to them where their parents must've been sleeping.

The giant roared again. Another gout of flame struck an empty oxcart just outside the door, which exploded into flaming shards.

Since I seemed out of the giant's way for a few seconds, I took one of those precious seconds to pull my wits together. The giant didn't emanate that nauseous feeling that daemons gave me, so I could rule them out. It was just big and scary. But something about the giant struck me as familiar, and I mentally scrambled through my Roman mythology until—

*Wait. Giant, breaths fire, we're on the Aventine Hill.*

*Cacus.* Not to be confused with my favorite Roman swear word, but I was literally facing *the* Cacus. According to Roman myth, Cacus lived in a cave on the Aventine Hill before the founding of Rome. He was a fire-breathing giant who kept stealing the cattle and daughters of the nascent Romans. But then Hercules came to town, choked Cacus to death, and earned the eternal gratitude of the locals. It's why there's an Ara Maxima in front of the Circus Maximus: It's the altar dedicated to Hercules for his slaying of Cacus.

Okay, I had the monster's name. Now question number two: What in damnation was it doing here? Did Silanus somehow cook him up? Was it another one of the random supernatural events that plagued Rome from time to time?

Cacus bellowed again, the sound like gargling stone and roaring flames, and then it sounded like he punched the second floor of the apartment building I was in. More screams from upstairs.

Whatever he was, it looked like he was after me. If I didn't get out of this building, he'd bring it down with all the people inside.

So I followed my own advice. I didn't think about what I had to do, I just did it. I ran out the front door, just as Cacus gave the second floor another punch with his massive, sledgehammer fists. I ran past him toward Balnor's shop, praying that Helva was still inside. I was going to need her help with this one.

As I guessed, she was already coming out the door and up the steps from the garden-level shop as I charged toward her. She looked at the giant, her eyes widening, and then she beckoned me inside. Once I charged past her, she slammed the door. Cacus bellowed his strange stony roar again and stomped toward Balnor's shop.

Balnor and Tanith appeared in the front room, both looking understandably frightened by all the noise.

"What is happening?" Tanith asked, eying the closed door and the heavy foot falls coming toward it.

"Aunt, Uncle," Helva said, "please go into the back room and stay there." Helva's voice took on the same slightly reverberating quality as earlier when she calmed Balnor about talking to me. Both Balnor and Tanith nodded and returned to the back rooms.

"This is Silanus's work," she said.

"You think?" I cried. "How'd he do it?"

Cacus struck the door to the shop, but the door somehow held. It must have been warded, for there was no way the flimsy door could've held without magical aid. I couldn't see the wards, so I assumed they came from Helva's earth magic.

"This hill holds the beliefs of many generations," she said, flinching from another Cacus strike. "Silanus can pull those beliefs and mold them into an apparition with substance."

The legend of Cacus was one of the most popular myths in Rome, especially on the Aventine. It was better than any explanation I could think of, so I went with it.

"Okay," I said, "let's say that's true. Can you banish it?"

She nodded. "I can sever the creature's connection to the earth. But the spell takes many heartbeats, and I must not be interrupted." She gave me a meaningful look. "You must distract it."

I exhaled sharply and said, "Of course I do. How long?"

"As long as you can give me," she said.

Cacus slammed his fists into the door again. This time it cracked, and one of the boards splintered.

"This place have a back door?" I asked.

"No," she said, "but I can gate you behind the monster."

She held her arms at her sides, palms facing down, said something in her arcane language, and then a *reizen* gate popped into existence right in front of me. Through the gate, I saw Cacus's massive, stony back as he knelt before Balnor's shop and rained blows upon the door. Those blows were matched by the ones I was hearing and feeling just a few steps away.

If we survived this, she was gonna *have* to show me how to do this spell.

"Hurry," she said, "he's about to break through!"

I leaped through the gate. It was no different than running through the doorway to a different room: One moment I was in the shop, and the next, I was standing on the brick alley behind Cacus, my own shop to my left. Cacus had just pulled one fist back and slammed it through the unwarded door. The top part of the door was gone, but the bottom with the latch still held.

"Cacus," I shouted. "Over here, big guy!"

Cacus had one fist raised to punch the bottom of the door, but he paused, turned to look at me, and then jumped to his feet faster than I'd have expected from a giant his size. Supernatural strength meant you could ignore the laws of gravity. His eyes still glowed orange, and his gray stony head was riddled with black cracks that looked like veins. Flames still flickered from his open mouth. The rest of his naked, muscled body looked like a body builder covered in gray ash.

"Yeah," I said, fear suddenly swelling from my gut and into my limbs. "You're as ugly as the myths say you are."

I started backing up on trembling legs now that I had his attention. I tried not to look at the door to Balnor's shop, but in my peripheral vision, I noticed Helva emerge quietly and sneak behind Cacus. She stopped about ten paces from him and pointed her palms toward the ground. She closed her eyes, and her lips began to move with the cadence of her spell.

"So...Hercules. Not a fan, eh?"

Cacus issued another bellow that startled me. It took every bit of my willpower not to run like every daemon in hell was after me.

"Right. Sore subject. Why are you here, Cacus?"

A deep rumble came from Cacus, and it sounded like the old furnaces firing up in my Pingree Hall lab back in Detroit. He didn't look like he was taking in a deep breath, but I thought he was actually going to say something.

But instead of words, a flood of black smoke shot out like footage I once saw of an exploding volcano. The smoke enveloped the entire street before I could move out of the way. The smoke was everywhere; I couldn't see a thing, and I immediately began to cough as if I were drowning.

"Natta Magus, I need to see him!" Helva shouted from behind Cacus.

I couldn't respond because I was too busy coughing up my kidneys. The smoke smelled like a combination of a musty cave and sulfur. That alone was enough to make me gag.

A lance of fire struck the ground immediately to my right, so I instinctively dove to the left. Fortunately, judging by Cacus's aim, he couldn't see anything in his own smoke either. Neither could I, for I rammed right into the wall of the building on the other side of the street face first. I fell backward, stars now filling my eyes instead of black smoke.

Another lance of fire struck the building wall where I'd just left my facial imprint. Screams came from inside where the lance must have pierced the wall. If I'd been standing there, it would've impaled me.

Cacus roared again, and a third lance shot into the building, but several paces away from me. I crawled and scrambled in the opposite direction, trying to suppress my coughs while raking my shins across jagged rock in the process. I wanted to help the people inside the building, but first I needed to stay alive to figure out *how* to help them. I reached my hand out to the building next to me—I still couldn't see anything beyond my throbbing nose—and slowly stood. I stifled a curse as I slammed my wounded shin against the clay water urn directly across from my shop. At least I knew where I was now.

Cacus continued to bellow. And his fire lance came back in my direction.

"Natta Magus!" Helva cried again.

I struggled to bring my mind back to figuring a way out of this. Helva needed to see Cacus, so I needed to clear the smoke...

And I knew just the thing to do it. If I could somehow cross the street back to my shop. Cacus couldn't see me, so maybe that would give me the edge to survive a sprint across the street. Maybe. If my sore shins held out. Or I didn't trip over a rock, or a loose brick, or simply run into the side of the building.

Regardless, I had to go now. His fire lance was just paces away from me.

I said a quick prayer to the Unknowable Will, drew in some cell magic to throw a spark globe behind me, and then sprinted across the street. The fire lance split the air behind me as it targeted the spark globe. But I was halfway across the street by that time. I knew the number of strides it took me to go from one side to the other, so I stopped when I hit the limit and then reached out my hands to feel my way to my shop. I almost tripped down the steps to my door, but once I found them, I scrambled down and charged inside. The smoke wasn't as thick inside my shop, but I could've navigated in it blind.

I grabbed my feathery air freshener ring from above the door. I cupped my hands over it, drew in as much cell magic as I could siphon without passing out, and yelled, "*Vers!*"

I threw the air freshener outside my door just as Cacus heard where I'd slipped off to. He came charging toward my shop, his fire lance scorching the ground before him, bellows echoing up and down the Aventine alleys.

And then the smoke abruptly swirled and flowed directly into the air freshener ring laying on the cobblestone street. I felt a rush of air around me as all the stenches and smoke particles that were not part of the natural breathable air flew into the freshener.

There was Cacus, not five feet from my door, staring at his smoke disappearing into the feathered ring. He looked down at the freshener and then at me.

I'd faced "imminent death" several times since I landed in ancient Rome, and each time came with a moment of peaceful acceptance, as if my soul simply shrugs and says, "Ah, well, we had a good run. Time for the next life." That's how I felt again when I watched Cacus raise his fists to crush me flat.

But as you no doubt suspected, Helva fired off her banishment spell as soon as she saw Cacus again. The giant didn't bellow or issue a satisfying scream of "I'm melting!" He simply collapsed into a huge pile of mud, wet leaves, and twigs.

It was the moment *after* I had survived "imminent death" that was the worst. My shaking legs wouldn't hold me anymore, so I plopped down onto my bottom and leaned back against the brick wall as I stared at the pile of mulch that had almost killed me.

Helva ran over and stopped at the top of my stairs. "Your face is bleeding. Are you hurt?"

It took her question to remind me about my possibly broken nose and bloody shins. "I'll survive, I suppose." My voice was already sounding nasally from my swollen nose. "You don't happen to know how to heal, do you?"

She shook her head. "Not with my earth magic."

"Right," I said, then slowly stood. Now that the monster was gone, I saw people streaming out of the burning tenement across the street. Cries for the fire brigades were already ringing up and down the Aventine. "Finally," I muttered, "a fire I can put out on my own."

I limped to the top of the stairs and held my hands out in front of me. I drew in the last of my cell magic and said, "*Blussen!*"

My magical sight watched the *blussen* dome descend over the entire burning building, which was only fifteen paces wide. The fires didn't have a mind of their own, so they winked out as soon as the dome fell over them. About a dozen men who had arrived with buckets of water stared in stunned silence as the fires went out, and then they looked at me with open mouths.

I grinned, which must've looked ghastly with the blood flowing from my nose and over my mouth. I was about to apologize for giving them nothing to do when Helva gasped.

Her head snapped in the direction of Balnor's shop. "No," she whispered, and then ran toward it.

I shambled after her as best I could. She charged down the shop's steps with me just a few paces behind her. I arrived in the shop's front room just in time to see Silanus standing in before a gate. There was a dimly lit room on the other side of the gate. Several oil lamps sat atop stone pedestals providing the meager light. I saw Balnor and Tanith standing beside the lamps, looking completely enthralled.

Silanus was speaking to Helva as I came through the door. "They will be safe here, sister." Upon noticing my arrival, Silanus glared at me briefly before returning his steely gaze to Helva. "Do not help him. Or they will die."

"Silanus," she said, her voice taking on a pleading that I had never suspected she could possess. "Please."

He gave her a grim, serious look and then stepped through the gate, which closed as soon as he was through.

She stared at the empty space for several moments. When she turned to me, her eyes seemed to have the same fire as Cacus. "You still want my help?"

At that moment, I couldn't help but feel Silanus had made his first blunder: Instead of frightening his sister, he'd only pissed her off.

# THIRTY-SEVEN

All the people in the apartment building across the street had escaped Cacus's fists and fire lances with only minor cuts and bruises. (I thanked the Unknowable Will, Fortuna, and any other god/goddess that would listen). That left me free to cast a self-healing spell on my swollen nose and equally swollen shin. Magical self-healings are problematic because they suck out all the cell energy your body needs to naturally heal itself. So I could only do a little at a time or risk weakening myself to the point of total exhaustion—as in, sleep-for-days exhaustion—and my tight timetable didn't allow for that.

I healed my shins and nose to the point where they stopped bleeding. They were still swollen and painful, but at least the open wounds were closed and I'd minimized the infection risks. I just hoped I wouldn't have to run from a monster or make a speech before the Senate anytime soon.

While I lay on the cot in the back of my shop healing myself, Helva was busy gathering the components from my shelves that I'd asked her to grab. Many of them had fallen on the workbench and floor due to my fight with Silanus and Cacus's attack. I had to tell her several times to watch where she was stepping lest she crush a dried starfish or a desiccated spider, items that had taken me weeks to prepare and preserve.

"These materials are so inefficient," she growled as she picked them up. "It's a wonder you can use magic at all."

"Not all of us are blessed with an infinite source of energy," I said, as I lay on my cot. "Did you find the *elementair* pebbles? It took me a week to enchant just one of them."

She tossed a handful of components onto my workbench with a bit more force than I would've liked. "How would I even know what those are?"

"Oh they're great! They're smooth, white pebbles about an inch long. We use them in my time to recycle toxic components into their base elements. Mine can only recycle a twelve-inch sphere, though. Make sure you look for those before you..."

She glared at me and began to point her palms down.

"No bother," I murmured. "I stored a few extra at Vitulus's."

"Balnor and Tanith are languishing in my brother's prison, and I'm cleaning your home. Just how much longer must you heal?"

"I'm just as impatient as you, but I'd rather not faint the next time I cast. I need to recover and that takes time. Plus I'm going to need some of those components when we do...whatever it is we're going to do. What are we going to do again?"

Helva gave me the same stony silence on that topic that she'd given me since we got back to my shop.

Lares had been relatively silent since Helva arrived, and I was pretty sure it was out of chilly jealousy toward Helva: Her statue's aura shifted from crisp blue to a frosty white. So when she finally spoke up, it was with a tone that could've frozen lava. "My heart, I believe your friend kicked an *elementair* pebble under your workbench during her cleaning. Rather clumsy of her, I fear."

Helva's frown deepened as she gathered my components, but she refused to respond to the house spirit's gibes.

"Lares, be nice," I said. "Helva's a guest."

"And I will treat her with the courtesy due a guest," Lares said. "But I was simply pointing out facts, dearest. Her feet did indeed kick the *elementair,* and it did indeed fall beneath your workbench. I did not jump to the dishonorable conclusion that she did it on purpose, so therefore I believe it was clumsiness. Is that not courtesy?"

Helva gave me a level stare. "It is not too late for me block her again," she growled.

Lares's statue turned a fiery red for a moment, but then calmed to a more self-controlled golden orange. "She does not have to threaten me, love of my lives," Lares huffed. "She is in my house, after all, so I believe I have a right to speak my mind here."

Helva suddenly grinned mischievously and strode over to the plump statue. She leaned toward it and said, "That was not a threat, *dearest*, but a simple stating of facts."

Before this could blow up into a full-blown shouting match, I said, "Lares, what were you going to tell me about the Sibylline Books earlier?"

"Yes," Lares said, "before I was so rudely kicked out of my own home, I was about to tell you the books contained knowledge on channeling the belief magic of many people."

I slowly sat up in my cot and brought my feet down onto the floor. I stood on wobbly legs. I felt weak and tired from my self-healing, but at least my shins could support my weight while I slowly paced in front of my cot. "Paetus told me that he suspects Silanus is trying to summon Invidia, the goddess of revenge, and that the books might contain a way to stop him from doing that."

"If this magus is trying to summon a goddess," Lares said, "then the books may indeed help you stop him. Perhaps that is why he stole them."

I looked at Helva. "Can Silanus do that? Can he summon a goddess?"

"Silanus is powerful," she said, "but to summon a goddess?" She shook her head. "Not even William was that powerful. Whatever Silanus is going to do, I do not think he could summon a goddess to do it. It seems to me the gods are too powerful for a mortal—even a strong magus—to force them to do anything."

I glanced at Lares's statue. "Could a strong mortal summon a god?"

The statue shifted to the ethereal, calming white that it usually glowed when I asked about the nature of gods and goddesses. And as I expected, she gave me a vague answer. "The celestial planes will always be a mystery to mortals, my honey fig."

I frowned. "That's what I thought." I looked back at Helva. "Do you think Silanus would keep the books in the same place where he took Tanith and Balnor? It was pretty dim, but I thought I saw hieroglyphs all over the walls. Did you recognize that place?"

She looked uncomfortable for a moment as she placed some components back on my shelves. "I think it was the tomb of our ancestors."

"Are you both Egyptian?" She gave me a sharp look, and I said, "Sometimes I can add two plus two. Silanus said he was trained by 'Egypt's best swordsmen.' He also mentioned the 'Duat,' which from my mythology studies back home, was the Egyptian afterlife. Not to mention your Coptic words when you cast spells."

She sighed and then nodded. "Yes, Silanus and I are Egyptian."

"Why did you want to keep that a secret?" I tried to give her a piercing stare. "You were both important, weren't you? Egyptians don't build tombs for the common folk. Who were your parents?"

She clicked her teeth as she tried to ignore me by continuing to clean, which she suddenly found very interesting.

"Helva, if you don't tell me the truth, I'm going to speculate wildly and probably come up with explanations that—"

"I'm the granddaughter of Cleopatra Ptolemy," she said, turning to me finally. "My father was Caesarion, son of Cleopatra and Gaius Julius Caesar. Can your speculations match that?"

I stared at her a few moments and then forced my mouth closed. "Well," I said, "that would explain a lot. The tomb. Why Romans killed your parents. Silanus's sword training...and his sense of royal entitlement."

Helva sat on the cot next to me, her shoulders slumped. She looked like she had unloaded a great weight, yet it had done little to relieve the burden she still carried. "All my life," she said, "my family was on the run. From Egypt to India to Africa. Always looking over our shoulders for Roman assassins. All because *Augustus*"—she practically spat the word—"couldn't have potential rivals to his rule. My father never wanted to rule Rome or even Egypt. He'd had enough. All he wanted was to raise his family in peace in some quiet corner of the world. The Romans finally caught up with us three years ago. They killed everyone I ever knew and loved: my parents, my nurse, the loyal men who guarded us. Silanus and I escaped only because of our magic, which we could barely control or wield at the time. William found us soon after. He was like a god who appeared to us and guided us in our moment of greatest need. We could not have survived without him."

I wanted to put a hand on her shoulder, or something, to comfort her, but I wasn't sure how she'd take it. Instead, I said, "This is a pretty big secret. Why are you telling me this?"

"Because it doesn't matter now. You're going to find out from Silanus soon anyway. Besides, Silanus and I enthralled all the Roman assassins to believe they had killed us, too. Everyone thinks we're dead."

"Thank you for telling me."

She nodded bleakly.

"So that tomb was the tomb of your ancestors? The Ptolemys?"

"Yes. But the tomb is sealed and buried, and I can't gate in. I've tried, but Silanus has set up wards around it. Only he can gate into it now. I could take us to Egypt, but it would take us days to walk the rest of the way. And even then, the tomb is buried into the side of a mountain. We don't have the time dig for it."

"Then how are we going to rescue Tanith and Balnor?"

She glanced at Lares's statue. "I have an idea, but you may not like it."

I followed her glance and said, "What...?"

When she explained it, Lares' statue turned from enraged red to fearful gray to a tearful black to a protective sky blue. "She is mad, Natta Magus! You cannot possibly consider this! You have no idea the powers you'd be taunting with such a scheme! Why, it would be—"

"Lares," I said, "let her finish." I was inclined to agree with everything Lares said, but I wanted to at least hear Helva's idea in its entirety. Maybe it would get a little saner.

But it didn't. It got worse.

When Helva finished, Lares was so uncharacteristically quiet that I wondered if Helva had blocked her again so she could finish her idea. Helva fixed me with a neutral stare and said, "This is the only way to rescue Balnor and Tanith and retrieve your books."

I sat back down on my cot again, suddenly so exhausted that I could barely keep my eyes open. Helva stared at me. "How badly do you want to save Rome, Natta Magus?" she asked quietly.

I thought of Vitulus, Claudia, and little Lucius, the only real family I had here. Hell, I'd even throw Paetus in with them. And Aper, when he wasn't so intimidating and making me feel like he was going to arrest me at any moment. I couldn't let them die because Silanus had some kind of twisted jealous rivalry with me. Even though I knew Vitulus would've had me chained and thrown into Rome's deepest dungeon before he allowed me to do what Helva was suggesting.

It's a good thing he wasn't in my shop.

"Well," I said, "today is as good a day as any to die."

Lares moaned, Helva gave me a grim nod, and I struggled to remember my mythology studies of the Egyptian underworld.

# THIRTY-EIGHT

"Remember," Helva said, as we stood next to Lares's cherubic statue in my shop, "when the spell begins, you'll feel a little shaking, but it's important you continue holding my hand throughout. And once we arrive, stay within ten paces of me or we both will be lost forever in Duat—my magic will not maintain your body there, and your connection to Lares will not bring me back to the mortal plane."

"I know," I said, turning my ball cap around so that the bill faced backward. "That's the third time you've warned me."

I also checked to make sure my gladius belt was secure beneath my spell components belt. I didn't know what good a gladius or my magic would do in the land of the dead, but I'd be a fool not to bring every weapon I had. Besides, I was eager to practice my *magical* gladius skills on a real threat.

"And our magic will not work on the Duat's denizens. Only the spells I recite from the *Book of the Dead* will affect them. There will be temptations, places you once knew—"

"I know, Helva. Damnation, you sound like Lares now."

Right on queue, Lares's statue glowed orange. "Natta Magus, my love, my sweet, I once again protest this foolish idea. I fear I will lose you for all eternity, and then I will be alone in this shop. I don't want to share it with a tanner, or a brothel, or, gods *forbid*, a practice home for another acting troupe!"

"Look at it this way," I said, "at least you'd be with *me* for all eternity."

"No, I won't," she wailed. "You'll be in Elysium with all the other blessed, beautiful souls!"

"We're wasting time," Helva murmured.

"Lares, we need to do this now." *Before I lose my nerve.* "Are you ready?"

The colors on her statute seemed to make it tremble a few moments, and then she said in a shaky voice, "Yes, I'm ready."

Helva held out her hand to me. "Take my hand and then put your other hand on the statue."

I did as she asked. Her hand was warm and dry compared to my sweaty, cold hands. I put my other hand on Lares's statue. From a tactile sense, all I felt was cool stone. But from a magical sense, I felt a warm twinge from Lares' spirit. I could feel her fear and worry over what I was about to do, and I got the sense that she could feel my resolve, too.

"Oh, Natta Magus," she said, weeping softly, "why must you always be a hero?"

I didn't respond, for Helva had begun her spell. Her Coptic words began softly, and I quickly recognized that they were a mantra that she repeated over and over. A misty, black oval about my height coalesced near my shop door. She stepped forward into the black oval, gently pulling me along. When I stepped into it, everything went black.

Though I couldn't see anything, I still felt her hand in mine, and I heard her chants. A slight vibration began in her hand as if she had started trembling. But the vibration grew stronger and even began to make my arm vibrate. It grew with every moment, and I soon felt it over my entire body. Helva's chanting seemed to get louder as well, but I couldn't tell if they had increased in volume or if it was the magical vibration enhancing them. Whatever the cause, it became painful. I felt like my bones were about to explode. My organs felt like they were turning to jelly. I think I screamed, but I wasn't sure since I couldn't have heard myself if I had. I shut my eyes tight, praying for death—

And then all was quiet. I slowly opened my eyes just as Helva was opening hers. We held each other's gaze for a moment. I still held her hand. Then I glared at her and said, "A *little* shaking?"

She let go of my hand. "That was the first time I'd ever done that spell. I apologize for your *discomfort*, but it was necessary to get our bodies vibrating at the same level as the Duat. It was either that or we kill ourselves to come here in spirit—"

I held up my hands. "A little shaking is fine."

We both glanced around at the complete darkness to our left and right. We stood on a log raft about ten paces long and wide, covered with a weaved papyrus rug. The water on either side was just as black as the air. I couldn't see anything beyond the raft or the water immediately around us, yet I could see Helva and the raft clearly as if they emitted their own light. Our voices didn't echo at all, and this place gave me unnerving flashbacks to the underground temple at Aventicum.

I glanced behind us and nearly jumped out of my sandals.

A hooded figure stood about five paces away holding the rudder to our raft. The figure wore a yellow stolla dress with a light purple palla draped over its head, its face in shadow. It looked like the clothing of a Roman equestrian woman.

"Lares?" I said.

The figure pulled the palla down around her shoulders. I stared at her, stunned. All I can say is that when Romans painted their frescoes depicting beautiful goddesses, Lares must've been one of their models while she was alive. She had the classic Roman beauty: Long, thick dark hair tied in braids around her head, olive complexion, sharp cheek bones, long lashes, and bright green eyes that smoldered with the same passion I always heard in her voice.

"Salve, Natta Magus, my love," she said. Her smile seemed to light up the entire raft.

"Lares," I stammered. "Wow. Um. You're...not what I expected."

Her brow furrowed. "Do I not please you, my honey fig?"

I took a few steps toward her and said, "You're one of my best friends. Of course you please me." Then I sighed. "I was just hoping to see the *real* you."

She opened her mouth to protest, but then closed it when she understood that I wasn't buying her mask. She knew me well enough to know that she couldn't trick me, pouty protests to the contrary. Instead, her beautiful face took on a defiant expression. "This is what I look like on the inside whenever I'm with you, Natta Magus. Besides, which 'real' me did you want to see: The newborn; the adolescent; the unmarried, pimply woman; or the old woman who died in your shop of a sudden heart affliction? Does it really matter?"

I smiled. "No. Just know that I don't care what you look like now or what you did in life."

"This is pleasant," Helva growled from behind us. "You both realize we are in the underworld, yes? I suggest we focus on our surroundings."

Lares scowled at Helva, but then gave the surrounding darkness worried glances. "The child is correct," Lares said, and then she began to move the rudder in a sweeping motion to propel the raft. The raft barely made a sound as it sliced through the still waters. "I will find this tomb, love of my lives. I don't want you here any longer than you have to be."

"I second that," I said. "You know how to navigate in this...darkness?"

Lares nodded. "I do not see the same way you see, honey cake. I will guide you there."

I nodded and then walked a few paces ahead to Helva, who stood at the very front of the raft facing the darkness. The entire raft was remarkably stable, like walking on the floor of a house. Not like the shifting and undulating you'd expect on a real raft. I hoped our entire journey went this smooth, but considering my luck and life, I didn't count on it.

"Won't Silanus think of this, too?" I asked.

She shook her head without looking at me. "I learned of this spell after he and William fought. He will not know of it. He believes that the tomb of our ancestors is inaccessible to all besides him."

"So if the tomb is buried, then how did Silanus get in? Don't you have to have been to the place where you gate into it?"

She nodded. "Our father gated him in once. As our father's ancestors did for him, which they did for each other all the way back to the original builders before they sealed the tomb."

"Your father was a magus?"

"Yes, though he was very weak compared to Silanus and me. I had only seen him use the gate spell to the tomb, and doing that made him weak for days. He did not cast any other spells or allow Silanus and I to use our magic. He said it would only draw attention to us all."

"Your mother?"

Helva shook her head.

We stood in silence for many minutes, staring at the darkness. There wasn't even a breeze to tell me that we were moving. Only the water lapping at the raft suggested movement.

"The underworld is kind of boring," I said.

She snorted. "You crave action. Like me."

"I don't *crave* action. I just don't like waiting for things to happen."

"No, you crave action," she said with a knowing smile. "I've watched you a long time, Natta Magus. I've seen the difference in you when you take a finder job from a citizen versus when you help your friend Vitulus. With the former, you shuffle about as if you just want to get it over with. With the latter, you bounce out of your shop as if you are on holiday. You crave this."

"'Bounce'? I don't bounce. Stride, maybe. Besides, adrenaline makes every-one jumpy."

"Whatever 'adrenaline' is, it is a synonym for 'crave action.'"

"Only if you mean that I'm about to *cac* my pants every time I go up against some daemon or monster or angry spirit, then yeah, sure."

"Everyone feels fear. But what do you feel when you know victory is at hand? What do feel after you've used your magic to bend nature's laws to your will and defeat your enemy?"

*Like I could do anything,* I immediately thought.

"Exactly," she said, staring at my expression victoriously.

I laughed despite where we were and what we were about to do. "You don't give up, do you?"

"Not when I'm right," she said. She continued to regard me with that bright smile. She had a small dimple in each cheek that I hadn't noticed before. A pretty smile, really...

She seemed to notice something change in the way I looked at her, so she turned away and returned her gaze to the darkness before us. "Silanus was right about one thing, though," she said quietly. "We *should* be ruling them."

I groaned. "Now don't you start with that."

"William once told me there is no slavery in your time. That you abhorred it." She turned back to me. "If you ruled Rome, as you have the power to do, then you could eliminate slavery there."

"It would still exist everywhere else," I said, shifting my feet. "And even *if* I wanted to rule Rome *and* I issued a decree like that, I'd be assassinated faster than you can say 'Ides of March'. I can't fight an army. Look, I hate slavery. But I'm not here to right every wrong I see in the ancient world."

"Then why are you here?"

Oh, that question again. The question I'd asked myself every day since Aventicum. *Why am I here?* What universal decree made it so that I was the one person—out all the billions of people who've existed and were yet to exist—who had to live in a place 2,000 years before my time? Who had to give up the love of his life in order to keep the world he loved from dying?

Was I bitter? Some days that word didn't even come close to how angry I felt about all this. But most days I had figured out how to live with it. To do some good, where I could. I mean, isn't that what everybody was supposed to do with their lives?

But sometimes I *knew* I had to do more. I'm all about live and let live, but damnation there were a lot of things in the ancient world, and Rome in particular, that I could change if I had a little power—

And that's pretty much when I shut myself down and stopped thinking that I could fix things if only I had absolute power. It was the people who thought that who ended up screwing things up the most.

I gave her a sad smile. "I'll tell you why I'm here when I figure it out."

"Natta Magus," Lares said in a curt voice behind us, "it pains me to end your discussion with the *child*, but we are nearing the shore. You should be wary now, love."

I peered into the darkness. At first I couldn't see anything, but after several moments I noticed a brightening in the sky directly ahead. Shapes began to form in front of the sky. At first I thought they were shadows of mountains, and that we were approaching a vast continental landmass. But as we grew closer to the shore, the shapes became clearer, even though the gray light did not grow brighter. Like Helva, Lares, and the raft, I had no trouble seeing the shapes despite the meager light.

I was looking at pyramids. Hundreds of them. No, thousands. Smaller ones lined the shore of the quiet, black ocean we traveled upon. Much larger ones behind them trailed off into the distance as far as I could see. Some were crumbled and falling apart like the pyramids at Giza in my time, while others looked brand new with smooth stone surfaces and gleaming gold tips that seemed to reflect their own light. The closer we got, the better I could see the tall obelisks scattered throughout the spaces in between the pyramids, each one in the same seemingly random state of newness or disrepair.

I really hoped Lares had a good tracker sense on Silanus's Ptolemy tomb because I didn't see any neon arrows pointing the way.

"Why so many?" I asked Helva. "Even in my time, we never found more than a few dozen pyramids. Certainly none as big as the far ones."

Helva shook her head, looking just as confused at me.

But Lares spoke up behind us. "These do not represent real structures on the mortal plane, honey fig. They are the honors given to souls whose bodies were buried after their hearts are weighed on the Scales of Ma'at." I turned and stared at Lares. This was the most information she'd ever given me on the afterlife since I'd known her. Before I could ask her another question, she continued. "Anubis weighs each heart on a scale. If the heart is lighter than an ostrich feather taken from the headdress of Ma'at, the soul can pass into the realm of Osiris. The lightest hearts that led a life of truth and justice are given the largest, most beautiful pyramids that you see ahead of you. Those whose hearts are...not so light are given the small crumbling pyramids." I saw an unnerving gleam in her eye. "And then the crocodile-headed Ammut comes along and eats them alive."

I glanced at Helva, who did not seem nervous over Lares' description at all. She shrugged and said, "The spirit speaks the truth about the Scales of Ma'at. But I was unaware about the pyramid honors." Then to Lares, she asked, "You can find Silanus's pyramid amongst all these?"

Lares nodded. "All souls have a pyramid here: past, present, and future." Her eyes stared ahead as she continued to swing the rudder. "Silanus's is up the river."

"The river?" I said. And as soon as I said it, I noticed that we were sailing straight toward the mouth of a wide river. It was as if it appeared immediately after Lares mentioned it. The river split the endless shoreline in half, each side a mirror copy of the other.

As we sailed past the shore and onto the river, Lares said, "Beware, my love. The trials begin now."

# THIRTY-NINE

W hen Lares said the "trials begin now," she wasn't kidding. We entered the mouth of the river as she said it, and the raft started to buck up and down like a cork in a fountain. Water frothed and splashed over the sides of the raft. Helva and I had nothing to hang onto, so we both sat down in the middle of the raft to avoid getting tossed into the black, angry water.

Lares, however, seemed to have no trouble standing, and she continued to guide the rudder with a steely expression and an occasional worried glance at me. I felt like she'd let her spirit be scattered throughout the underworld before she allowed something to happen to me.

The first monster attacked soon after the rough water began.

"Natta!" Helva cried, pointing behind me.

At first I thought a small crocodile was trying to get onto our raft. Its head had risen from the black water and its croc snout was leaning on the raft. Then a pair of human hands rose up from either side and tried to pull its body onto the raft. That's right. We were being attacked by a human being with a crocodile head. A similar creature was trying to get onto the raft next to the other one.

"Keep them busy," Helva told me, and then closed her eyes and began a Coptic chant.

My role in the plan we discussed earlier was that I ran interference against the monsters we encountered during our journey while she recited the spells that should pacify said monsters. *Should* being the keyword there, because we were going on the bedtime stories of Helva's father, who got his information from stories told to him by Egyptian priests in his mother's court, who got their information from texts that had been copied and re-copied for thousands of years. I couldn't touch my cell magic at all since we got here, so I had no idea how her magic worked in the underworld. So I had no choice but to trust her.

I drew my gladius and thought, *Now I know how Vitulus feels.*

A gladius is more of a stabbing weapon, but if you get a good angle—as Vitulus had instructed me during our training—you can certainly hack through limbs with a sharp one. I swung my sword down on the wrist of a croc-man. The sword cut neatly through the limb as if I were chopping a loaf of crusty bread. Muddy water spurted from the stump, while the hand itself seemed to dissolve into a gray, muddy mass. The croc-man opened his long, toothy snout and bellowed an enraged croc roar. I caught a whiff of its rotting meat breath, which made my eyes tear up.

But I had no time to gag. I followed up my chop with a quick backhand swipe at the beast's neck, which it had been kind enough to show me when it roared. More brown, muddy water spurted from the neck wound. The croc-man ceased its roaring and slipped back into the frothing waters.

Lares screamed. "Behind you, love!"

The second croc-man was halfway onto the raft and had swung its all-too-human legs onto the papyrus surface. I tried to rush over to it, but a wave pushed the raft up from the front, and I had to pause to regain my balance. Unfortunately the wave helped the croc-man leap to its feet all the faster. The croc-man roared and lunged at me, its toothy mouth snapping as it came. I only had time to assume the defensive stance Vitulus taught me before the creature barreled into me, knocking me backward toward Lares.

But I stopped myself before hitting her. I assumed another defensive stance despite the rocking raft, and thrust my gladius forward just as the croc-man lunged at me again. The gladius point ran through the croc-man's chest, muddy water splashing down my wrist and arm. The croc-man snapped once at me, and then disintegrated into a pile of gray-brown mud on the raft's surface.

"Oh, Natta Magus," Lares breathed, "you were wonderful. So brave and...manly." Her lips were slightly parted and the tip of her tongue lightly touched her top lip. I wanted to believe Lares's praise. I felt like shouting, *Yes, I am the destroyer of otherworldly monsters*.

But my primal scream of triumph died as soon as I noticed what was really making the water froth and roil. All around us, hundreds—no, thousands—of croc-men were slithering around and over each other to get to our raft. Many snapped and fought in their frenzy to get to us. In the gray light that permeated this place, I could actually see the banks on both sides and noticed thousands more leaping into the river and swimming toward us.

The first wave would arrive in seconds.

"Helva," I breathed, unable to manage more than a whisper. She still sat in the middle of the raft, her eyes closed, her mouth moving in time to her chanting.

"Helva!" I said again, louder this time. Her brow furrowed, but she continued her chanting. I knew that me yelling her name would only distract her from the spell, but I didn't know what else to do. My knees and gut were filling up with panic.

"Lares, what happens if those things swamp us?"

Her face was bleak as she looked around at the swarming croc-men. "I will lose you, my love."

She suddenly reached out with both hands, grabbed my face, and pulled me toward her in a kiss. It was deep, warm, and probably the most passionate kiss I'd ever received in my life. Lares put into her kiss all the words of longing she had claimed to have for me over the years. Gods help me, I don't even remember Brianna kissing me like that, and she had given me some doozies while we were together.

The difference, though, was that I had loved Brianna. I loved Lares after a fashion, but not like that.

When she pulled away, her startling green eyes glistened in the gray light, and she gave me a coy smile. "I know you do not share my love, but I could not let you die without you knowing that everything I've ever said to you was true."

I nodded, not knowing what else to say. And then I realized we were still alive and all was quiet.

I glanced around at the river and the army of croc-men, almost afraid that doing so would break whatever spell had given Lares and me this moment of peace.

All the croc-men swam up the river alongside the raft, only their croc heads visible on the water's surface. The croc-men were no longer trying to board the raft either. In fact, they all seemed to be guiding the raft up the river like some sort of reptilian honor guard.

Helva stood in the center of the raft glaring at Lares and me. "If you two are finished," she growled, "our way to the tomb is clear."

Then she sat down again near the front of the raft, facing forward.

Lares looked at her smugly, but her smugness evaporated when she noticed me frowning at her. "No more games, Lares. Just take us to the tomb."

"Of course, dearest," she said, watching me beneath her dark eyelashes, and then she began to sway the rudder. She still wore a satisfied smile as she gazed up the river, shooting periodic glances at Helva's back.

I went and sat down next to Helva, facing forward like her. "It got pretty dicey for a minute there. You know your *Book of the Dead*. Well done."

She shrugged. "It took longer than I had hoped. Either my father taught me words that were slightly different, or I did not remember them correctly. These creatures will keep other denizens from bothering us. At least as long as we stay on or near the river." She said all that in clipped tones, which told me she was even grumpier than usual.

"Listen, that kiss—"

"What you do with your house spirit is your business," she said, "but our plan today was that you watch my back. You know what's at stake, and yet you let yourself get distracted. That concerns me."

"I didn't kiss her, she kissed me," I protested, which sounded lame even to my ears. "Besides, she thought we were all goners, with that croc-man army about to turn the raft over—"

"She knew that wouldn't happen," Helva hissed. "She knew the spell I was reciting, and she knew it would work. She *knew* you weren't going to die. She used that moment to distract you." Helva leaned toward me and lowered her voice so that I could barely hear it. "She says she wants to spend eternity with you. Think about it."

"That's ridiculous," I said, matching her low tone. "Lares is my friend, and she only wants to help. She may be a little possessive, but she would never hurt me."

Helva sniffed and said, "Think about it." She leaned away from me and stared ahead.

I also returned my gaze up the river toward the gray, sunless sky. Pyramids of all shapes and sizes, crumbling and pristine, moved past us. I nervously eyed the army of croc-men heads swimming in the black waters alongside the raft, each head leaving wakes in the water that did not affect the stillness of the raft. In fact, they seemed to bear the raft on a smooth wave that felt as if we were sitting on the shore.

And I thought about what Helva said. Ever since I'd discovered Lares' cherubic statue when I first moved into my shop, I had never sensed any maliciousness from her. She had done nothing but help me since I'd known her. I doubted I would've survived in ancient Rome for as long as I had if not for her.

Yes, she was possessive, and she had a huge jealous streak. And she constantly told me how lonely she would be without me. Did that mean she would kill me so that my spirit would stay with her? She'd had plenty of opportunities to do so by giving me false information during my many supernatural fights, yet she hadn't.

But the rules were different in the underworld. She knew them, and I didn't.

No. Lares was my friend. I'd already been betrayed by a good friend once before. I refused to believe that all my friends were fated to do so.

I kept my gaze forward, but I could feel her bright green eyes on my back as we sailed up river.

# FORTY

Once again I was treated to the strange lack of time in a timeless place. Last year, while I was stuck in the Ring of Saturn, years had felt like moments and moments felt like years. Here in the Duat, I got the same sense that time did not exist the way mortals perceived it; it was another eternal now.

So when Lares pulled the raft toward the shore for us to disembark, it felt like we'd been riding the raft for eons, while at the time I could still feel Lares's saliva on my lips from her kiss. Damnation, I hated these celestial planes.

As soon as the raft bumped up onto the shore, our army of croc-men disappeared beneath the black water with barely a ripple. I'd gotten used to having them around for the years—or seconds?—it took us to travel the river, and now felt a little naked without the buffer zone they'd created. Granted, nothing had attacked us during our journey, but I figured the croc-men had scared everything away. Now that we had reached the shore, we were on our own.

Helva and I stepped onto the sandy shore. No waves lapped at the shore, for the river was a calm sheet of glass. Lares glided off the raft and stepped down just behind me. She weaved between Helva and me and came to a stop a few paces in front of us. Her veiled head slowly scanned the field of pyramids that ran from left to right toward each horizon.

"That way," she said, nodding her head slightly to the right. Her voice sounded low and serious, not at all like the flighty Lares I'd always known. She began walking in that direction with all the grace of a Roman matron without turning to see if we were following.

I felt Helva's eyes on me, but I didn't want to look at her. I didn't want her to see any doubts on my face, because I was doing my damnedest to convince myself that there was no reason to doubt Lares.

"We stay together," Helva warned again.

I nodded, still not looking at her, and said, "Let's follow our guide before we lose her." I strode forward with Helva beside me.

The gray light had not grown any brighter this far up the river, so the spaces between the pyramids were blanketed in shadows. But as with the strange way time worked here, the shadows didn't prevent me from seeing Lares or Helva. In fact, whenever I focused my sight on a particular place, I could see what I was looking at: the finely chiseled hieroglyphs covering the entire pyramid on my right; painted statues of the jackal-headed Anubis guarding the open entrance to the pyramid on my left. It was like the shadows preferred to dance in my peripheral vision or my quick glances, but retreated whenever I focused on something.

And then there was the absolute silence. I could hear our footfalls and even the thumping of my own heart in my ears, but every noise the three of us made sounded as if we'd made it in a closed wardrobe filled with coats. I wasn't as up on my Egyptian mythology like my Roman mythology, but I wondered if it was because this place was meant for rest. It didn't feel evil, but it sure creeped the hell out of me.

As with the river, it was difficult for me to measure how long our journey took. After we had passed two—or two thousand?—pyramids, Lares stopped in front of a smallish pyramid.

"Here," she said.

The pyramid was about twenty feet high, well-built, painted in bright colors, and covered in neat hieroglyphs. It had a square outcropping with a set of solid wood doors, each with a ring latch made of bronze. Like the pyramid, the doors were solid, had finely worked edges, and fit precisely into their frames. They, too, were covered in carved hieroglyphs that I had no hope of interpreting. The whole thing looked, well, nice.

Which was surprising; I would've thought an evil magus like Silanus would've had something far more run down. Instead, he'd earned a "quaint" tomb for someone who'd had an honorable, though not perfect, life. Did that mean his crimes against Romans didn't count in the Egyptian underworld? Or did he somehow redeem himself later in life to balance the scales?

Lares stepped to one side, but her expression told me she was nervous about something.

"What's wrong?" I asked her.

She sighed, and then her voice returned to the Lares I knew and loved. "Oh, Natta Magus, my sweet, I cannot see beyond that door. There could be anything in there: monsters, magic, that terrible magus waiting to burn you alive—!"

"Lares, we can't turn back now."

She sighed. "I know. It's just that—I cannot go in there with you. You will be on your own." She then gave me a pleading look. "So please do not die."

"Trust me," I said, putting my hands on her shoulders, "I don't want to die. But we're going in there, and we will stop Silanus. You'll be here when we get back?"

"Of course, honey fig," she said with a sad look. "I have nowhere else to go."

I kissed her forehead and turned to Helva. She regarded me impatiently and said, "Ready?"

I nodded, drew my gladius, swallowed once, and prayed my magic would work in this tomb. At the same time, Helva and I put our hands on the bronze latches to each door and—

# FORTY-ONE

"Remi, wake up, we're late!"

I sat up in bed, my heart pounding. Brianna was already up and rummaging through her clothes dresser next to our bed.

"Damnation, I forgot to set our alarm last night," she muttered, searching for underclothes. "You want to shower first or me?"

I stared at her, my brain struggling to process what I was seeing and hearing. I was lying in our bed in our Detroit apartment's bedroom.

*Our Detroit apartment's bedroom.*

Everything was exactly how I remembered. It was a small bedroom, about ten feet square, yet we managed to cram all our clothes, most of our books, a com mirror, and various knickknacks. There wasn't a "my side" and "her side" as our stuff mingled. Her dresser top had all her prized Detroit Cougar hockey mementos—like the puck she caught during game five of the '97 Derby Cup finals and the autographed '98 team photo—mixing with photos of both our families and friends. Right next to her dresser stood a tall bookshelf filled with her Communications arcanum textbooks and hockey histories mingling with my Finder arcanum, Roman histories, and graphic novels. The cream walls were covered with *my* geological maps of the Great Lakes next to *her* Magritte prints next to *our* Wayne State University pennants and coats-of-arms.

"Remi?" she said, turning to me. Her long brown hair was wispy and disheveled, she wore a white t-shirt with a faded Detroit Cougars hockey logo emblazoned on the front, and she squinted at me since she hadn't grabbed her spectacles from the nightstand on her side of the bed. I opened and closed my mouth, but no words would come out.

*This can't be real.*

"Fine, I'll shower first while you wake up. Could you be a dear and put some coffee on once you're lucid?" She leaned over the bed, put a warm hand on my naked chest, and gave me a quick kiss on the lips. She then hurried into the hallway, one butt cheek endearingly exposed beneath her scrunched up panties. I heard the bathroom door shut and the shower faucet turn on.

*This. Can't. Be. Real.*

*Can it?*

My memories of ancient Rome were still vivid, but were already fading as if I'd just awoken from a dream. I felt like I was supposed to do something. Something important, but...I just couldn't remember.

Just like a dream.

Damnation, that was the most intense dream I'd ever had in my life.

I swung my legs out of bed and put my feet on the smooth wood floor. I shuffled over to the window and opened the blinds to let in the bright sunshine and blue sky. I looked down on a winter wonderland kind of day in Dee-troit City. Snow was piled up along the sides of Woodward Avenue from yesterday's storm, so the trolleys and autocars had no trouble cruising up and down the street. People walked the sidewalks dressed in thick coats, hats, and gloves of various colors. Most were students, heading to their classes at Wayne State a few blocks north. Across the street and a block south was the castle-like structure of the British Consulate, where maintenance men magicked snow off the cobblestone walkways with their raised gloved hands. I could feel the cold wafting off the window.

*Is this real?*

I whirled around and practically dove onto the bed toward Brianna's nightstand on the other side. I opened the single drawer at the top, took out the small blue box sitting on top of some books, hand creams, and hair clips. I opened the box to see the engagement ring that I'd given her two weeks ago. She never wore it to bed because she was too afraid it would slip off and be lost forever somewhere in our mattress. Some people would've said she was paranoid—the ring fit perfectly—but I took it to mean how important she thought it was.

I put the ring box back in her drawer and then lay on Brianna's pillow staring at the ceiling. I could still smell her hair and feel the warmth of where she'd been lying just a minute before.

This was crazy, of course it's all real. *Rome* was just a dream. And a fading dream at that; I could barely remember what I'd done there. It felt like something important...but then it was just a dream.

I got up, put on a robe, and padded into our apartment's small kitchen. I lit a fire on the stove with a flick of cell magic and started heating some water for coffee. I opened the coffee canister and took a long sniff from the ground beans. Damnation, it smelled so good. Like it had been years since I'd smelled it. If anything, that intense dream was giving me a new appreciation for the little things in my life. Stoves, coffee.

I glanced at the closed bathroom door. *Brianna.*

I walked over to the door and opened it. Steam flooded out of the bathroom, and the large vanity mirror to my right was covered in it. Brianna peaked from behind the shower curtain and said, "Sorry, I'm almost done."

"No, no," I said, "take your time."

I took off my robe and hung it on the peg behind the door. Then I slipped out of my underwear and stepped into the shower with her.

Brianna was confused at first, but she smiled. Her dark hair was pushed back from her face and hung in wet strands over her shoulders. Soap lather still clung to her wet, naked body, concealing and revealing in maddening ways. I pulled her close, feeling her soft warmth against me. And my own desire, for the first time in what felt like years.

She gave me a coy smile and an arched eyebrow. "We're late for work."

"William's in Europe and Dr. Hapsburn thinks you're the bees knees. A few more minutes of 'late' won't make a difference."

She giggled, and my heart did a high jump. "A few minutes?"

I shrugged. "Well it's been a long time, so..."

"Last night was 'a long time'?"

I looked into her playful green eyes and felt myself get serious. "It feels like it. I had this crazy dream that..." Even while the memories of that dream had faded to almost nothing, the emotions of it seemed to remain. And the one emotion that I could still feel was a terrible sense of loss—specifically, losing Brianna. "Well. I feel like I haven't held you in years. So I don't want to let you go again."

She put her hands on my scruffy cheeks and pulled my head down to her lips in a deep kiss.

And, as I figured, we were done by the time the coffee kettle started whistling.

Brianna and I stepped out of our apartment building and into the frigid cold, gloved hand in gloved hand.  Even though I wore a thick coat, a knitted hat over my Wolverines ball cap, and insulated gloves, the cold air was still a shock to my system. As if I'd spent way too long living in a warmer climate.

Damnation, it would take all day to get over that dream.

Brianna wore an equally thick coat, but she had a scarf wrapped around her face with red earmuffs over her wavy brown hair, which she had pulled back in her traditional ponytail. She pulled down her scarf and said, "Have a good day, Dr. Blakes."

"You too, Dr. Romijnders." I leaned forward and kissed her warm lips. Not deeply, but I did take my time about it.

She finally pulled back with a smile and said, "What is with you today?"

I shrugged. "I just really love you, and I want to make sure you know it every moment I'm with you."

"Remi, I love you more than I can say. But I'm going to gag if you keep talking like a trashy romance novel."

"Got it," I grinned. Then I kissed her one more time, my normal goodbye peck, and we both parted ways—me to my trolley stop a block north and she to her stop a block south.

I took a few steps and was seized with panic. I turned and was half tempted to run after her as she jogged down the sidewalk to her stopped trolley. But she jumped onto the trolley before I could move. If she hadn't, I think I would've ran up with her and...what, clung to her?

*Yeah*, I thought. *What* is *with me this morning?* One *caccing* dream and I become more paranoid than my mom when I learned to drive an autocar.

I started walking north again, but stopped. *And who says* caccing?

"Snap out of it," I muttered to myself.

"Yes, my love, snap out of it."

I whirled around, but nobody was behind me for at least a dozen paces. And I had just passed the long glass windows of the apothecary below my apartment. So where did that voice come from? It was so familiar...

I gritted my teeth and resolved to get more coffee once I arrived at William's lab. I was obviously still groggy from the shock of waking up from the most vivid dream of my life.

My trolley was pulling up with a crunch of tires on the slushy street, so I jogged toward it and was the last one on. The time was well past rush hour, so open seats on the benches alongside the windows were plentiful. I took a seat across from a grandmother who was twirling three paper stars in the air for her delighted grandson. It seemed kids delighted in the most basic of magicks just like kids delighted in polished stones back in Rome—

I shifted uncomfortably in my seat.

I rummaged through my leather satchel for my morning issue of the *Detroit Times*. Before I opened it to the pre-season baseball updates, I glanced across the aisle.

The grandmother and grandson were gone. In their place was a beautiful woman wearing a yellow stolla dress with a purple palla draped over her head. I frowned, the shock over how I knew what kind of dress she was wearing pushing away my confusion over where the grandma and kid went.

"Natta Magus, my heart of hearts, you cannot stay here." The woman said this with such sad tenderness that I wondered if she actually knew me. I felt like I knew her, too...or at least I should've known her. But at the moment, I couldn't place where I might have met her.

"Who's Natta Magus?" I asked quietly.

She sighed, tears brimming in her eyes. "You are, my love. And you need to be again." Then she reached over and put a soft hand on my knee.

White hot pain exploded between my eyes, and the world seemed to melt like a wax patrician bust set too close to the fire. I heard screaming, knew it was my own voice, but didn't care. Along with the horrible pain came memories of my years in Rome, from the moment William dropped me in the Circus Maximus, my jobs with Vitulus, Aventicum, losing Brianna... It all came crashing back into my mind in all its painful, glorious, heartbreaking detail. Including my journey through the Egyptian underworld, Helva, and the reasons we were there.

When the pain and flood of memories subsided, I opened my eyes. I still sat on the trolley, which continued to crunch through the icy, slushy snow up Woodward Avenue toward Pingree Hall. But Lares was the only person there besides me. She continued to watch me with those brimming eyes.

"You cannot stay here," she said.

I looked out the windows at the buildings and people the trolley passed. Detroit, my city. The city where I grew up. Where everyone I ever loved lived. I recognized the hot dog place where my parents took ten-year-old me after Wolverine ball games in the summer. Less than a mile east was Lake St. Claire, where I spent many summer afternoons fishing with my friends and my parents. My parents had died in a boating accident on the lake four years ago, but I preferred to remember the good times we had on the lake, not the tragedy. I knew that's what they would've wanted. And just a half-mile down Woodward was red-stone chapel where Brianna and I would get married in four months.

Detroit was my city. Not Rome.

"What if I don't want to go back," I said, staring out the window.

"This place is not real," Lares said. "It is only a trap to distract you from entering Silanus's tomb. It is part of his wards."

I touched the frost in the corner of the window next to me. Even through my gloves, I could feel the cold winter day. "Feels real to me."

"This world is built from your memories. That is why it is so insidious. If you do not leave soon, your mind could remain trapped here forever."

I snorted. "Eternity with the woman I love. I'm not seeing a downside."

Lares looked as if I'd just punched her in the stomach, and I felt like eternity's biggest jerk. I was about to apologize, but she quickly recovered.

"Time has not stopped moving on the mortal plane," she continued. "If you stay here, you will not have time to stop Silanus from killing thousands of people. And since I've given you your memories, you will always know you could've done something to stop it. You will know that you sacrificed all those lives so you could remain in an illusion." She shook her head at me, pleadingly. "That regret will stay with you for eternity. And it will destroy your soul."

"Damnation, Lares!" I yelled. I stood up suddenly, my satchel falling to the floor. I paced back and forth, up and down the trolley's aisle. "Look at all these people out there on the streets. They all have magic. Most of them are probably stronger than me. So why weren't they chosen to stay in Rome. Why did I have to give up everything I knew and loved? *Why me, Lares?*"

She didn't flinch from my outburst, but she stared at me, her lower lip quivering. "I wish with all my being," she whispered, "that I could tell you everything you want to know. I've already broken some laws as it is." She seemed to flicker, and then her eyes widened as she sucked in a startled breath. She licked her lips once, and said, "My time with you is short. You simply need to will yourself back to the tomb."

I looked at her, concern seizing my chest. "Why is your time short?"

"I told you I was forbidden to go with you into the tomb," she said, tears now streaming down her face. "But I did it anyway so that I could come here and bring you back. Now I must pay the penalty."

"What penalty?"

She flickered again, and this time she actually disappeared for a long moment before coming back. "I interfered by guiding you. My being here now was my last offense. I must now leave you and never again visit the mortal plane."

I stared at her. "You knew this was going to happen. When you agreed to guide us before Helva brought us here...you knew you were breaking a law. Why did you do it?"

She tilted her head and smiled, despite her flowing tears and flickering in and out of existence. "Because I love you, my honey fig."

Then she was gone.

And I was stuck in another one of those gut-wrenching, dig deep for the will to go on moments. Lares had willingly sacrificed herself to help me, knowing what the price would be. And yet she hadn't told me. Why?

*Because she knew you'd nix the plan,* the wise, rational part of my brain told me. *Because she knew you'd try to find another way, and she knew there* was *no other way.*

Over the last year I had told her all about my experiences in the Ring of Saturn, and the overwhelming regret I felt in each timeline where the world died with me knowing that I could've done something to stop it. That was why I had stayed in Rome: because the pain of losing Brianna to a safe world in the future was far less than watching her, our children, and our world die from a calamity that I could've prevented.

Lares sacrificed herself so that I could save innocent lives. And she knew that if I had tried a different plan just to save her, it would've been too late to stop Silanus.

She would rather sacrifice herself than watch me die a little inside each day because I had failed.

I had no idea what I'd done to deserve that kind of love from her, but at that moment I resolved that her sacrifice would mean something.

I willed myself back to Silanus's tomb.

# FORTY-TWO

"Lares!" I gasped, my hand still on the ring latch of Silanus's tomb.

Helva exhaled sharply. We both looked at each other with wide eyes. "Did you just have a—?"

"Yes," Helva said, nodding quickly. "I was tempted. But Lares guided me out. She...she sacrificed herself for me."

I looked around. Lares was nowhere to be seen among the living shadows and dark pyramids surrounding us. I didn't know where she would end up, but I knew she'd no longer inhabit my shop when I got back to Rome. A huge lump formed in my throat. and my eyes grew misty. But I gave a shaky sigh, and said, "We've wasted enough time. Let's go."

Helva's lips thinned. She reached for the tomb's latch and pulled open the door.

Complete blackness greeted us. Helva put her hand forward, but was unable to penetrate the darkness. It was like a solid wall of obsidian.

I glanced at her. "You have a spell for this, right?"

"Yes," she said, "but I do not know how long the opening will last. I will bind Silanus while you find Tanith, Balnor, and the books. And quickly."

I drew my gladius. "Well I wasn't planning on sightseeing."

Helva raised her hands and began reciting ancient Coptic words, saying the same phrases over and over again. They soon took on a rhythm that was almost musical; the tune was so catchy that I started to hum it a bit in my head.

A pinprick of light formed in the solid darkness, like the first star after sundown. The light grew brighter and larger, much slower than I would've liked, but it was steady. The light turned into a circle as it grew, with an ethereal white border and a hazy gray middle. Within the gray haze, I could make out vague shapes and...something moving.

I caught movement to my right out of the corner of my eye. I swung to face it, my gladius up, but nothing was there. I heard whispering, though, and it was getting louder. It came from all around us and then suddenly right next to my ear. I swatted empty air with my left hand, but the whispers and growls moved to my right. Movement seemed to be all around us in my peripheral vision, but when I tried focusing on it, I saw nothing.

*Damnation,* I thought with growing terror, *the Duat doesn't want us to leave.*

Helva stopped chanting. The solid darkness now had a door-sized, white-rimmed circular gate that opened into a shadowy room. A single lamp burned in one corner. It illuminated a stone wall covered in intricate, colorful, Egyptian art work. Painted pictures of gods sitting on thrones mixed with carefully drawn hieroglyphs.

A stone sarcophagus sat in the center of the room. Upon it were leather containers and various scrolls laid open.

To the left, Tanith and Balnor lay on their backs on the dusty floor, staring up at the ceiling.

To the right lay a man with his back to us and a blanket over his body. I noted his dark hair and prayed to every god or goddess that could hear me that we'd been lucky enough to catch Silanus asleep.

Helva seemed to notice everything that I did at about the same time. She stepped softly through the gate as if tiptoeing from one room to another.

I was about to do the same when Tanith and Balnor started shrieking at the tops of their lungs. They had both sat up, their eyes staring at us wide with terror. At first, Helva was about to shush them, but she realized the same thing I did—they were still enthralled, and they served as Silanus's alarm in case someone, somehow got past the wards on this tomb.

The figure to the right threw the blanket off his shoulders and leaped to his feet. He looked just as startled to see us as we were to have Tanith and Balnor screaming their heads off. But he quickly recovered from the shock and started gathering his magic the same way Helva did—palms facing down to draw in power from the earth.

I didn't wait for Helva to bind him; I charged forward, yelling a nonsensical battle cry with my gladius raised for a killing stab. I had to disrupt the spell he was about to cast, and the best way I knew to do that was to distract the hell out of him.

A blast of arcane energy flew past me from behind, even though I couldn't see it like I could cell or soul magic. Whatever spell Silanus had been about to cast must've fizzled, and I didn't care if it was Helva's binding or my charging.

Silanus snarled and threw his blanket at me. It blocked my view of him long enough for him to get behind the stone sarcophagus in the center of the room.

"Leave now, or they will kill each other!" he said.

I spared a glance behind me and saw Tanith and Balnor holding knives pointed at each other's hearts. They'd stopped screaming, but they stared at each other with slack indifference. Helva spotted them, saw the knives, and then turned pleading eyes to Silanus.

"Brother," she said quietly, "they're not Romans. They're Canaanites. Just like Yasha."

He sneered. "You think you can draw sympathy from me by naming our nurse? That you can distract me? You may have cut me off from my magic for a short while, but their enthrallment continues. If you try to move them, they will kill each other. If you harm me, they will kill each other. And you will activate all the other surprises I've put on this place in the event of my untimely death. So you can either maintain your binding on me or you can end their enthrallment. You cannot do both."

Earth magic was new to me, so I wasn't sure if Silanus was telling the truth. There was no such thing as a "binding" spell in either cell or soul magic, for it was impossible to cut a magus off from the magic in his or her own cells or soul. Such a thing would simply kill the magus even if it were possible.

But judging from Helva's expression, Silanus was right. She sent worried glances from her adopted aunt and uncle to Silanus. To end their enthrallment, she'd have to drop the binding on Silanus, which meant he'd either kill us outright or at the very least escape through another gate. But if she maintained the binding on Silanus, Helva would have to watch Tanith and Balnor slowly kill each other.

Silanus turned his dark eyes to me. "Is this stalemate, Natta Magus? It would be a shame for our game to end in such an unsatisfying manner."

"If you kill them, you will die," I said, pointing the gladius at him over the sarcophagus so that it was only inches from his throat.

I'd never actually killed a human being, and I sincerely hoped it wouldn't come to that now. But I had just watched one of my best friends sacrifice her spirit for me so that I could stop this maniac. I was going to make damned sure she didn't do it for nothing. Even if it meant breaking an old Oath that I'd sworn in a different life.

Silanus didn't move from the sword pointed at his throat, even though he had plenty of room to back away. "Oh, I'm sure you will try. But my sister will never allow it."

And now came the part where I had to put my faith in Helva's promise to help me, even if her brother's life was at stake. That she would see the same game board that I did and that our next moves would be obvious.

"Helva?" I said, without taking my eyes off Silanus. "You still plan on backing me up?"

She paused far longer than I would've hoped before she said, "Brother...please...William wanted us to protect him. William said he's important."

Anger suddenly smoldered in his eyes and face. He turned his fiery gaze to Helva, ready to snap at her with some jealous nonsense. That momentary lack of focus on me was the thing Helva and I had hoped and planned for.

Because it finally gave me the chance to use my gladius in the way I'd practiced.

As I've previously mentioned, Vitulus had tried to teach me a thing or two about using the gladius like a true Roman legionary. To say I was hopeless at it was an understatement, but at least it gave me the basics of how to stand and point and make my opponents *think* I knew how to use it. When most people—especially experienced swordsmen—see a guy with a sword pointed at them, they start thinking of sword tactics and strategies.

They typically don't think about the magic that might shoot out of the blade and into their faces.

As soon as Silanus's eyes shifted from me to Helva, I yelled, "*Slapen!*"

The sleep spell that I had enchanted into the blade did not require me to siphon my cell magic. It could've been activated by anyone who knew how to say the bastardized Dutch word correctly and with conviction. But it only worked on victims who were within a couple of paces of where I was aiming, and Silanus was at point-blank range. As soon as his unconscious body slumped to the floor, Helva screamed something in Coptic. I whirled around to see Tanith and Balnor gasp and then drop their daggers. They suddenly clutched each other tight, both of them weeping with fear, joy, and the incredible relief that they were free of Silanus's enthrallment.

Helva rushed over to them, but when they saw her approach, they recoiled from her. At first I thought it was a vestige of Silanus's enthrallment, but then I realized that Helva's spell had not only broken his enthrallment but also the one *she'd* put on them. Helva stopped, then held up her hands. "I just want to help you."

"You are just like him," Tanith spat. "You did something to us. We took you in, loved you. *You lied to us!*"

Balnor had grabbed Silanus's sword by this time and was pointing it at Helva. "Just stay away from us!"

I let Helva deal with the consequences of her enthrallments as I looked over the scrolls laid out on the sarcophagus. They were all written in Greek, so I had no idea what they said, but I searched for the Roman seal that Augustus had told me would identify the Sibylline Books. Silanus had many scrolls and clay tablets strewn about the place. I ignored the tablets, and searched every scroll for—

There, on the floor in front of the sarcophagus, was a satchel with three scrolls peeking out of the top. I lunged forward and opened each one a little to find the Roman seal on all three.

I exhaled sharply. *And Natta for the hat trick.*

Silanus groaned. His breathing seemed to quicken, but his eyes remained closed. Damnation, he was coming out of the sleep spell far faster than I'd hoped.

I glanced at the sword at my side and then at the prone, helpless Silanus. If I killed him now, it would all be over. It would be so easy: ram the sword through his heart. Done and done. Vitulus would've done it without batting an eye, and he would've screamed at me for not having done it already. I'd save the lives of thousands of people by killing one psychotic magus. One man's death versus thousands was certainly a bargain by any standard.

But at what cost to my soul? I was ready to kill in self-defense. But could I kill a sleeping man, even if it meant saving lives?

Well, we were about to find out. I picked up my sword and walked around the sarcophagus toward Silanus.

"Natta Magus!" Helva yelled. "If you hurt him I *will* kill you!" She stared at me, the fires of the lamp burning in her brown eyes, her palms facing down.

"What about your Oath?" I asked.

"He's my brother. I will help you stop him, but I will not help you kill him."

"We can end it right now," I said quietly, turning back to Silanus. He groaned again and his legs twitched. My grip tightened on the gladius. "I can't let him murder thousands."

"And I can't let you hurt him," she said.

"Kill him!" snarled Balnor. He huddled in the corner with his arms wrapped around Tanith.

"He enslaved us," she seconded with enraged eyes. "He almost made us kill each other!"

I felt a tingling in the back of my neck as the hairs stood straight. She was calling up her magic, but since it was a magic that was alien to me, I couldn't see what kind of spell she was preparing. But it felt damned powerful, and I knew she meant what she said.

But so did I. I was tired of being the one to react to the chaos brought on by madmen. I wanted to strike them down *before* they killed innocent people. Hell, Silanus deserved death for what he did to Capito's family alone, not to mention the Circus Maximus. I had the power to carry out his sentence right now. It was justice. No, it was common sense.

I raised my gladius, knowing full well that I only had a fraction of a second to strike before Helva released her magic at me—

And then a thought stopped me as if it had thrown a shield over Silanus, taking up that fraction of a second.

Silanus's pyramid. Why was it so nice?

I had no time to wonder further before my sword glowed like molten steel and burned the holy *cac* out of my right hand. I screamed and dropped the sword, which instantly turned back to normal. I looked down at my red, blistering hand, tears forming in my eyes, my mouth forming silent screams. By all the gods and the Unknowable Will, I had never felt such pain in my life. And it didn't stay in my blistering palm, but seemed to shoot up and down my right arm in waves of white agony. I fell to my knees, held my hand out, and stared at the horrible source of pain.

"You should've listened," she said from behind me.

My eyes were focused on my palm, but I sputtered curses at her that would make a Polish grandmother proud.

Silanus groaned again. His eyelids fluttered, but then stilled. I forced myself to my feet, turned to Helva with a murderous glare and snarled through clenched teeth, "Grab the *caccing* books and my sword. I can't hold anything right now."

She nodded once, as if I wasn't in a torturous agony that she had caused, and then hurried over to pick up my sword and Sibylline satchel. I went over to the still-open gate into the underworld, its white rimmed edges still glowing, and then looked at the two scared Canaanites.

"You're only chance to escape this place is to come with us," I said through gritted teeth. I glared at Helva as she held the satchel and my sword. She glanced warily at Silanus as she did so. "I'll make sure you stay free when you get home."

Balnor and Tanith looked at each other, gave Helva a wary glance, and then walked over to me, still holding each other.

"We trust *you*, Natta Magus," Balnor said.

Tanith leaned toward me and said, "You will help us be rid of her?"

I spared a look at Helva, who wore a pained frown. I took some petty satisfaction in it.

"I'll pack her bags myself," I assured Tanith.

Helva was suddenly beside me holding my sword by the hilt. I flinched before I realized she was simply putting it back into the scabbard on my belt.

"He's waking up," she said without looking at any of us, and then stepped through the gate and back into the underworld.

"Go," I said to Tanith and Balnor. They gave the gate a fearful look, as if expecting it to shock them or something, but then they slowly stepped through.

I stepped through just as I heard Silanus's enraged scream behind me. "Natta Mag—!"

Helva shut the gate and all was underworldly silence.

# FORTY-THREE

I leaned my back against the cool stone of Silanus's tomb, staring at my raw sword hand. Tanith and Balnor huddled near the door of the pyramid, their wide eyes staring at the shadowy Egyptian underworld around them. Helva tore strips of cloth off the bottom of her tunica dress with a small knife and stooped next to me.

"Hold out your hand," she said.

I held out my hand, palm up so that she could see the damage she caused. She didn't even flinch at the sight of the red blistering, which had taken on the same pattern as my sword's crisscross hilt. I winced as she wrapped the cloth around my hand. I winced big time. One time, while camping with friends on Lake St. Claire, I'd tripped over a root and my left hand landed on one of the glowing coals next to the campfire. But that was nothing compared to what my right hand felt now.

"Why did you hesitate?" she asked while slowly wrapping.

I hissed once when she finally tied the cloth tight. "A hunch," I said through clenched teeth.

"'Hunch'?"

"A feeling. Look at his pyramid. Is this the monument that the gods would give to an evil villain?"

Helva looked at the pyramid again and I watched understanding dawn on her face. She scanned the intricate carvings and the colorful frescoes that decorated every surface. It was by no means the largest pyramid around us, but it wasn't the smallest either.

"Can you interpret the hieroglyphs?" I asked.

"Yes, but none of it tells of his future deeds," she said, frowning. "It's all poetry. It feels...tragic."

"The way I figure it is that something balanced his scales. Now either he was the perfect angel before the chaos and death he caused at the Circus Maximus—"

"Or he redeems himself later," Helva said quietly, still staring at the pyramid. "I can assure you, Silanus did nothing in his life before the Circus to balance what he did there. It has to be something he is fated to do in the future."

I nodded. "Which is why I hesitated. And got my hand almost burned off as a reward." The wrappings did nothing to stop the agony emanating from my hand, but at least they'd keep dirt and gunk off it until I could get home and heal—

"*Cac,*" I swore. "Lares." The pain of losing her hit me with the emotional equivalent of how my hand felt. "How are we going to get back home?" I glanced back the way we came from the river. The path rounded the corner of a smooth, marble pyramid ten times the size of Silanus's. "I remember the path that got us here, but will it be the same? Do things...I don't know, *move* in the Duat?"

Helva shrugged. "It is the only option we have." Then she glanced at Tanith and Balnor, who had remained silent since we stepped through the gate. They were probably wondering if they'd just stepped off the Silanus frying pan and into the Duat fire. "We need to go," Helva said to them, her voice softer than when she talked to me. "Are either of you hurt?"

Balnor shook his head, and Tanith said, "No." They both refused to look at Helva.

I scanned the area around us. The pyramids were still bathed in the shadowy, gray light from the sunless sky. I suddenly felt uneasy, even though nothing about this place had changed. "I'll carry the books," I said to Helva. "You need to be free to cast if you need to."

She handed me the satchel, and I awkwardly slung the strap over my shoulders with my uninjured left hand. I hissed again. Even that movement was enough to send a fresh wave of pain up my right arm and across my chest.

I heard a similar hiss behind me. My muscles froze. Then the hiss seemed to wrap around me and come from up ahead. All at once I heard whispers, low growls, and skittering feet, but I saw nothing when I frantically searched the shadows. Or at least not when I looked *directly* at the shadows. In my peripheral vision, however, I caught monstrous, hungry faces that disappeared as soon as I focused on them.

I glanced at Helva, who was also looking at me.

"Do you hear that?" I whispered.

"That wasn't you?"

"No."

Tanith and Balnor screamed. I whirled around to see a wave of...things coming toward us. That's about all I could say to name them because they defied classification. *Damnation, they were waiting for us.*

Back in the twenty-first century we had toy dolls that allowed kids to remove the limbs and heads and attach them to other similar torsos, creating a whole new doll that had a boy's head on a torso with boobs, and vice versa.

The things coming toward us were similar, but straight out of Anubis's nightmares. I saw human bodies with the heads of flies, goats, and even torches and swords. There were man-sized preying mantises with human heads, gnashing teeth, and orange eyes. There were scarab beetles the size of wagons that skittered toward us on human hands rather than beetle legs. A gorilla body with a lion's head roared at us, and then reached to its hindquarters, took a handful of its own excrement, and started eating it.

Terrifying and disgusting do not begin to describe the Egyptian Duat.

It took half a second for me to process the wave of horror rushing toward us, and another half a second for Helva and me to start sprinting down the path back to the river, Tanith and Balnor close behind us. After we passed around the first large pyramid, I let Helva lead and then let Tanith and Balnor get ahead of me so that I could be the rear guard. I drew my enchanted gladius with my left hand—my right hand hurt far too much to hold it let alone wield it properly. I couldn't cast cell magic here, but I did have a pre-enchanted gladius with some sleep spells. Perhaps I could sleep one or two out of the one or two *thousand* creatures chasing us...

"Helva," I cried, "is there anything you can do?"

"I'd have to stop to cast," she yelled over her shoulder. "It could take a moment, or many moments like it did on the raft."

We wouldn't last a second, never mind *many* if we stopped now. I glanced behind us at the nightmare horde. They were gaining on us, only twenty paces behind me. If we didn't reach the river soon—

"There's the river!" Helva yelled.

I whipped my head around and saw the glorious river with its creepy black waters directly ahead. Our raft was even in the same place where we'd left it. Helva leaped onto the raft, followed closely by Tanith and Balnor. I jumped on just as Helva had unfastened the rudder and used it to push the raft away from the shore.

We were no more than three paces away from the shore when the water around us erupted into frothing fury, as if our raft had been flung into mountain rapids. I thought it was another nightmare horde come to eat us.

I was half-right. It was a nightmare horde made up of our old friends the croc-men. They rose out of the river like an army of angry hornets and leaped at the land horde trying to attack the raft. A vicious battle ensued at the water's edge with growls and shrieks and severed limbs and black ichor flying in every direction. Despite the onrush of croc-men, Helva was able to push us farther away from the slaughter so that we reached the middle of the river. The raft floated along the river's current, away from the chaotic battle.

Once I caught my breath, I turned to Helva. "Any ideas on how we get home?"

Helva had reattached the rudder to the back of the raft. Her lips were thin as she thought for several moments. "Lares was our connection to the mortal plane." She sighed. "I cannot open another gate unless I have that connection."

"I'm almost afraid to ask, but could we find one of our own tombs? Maybe get home that way?"

She shook her head as I said it. "How would we find them? We can only cast spells from the *Book of the Dead,* and none of them can guide us to our own tombs like Lares might have." She glanced at the shores and the myriad tombs on either side. "And even if we did find our own tombs, we are *here*. My gate can only take us to that tomb's *occupant* on the mortal plane."

I sat down on the papyrus surface of the raft, watching the pyramids float by. I bumped my wounded hand and hissed another curse. Now I knew how Balbus and his friends must've felt when Helva had saved me from them.

Balbus. Holy *cac* on a sandal.

I leaned my head back and barked laughter into the Duat's otherworldly silence. I just couldn't help it despite our situation. It seemed that twit was actually going to save my life, and that was the funniest thing in the world to me.

Tanith and Balnor looked at me with alarm from near the front of the raft. I turned around to see Helva giving me the same "what's with the crazy man" look.

When I calmed myself down, I said, "I know how to get home."

# FORTY-FOUR

I t had been so long since I had the mental freedom to think about Balbus
that I'd completely forgotten about the little finder spell in the back of my
mind, still sitting there and even now making my feet want to take me to where
I could find him.

Which in the Duat, I assumed would be his tomb.

Again, due to the strange way time worked in the Duat, I wasn't sure if it
took us twenty days or twenty seconds to traverse the river to Balbus's tomb.
But find its location we did—the finder spell telling my feet where to park the
raft—and thankfully on the opposite bank from the nightmare horde. The raft
crunched onto the rocky shore, and we all jumped off onto a pebbly beach that
seemed more like the shore of a glacial lake than a river. I let my feet do the
walking, so I took the lead.

Even though no nightmare horde was there to greet us, I still couldn't relax
since, once again, I saw the strange shadow movements out of the corner of my
eye. Helva, Tanith, and Balnor must've noticed the movement too, for all three
kept turning around quickly as if they expected something to grab them. Helva
muttered something in Coptic, which I hoped was a *Book of the Dead* spell to
pacify whatever came at us.

The pyramids on this side seemed more diverse than the opposite bank. We
passed flat-topped pyramids of the ancient Incas and Aztecs; tombs cut into
grassy hills with elaborately carved stone doors; painted, columned temples
with stone sarcophagi in the middle; lovingly wrapped bodies lying upon
golden beds held up by golden stilts twenty feet high. All of these were for those
whose hearts were light upon death.

I found it surprising that tombs for really bad people were not that common,
though they were pretty nasty when we came upon one. I figured the smat-
tering of forgotten, crumbling cairns was sad enough, but it was the rotting

corpses in ditches being picked at by feral dogs that seemed to be the worst fate. Luckily the dogs ignored us.

After another few seconds or hours, my feet finally stopped in front of Balbus's tomb. It was about twenty feet square with small columns holding up a red-tiled roof that had painted and carved bas-reliefs along the front. In the center was a marble statue of an older Balbus—I could make out his long nose—dressed in a senatorial toga and striking a distinguished pose. I wondered if he'd be cremated in the future, for there was no sarcophagus that I could see. His tomb was one of the smaller ones, but at least he had made it into the honored dead club. He certainly wasn't evil...though he may have died still a twit.

Helva stood her ground in front of the two steps that led into the small temple. "The denizens of the Duat are attracted to my gates, so as soon as I start the spell, it's likely they'll attack again."

Tanith groaned, and Balnor asked, "Why can't you subdue them now, like you said you did to the crocodile men?"

"That only works if they show themselves," Helva said, glancing around us nervously. "By the time they do, I will be in the middle of the gate spell."

"What should *we* do, then?" Tanith asked.

"Do not disturb me. And be ready to jump through the gate as soon as it opens."

Balnor gripped Silanus's sword and placed his back to the temple, with Tanith behind him. He watched the growing shadows with grim determination.

I gripped my enchanted gladius awkwardly with my left hand as I scanned the moving shadows all around us. My right hand still screamed with pain, but adrenaline and fear had dulled it enough for me to worry about other things. Like the whispers in the air just within my range of hearing. Though I still couldn't focus on any of the shadows or detect where the whispers came from, all the hairs standing up all along my arms told me something was out there watching us.

And as soon as Helva began chanting her spell, the shadows jumped from out of the corner of my eye.

It was not a wave of creatures like before, more like a dozen. But it was a dozen nightmares.

A black, hairy spider the size of a large dog, but with the head of a woman, crept toward me, stopped a moment to let its front legs test the air, and then crept forward a few more paces. The woman's eyes were wide open and looked multifaceted like a fly's. Her mouth opened and closed as the strange whispers reverberated from her. Behind her were several more spiders with human heads, men and women of different skin and hair color, but all with the same repulsive spider body.

I transferred the sword to my right hand. I clenched my teeth as my palm felt aflame again, but at least I could defend myself better than if it were in my left hand.

As soon as I did that, the first spider woman charged toward me. I stepped to one side, Vitulus-style, and brought my gladius down in a quick stab toward the center of the spider's body. My sword slid through the bulbous abdomen, pinning it to the sandy ground. Black ichor blood spurted from the body. The spider's human head screamed once before slumping down.

I yanked my sword from the body just in time to find another spider skittering at me. The white teeth in its long-haired, male human head clicked and gnashed at me as it came. I tried stepping aside for this one, too, but the creature didn't fall for it. The thing leaped, and its front legs hit me square in the chest, knocking me onto my back. It tried to pin me down with its talons, but I rolled out of the way as the talons struck the ground with a powerful thump. I managed to get to my knees and swing my gladius down. The edge of the sword embedded itself in the human head, like one of those fake arrow hats that comedians wore in my home time (I had to suppress an insane giggle at that image). But the spider thrashed about, yanking the embedded sword out of my hand. More black ichor spurted from the wound, bathing me in slippery, hot monster blood. I tried reaching for the hilt of my sword, but it kept flying out of my grasp with the spider's death throes.

Still on my knees, I heard clicking and thumping behind me. I turned to see a spider charging right for me, its human head like that of a bearded Viking. About all I could do was instinctively bring my arms up.

Balnor jumped from out of nowhere and severed the spider's Viking head with one graceful swing. He didn't take time to admire his handiwork, for another spider leaped at him. He sliced off three of its legs with one swing. He stepped away from the flopping, spraying spider to meet another spider skittering toward him. He gave it three deep stabs to the body, which stopped the monster almost immediately.

When he was done, there were no more spiders around us. At least none living.

I scrambled to my feet, yanked my enchanted sword from the spider head, and stared at Balnor. His eyes scanned the shadows for more threats. He noticed me staring and shrugged. "I was a pirate in my youth. Some skills you never forget."

"Lucky me," I said. "Thanks."

He nodded once, then whipped his head to the right. I did, too, and saw what I was dreading. The nightmare horde had found us. In addition to the mish-mash creatures in the first horde, I saw many more terrors that would stick with me for years to come: creatures with human male torsos, but torches for arms and centipede carapaces for legs; dog bodies with pelican heads; and most disturbingly—I kid you not—tall camels that galloped toward us with heads that looked like human buttocks spewing feces at everything around them. That last one was so disturbing, disgusting, and hilarious that I barked a mad laugh when I saw it.

Then the voice of an angel came from behind me. "It's open," Helva cried, "let's go!"

Balnor and I whirled around and bounded the five paces to Helva and Tanith, who were already holding hands. Balnor grabbed Tanith's hand as I grabbed Balnor's, and then we all leaped through like a train into the black, misty oval, the nightmare horde right on my heels. I felt the same intense, painful vibration as when I'd entered the underworld, as if my entire body were about to explode.

Then I crashed into some furniture and knocked over a bunch of items that I couldn't see, causing more crashes and collisions and curses. Once I came to a stop, I laid still a moment trying to figure out where I was.

I was in a dark room, that was for certain. I glanced up at where the portal had been, but there was nothing but a blank wall. I drew from my cell magic, and it felt like a cool drink of water after a desert hike. I produced a spark globe above my left hand, which bathed the entire room in its comforting ethereal white light. Balnor had his hands on his knees, taking heavy breaths. Tanith stood beside him with a protective hand on his back. Helva was next to me, slightly out of breath, but glancing around at the room in which we found ourselves.

Beyond Helva was a bed where Balbus lay with his blankets up to his nose and his wide shocked eyes staring at us all.

"Hey there, Balbus," I said.

He yelped, as if my speaking confirmed that I was really standing in his bedroom. He scrambled to the other side of the bed, rolled over the woman who had been sleeping next to him, and huddled in the corner of the room. He was naked, so he yanked the blankets off the woman to cover himself—a real gentleman, Balbus. The woman, also naked, screamed as well. She jumped into the corner with Balbus and fought with him over the blankets.

"Immortal gods," Balbus sputtered, "please don't burn me again! I swear I never meant to kill you! I just wanted to scare you is all!"

I raised my hands. "Calm down, I won't hurt you...unless you don't answer my questions."

"Ask me anything!"

"First," I said, glancing around the room, "where are we?"

He stared at me a moment. "The home of Gellius Canus."

"Yes, but where? Are we in Rome? If so, which hill?"

"Yes, Rome," he said, confusion warring with his fear. "The Caelian Hill."

"Good. Now where's the front gate?"

He pointed a shaking finger at the doorway behind me, which was covered in a thick curtain. "Go right. You'll find the atrium and then the gate."

Helva glared at Balbus. "Anyone else in the house?"

Balbus shook his head quickly. "No, Gellius and his household are in Capua this month. He said I could stay here if I wanted. I swear I'm not a squatter!"

Helva, Tanith, and Balnor were already heading toward the door, but I paused. I willed the spark globe over to Balbus and made it stop a foot from his head. He and his girlfriend screamed and continued to fight each other for control of the blanket.

"Balbus, go home to your father," I said. "If you really want to be a singer, fine. But if you have even a shred of honor in you, you'll make nice with your dad before he dies. When he's gone, then you can sell everything and come back to this life. But at least give him a peaceful death."

Balbus nodded throughout my orders, and said, "Sure. Yes. Of course. I'll go see him at dawn."

I didn't know how much of that was Balbus saying anything to avoid the horrors of my spark globe or if he really meant it. "Because if you don't, I will continue to pop into your room at night and visit tortures upon you that you can't even imagine."

His terrified eyes were already imagining such tortures, and he said, "I swear by Jupiter, I will go see him this day. Please..."

"Good. And tell him that I still expect triple my fee by noon today." The twit's finder spell had saved my life and, hopefully, the lives of many other Romans. If anything, I should be thanking *him*.

But replacements for the broken components in my shop weren't going to pay for themselves.

"Yes. Of course. I will," he said nodding quickly.

I turned and followed the others through the hallway and into the atrium. The house was about half the size of Salvius Aper's home, and we quickly found the front door. Balnor unbarred the door and swung it open. The door opened directly onto the street, and we all filed out into the night, breathing in the miasmic Roman air as if it were a spring meadow. I wasn't sure how late—or early—the time was, but there were not as many delivery wagons on the street as I would've assumed.

"We need to get these to Aper right now," I said to Helva, patting the satchel with the Sibylline Books.

"Do you need me to come with you?" she asked.

"It might be best if I go alone. Your presence may bring up some...awkward questions again."

"I'm sorry for Lares."

I nodded. My eyes misted over at the thought of losing yet another friend, in addition to the taste of what my life could've been like with Brianna. I had to use those sacrifices to ensure they were all worth it. To ensure that I stopped Silanus's plan. It all *had* to be worth it.

"Can I call on you later?" I asked. "I could still use your help."

She looked at me. "Are you going to kill him?"

"I don't think it'll come to that. Remember his tomb? But we have to stop him somehow, and he didn't sound like he had a change of heart when we left him. We still have some persuading to do."

"Then I will help you."

Balnor and Tanith stood nearby. Balnor nodded to me and said, "Our thanks, Natta Magus, for saving us from that...man." He eyed Helva and said, "And to you, too."

Helva's eyes softened as she looked at both of them. "I am truly sorry for what I—"

Tanith held up a hand to stop her. "We thank you for saving our lives." Then her eyes hardened. "But we will never forgive you for enslaving us. You will find your trunk of items outside our shop in the morning."

She turned her back on Helva. Balnor gave Helva a pained look, part anger and part sadness, and then also turned his back. They started walking down the winding street.

Helva took a step toward them, but stopped. "Don't go home," she said to their backs. "He may try taking you again. Go stay with friends or family until this is all over. But don't tell me where."

They stopped and looked at each other. Balnor half turned, gave Helva a nod, and then they resumed walking into the night.

Helva stared after them silently for many moments.

"Even when I was enthralling them," Helva said quietly, "I still believed they loved me. I still believed that I had a family again."

What could I say to her? I doubted a lecture on why enthrallment was a magical taboo for a reason would help. Her parents had been murdered, her mentor had died, her brother wanted to kill thousands, and now the only people in her life who had treated her kindly—albeit under enthrallment—wanted nothing more to do with her. I could *partially* relate to a couple of those things, the big one being that she felt utterly alone.

Yeah, I could definitely relate to that one.

"You can stay at my shop, if you want," I said. "It's no palace for a princess, but it has a cot you can sleep in."

She gave me a sideways glance, her eyes narrowed.

"I mean, I'm not saying it would be a permanent thing," I added, "just for the night. But not with me! Just while I give the books to Aper. Then you can leave. Not that I want you to, but only if you want..."

I groaned inwardly and wanted to pull out my tongue for making these foolish sounds.

But Helva continued to watch me. The way she looked down at the ground and then back up at me with a little smile was very...interesting.

"Thank you for the offer," she said, "but I want to walk for a while. I need to think on what has happened tonight."

"Of course," I said. Then I gave her shrewd look. "You still plan on following me around, don't you."

That interesting smile didn't waver. "I told you, I need to think on what has happened tonight."

"Well, if you get bored skulking in the shadows, I won't mind it if you walk with me."

"I will keep that in mind," she said, and then turned and walked away from Aper's home on the Palatine Hill.

I shook my head and headed toward the Palatine.

# FORTY-FIVE

P aetus's home was on the way toward Aper's, so I decided to stop there first to see if he'd made any progress on figuring out how Silanus could summon Invidia. Second, I wanted to get his take on how the Sibylline Books could stop Silanus before I turned them over to Augustus. I knew Augustus had plenty of flamens ready to interpret the books from a Roman pantheon perspective, and I doubted I'd see them again once I handed them over. I had a feeling Paetus's daemonology perspective would be far more useful in stopping Silanus than a flamen's prescription to sacrifice a goat with sixty-three black hairs at dawn next Tuesday.

I kept my burned right hand on my gladius and my left hand on the satchel strap over my shoulder. My burned hand didn't issue the waves of agony it had earlier, and I chalked that up to my body's natural magic-infused healing processes. It still hurt like hell, and I'd still need to heal it soon before it got infected. But to do that I'd need at least a day of rest afterward. My day was looking kind of full.

Usually at this time of night, only drunkards, beggars, and bandits were out. But tonight I had to fight through trains of people pulling hand carts, people on horseback, and people being carried on slave-driven palanquins, all hightailing it out of Rome. They all looked scared and desperate. While I saw many fistfights as people grew frustrated with the traffic, I didn't see panicked flight. I wondered how much longer before that changed.

Fortunately it was the main *vias* that were crowded, so I made my way through the narrow alleys, of which I had a mediocre knowledge in this neigh-borhood. The danger of that, though, was that all the bandits would be forced off the main *vias* due to the crowds, so they might lurk in the darker alleys. Men huddled in alcoves and doorways here and there, most of them sleeping, but some staring at me with hollow eyes. I tried to strike an imposing figure as I strode through them. It wasn't hard, considering I was a head taller than almost everyone in the ancient world, though it also made people notice me and made me a tempting target. Apparently my scowl and bearing did the trick, for no one accosted me along the way.

I got to Paetus's home, ignoring the raucous laughter coming from the brothel next door, and pounded on his door. I got no answer. I didn't even see a candle or lamp lights coming from the small porthole on his heavy wood door.

"He ain't there," said a young woman's voice from the brothel. I glanced up and saw her standing in the light of the open doorway. I could barely see her face in the shadows, but I could tell it was heavily painted.

"Do you know where he went?"

She shrugged. "Some men came by a few hours ago, and he went with them. Don't know where."

I frowned. I didn't want to hand the books over to Augustus until after Paetus had looked at them. But I also didn't want to sit outside Paetus's door waiting for him to come back, considering I carried a priceless relic and I was just asking for bandits to jump me.

Damnation. I was going to have to take my chances with Aper.

"Thanks," I said to the young woman. "If you see him come back, could you tell him to meet me at Salvius Aper's home?"

"I might be busy. But I'll tell him if I see him." When I nodded my thanks and turned to leave, she said, "I saw what you did earlier today. Are you that magus everyone's talking about? The one who fought the sand giant and monsters at the Circus?"

I stopped, turned slowly, and bit my lower lip. I glanced around at the few drunks and gamblers on the street, who seemed too busy being drunk or gambling to listen to me and the woman. "Yeah," I said in low tones. "Although I did have help. The Praetorians and another magus—"

"Will all firstborn die tomorrow night?"

"I'm going to try really hard to ensure that doesn't happen," I said. "Still...if you have friends or family outside of Rome, I'd recommend you go visit for a few days."

She smirked. "I ain't got no one outside of Rome. All I have is here." She said it in a slightly bitter tone that told me she didn't think all she had was so great. "Everyone who works here ain't got nowhere to go either. Even the boys inside. They all think it's the end of the world, so they're spending all the money they have. Elsewise we'd all be running like everyone else." She glanced at the occasional citizen hurrying down the alley with a loaded pack on his back, then she looked back at me. "But the people who have nowhere else to go are hoping you'll save us all again. Me and the other girls are gonna sacrifice to Jupiter for you on the morn."

*No pressure,* I thought. But I gave what I hoped was a reassuring smile. "I appreciate that."

She returned my smile with a worried look and then went back into the tavern.

"Natta Magus!"

Vitulus was jogging up to me from the darkened alley, weaving around the fleeing citizens. I grinned at seeing my friend again, but got wary when I saw how serious he looked.

"I've been looking for you for hours," he said, breathing heavy when he finally stopped in front of me. "Where have you been? And what happened on your street? Buildings were smashed, including your shop. People were talking about Cacus...?"

"Well not *the* Cacus, but a pretty good copy of the mythological Cacus."

Vitulus just stared at me.

"Long story," I said. I patted my satchel and said, "The good news is that I found the books."

His eyes widened and stared at my satchel. This time he actually smiled and clapped me on the shoulder. "I knew you'd find them, my friend! I told them, if anyone can find the books, it is Natta Magus. But where were they? How did you get them from Silanus?"

"Another long story. Do you know where Paetus is? I wanted to get his interpretation before I returned them to Aper."

"He's actually at Aper's home now. That's why I've been searching for you half the night: Augustus has discovered a prophecy regarding the books. He wants to talk it over with you and Paetus."

"What did he discover?"

Vitulus shrugged. "He wouldn't say, only that the prophecy involved you."

"Me? Where did this prophecy come from?"

"I don't know," he said impatiently. "We'll find out when we get to Aper's."

Prophecy? Involving me? Could it be a clue as to the reason I was supposed to stay in Rome? My heart quickened at the thought of finally learning why I had to stay in the ancient past and give up all that I knew and loved. But my brain tried to put the brakes on my rising hopes; I'd been disappointed many times before. This could simply have something to do with Silanus's attack, or it could be utter nonsense.

But I'd never know if I didn't go to find out.

I nodded absently. "Let's go."

"And you can tell me your 'long stories' on the way," he said.

So I told him about everything that happened, from Silanus's visit to my shop, to Cacus, to my visit to the underworld with Helva to rescue Tanith and Balnor and retrieve the Sibylline Books. I even told him about my brief illusory visit to Detroit and Lares's sacrifice to break me out of it. Just telling him everything exhausted me and brought back the horrible sense of loss, not only over losing Brianna all over again but also my spirit friend. I was stunned that all that had only happened over the last six hours. I wanted nothing more than to curl up on my cot in my shop and sleep for a week.

But Rome wasn't going to save itself, so I kept walking.

"How does a creature with an arse for a head see or eat or hear?" Vitulus asked.

I glanced at him in the darkness. "Out of everything I just told you, *that* is your first question?"

He gave a little chuckle, which sounded like he was holding back a huge belly laugh. "I'm sorry, but I find such a creature hilarious."

"Yeah, well you wouldn't if you saw one coming at you at the head of a—Will you stop laughing?"

"Forgive me." When he finally got himself under control, he said, "I suppose it does disturb me that the underworld is so...Egyptian. I mean there are many similarities: The river you spoke of could be Styx, but I am surprised Mercury or Charon was not there to meet you. And the pyramids and these creatures you fought are just not known in the Roman Religio."

"Every religion's underworld has a place of judgment where the soul stops before moving on," I said. "Helva controlled the spell that opened the gateway, so perhaps we encountered *her* vision of the underworld." Then I shook my head and said, "Anyway, the point is that we got the books back at considerable cost. They'd better be worth it."

I was silent for a while, and then Vitulus said, "I'm sorry for Lares, my friend. I know she was important to you."

I tried to keep my voice from cracking when I said, "I appreciate it."

It wasn't long before we reached Aper's home. After we knocked on the main door, Nicio let us in immediately, as if he'd been waiting for us. A dozen or so Praetorians stood around in the courtyard, either throwing dice, snacking on fruit or bread, or polishing their swords. I recognized a few as Augustus's men, and some were Aper's. I traded nods with the two Praetorians who had stood by Vitulus and me in the Circus. It felt good to have them look at me now not as some freak; now I saw respect in their eyes. To have such hard men look at me like that raised my chin a little higher.

Nicio guided us into Aper's atrium where I got a major sense of *deja vu* from last night. Aper and Capito stood off in one corner speaking in low, heated tones. Paetus stood next to a table where he had several scrolls rolled out, one upon the other. He glanced up at me as we entered, and as always, he looked like he'd rather be anywhere else than in the same room with Rome's most powerful men.

When he saw me, Augustus himself rose up from a couch near Paetus. His eyes glittered when he noticed the satchel I carried and the familiar scroll cases poking from it.

"Are those...?" he asked quietly. Aper and Capito had stopped their hushed argument and stared at me. Capito watched me with surprised eyes while Aper gave me his usual blank expression (I swore I caught a hint of a smile, though it could've just been the shadows).

I hated turning the books over to him so quickly without letting Paetus take a look first, but time was short, I was exhausted, and I pretty much didn't have a choice at the moment. I unslung the satchel, made my way around the atrium's stone planters, and handed the satchel to Augustus.

"I hope they're all there," I said. "I was a little rushed when I found them."

Augustus set the satchel down on top of the scrolls that Paetus had been reading and then opened each of the three scroll tubes. He reverently pulled each scroll from the tube, scanned it once, and then put it back. He did this for all three before sighing, a relieved expression dominating his usual cool demeanor.

"You've done well, Natta Magus," Augustus said. Then he suddenly looked as tired as I felt. "I am sorry it has to be this way."

My first clue that something was wrong came when Vitulus cursed loudly. My second clue came when a club smashed me in the back of the head. I don't remember falling down, but I do remember looking up for a few seconds. Vitulus fought with two Praetorians who were struggling to hold him against a nearby column, Aper and Capito looked down at me with the same grim expression, Paetus looked like he was about to throw up, and Augustus's cool demeanor had returned as he took the Sibylline Books and walked away.

Then another Praetorian club—wielded by the same guy I had traded respectful nods with in the courtyard—brought stars and then darkness.

# FORTY-SIX

T he mirror dramas I once watched in the twenty-first century often showed characters clubbing people in the head to knock them out rather than kill them. Brianna, my favorite nit-picker ever, often scoffed at this.

"If you hit someone in the head that hard," she'd say, "you can just as easily kill them as knock them out!"

It's true. The fact that you're unconscious means you literally have brain damage. The extent of that damage varies on the force of the blow, where you were struck, and pretty much luck.

So when I started coming back to consciousness, Brianna's scoffing was the first thing I thought of. Then the fact that I was *not* waking up next to the River Styx handing a coin to Charon. I'd gotten lucky. Of course, when I opened my eyes to see where I was, I had to amend that lucky part.

My prison was dark, dank, and stank like the Cloaca Maxima. I laid on my back on cold, wet stone. My head throbbed all over, and I couldn't immediately tell where I'd been hit. But when I moved it a little, a sharp blast of pain came from behind my left ear as if a dagger were sticking out of my head. I cursed loudly as I slowly sat up. I put my left hand behind my head to explore the wound. There was a huge, crusty knot back there, and my hand came away with flecks of semi-dried blood.

And then despair hit me when I realized my hat was gone along with my components belt. Both were enchanted to remain on my body so long as I was conscious. But then they would've known that because Aper knew it.

*Cac.*

I slowly raised my head toward the source of light that enabled me to see my hands. Even that motion was enough to send pain knifing through my head, but I forced myself to look up nonetheless. There was a circular hole in the ceiling about the width of my shoulders. It was covered by a metal grate that was locked from the outside. Torches or lamps were burning in the room above me, casting some flickering orange light into my pit. Even with my hat gone, I saw the faint aura of an anti-magic shell covering the hole. I probed for my cell magic, but it was gone. It was the same shell I'd used to trap Silanus in my shop...and the same one that I'd shown Paetus how to use in his home.

*Et tu, Paetus?*

I scanned the circular dungeon. It was about twenty paces wide and had a domed ceiling that topped out at the grate a little over six feet high. I was the only prisoner. A large jug sat nearby along with a plate full of hard rolls and fish jerky. A few paces from the jug was a circular hole about a foot in diameter. Judging by the horrid smell coming from it, I figured it was my latrine.

So this was how Augustus thanked people who retrieved his priceless religious artifacts.

"You're welcome," I cried out in a raspy voice. Simply speaking made the dagger in my head twist and turn, and I cursed loudly again.

"Natta?"

I looked up, wincing from the pain. Paetus looked down at me through the circular grate, looking as nervous and sick to his stomach as ever. *Good, the little bastard deserved all the nausea he can get.*

"Ah, one of my *friends*," I tried to growl, but which came out as more of a groan. "Nice work on the shell."

"Natta, I'm so sorry," he pleaded. "I had no choice! They said you betrayed us, that you were working with Silanus. If I didn't help them, you and Silanus would destroy Rome!"

I tried to stand, gritting my teeth from the agony in my head. I never thought it would happen, but the pain in my head almost made me forget my burned right hand. "Paetus, what the hell are you talking about?"

"They saw you with Silanus," he said. "They watched Silanus leave your shop last night. They said you parted like old friends."

*Damnation, they were spying on me?* Of course they were spying on me. I'm a magus; they didn't trust me and never would.

"When Augustus found out, he flew into a rage," Paetus continued. "He said Rome would defeat this menace on her own, just like she always has—"

I started laughing. Even though I was in the worst pain of my life, I couldn't help it. "How is Rome going to defeat an army of Dea Tacitas and the goddess of revenge?"

"Augustus will use the books tonight," Paetus said miserably. "He is the *pontifex maximus*, so he has the divine authority."

"So you believe all this?" I asked, squinting at Paetus's shadowy form through the grate and foggy anti-magic shell. "You believe I'm working with Silanus?"

Paetus was quiet for several moments. "Was Silanus at your shop last night, Natta?"

"Yes," I said, then wearily sat back down again. I was getting a nasty case of vertigo and didn't trust that I could remain standing without throwing up. "But he came to taunt me. This is all a game to him. He hates me because William thought I was more important than him. And he hates Romans because Roman assassins killed his parents. He's the grandson of Cleopatra and Marcus Antonius."

"Gods below," Paetus breathed. "This is starting to make sense..."

"And you know as well as I do that reciting ancient prophecies to Silanus won't stop him. They're not magic. The only thing that can stop a bad guy with magic is a good guy with magic."

"Are you a 'good guy', Natta Magus?" Paetus asked quietly.

I closed my eyes, and said, "If my actions haven't proven that by now, then my words never will. Why didn't Augustus just kill me? Why throw me in here?"

"You're a valuable weapon," he said. "He won't kill you until he's sure you're no longer of any use to him."

I grunted, then asked, "Where's Vitulus?"

"He wanted to be here, but he's under house arrest. He's refusing to follow orders to protest your detainment. If it makes you feel any better, Aper vehemently disagreed with this, too. But his duty and loyalty to the Princeps will always come first. Unlike Vitulus, apparently."

I felt a smile creep across my lips. I worried for Vitulus's future, and the future of his family, if he persisted with his protest. But it felt good, nonetheless, to know that at least Vitulus never suspected the worst of me.

"Why are you here?"

"I told them I needed to maintain the anti-magic shell to ensure it stayed intact once you awakened. Your hat and sword and components were most helpful." He then gave a meaningful glance with his eyes at the corner of the room above me.

I frowned. "You don't know how to maintain a—"

"I also wanted to find out," Paetus interrupted, his voice louder this time, "whether you really are a traitor to Rome. But I think I've heard enough, Natta Magus. I must now return to my library so that I can obtain the knowledge that the Princeps needs in his heroic efforts to save Rome from Silanus." Paetus sounded like he was reading off a cue card. "I bid you farewell, and I hope the Princeps forgives your treachery."

I just stared up at Paetus's shadowy face, my pain-addled mind not knowing what to think of his weird performance.

But the way he "accidentally" kicked a rock through the anti-magic shell and the grate when he turned to leave was truly inspired. The rock, a piece of brick no bigger than my palm, poked a hole through the shell when it came through. The hole opened briefly like a bank of heavy fog that had been pierced, and then it tried to reform. But the hole did not close up completely, and I saw a tiny point like a dark speck still in the shell.

It was enough. I could feel my cell magic again.

I considered my options. Based on Paetus's performance and his subtle way of helping me, there had to be guards nearby. I was exhausted, concussed, and in terrible pain. And I didn't have my Wolverines ball cap or my components belt, so focusing my magic would've been hard even if I was in optimal health. In my condition, a spark globe would be the most powerful spell I could cast.

I briefly considered the old spark globe trick, which had helped me bluff my way out of dangerous situations before. It was harmless to people and things, but scared the *cac* out of anyone unaccustomed to magic. But even if I got the guards to peek into the dungeon at me, there was no way I could fit the spark globe through the pinprick hole in the anti-magic shell. And I couldn't cry out for food and water because they'd already left enough down here with me to last the day.

I sat up again and winced when I unconsciously put my right hand on the—

I stared at my right hand. It was still wrapped in the black cloth that Helva had given me. The black cloth she had ripped from her own tunica.

Finding spells were my specialty and had been my career focus before I was flung back into the past. In the twenty-first century, I had reached the point where I could cast them almost subconsciously with very little effort and concentration, and my jobs in Rome had only made me better.

Though I had never tried, I assumed I was efficient with them by now that I could cast them without my ball cap to focus my magic.

Casting a reverse finder spell was, in principle, the same as casting a normal one. In this case, I was going to use Helva's tunica cloth to broadcast *my* location to *her*. The spell itself would be easy.

But would she get it? If she was a cell magus, then I'd have no doubt. But she was an earth magus, something entirely new to me. Hell, I could only see her aura when she lost concentration or chose to let me see it. Would she feel a reverse finder from a cell magus? It's not like I had many options at the moment.

The tunica strip was already in my hand, so I made a fist around it, grunted from the pain, and tried siphoning my cell magic. It was slippery without my ball cap, like trying to catch a fish with my bare hands. I could feel it there, but when I tried siphoning the magic, it squirmed away. Something that would've been instantaneous with my ball cap took me several minutes to accomplish. Once I did connect, my skin tingled with the power running over it and through it. I began to recite the bastardized Dutch finder spell: *"Vinden me, Helva."*

Rather than feel a connection with my quarry snap into place and my feet urged to walk toward it, I felt my aura blast through the tiny hole in the anti-magic shield and then quickly expand into a sphere of spiritual energy. That invisible energy would encompass the city limits of Rome within seconds. If Helva was in Rome, and her earth magic enabled her to hear my finder spell, then she would suddenly have the urge to walk toward my location. I just prayed she'd understand what that urge meant.

With the reverse finder sent, all I could do was lay back down and wait. I curled up into a fetal position on the damp stone floor. I still held my cell magic, so I tried channeling a bit of it into my hand and my head to at least heal myself enough so that I wasn't in so much agony. It worked because I began to doze into a healing recovery sleep soon after I began.

But then my eyes snapped open when an idea came to me. An insane idea, but a better one than trying to take on Silanus by myself.

And it had the added bonus of scaring the hell out of Augustus.

I mentally filed it away and let myself fall back into the healing sleep while I waited for Helva.

# FORTY-SEVEN

An explosion woke me up.

I sat up way too quickly from my stone floor bed. Vertigo assaulted me and blackness crept into the corners of my vision, but at least the horrible agony in my head was gone. I still felt the dull throbbing welt, however, and my burned hand felt scabby rather than raw.

But I had no time to marvel at my healing abilities despite not having my ball cap; another explosion came from somewhere above me. It seemed closer this time. The stones around me cracked, and little pellets of dirt and mortar hit me. I heard men curse through the ceiling gate, then pause. Then they started shrieking in terror.

*Damnation, Helva, don't kill them...*

Despite having lived over two years in the ancient world where life was pretty cheap, I still couldn't stomach the killing of other human beings, especially people who weren't actively trying to kill me, like my guards. It even made me sick thinking that I might have to kill Silanus, but at least with him, I knew that I'd be saving many lives.

It still made me sick, though. And to be honest, I hoped it always would.

"Natta Magus?" Helva said from above. I saw her serious face look down into my dungeon and then break into a satisfied grin when she saw me. "I got your message," she said over the screams and curses of the men behind her.

"Great," I said. "What the hell did you do to the guards?"

She waved a dismissive hand. "They'll be fine. Eventually."

It took far too much effort to stand than I thought it would. My muscles were terribly cramped from lying on cold, wet stone for so long, not to mention I was still exhausted from the healing and breakneck pace of the last couple of days. "Can you get rid of the anti-magic shell over the grate? I can't do it from this end."

She hovered her hand over it, muttered something in Coptic, and the shell disappeared. She then unlatched the grate, swung it open, and lowered a rope ladder. The three or four feet I had to climb felt like miles, but I managed to crawl out of the dungeon and through the hole into the torchlit room.

I glanced behind Helva and stared at the guards. There were three of them, and all three were stuck in either the walls or the floor. One guy was up to his kneecaps in solid stone, a second hung from the ceiling in which his entire right arm was stuck, and a third man's back was encased in the wall, as if he'd leaned in wet cement that instantly solidified once he'd sunk into it. All three seemed more terrified than in pain.

Helva glanced at the guards and then at me. "What?"

"Um. They won't stay like that, will they?"

She rolled her eyes. "The spell releases in a few hours. Or perhaps a day. Come to think of it, I was always running for my life every time I cast it. Maybe it never releases."

The men heard this and renewed their pleas for mercy. I stared at Helva until I noticed a slight twinkle in her eyes that told me she was playing with them.

"Your things are over there," she said, nodding behind me.

I turned to see my hat, sword, and components belt lying on a table with a lit candle in the middle. It looked like my components had been rifled through, for the pouches and clay vials were sitting outside the main pockets of the belt. I didn't worry about ensuring their correct order and stuffed everything into the nearest pocket, then wrapped the belt around my waist. After strapping my gladius belt on, I finally put on my old Wolverines ball cap.

My cell magic came into such focus and clarity that I almost wanted to cry.

"I have never been here before," Helva said, studying the dark room. "It is useful to know this place for when you get into trouble again."

"Thanks. Can we leave now?"

"Where do you want to go?" Helva said. She had her palms facing down, readying a gate spell.

I eyed the struggling guards ten paces behind her and whispered, "Take me to Vitulus. You should know where he lives if you've been following me for months. I have an idea on how to stop Silanus."

From the look on her face, you'd think I'd just asked her to drop me off on the sun. "Are you mad?" she said in a harsh whisper. "He is a Praetorian! The Praetorians put you here."

"*He* didn't put me here. Besides, he's under house arrest for refusing to follow orders. He's protesting my detainment."

"Even if that's true, so what? They will be guarding him. I've never been inside his home, so I can only get you to the street. The sun is up now. You will surely be seen."

"Between you and me, I think we can disable a few guards," I said, glancing at the men in stone behind her. "We just need to get inside for a few moments and then you can gate us out."

She exhaled sharply. "Why do you still want to help them? I've told you: The Romans don't trust you, and they never will. They beat you up and threw you into a pit, and that was *after* you returned their precious books. They don't deserve your loyalty or protection! I can take you to the other side of the Mediterranean in the blink of an eye. You can be far away from them forever. They will never betray you again."

Oh, she was telling me things that I'd argued back and forth with myself ever since Aventicum. I still had so many questions raging in my mind from my experience in the Ring of Saturn, but one thing was made crystal clear to me: I hated feeling regret. Over and over again, when the Ring showed my world ending while I watched, that was the last thing I always felt. Horrible, crushing regret that I could've stopped it all if I had just stayed in Rome like I was meant to.

I still didn't know what grand destiny the Ring had in store for me here, but I knew that I would do everything in my power to avoid feeling that regret again. That I would always fight for right, even if it meant my death. The young woman outside Paetus's home reminded me there were a lot of Romans who still believed in me, Romans who didn't have patrician or even freedmen resources to flee the city. I was fighting for them as well as for people who hated me. Because it was right.

I wanted my heart to be lighter than a feather on whatever celestial scale greeted me upon death.

But I didn't think I had the time to persuade Helva to join me, let alone explain my complex feelings on the matter.

"Look," I growled, "this is not the place to discuss this. Between you blasting holes everywhere and their yelling, it's a wonder the whole Thirteenth Legion hasn't arrived yet. Please just trust me."

As if on cue, I heard the sounds of many feet and clinking armor coming down the stairs behind Helva. The enspelled guards heard them too and cried out for help.

Helva cursed something in Coptic under her breath, but then gathered her earth magic and opened an oval gate right behind me. I turned to see a narrow alleyway that was still in shadows despite the glow of the rising sun bathing the street beyond the alley in orange light. I jumped through the gate into the relatively fresher air of the Roman street with Helva right behind me. I turned around just in time to see the armored guards come rushing down the stairs, stop in shock when they saw the guards, and then stare wide-eyed at us. Helva closed the gate before they could gather their wits.

# FORTY-EIGHT

I recognized the alley as it was one block from Vitulus's home on the same side of the street. I peeked around the corner toward my friend's house and looked for any obvious guards. The street was practically deserted for a typical morning, and the people I did see were either carrying large rucksacks and heading out of town or were drunkards stumbling home after celebrating the end of the world. Even the shops next to Vitulus's home were closed. I saw no one standing around outside Vitulus's door, nor did I see anyone standing on the rooftops of the buildings nearby. Either the Praetorians had multiple teams circling the block in disguise, or they just didn't have any guards posted.

Helva and I erred on the side of caution, though, and waited for about a half-hour to see if we noticed the same people walking by. After enduring a final sour look from Helva that said we should be sitting on an African beach sipping wine, I decided to head over to Vitulus's door. I briefly considered searching for an open shop to buy a shawl to disguise myself, but I figured there'd be no disguising my height no matter how many shawls I draped over my head. Our only option was to make a run for it and hope our powers of observation were correct.

I waited for a lull in the traffic—an elderly couple shuffling off to market with their grocery sacks—and then we hurried from around the corner and did a fast walk to Vitulus's door. My neck tensed, expecting either a shout of recognition or an arrow in the back at any moment.

When we arrived at Vitulus's door, I pounded on it with my fist. Helva had her back to the wall, and her eyes darted to every noise and motion on the street, as did mine, while we waited for the door to open. The elderly couple had already passed us by, but they were followed by three young men dressed in off-white togas. None of them gave us a second glance.

The barred porthole on the door opened, and Ambio's pale, Gallic face peeked through. He frowned and shut the porthole. I did not hear the bar lift on the other side.

"Ambio!" I hissed to the closed porthole. "It's Natta Magus, I need to see Vitulus now!"

I knew Ambio was fiercely protective of Vitulus and his family. Knowing that I was the reason why his master was under house arrest probably made him want to ignore me out of spite. As someone who grew up in the twenty-first century, slavery was abhorrent to me, so it always came as a surprise to find slaves who were so loyal to their Roman masters. Figures I'd encounter one at the worst time possible.

"Ambio!" I hissed again, glancing to my left and right. That feeling of an imminent arrow was getting stronger.

Then I heard the bar on the other side raise, and the door cracked open. Vitulus stared at me open-mouthed.

"How did...?" he stammered.

I didn't wait for an invitation. I slipped through the opening with Helva practically on my back. Once we were through, Vitulus closed the door and barred it. He turned, opened his mouth to say something, but shifted his eyes to the ground.

"I'm so sorry, my friend," he said without looking up at me. "You are a hero of the State, and they cast you into the Tullianum like a criminal. The injustice wounds my honor as a Praetorian and a Roman."

"I appreciate that," I said, "and I know you had nothing to do with it. But we can't stay long. I just came to get my components, and then we'll leave. Is your house being watched? I didn't see anyone outside."

Vitulus led us into his home. "Watched?" he said as we passed through the small atrium. "Why?"

"You're under house arrest. I assumed they'd watch your house to ensure you stayed put."

Vitulus snorted. "Nobody is watching this house. My honor will ensure that I 'stay put.' I swore an oath to Aper that I would do so, and he trusts my word."

"Too bad *I* can't trust *Aper's* word..."

Vitulus eyed me as he led us to his library toward the back of his home. "Do not judge Aper too harshly. He disagreed forcefully with Augustus over having you arrested, and I'd never seen him do that. Unfortunately Capito has a stronger influence on the Princeps than Aper. Capito's words of fear only fueled Augustus's mistrust."

I shook my head. "Damnation, I saved the guy's family, and he *still* doesn't trust me?"

*Remember,* I told myself, *fight for right, even for those who hate you.* It was a noble sentiment, but did nothing to stop the urge I had to give Capito a huge, open-handed slap in the face.

I didn't even look at Helva behind me, who hadn't said a word since we entered Vitulus's home. But I could feel the *I told you so* wafting off her.

"If it makes you feel any better," Vitulus said, "Capito doesn't trust anybody."

"Where's Claudia and Lucius?"

"They left the city last night upon my urging," he said in a clipped tone, which conveyed all the worry and fear he felt for them. "They're with her father and should be far from Rome by tonight." He paused, and then asked quietly, "Will this firstborn curse affect Romans *outside* Rome?"

"I honestly don't know," I said. "I'm sorry."

He nodded once, his face a stony mask.

When we entered the library, Vitulus went to an alcove where a marble bust sat of ancestor Gaius Aurelius Cotta, the first Aurelius to be named consul of the Republic over two hundred years ago. Vitulus reached behind the bust, hit some kind of switch, and then a click came from the floor immediately in front of the bust. He stooped to the wolf pelt rug below the bust and flipped over a corner. A rectangular section of the tiled floor, about three feet by two feet, was partially raised. Vitulus opened the section and pulled out a chest about the same size.

"You kept my components with your family treasure?" I said with a raised eyebrow.

He shrugged as he opened the chest. "You said they were valuable."

I inspected the contents of the chest, ignoring the jewels and gold coins, and reached for the five component pouches that I had given Vitulus to keep safe. I had another stash of these components back at my shop, but considering their value, the time and money it took me to acquire them, and my shop's propensity for getting trashed, I thought it wise to not keep all my eggs in one basket, so to speak.

Sometimes I do plan ahead.

I held up a smooth, white pebble to Helva. "For future reference, this is an *elementair* pebble. Keep an eye out next time you clean my shop."

She scowled at me.

I slipped the pouches into some larger pouches on my belt. "Thanks again, Vitulus. I know you're putting your neck out there for me."

Vitulus gave another shrug. "You're my friend." He said it as if it were so self-evident that it required no explanation. It made me want to give him a big hug again. He nodded toward the components that I'd just slipped into my belt and asked, "What are you going to do?"

I took in a huge breath and exhaled slowly. "Something that'll make Augustus trust me even less. But I think it's our best shot to stop Silanus."

When I explained the gist of my idea, Helva actually smiled for the first time in hours, while Vitulus's skin paled before my eyes.

"You're right," he said, after I finished. "Augustus will *not* like that."

"I don't see any other way," I said. "Helva and I cannot defeat Silanus on our own, especially after he's summoned a possible goddess."

"*Possible* goddess?" he said. "You don't think he will summon the *actual* Invidia?"

"Well that's for Paetus and the flamens to interpret. But it's more likely he will summon a daemon that embodies revenge. Daemons are just negative energy; magical principles dictate that it's the summoner who gives it form. If Silanus thinks he's summoning Invidia, then the revenge daemon will take on the form of Invidia. Given his hatred of Romans, I'm sure he wants it to be Rome's own revenge goddess who kills its firstborn."

Vitulus nodded reluctantly through my explanation of daemon physics. "If this is the only way to save my son," he said quietly, "then you should do it. How can I help?"

"Since I'm no longer in jail, you can end your protest and go back to your duties. Aper's going to need your advice and experience more than ever once I really get the puck sailing tonight. And if possible, do everything you can to stop Augustus from trying to take on Silanus with the books. It won't work; I don't care what the prophecies say."

"I will try," he said grimly, "but once Augustus sets his mind to something, not even Atlas could budge him."

Pounding came from the front door along with distant shouts for Vitulus to open up. I glanced at Helva. "I think that's our cue to leave."

She nodded and immediately opened a gate in the middle of Vitulus's library. On the other side, I saw the sun shining on a sandy beach and the waves of a sea.

Ambio rushed into the room with a dagger in hand. He stopped short in the doorway when he saw the gate, then looked to Vitulus.

"*Dominus?*" he said questioningly, glancing from Vitulus to the gate.

"Put away the dagger, Ambio," Vitulus said. "Natta Magus is leaving, but we must greet the friends at our door without weapons in hand. But, um, keep Natta Magus's visit between you and me."

Ambio nodded, placed his dagger on a table next to the library's entry, and then hurried toward the front door without a second glance at the gate, me, or Helva.

Vitulus and I embraced again. "I'm sorry for any trouble I've caused you and your family," I said.

"And I'm sorry my Republic has forgotten how to treat its heroes," he replied. When we pulled away, he said, "May Fortuna go with you."

"You, too, buddy."

Then I turned and jumped through the gate onto the sandy beach. As the warm sea breeze greeted me, I glanced back through the gate just in time to see it close while Vitulus stood on the other side watching me. I hoped it wasn't the last time I saw him.

# FORTY-NINE

I scanned up and down the beach as far as I could see. It was all sand, dunes, and limestone cliffs, some covered in green shrubs as tall as my waist.

Helva stared at the sea. "We are on the Egyptian coast of the Mediterranean. My father brought Silanus and me here when we were very young. It was the first time I'd ever seen it. I remember him pointing out toward the sea and saying, 'The people who want to kill us live that way.'"

I just stared at her.

"I swore an Oath to William to do everything in my power to keep you safe," she said, still looking at the sea. "The easiest way to do that would be to just keep you here until tomorrow."

"Helva," I said quietly, "*Augustus* ordered your parents killed, not 'the Romans.' If you don't gate us back to Rome, innocent people will die. Children will lose their parents today."

She finally looked at me. Her was face a stony mask, her voice as steady as always. "I spent my whole life running from the Romans. Hating them. Now you want me to help save them. Forgive me, Natta Magus, but that is not a readjustment that is easy for me to make."

"I get that. But I see honor in you. Where is the honor in killing innocents? Where is the honor in allowing Tanith and Balnor to die? They're Roman citizens too, you know."

She closed her eyes, her lips suddenly curled into a snarl. Then she thrust her palms downward and screamed something in Coptic. The words were indecipherable to me, but they were arcane, for all the hairs stood on my body as she drew in an incredible amount of power from the earth.

"Helva!" I said. "You're going to burn yourself—!"

With a scream of rage, frustration, and unfathomable sadness, she threw her hands toward one of the cliffs about a hundred paces behind me. The entire cliff face exploded into boulders, pebbles, and sand. She screamed again and swiped her hands toward a cliff in the opposite direction. That cliff, too, exploded when her earth magic struck it. She continued screaming arcane words while sweeping her hands in every direction, the earth erupting in violent explosions wherever she directed her magic.

Damnation, I'd never seen such power from anyone outside the twenty-first century. I wanted to yell for her to stop before she burned the magic out of herself, as I had done at Aventicum, but I wasn't sure she'd even listen to me if I tried. All I could do was hope she didn't kill herself—or me—before she was spent.

She finally slumped to her knees, put her hands to her face, and wept. "I've lost everyone I've ever loved," she shouted through her sobs. "My parents! William! Silanus! Tanith and Balnor! I can't lose you, too!"

I stared at her. "What?"

She just sat on her knees, staring at the sand, shaking her head slowly. "I'm such a fool," she muttered. "I've watched you many months. I've seen how all you want to do is help people. I've watched you help Romans, Gauls, Germans, Africans, it doesn't matter. Patricians, plebeians, slaves. You don't care who a person is. You help them." She looked up at me, tears brimming in her eyes. "I want to be like you. I really do. But I have so much *anger* in me. I hate the Romans for what they did to my family. I hate William for abandoning me just when I had learned to trust him. I hate Silanus for making me fight him. But mostly I hate myself for being incapable of knowing what the right thing to do is, which you seem to know instinctively."

I slowly sat down on the sand in front of her, cross-legged. I felt that I had to say something to Helva, but I had no idea what. I'm no psychologist. She'd been through hell her entire life and really wanted to turn it around, but didn't know how. I totally understood how she felt about being abandoned and not knowing what to do. These journals are filled with those feelings.

How could I advise someone on something that I was still trying to figure out?

I guess I'd do what I always did: make it up and hope for the best.

I picked up a piece of driftwood half-buried in the sand. I stared at its smooth surface, polished by months or years by the sea. "Did William ever tell you that a lot of people keep dogs as pets in the twenty-first century?"

She stared at the piece of driftwood I held, but shook her head absently.

"I had one growing up. She was a brown and white sheep dog. Smartest dog ever. Her name was Leeta. Every time I came home, Leeta would be *so* excited to see me. She would jump up and down and bark and try to lick my face. Most of the time I let her." I grinned with the memories of trying to fend her off while laughing. "One day when I was seventeen, I'd had a bad day at school—I can't remember why—and was in no mood to have my faced licked when I came home. So when I walked in the door and she jumped on me all excited as usual, I yelled at her to go away. She stopped jumping on me, but she didn't go away. She just stood there and stared at me, her ears up. And then she followed me around for the next hour or so. Once I finally cooled off from whatever was bugging me, I stooped down to pet Leeta. She jumped on me and tried licking my face as if nothing happened, and then we went outside for a good game of fetch."

Helva sighed. "I do not understand the lesson of your dog parable."

"I'm not finished. The next day, Leeta was hit by an autocar and died. I was pretty devastated, but I knew I'd have been even more devastated if my yelling at her had been the last memory she had of me instead of that last game of fetch the day before. I told my dad this as we dug her grave in our backyard that day. He thought about it and said, 'Dogs love unconditionally. That's what she would've remembered. The best way to remember her is to try to be the person Leeta thought you were.'"

I paused a moment to let that sink in. Helva continued to stare at me with a blank expression, and I began to think that parables were line item number 2,983 of skills that I needed to work on.

"In other words," I said, "think of the person you want to be and then make choices in life that make you that person. All those things you said that you admire about me? I didn't have any kind of master strategy for any of that. Every time I help someone, I do it because that's the person I want to be. Does that make sense?"

She stared at me several moments. "So I should only make choices approved by dogs?"

"No, that's not what..." I stopped when I noticed the mischievous smile creeping across her tear-stained face. "Was that humor, Helva Magus?"

Her smile seemed to run out of energy. "I understand what you are trying to tell me. But it's...not easy."

"I never said it was easy. Look, I don't have all the answers, and I don't know what will work for you. Hell, I know all about being angry at fate, trust me. But for me at least, helping other people eases that anger. Maybe it can do the same for you. Don't let your anger tell you what's right and what's wrong." I raised an eyebrow at her. "I ate a lot of Chinese food in my time and opened a lot of fortune cookies, so I'm gonna keep saying these proverbs until you take me back to Rome."

"I won't kill my brother," she said. "I don't care what he does. I won't do it." She looked at me, her eyes as firm as her voice. "And I won't let you do it either."

"Like I said, I don't think it'll come to that. I don't know much about the Egyptian underworld, but I don't believe they give out pyramids like his to mass murderers. He must do something pretty damned heroic in the future to make up for the lives he's already taken. And I don't think he could do anything later to balance out the lives he'd take if his plan succeeds tonight."

She still didn't look convinced, but at least she was no longer crying and blowing up the North African coast. I put a gentle hand on hers, which were absently poking at a pebble in the sand. She grew still as soon as I did, but did not pull away.

"Helva. Be the person you *want* to be. Please take me back to Rome."

"Swear an Oath to me that you won't kill my brother."

"Helva..."

"I want to help you, Natta Magus. I want to be a better person. But not at the cost of my brother's life. Swear an Oath, and I will use all my power to help you stop Silanus without killing him."

Oaths with a capital "O" were a far bigger deal in the twenty-first century than in the ancient world. If you broke an Oath in my time, your aura was tainted for every magus to see, and then good luck finding a job, making new friends, or simply going to the grocery store without enduring the whispers and wary looks. It was the kind of thing where mothers pulled their children to the other side of the street to avoid walking near you. An Oath-Breaker was the twenty-first century's equivalent of a leper in the ancient world.

But swearing an Oath in the ancient world didn't have the same importance because 99% of the people were not magi and therefore could not see an aura and an Oath-Breaker's shame. Breaking an Oath did put a magical dent in your soul that hurt far worse than a mundane oath, but it didn't make you an outcast to everyone you'd ever meet. It could be hidden the old fashioned way: by keeping it a secret.

Despite the lesser penalties of Oath-Breaking in the ancient world, I did take it seriously due to that soul-denting thing. As I've explained before, I'd rather die than feel deep regret, and Oath-Breaking brought on a heaping helping of it, which someone like me couldn't live with.

I hated to swear an Oath that I might not be able to keep, but I'd much rather feel the regret of breaking that Oath than the regret of standing by while Silanus slaughtered thousands. Talk about a lose-lose proposition.

I still had that same feeling, however, that made me hesitate in Silanus's tomb—that it wouldn't be necessary in the end. I used that to console myself as I nodded to Helva. "I will swear the Oath."

I gathered my cell magic and focused it into my aura. My skin prickled like it always did, but rather than the hairs standing high, it felt more like they were pointed inward, toward the source of my aura. Then I said the words, "I swear this Oath: I will not kill Silanus, brother of Helva Magus."

The words reverberated through my body, and then I felt them imprint upon my aura as a new sense of purpose. I'd always felt an abhorrence to killing, but with Silanus, it was now so deep that it made me nauseous and tremble.

"Oath sworn," I said. "Now can we go?"

She stared at me with distant eyes, like any magus would when inspecting the aura of another magus. When focus returned to her eyes, she nodded and then stood.

"You know," I said, standing up next to her, "it's really unfair that you can see my aura, but I can't see yours. It's like you know exactly what I'm thinking, but I have no idea what you're thinking."

"You can see mine if I let you," she said. "I just choose not to let you."

She directed her palms toward the earth, muttered some Coptic words, and a gate sliced the air in front of us and became a blue-rimmed oval. Beyond it, I saw another quiet alleyway with a brick road surrounded by wooden and stucco buildings.

"Well I know you love me, so I guess we're even," I said, and then jumped through the gate before she could close it out of spite.

# FIFTY

Helva's gate opened onto an alley near the desolated Circus Maximus, which at first you'd think was insane. I mean, that's right next door to Caesar *caccing* Augustus's palace. But the Circus was surrounded by the homes of wealthy patricians and equestrians who had the resources to flee the city before Silanus's attack tonight, so I figured it was likely the most deserted place in Rome. Plus, the superstitious Romans wouldn't want to be anywhere near a location that was the scene of a recent attack by daemons and sand giants. At least not until it was thoroughly re-sanctified to the Roman Religio, which I doubted Augustus, in his duties as *pontifex maximus*, had gotten around to yet.

My hunch turned out to be true. Helva and I weaved our way through the alleys a few blocks from the Circus and saw maybe a dozen people, all who looked like slaves running errands for their absent masters. Every home and shop we passed was locked up, and even most of the taverns were closed. I saw one intrepid tavern still open, but heard only a few voices inside.

"I never said I was *in* love with you," Helva explained as we weaved our way through the alleys. "I simply meant that I admired you. I loved William, but I was not *in* love with him."

"Uh-huh."

Even though the streets were relatively deserted, I still tried to keep an eye out for roaming Praetorians who might recognize me, or even one of Augustus's cronies. I couldn't blend into the crowd on the busiest of days; today I'd stand out like a rampaging strix.

"I love Tanith and Balnor because they are good people and they were kind to me," Helva continued. "It's a similar sort of love: one of *admiration* and *respect*."

"Okay."

"What I'm saying is this: If you tease me one more time about a moment of weakness, I will rip the ground apart on which you stand and reform it again so that you are sunk up to your neck. And then I will leave you there for the crows to pick out your eyes."

I frowned at her. "That's a terrible thing to say to the one you love."

She thrust her arms to her sides, palms down, and I felt her earth magic build with the tightened hairs on my body. I raised my hands in surrender. "I'm sorry! That's it, I swear. No more teasing!"

She stared at me a few more moments, her brown eyes flashing, then she took several deep breaths and released her building magic. "Your Detroit humor is biting and annoying," she grumbled.

I turned around. "You're not the first one to tell me that."

We exited an alley onto a deserted street right next to the hulking and blackened walls of the Circus Maximus. As soon as we had exited the gate, I smelled the burned wood and flesh that still hung in the air, but it was almost overwhelming this close. Wisps of smoke still rose here and there from the center of the Circus. More sections had collapsed since yesterday, and I could partially see the dirt racing track from across the street. Crows circled the sky above the Circus, and some were perched in the stands and among the rubble, picking at bodies that had yet to be retrieved by the cleanup crews. Helva stared at the corpse of the Circus with the same grim expression I was sure I had. I could even feel the residue of the powerful magics that had been thrown around here, one so potent that even capped people could sense it as vague unease. None of the shops or homes on the other side of the street looked occupied, and I didn't see one person in any direction. It was a surreal change from the bursting crowds of yesterday.

Yes, the Circus was the perfect place for a meeting.

We hurried over to a spot on the street that put the ruins between us and Augustus's palace on the Palatine Hill, just in case he or one of his men happened to be looking out from the balcony. The spot was also surrounded by Circus rubble, which made it a kind of alcove that could only be seen into if one were looking directly at it from across the street. I stopped in the center of the alcove with the Circus wreckage to my back, dug through the component bag that I'd retrieved from Vitulus, and pulled out a small clay vial.

It contained some of my dried blood.

Dried magi blood was very useful as a spell component because, once all the water and wet material in the blood evaporated, the magical properties in the blood were actually enhanced and grew more enhanced over time. This was especially useful for healing. In the twenty-first century, we had healing spells that were far more powerful without needing blood of any kind, so it was rarely used any more. But here in ancient Rome, I didn't have access to the components needed for those spells, so I figured saving some of my blood would be wise in case I needed a healing with a lot of punch.

But this was not for the pain that still raged in my burned hand and my head.

I turned my Wolverines ball cap around and poured the vial's dark red flakes onto my open left palm. It filled up the center of my palm with a small pile about an inch in diameter. I closed my palm, siphoned my cell magic, and said in my arcane Dutch, "*Vinden me, magi.*"

I concentrated on the magical properties within my dried blood. They danced like red and blue sparks in my mind's eye, my aura's colors representing my magical abilities. Like the dungeon when I called Helva to me, I felt a wave of magic blast out of me and expand exponentially like the ripples in a pond where I'd just tossed in a brick. I sent the reverse-finder wave out only a few miles since I didn't think anybody farther than that would get here in time.

No use giving naturally born magi the urge to travel here if they'd only arrive after the fun was over.

After the spell went out, I slumped to the ground and sat cross-legged on the brick street. Exhausted, I leaned back against a large hunk of stone that had fallen from the Circus and shut my eyes.

Helva remained standing, but leaned against the same stone. "Won't Silanus hear your call?"

"Doubt it," I mumbled. "I called all the *cell* magi to me. He's an earth magus."

"But I heard your call from the dungeon."

I held up my burned hand, my eyes still closed. "That's because I had this. I called you, specifically. This call went out to everyone with the same cell magic in their blood as mine. You don't feel like walking toward me right now, do you?"

She shook her head. "Now what?"

I sighed. "I nap, you take first watch. And we hope there are enough magi in Rome to help us kill a goddess."

# FIFTY-ONE

The first magus arrived about an hour after I cast the reverse-finder spell. Helva had to poke me awake. I woke up with a start and was on my feet before I was even lucid.

"Are they here?" I muttered blearily.

She nodded to the young man walking purposefully toward us. Judging by his tunica, which had two vertical purple stripes on either side, he was of equestrian social rank. He had short, curly black hair and was about the size of the average Roman male. He looked ten years younger than me, barely out of his teens. His eyes never wavered from me as he crossed the deserted street and stopped in front of me. He glanced from me to Helva and back to me again.

I allowed my eyes to stare at him, unfocused, and I saw his magus aura: a clear shimmer with gold and purple streamers flitting around him.

"Why am I here?" he asked, the first hint of confusion clouding his face.

"Before I answer that," I said slowly, "what made you want to come here?"

He blinked several times and said, "I *had* to. I don't know why. This place is cursed, and yet...I had to come to this spot." He glanced at my hat. "You're the magus from the Circus yesterday. Did you curse me?" He put his hand on the hilt of the dagger on his belt.

"I did not curse you," I said with a soothing tone, "but I did call you. Rome needs your help. You heard about the other magus who wants to kill Rome's firstborn, right? The sand giant?"

The young man gave one quick nod, his hand still on his dagger.

"The only way we can stop him is if you and me and Helva and..." I glanced around the empty street. "And hopefully a lot more like us work together."

"What do you mean 'like us'? I'm no magus."

"What's your name, my friend?"

"Decius Subulo."

"Decius, have you ever done things that you can't explain? Have you ever wished for something to happen and then it did?"

He shifted his feet nervously and looked away from me. "I'm no magus. I'm a gods-honoring Roman of the Religio, not some kind of witch." He said it in a rote way as if it were a litany he'd been reciting to himself all his life. But one he had grown to doubt over the years.

"You may not be a magus," I said, "but you have magus talent in you. Otherwise you wouldn't have heard my call."

He closed his eyes tight and shook his head. "I can't be a magus. I'm supposed to swear oaths to Jupiter this very night to join the *auguria*! I am the first of my gens to set upon the equestrian *cursus honorum*! How can I bring honor and wealth to my gens if I'm some kind of freak?"

I kind of expected this. As someone born as a magus, raised as a magus, and culturally brought up to believe that anyone who *wasn't* a magus was "capped," it was still hard for me to grasp how that feeling could go the other way. I always described my arrival in ancient Rome to my capped friends like this: Imagine arriving in a city where everyone was blind from birth and you were the only one who could see. Now try describing the color blue to them. At best they wouldn't understand a word you were saying; at worst, you'd be labeled a "freak" and become an instant outcast.

I understood Decius's hesitation. A good Roman who wanted status and wealth *always* followed the rules and rituals of the Religio and the State. A good Roman never believed in foreign religions or philosophies. Because then you weren't a good Roman anymore. And to someone who *wanted* to be a good Roman, any deviation from the path was to be avoided at all costs.

So I needed to persuade a good Roman like Decius to deviate.

"Look," I said, "after today you can go live your life any way you want. I won't bother you again. But today, Rome needs your talent to save the lives of thousands of people. What Silanus said about killing all Roman firstborns is true; he *will* do it if we don't stop him."

"What about the Princeps?" Decius asked desperately. "I heard he will use the Sibylline Books to stop this curse himself."

It was a physical struggle for me to avoid rolling my eyes and snorting with derision. I managed to keep a straight face, but Helva was not as disciplined as me. She actually laughed. Decius glared at her, but I quickly said, "The Princeps has a plan, yes, but he needs our help. While he keeps Silanus busy on the Capitoline, we will attack the magus from another direction. Our side of the plan is very secret, known only to a select few."

He narrowed his eyes. "So...you're part of the Princeps' plan?"

*More like* he's *part of* my *plan, but tomato-tomahto...*

"As I said, we are a vital part of the plan that will save the lives of thousands of Romans. Decius, will you serve your country and your Princeps today?"

As Decius agonized over his decision, Helva nudged me and pointed to my right. Two more people, a young woman dressed like a patrician and an older man dressed in a slave's drab tunica, walked toward us on opposite sides of the street. They both had the wary gait of people who were practically sleepwalking, but I could see that their eyes were focused on me. When they got closer, Decius turned and paled as he saw them approach.

"Oh gods, there are more of you?" he moaned.

The patrician woman was about Decius's age, dressed an elegant yet practical stola dress, and her long black hair was braided expertly. The old slave was balding, thin, and wrinkled, but seemed to have a wiry strength about him as his back was straight, and he walked with the surety of a twenty-year-old. Both stopped next to us with the same questioning expressions Decius had.

So I gave them pretty much the same spiel.

The woman, whose name was Lucia, looked nervous, but she agreed to help with a resolute nod. "My father will be on the Capitoline tonight with the rest of the Senate. I want to do what I can to help him, Natta Magus."

The slave, Hughard, agreed without hesitation. "Me master was among the first to flee the city," he said in a heavy Germanic accent, "so I got nothing better to do than watch his house. Knew there was something off about meself all me life. Will be right interesting to figure what me can do with it."

When first Lucia and then Hughard agreed to help, Decius's ears turned red with shame. In his eyes, he was an honorable Roman man following the duty and career path that honorable Roman men in his social rank followed. To have a woman and a slave agree to fight for Rome while he vacillated must've made him feel like his manhood was shrinking by the moment. As I figured it would. Romans were pretty easy to manipulate once you knew how to kick them in their cultural tender parts.

Decius lifted his chin proudly and said with a shaky voice, "I will do my duty as a Roman. What do I have to do?"

Helva and my new recruits looked at me expectantly. I suddenly felt the weight of leadership fall upon my shoulders like a lead blanket. What if I was leading them to their deaths? What if my idea didn't work?

*Then run,* part of me said.

Well that wasn't an option. This was it. This was the only way, and if it didn't work, I guess I'd be too dead to care.

Which was better than a life with decades of crippling regret.

"Here's what I have so far..."

# FIFTY-TWO

One pleb women, Cana, and one male slave, Eudo, arrived within the hour, both curiously the same age as Decius and Lucia. I wondered if more "proper" Romans had heard my call, but had either refused to believe it or had decided their duties to their families were more important. I couldn't fault anyone for such a decision, for duty to gens and children was noble as well.

And I *really* hoped I wouldn't see a bunch of little kids coming down the street. I'd certainly turn them away, for I felt bad enough as it was bringing other adults into this; no way I was going to draft eight-year-olds to fight daemons and a crazy magus. I prayed little Aula, the only other natural cell magus that I'd met in Rome, was already far away with her patrician family.

I just hoped that six cell magi and one earth magus would be enough.

The sun was getting low in the sky when I decided that we should make our way to the Capitoline with what we had. Along the way, we learned that it wasn't just the streets around the cursed Circus Maximus that were deserted, but also every other street we took. It was eerie as hell as I was used to the crushing crowds at this time of day. People had either fled the city or were taking shelter wherever they could find it. Which seemed to include most of the taverns we passed: Each one was filled with raucous laughter and shouts. Many Romans seemed to want to face the end of their city with a posca in one hand and a lover in the other.

Decius stared longingly at each tavern we passed. "I could use some wine."

"Wine will dull your magic, my friend," I replied. But I also knew the feeling. I sure could've used something to dull the knot of fear in my gut that got bigger as we closed in on the Capitoline.

"What does it feel like?" Decius asked me.

"Magic? Well, it's hard for me to describe something I've taken for granted all my life. I can tell you how I felt when I couldn't touch my magic once last year:

It was as if I'd lost two limbs and one of my senses. All at once. Magic helps me experience the world. If I don't have it, I feel lost and crippled."

The young pleb women, Cana, said from my right, "So when we use our magic for the first time, it will be like we gain two limbs and a sense?"

I smiled. "Yeah, something like that. Your lives will change forever."

Cana smiled with anticipation, but Decius looked ill and glanced desperately at another loud tavern. The faces of my other would-be magi had a combination of Cana's eagerness and Decius's fear.

It was true, their lives were about to become far more interesting. But for how long was a different matter that I didn't want to bring up or even dwell on myself. If we somehow stopped Silanus, then they would want to know more about their talents. Even Decius, for how could he willingly abandon magic once he'd experienced it?

But who would teach them? Me? And even if I did become their teacher, could we stay in Rome? Augustus was going blow his top once he learned there were at least six other magi inhabiting his gods-fearing city. Would he try to imprison them, kill them, or worse: make them tools of the Roman state?

I was already thinking ten moves ahead when I should've been thinking about my current move. Dwelling on the sacrifices I had to make now would only distract me from winning the game.

Damned Silanus and his chess obsession...

We got to the foot of the Capitoline by late afternoon. The blocky, columned facade of Tabularium, where the state kept its official records, was eerily quiet and in shadows as we passed it on our way up the hill. Once we passed the Tabularium, I could see the four horse sculptures that stood at the apex of the Temple of Jupiter Optimus Maximus. And the closer we got, the more I heard the nervous murmur of the crowds gathered in front of the temple.

When we rounded a corner, we encountered hundreds of people—patricians, plebs, slaves, freedmen—all gathered in front of the columned temple fifty paces in front of me. I saw squads of armored Praetorians and urban *vigiles*, which was a rare sight in Rome due to the ancient taboo of maintaining an army within Rome's city limits. The warriors were stationed at the intersections of streets and alleyways surrounding the crowds and on the temple steps to protect all the VIPs gathered in the temple colonnade. I quickly scanned the cohorts for Vitulus or Aper, but couldn't find either one.

Augustus stood at the top of the temple steps wearing a purple and gold trimmed toga. He was surrounded by a couple hundred senators wearing their bright white togas with broad purple stripes down the middle. They crowded the entire colonnade. I spied Paetus standing a few paces behind Augustus, his dark blue tunica standing out among the senatorial white. He looked about as terrified as I figured he'd look in this situation.

In fact, fear hung in the air as thick as the city's usual miasma.

"It's not too late for me to take us out of here," Helva murmured next to me.

The part of my brain interested solely in self-preservation screamed, *Good idea, let's go*. It was so powerful that I actually opened my mouth to say something like that without realizing it.

But I was saved from my own flight reflex when the people around us noticed me.

"It's Natta Magus," one man said to another.

"It's the hero of the Circus Maximus," said a woman to my left.

"He's come to save us!" cried a male voice ahead of me.

Heads turned in my direction, and the expressions that were fearful moments before turned hopeful. Excited murmurs began to replace the nervous ones, and a few cheers began to ripple into the crowd surrounding me.

I turned to Helva who looked up at me with questioning brown eyes. "Too late now," I said to her.

Then I began to make my way through the increasingly buoyant crowd toward Augustus.

# FIFTY-THREE

To be honest, the part of my plan that had me slowly make my way through the crowds toward Augustus was the part that made me the most uncomfortable. Whereas combat scared the hell out of me, those fears always melted away as soon as battle was joined. But this—the cheers, the hope, the expectations, the adoration—scared me far more than battle.

It scared me because I could grow to love it.

I kept my eyes on Augustus as I made my way through the crowd, sensing more than seeing Helva at my side and my cohort of five magi behind me. Augustus was looking toward me, scanning the crowd for the source of the cheering and excitement. Once I got within twenty paces of the temple steps, his eyes locked on mine, and his face became the same blank mask it had been when he had ordered his Praetorians to beat me silly. Capito was suddenly at Augustus's side, his eyes on me while he whispered something into Augustus's ear. The Princeps glanced at the crowds then back at me, and then he gave Capito a quick shake of his head.

I allowed myself some tentative relief. My gamble—based on my brief talk with the prostitute outside Paetus's door before my arrest—that Augustus would not attack me in public had paid off. He may have been Rome's king in all but name, but he was still acutely aware of maintaining the appearance that Rome was a republic governed by laws. Making me disappear from Aper's home was doable; making me disappear in front of an adoring crowd was impossible. He had no choice now but to share the stage with me and accept my help.

I arrived at the temple steps without a Praetorian or vigile shooting an arrow into my eye, so I figured my chances were good.

However, a line of armored Praetorians with shields stood in front of the steps, the men all giving me hard, unyielding looks.

"Let him through!" came a shout from my left. I glanced that way and saw an officer wearing a red plumed helmet striding toward me behind the line of Praetorians. It was Salvius Aper, wearing the same blue breastplate that I had found for him two years ago, a job that had secured his trust in me and introduced me to Vitulus, my best Roman friend. It's funny the unrelated flood of memories that pop into your head when you see such a trigger object.

Aper was also a master of the blank face, but over the last two years I had come to notice the cracks that came with strong emotions. Right then he looked relieved and annoyed. Considering he hadn't ordered his men to run me through, I figured his relief took precedence.

Two Praetorians stepped back to allow me and my magical cohort to slip through the line. Aper stopped in front of me, fists on his hips. He then said in a low voice, "Vitulus told me you were coming."

"Glad you let him come out to play," I said. "Where is he?"

"Commanding the cohort searching for daemon *fascinus* tokens. Thankfully he hasn't found any yet." He shook his head at me. "You have balls, Natta Magus, I'll give you that. But I don't know what you hope to accomplish. *He* will never forget or forgive you for this."

"I don't really care what *he* thinks about me," I growled. My head still hurt from the beating, in addition to my sense of justice at being thrown into a dungeon for helping the bastard. "Come on, Prefect, we both know he has no chance of stopping Silanus alone. I want to help!"

Aper glanced behind me at my cohort, his eyes narrowing. "He's afraid you're in league with Silanus."

"No, he's afraid I'll become more popular than him."

Aper scanned the cheering crowd. "A fear that seems warranted, Natta Magus."

I stepped forward, closing to within a pace of him. He was shorter than me, but since he stood on the first step, our eyes met at equal height. "You know me, Prefect," I said quietly. "Now I'm guessing you're going to let me help since you would've stopped me by now if you weren't."

His blank face cracked a bit, and he gave me a sad smile. "I trust you, Natta Magus. And I take no joy in what we did last night. But, yes, if I had been ordered to do so, I would've stopped you again. I respect you too much to give you anything less than the truth." He then turned and said, "Follow me." He strode up the marble steps toward Augustus.

*So I can trust Aper,* I thought as I followed him up the steps. *Trust him to do whatever Augustus tells him to do...*

The crowds seemed to cheer all the louder as I ascended the steps toward Augustus and the gathered senators. The Princeps watched me with the same cool face, so I had to glance at Capito to get a feel for Augustus's real emotions: Capito scowled at me as if I were a wet rat climbing out of the Tiber.

"You are not welcome here, Natta Magus," Capito said once I came within a few paces of them. "Your very presence is a blasphemy to Jupiter and the gods at the exact moment when we need their divine attention the most."

I didn't even look at Capito, but kept my eyes on Augustus. "Princeps, with respect, we have very little time. Let us help you."

"Help?" Capito said. "You're in league with the sorcerer! You were speaking to him at your home just last night! How can we trust that you'll—?"

Augustus put a gentle hand on Capito's arm. Capito immediately shut his mouth and looked at the Princeps, who shook his head slowly.

"It doesn't matter whether or not he was in league with Silanus," Augustus said quietly, though I could still hear him over the excited crowd behind me. "None of it matters now."

"Augustus," Capito said, "please reconsider. We cannot give in to the whims of this magus. How do we know he will—"

I couldn't take Capito's accusations any longer. "Hey, buddy, I saved your *caccing* family's lives! You saw me fight Silanus in the Circus! Why can't you trust me now when I say I want to help?"

Capito glared at me with murder in his eyes, but it was Augustus's hand on his advisor's arm that I think kept him from lunging at me. I get it, this was a stressful situation, but damnation, I was getting really sick of everyone thinking I was the bad guy here.

"Natta Magus," Augustus said, "Capito was not referring to you. He was referring to Silanus."

I stared at the Princeps for several moments and then felt my mouth fall open. "You're going to *surrender* to him?"

Augustus's blank face sagged, and he suddenly looked like the old man he was: heavy wrinkles, dark patches around the eyes, pale skin. "We consulted the Sibylline Books all night and most of the day. Your friend Paetus was most helpful in that regard. My flamens took the auspices and read the omens and performed every divination ritual under the law. Everything pointed to one simple fact: Any attempt to fight Silanus will result in Rome's destruction. But under his rule, Rome will survive."

I just stared at Augustus in shocked confusion. It had never entered my wildest dreams that he would simply give up. History said that Caesar Augustus was the strongest willed emperor that Rome ever had. He was the last guy that I figured would surrender the republic to another man. I didn't know what kind of cockamamie rituals his flamens performed, or what they saw in some raven's entrails, but the idea that Silanus would rule Rome with benevolence was ludicrous.

Augustus looked out over the hopeful crowd, his eyes glistening. "I love Rome. I've spent my life serving her and making her great. But sorcery and monsters...I cannot fight these things and hope to win. As you've ably demonstrated, Natta Magus, by your simple presence here and not the Tullianum."

I opened my mouth to protest, but Helva beat me to it.

"Respectfully, Princeps, you are making a terrible mistake," she said, stepping forward. Capito gave her the same wet rat scowl he'd given me, but Augustus merely shifted his tired eyes to her. "Silanus does not want to rule Rome. He wants to destroy it. Surrendering to him now will only make it easier for him to do so. I know the hatred for Rome that burns in his heart, for it is the same hatred that burns in mine. He will *not* let Rome survive."

Augustus sighed and said, "What would you have me do, young lady? We barely have three cohorts of Praetorians in the city. Judging by what we saw in the Circus Maximus, I doubt they would be enough to stop the monsters Silanus would unleash upon us. And with all respect to your skills, can you really stop an army of monsters directed by a goddess?"

"We're ready to try," I said, glancing at my cohort of magi. All five of them looked fearful, but also resolute.  Even Decius struck a bold posture, though I was sure that desire for wine was killing him. "We're still ready."

"We?" Augustus said, his eyes narrowing as he glanced at my cohort.

"Yeah," I said. "Contrary to my own marketing, turns out I'm *not* the only practicing magus in Rome."

Capito issued a small groan, but a fresh calculating look took over Augustus's eyes and his face returned to that same blank expression he'd had moments before.

"Are they as powerful as you?" He gave them the same assessing stare that I imagined a *dominus* giving a slave in the Forum. Made me feel a bit creepy for them.

"Not yet," I said. "But they are willing to fight for Rome as *free* citizens." I gave the two slaves, Hughard and Eudo, pointed looks. They both looked even paler than Paetus at being in the presence of Augustus, and their gazes were directed at the ground in proper slave fashion. Augustus glanced at them, seemed to understand my terms, and nodded.

"Yes," he said, "free citizens."

Hughard and Eudo took deep breaths, and eagerness replaced their fear.

Augustus turned his shrewd eyes to me and asked, "*If* I were to allow your help, what form would it take, Natta Magus?"

I glanced at Paetus. He still clutched the same satchel in which I'd placed the Sibylline Books, and I saw the tips of the three scroll cases poking out of it.

I then scanned the murmuring, excited crowd. I saw hope in their eyes as they looked up at me. And a lot of belief.

I gave Augustus what I hoped was a confident grin. "How about the form of our own god?"

# FIFTY-FOUR

I 'd been so busy for the last day and a half that I hadn't had time to grieve Lares'...dissolution...or moving on...or whatever happened to house spirits who left the mortal plane. Her loss hit me as I quickly looked over the Sibylline Books with Paetus and tried remembering what Lares told me about channeling belief magic.

But it really hit me after we had found the relevant passages to cast our spells and were standing on the temples steps watching the sun go down. I knew it would be worse later, alone in my shop, when her statue didn't light up as she called me some dessert.

Assuming, of course, that I lived out the night.

I hate waiting because that's when I think about these things.

Augustus, Capito, Aper, and various Roman senators stood a few paces from me on my left, murmuring to each other and casting furtive glances between me and the setting sun. The Princeps continued to look as if all was proceeding according to his plans. I wondered whether he actually felt that or if he was the greatest actor of all time. If the latter, he was playing his part well.

I glanced at my cohort of magi to my right. The rookies stood behind several senators, and though I couldn't see it, I knew they were holding hands. But I could definitely see their faces: They all had the same contentment and ecstasy that came with siphoning cell magic. They all had a unique aura flitting about them as they concentrated on their spell. None of them had had any trouble siphoning their magic in the way that I briefly taught them. While they had seemed ready for combat, I still felt like a general in the moments before battle who wondered whether his draftees would fight or flee.

Helva stood two paces from me, staring at the setting sun with a thoughtful expression, her left hand idly twirling the black palla she wore over her left shoulder. The sunlight made her smooth, bronze skin practically glow and created shadows that accentuated her high cheekbones and parted lips. At that moment I could see the feminine strength and elegance that Renaissance painters hundreds of years from now would struggle to capture on their canvases. Yeah, she was beautiful.

Which only brought a pang of guilt that I was somehow cheating on Brianna for thinking that of Helva. And then another pang of guilt that if Helva's feelings for me were true, that I could never really be with her while I still loved a woman from the future. Why I sought to add further complexity to an already complex life is beyond me.

Which is why I hate waiting.

Her brown eyes suddenly turned to me. I was a little startled that she'd caught me staring, but I didn't turn away. She held my gaze, her face softening and a little smile creating a dimple in her right cheek.  Damnation, now *that* was a smile that could launch a thousand ships.

Then the smile evaporated and her face turned to a stony mask.

"He's coming," she said.

My heart skipped a beat. *Here we go.*

A blue point of light appeared on the steps of the temple and then expanded into a blue-rimmed oval about my height. Through the gate I could see the same torchlit tomb we had entered in the Egyptian underworld. Standing in front of the gate was Silanus dressed in the same exact purple and gold toga as Augustus. When he stepped through the gate and onto the temple steps, I gave Helva a quick glance.

She shook her head, and then I turned to shake my head at Aper. He frowned and nodded. Helva had seen an earth magic shield surrounding Silanus.

So much for the easy arrow take down.

Silanus strode toward Augustus wearing a confident smile. His face was freshly shaved, his short black hair shined with styling oil, and his purple and gold toga was expertly arranged. I caught a whiff of irises from the perfume he wore. He didn't even look at me or Helva as he passed us by, but he did murmur, "Try cutting me off now, sister."

Helva clenched her teeth, but said nothing. Based on her reaction, I gathered she was unable to cut him off from his earth magic the same way she had in the tomb when he was half-asleep. There goes Plan B.

He stopped in front of Augustus and his Roman dignitaries. Silanus looked Augustus up and down, glanced at his own toga, and said with a smile, "Well, isn't this awkward."

"We have followed your instructions, magus," Augustus said. "We are prepared to hail you as king. On one condition."

"There are no conditions," Silanus said.

Augustus glared at Silanus. "On one condition. That you swear to uphold the laws of Rome and honor her gods."

Silanus snorted. He reached into his toga, pulled out a small item, and held it in his palm.

"Natta Magus," Silanus said, without looking at me. "Can you tell Octavius what I hold in my hand."

I hated doing anything that Silanus ordered, but at this point, I really needed to pick my battles.

"A chess piece," I said. "A king."

"Exactly," Silanus said. "And what do kings do?"

"Uphold the laws and honor their nation's gods."

Silanus gave me a sideways glance and chuckled. "Maybe in your time. But here, in this time, they *are* the law and they *are* gods."

Silanus closed his fist around the king piece while his left hand opened up at his side with the palm faced down. He was blocking his aura from me, but I didn't need to see it to know he was casting earth magic.

A misty red aura appeared around Aper and then most of the senators behind him. I looked out onto the crowd and saw red auras appearing around nearly a quarter of the people present—men, women, and even a some children.

"Would you look at that?" Silanus said, waving the fist in which he held the king piece to the crowd. "There are a lot of firstborn Romans here tonight." His face became a mask of rage that made me want to take a step back. Augustus, to his credit, stood his ground. "This is checkmate, Octavius; there are no conditions. I will rule the way I want to because *I* will be the god here. If I see a house I want, I will take it. If I see women I want, I will take them. If a temple offends me, I will tear it down. I am going to take all the gold in your treasury, melt it down into a statue of me, and mount it on these very steps. And you will be at my side watching it all, your body enthralled and your mind lucid, as I *rape* Rome."

Shocked murmurs began to rumble through the crowd as they noticed the red glows surrounding each other. Some of the people closest to us, who could hear Silanus's words, stared at him in horror. I knew we'd have to act soon or we'd lose the crowd's belief.

I turned to Helva on my left and held my hand out to her. She took it in her right, which also held the horsehair braid we'd used in the Circus. She made her left palm face down, muttered some words in Coptic, and—

I knew that belief magic could be very powerful when enough people believed the same thing in the same place at the same time, but it was also very fragile. Based on Paetus's interpretations of the Sibylline Books, we could tap into that power when belief surged through a crowd. But if one thing came along to shake the crowd's belief, all that power would dissipate like smoke in a wind gust.

That was why my rookies and I had used the incantations we learned from the books—along with the Energy arcanum that my parents crammed into me years ago—to draw in that belief power and store it in our cells until we needed it at this very moment. Each one of us had become a magical battery humming with belief energy.

But I had no idea exactly how powerful belief magic could be until I felt it surge out of me.

I felt like I was trying to stand in the middle of a hurricane eye wall. I could barely hear anything as the magic filled my ears with a roar that not even a hurricane could produce. I shut my eyes tight, but even then I felt blinded by the magical white light before them. Despite the pain, I even threw in a healthy dose of my own cell magic.

It took Helva a precious moment to gain control of the belief power that I was sending her through our link. With a guttural scream, she released her earth magic spell that was multiplied by a hundred from the belief magic and my own cell magic. I couldn't see the earth magic she cast at Silanus, but I felt it pull in all my stored up belief.

During that precious moment when Helva threw everything she had at Silanus, her brother turned to her wide-eyed, obviously sensing the growing power she was about to unleash. And in that same precious moment, when her earth spell was supposed to slam through Silanus's defenses and cut off his access to earth magic, Silanus held the king piece out to her.

And damnation, he actually *smiled*.

I couldn't see any colors to the earth magic, but I did see distortions in the air around the king like heat waves off metal on a hot, sunny day. The distortions swirled around the king, faster by the moment, until they became so fast that I could actually see the king glow with magically powered red light. The distortions suddenly stopped, but the king in Silanus's hand continued to pulsate with a red glow that matched the glow surrounding the first born in the crowds.

I stared at Silanus. Helva stared at Silanus. Everyone seemed to be staring at Silanus. But he stared directly at me.

"And that would be checkmate for you, too, Natta Magus."

He calmly placed the king piece on the marble steps in front of him and said some Coptic words. A tremendous burst of magical energy exploded from the piece, knocking me and most of the people within a twenty pace radius backward several steps. A black and red cloud began swirling around the spot, growing bigger and taller until it rose to the height of the red-tiled roof of the Temple of Jupiter Optimus Maximus. The tornado's height stabilized at the top of the temple, and then it coalesced into a human form.

Invidia took shape on the steps of Jupiter's temple. Though her form retained black and red hues, she wore a thin stolla over a lean and wasted body. Her neck and back were hunched. She squinted at the people around her. Her mouth was open in an angry snarl, where many teeth were missing; those that were still there were jagged. She looked as if she were about to take a step toward the suddenly screaming crowd, but then she stopped.

Aper came out of nowhere and thrust his gladius toward Silanus. The sword deflected off Silanus's skin as if he were a marble wall. Arrows came at Silanus from various directions, but they too shattered upon his magically shielded body. Silanus didn't even blink or seem to know they were there.

I couldn't find Augustus anywhere. All the senators that had once filled the portico were fleeing into the temple behind them. I couldn't fault them for running, for what could a bunch of unarmed old men do against an angry goddess?

"You are enthralled to me, Invidia," Silanus cried out. "I have created an army for you. You will direct them to kill all of Rome's firstborn. Obey me, revenge goddess!"

Invidia snarled in an incomprehensible language and shook her head in jerky, unnatural motions as she fought Silanus's enthrallment. But his spell—magnified by the belief magic that Helva and I had just helpfully given him—was too powerful for her to overcome. She stopped struggling after several moments and then looked down at the crowd of panicked Romans before her.

More screams erupted from the crowd, not just from seeing a goddess come to life, but also from the Dea Tacita daemons that were now leaping down from the temple's red-tiled roof. I scanned the buildings surrounding the crowd and, to my horror, saw more Dea Tacitas leaping down from the rooftops. Their pale, naked bodies landed silently on the brick streets with barely a bent knee from the impact of a two or three story drop.

*Damnation, the rooftops!* No wonder Vitulus hadn't found any bishops lying around the Capitoline. They were all on the roofs where only construction workers or magi with gates could go.

When the daemons charged toward the crowd, the Praetorian and *vigile* cohorts stationed throughout the area leaped into action, forming up small units of about five men that covered each other with their shields. The daemons tried to get around the soldiers and at anyone with a red glow. But the soldiers were able to hold many of the daemons back while the crowd streamed toward one of the main streets that led off the Capitoline. I prayed there wasn't a daemon ambush awaiting them.

One daemon landed in front of me. Its milky white eyes studied me a moment, and then it turned away as if I were no threat at all. I was an only child and technically a firstborn, but apparently I wasn't Roman enough. But I felt its succubus aura, which only dialed up my supreme frustration and anger at this turn of events.

*Don't think I'm a threat, eh?* I quickly drew my enchanted gladius and lopped off the daemon's head. Its head and body turned into yellow-white pus before they hit the ground. The pus sizzled and boiled before evaporating into the air.

I turned around and found Helva staring in dismay at the chaos her brother had created. Behind her stood my cohort of magi, still holding hands, but each was pale, wide-eyed, and sweating.

But they hadn't run. By the Unknowable Will, they hadn't run. They were ordinary Romans given an extraordinary power *just today*, and they were choosing to stand and fight a nightmarish enemy. I was never so proud of anyone. *We can still survive this.*

"All right, team," I yelled over the din of battle, "time for Plan C."

# FIFTY-FIVE

S ilanus had been ready for us. Somehow he'd found out we would use belief magic on him, so he had enchanted the king piece to draw it all in and manifest his revenge goddess to direct his army of Dea Tacitas. But how? We'd only come up with the idea today with Paetus's translation help...

Or had this been his plan all along?

Things began clicking into place. He knew he needed the magic of belief and hope detailed in the Sibylline Books to enthrall Invidia, and he knew he'd never be able to generate it on his own. He could've gotten the same basic knowledge on the books from any house spirit like I had—I'm sure William taught him how talk to them. So he'd made a huge deal out of stealing the books, making me desperate to retrieve them because he knew I'd assume they contained knowledge on how to stop him. He set up the Circus massacre, knowing that I'd try to save the day in a very public place...and knowing that my fame would spread belief and hope throughout Rome. When I inevitably stole the books back from him and tried using the belief magic on him, he'd be there with his enchanted king piece to steal it.

Gods above and below. The bastard *was* a chess master.

But even chess masters can't anticipate *everything*.

Enter Plan C. It was Plan C for a reason because its chances for success were equal to its chances of killing us all and leveling Rome. It was the plan we would implement if Plan A—the quick arrow take down—and Plan B—cutting Silanus off from his earth magic—didn't work. It was crazy, but it was all we had left.

Helva rushed over to the rookies and took Decius's hand to begin their own summoning spell.

I turned back toward Silanus and wondered how I was going to get by Invidia to attack him. Fortunately it seemed like they were both heavily preoccupied at the moment: Invidia was squinting at the rapidly fleeing crowd and directing the Dea Tacitas to attack all the red glowing firstborns, while Silanus was staring intently at Invidia with bared, clenched teeth. Apparently enthralling a goddess was hard work.

I ran around Invidia's red and black spindly legs, up the steps of the temple, around a large painted column, and toward Silanus's back. I raised my enchanted sword, praying my magical enhancements would do more than Aper's gladius or Roman arrows. I briefly regretted not keeping my promise to Helva to spare Silanus, but I'd rather feel that regret than the regret of letting him kill thousands.

My sword clanged off Silanus's head same as Aper's.

I struck at him again and again with stabbing and cutting swings, but nothing penetrated his shield. I even released my sleeping spell from the tip of the sword, but the magic fizzled when it hit Silanus's barrier.

I had one job—distract Silanus from concentrating on Invidia—and I was failing miserably.

A flash of white light and a crack of thunder split the air behind Invidia. I stepped away from Silanus so that I could see past him and Invidia's legs. The first thing I saw were massive sandaled feet and then golden shin armor with lions carved into it at the knees. Muscular thighs led up to an equally muscular torso and bare chest. The head was that of a late middle-aged man: a long, brown and white beard with curly, brown and white hair held back by a pointed, golden crown. In one hand he held an actual sizzling lightning bolt, and in the other he held a shield that looked like the blazing sun. He was just as tall as Invidia, and his fiery white eyes took in the chaos upon the hill as if he were a father about to reprimand his misbehaving children.

*Cac, they did it. They summoned Jupiter.*

The Capitoline Hill had been the center of Jupiter's worship since before the Republic, so there were hundreds of years of belief stored up here. Now the question was whether Helva's manifestation of Jupiter—essentially the same manifestation Silanus had done with Cacus on the Aventine—would run amok and destroy the hill, or would it perform the duty that everyone who'd ever worshiped in this temple believed it would do.

Silanus snarled something in Coptic, staring at Jupiter in surprised anger. Invidia turned toward Jupiter, her clawed hands bared and snarling her own divine words at the ruler of the Roman gods. Jupiter drew back his muscular arm holding the lightning bolt and flung it at Invidia. She brought up emaciated arms in the form of an X. The lightning bolt blasted into a red and black shield that her crossed arms had created. The bolt pushed her backward several paces, though, forcing me to leap behind a marble column to avoid getting trampled by the goddess. I peeked back around the column. The bolt had not fried Invidia, but it seemed to have stunned her a moment.

Another bolt appeared in Jupiter's hand. His voice boomed something in an archaic form of Latin that I could barely decipher, but I got the gist: *"This is my temple, crone. Back to Hades with you!"*

He flung the lightning bolt at her, and she crossed her arms again to deflect it. The bolt bounced off her shield, but again it pushed her back. This time she tumbled down the steps of the temple and landed with a crash onto the brick street. She dug her clawed hands into the street, tearing through the brick as she did so, and jumped back to her feet with a speed and strength that belied her wasted form.

"Helva, the gate!" I yelled.

Part two of our insane Plan C involved opening a gate to the Egyptian underworld just as Helva had done back in my shop. But this gate had to be huge, big enough to push a goddess through, and that took quite a bit of belief magic. Helva and the magi behind her groaned with the effort: My rookies poured all the belief magic they had stored up in the last hour into Helva. Helva screamed her Coptic words, and then a black, misty oval materialized behind Invidia. The gate seemed to pull at Invidia as if she were a chunk of iron trying to get away from a powerful magnet. The energies of the underworld called to the gods, and Invidia had to struggle to simply stand. All Jupiter had to do was throw another lightning bolt at her and she would fall into the underworld where Helva would seal her off from the mortal plane.

But Invidia growled something in her infernal language and dug her claws into the brick streets to stop the backward pull of the gate. When Jupiter pulled his arm back again to throw another lightning bolt, dozens of Dea Tacita daemons leaped upon him and began clawing and digging at him. Jupiter roared with pain. He dropped his sun shield and began tearing the daemons off him like they were leeches. But as he did so, more and more daemons, abandoning their original orders to kill firstborn Romans, filled the temple steps and swarmed Jupiter. He stabbed at the daemons with a lightning bolt dagger, killing many, but only to have more replace them.

I looked at Silanus. He was sweating and panting as if he were running a long race. The effort to enthrall Invidia must've been straining him to his magical limit. If he tried to cast another spell, he wouldn't have the will to maintain the enthrallment. Damnation, I had to distract him somehow, but nothing could touch him through his shields.

I glanced up at the temple portico where Helva stood with my rookie magi. It was all they could do to feed Jupiter enough belief magic to keep him alive, so they looked as strained to the breaking point as Silanus. Jupiter was now covered in swarming Dea Tacitas, and he tumbled down the temple steps and onto the brick street. He flailed on the ground, rolling over and over as if trying to put out flames on his back. His outraged roars split the air like thunder. He crushed many daemons into yellow-white pus, but more kept arriving to take their place. Once Jupiter was dead, we'd have nothing left to stop Silanus from redirecting Invidia at Rome.

*How was I going to attack a magus who stood behind an impenetrable shield?*

My eye was drawn to the temple steps where Invidia had manifested. The king piece.

*By not attacking* him.

I ran toward the king chess piece still sitting on the steps, a red and black glow surrounding it. I raised my enchanted sword and swung it down at the piece with all my strength.

My sword deflected off the piece and hit the marble steps with a clang that reverberated painfully up my hand and arm. I transferred my sword to my injured right hand and shook out the tingling in my left. I tried kicking the damned piece, but my foot bounced off it as if I'd tried kicking a twenty-first century fire hydrant. I cursed loudly. Of course he'd have enchanted the piece with the same shield.

"Natta Magus!" Helva cried out from the steps above me. She visibly shook with the effort of channeling the magic into Jupiter. She didn't look at me, but she said, "We're losing him!"

Jupiter's struggles were indeed slowing down under the Dea Tacita on-slaught. Invidia fought the pull of the underworld gate, slowly making her way toward the thunder god one step at a time, her claws raised and ready to finish him off. A satisfied grin appeared on Silanus's strained face as he watched Invidia, his enthralled goddess, making ready to dispose of—

*Dispose. Like garbage.*

I barked an insane laugh, and then fumbled for a pouch on my components belt. I pulled out the smooth, white *elementair* pebble and placed it on the step next to the king piece. It would recycle everything within a six-inch radius, but would it recycle an enchanted object? Theoretically, yes...

With the pebble's activation command on my lips, somebody tackled me. I fell onto the marble steps hard. My shoulder screamed with the impact, and I wondered if I had dislocated it. And then Silanus was on my back, straddling me and choking the life out of me with iron fingers around my throat.

"You've lost, Natta Magus," he snarled. "Your god is dead. Invidia will destroy Rome and free the world from their arrogance."

I couldn't breathe, I couldn't move. I reached out for the *elementair*, knowing that all I had to do was say the arcane word that would activate it, but Silanus wouldn't let the air out of my lungs. My shoulder screamed, my lungs screamed, my throat was imploding, and a dark haze was forming in the corners of my eyes.

"Now I will kill you myself," he said, spittle flying from his lips. "My Oath to William be damned. You didn't deserve his respect! I was his son, not you! I served him, did everything he asked of me, and *he still loved you more!*"

"Silanus!" Helva screamed. She stood about ten paces away, giving Silanus a pleading stare. "Don't."

"Would you kill me to save him, sister?" he asked her, his voice cracking. "Do you also love him more than me?"

"I won't kill you, brother," she said. "Release him and stop this madness, and I swear an Oath that I will go with you wherever you go. We will be a family again. Please."

I felt Silanus grip loosen just enough for a trickle of air to enter my throat, but he said nothing for several moments. I slapped my good hand on the marble steps just to remind everyone that I was still choking to death here.

"It's too late to stop this, sister," Silanus said wearily. "Rome must pay for what it did to us."

He wasn't going to stop or let me go. And in that split second before he renewed his chokehold on me, I siphoned my cell magic and gasped, "*Verminderen*!"

A white flash burst from the pebble, and then a semi-circular divot appeared in the marble step as if it had been carved there and smoothed down. More importantly, the king piece was gone.

Silanus stared at the empty divot, his mouth opening and closing in disbelief. Then Invidia cackled a triumphant laugh. She swooped one clawed hand down and picked Silanus up, screaming and kicking. I turned over on my back, gasping for air and grunting at the pain in my shoulder. Invidia held Silanus up to her twisted, ugly face and leered at him with cracked, jagged teeth.

The revenge goddess was free, and she was about to take her revenge on the man who'd enthralled her.

"Silanus!" Helva screamed.

Invidia turned toward the misty, black oval hanging in the air, still holding Silanus like a rag doll, and then leaped through it. If I remembered my mythology, the underworld was the revenge goddess's home. Even after the man had tried to murder thousands of people and almost choked the life out of me, I still shuddered to think of the tortures she would visit on Silanus for enthralling her.

"Helva!" Silanus screamed as he disappeared into the black gate.

I looked up at Helva, and by the horror on her face, I figured she thought the same thing. She looked down at me, and her face turned to a calm resolve.

*Don't you dare,* I wanted to say, but it came out as a choking cough.

"Farewell, Natta Magus," she said. "My Oath to you is fulfilled."

She ran past me, even as I tried to grab her ankles to at least trip her up. But she easily jumped over my feeble attempts and charged into the black gate just as it winked shut with an ear-popping whoosh.

As soon as it did, Jupiter and the Dea Tacitas covering him turned into yellow and white jelly. Without Silanus's will to power the daemons and Helva's will to power Jupiter, they all returned to basic elements and then sizzled as they evaporated.

I scanned the streets in front of the temple. Bloodied bodies lay strewn about from the daemon rampage, soldiers and citizens alike. The *only* thing I could console myself with at that moment was that there weren't as many dead as I had expected.

*Although a fine consolation that will be to their families,* I thought bitterly.

I lay my head back on the marble steps and looked up into the darkening sky. Venus was rising in the east, and I noticed several more stars twinkling around her. I was in so much pain in body and mind that I barely heard the things my rookies said as they gathered around me, holding up my head. I also saw Vitulus in his armor and helmet, dirt and blood covering his face and arms. He knelt down and shouted something at me, but it was like I heard him from under water. All I wanted to do was shut my eyes and forget the pain in my body and the pain of losing another friend.

So I did.

# FIFTY-SIX

A few days later I stood in Augustus's office, or throne room, or whatever a "First Citizen" who was actually a king called his private meeting chambers. They were not as opulent as you'd expect of Rome's ruler: In fact, they were rather modest and workaday—a large room filled with several tables and shelves overflowing with scrolls, books, and clay tablets. The walls were painted in geometric shapes, not the frescoes with people or animals that were popular throughout the empire. It was a windowless room, so several lamps and candles burned throughout the shadowy office, adding to the overall stuffiness brought on by the musty smell of papyrus.

With the help of my rookies—although I couldn't call them "rookies" anymore—my body was healed and as good as new without a scar or pain. Even my burned hand was back to normal.

Too bad they couldn't do anything about my pain over losing Helva.

Augustus stood over one of the scroll-filled tables scanning the scroll containing the report that I'd help write for him. Capito stood to one side, reading the report over Augustus's shoulder. Aper stood silently next to me on my right with a legion-straight back. Paetus stood to my left, holding a cup of wine that Augustus had offered him to calm his ever-present nervousness.

"So the Sibylline Books were a ruse all along," Augustus said quietly. "Meant to force you to tap into this...belief magic."

"But why?" Capito asked.

I suppressed the urge to tell Capito to read the damned report that *he* had told me to write, but I held my tongue. Instead, I said, "Silanus knew he couldn't control Invidia with his own power, so he decided on belief magic. But he also knew he couldn't generate the belief magic he needed on his own, so he played me into using the Sibylline Books to generate it for him. When we used it on the Capitoline, he was ready with his chess piece to redirect it."

"Why the game?" Capito asked. "Why did he hate you so much?"

"He was William Ford's apprentice for a while. He thought that William...didn't appreciate him as much as he did me."

Augustus said nothing as he read my report. It seemed he was letting Capito interrogate me for him.

"Gods," Capito said, shaking his head, "how many mad sorcerers did this William train? Silanus, Helva—"

"Helva wasn't mad," I said quietly, staring at Capito. "She was a hero. She deserves your gratitude."

Capito scowled at me and was about to retort. But he must've seen the growing anger in my eyes. So he kept his mouth shut, though he maintained his scowl.

"Capito makes a valid point," Augustus said, his eyes still scanning my report. "How many did he train? When will we have to contend with the next one?" He finally looked up at me. "And to whom is *your* cohort loyal, Natta Magus?"

I laughed for what felt like the first time in days, but it was not genuine mirth. "No, I am not building my own magus army, if that's what you're asking. Decius and Lucia just want to go back to their old lives and never want to use magic again. Eudo wants to go back to Greece and Hughard is already on his way back to Germania Superior. Cana is the only one who wants to learn more, but her magic is so weak that I doubt she'd ever be able to cast more than a spark globe. Hell, all five of them are that way. It's going to take generations before this world regularly produces cell magi at my level."

"It produced Silanus and Helva," Augustus said.

I nodded slowly. "They are...different. They power their magic by tapping into the world's geomagnetic forces. We didn't have them in my time or even any historical evidence of their existence. I don't know how common they are." I glanced at Aper out of the corner of my eye. "Say, you're not going to arrest me again, are you?"

Paetus was taking a drink from his cup when I said that; he began coughing loudly. He set his cup down on a nearby table, coughed a few times more, and then said, "My apologies."

Once Paetus had calmed down, Augustus put both hands on his table and regarded me with that unreadable expression. "Gentlemen, I would speak with Natta Magus alone."

Capito's scowl deepened, if that were possible, but he nodded once and then walked toward the door. Paetus almost beat him to it. Aper paused, glanced between me and Augustus with that same damned unreadable face, and then left the room.

Augustus continued to stare at me with his hands on the table. "What am I to do with you, Natta Magus?"

"Let me walk out of here and live my life?"

A smile actually cracked his mask, which should've relaxed me. Instead, it sent a chill down my back.

"If only it were that easy," he said. "I still don't trust you, but I'm not going to arrest you. What would be the point? I could certainly let you walk out of here and then have my best archers shoot you full of arrows. But killing you wouldn't serve my purposes either. You're too famous now and would only become a martyr. Or worse, make it look like I had something to fear from you." He clasped his hands behind his back. "There's always the standard rumor campaign which I've used to great effect to destroy reputations in the past. But you're too valuable of an asset to ruin that way. And it doesn't feel...sporting. You did, after all, save Rome twice."

"There is that," I agreed.

"Yet you cannot simply 'live your life' anymore. You cannot walk the streets of Rome, wearing that cap, and not be recognized by everyone. And word of your deeds is already spreading throughout the known world with every ship that leaves a Roman port. Soon all of Rome's enemies will send agents here to either recruit you or kill you."

I knew there was a reason why Augustus's smile had sent a chill down my back. Damnation, everything he said was true. There wasn't anywhere in Rome I could go now without someone recognizing me simply based on my height, never mind my Wolverines ball cap. How would I be able to sleep in my shop again wondering if the next time I walked out the door some Praetorian—or Germanic, or Parthian, or Judean, etc.—assassin wasn't lurking in the shadows.

Augustus walked from around the table and stood in front of me, his face back to that unreadable mask.

"When we first met you told me that you served 'a future where humanity lives forever'. A noble sentiment, which judging by your recent actions, includes saving as many human lives as possible." Augustus exhaled slowly. "Romans love their republican institutions and history...but they *want* a strong hand to lead them, even though they speak of liberty. The gods have chosen *me* to be that strong hand. I cannot allow you to compete with me for the respect of the Roman people, for that breeds doubt in me. And as recent decades have shown, doubt in Roman leadership breeds civil war. I don't care how deserving you are, Natta Magus, but your freedom is not worth that many lives."

Damnation, he knew exactly where to hit me. I licked my lips and said, "What do you suggest?"

"The way I see it, you have only one option." He reached up and put his hands on my shoulders. The gesture was so sudden that I flinched. "I will adopt you as my son and make you my sole heir."

I don't remember much in the moments after his offer, for the world seemed to swirl and turn into a white haze. But I imagine my face took on the expression of someone who'd just been sentenced to a gruesome, torturous execution. I think I choked a bit, too, and probably made some noises that might have resembled words.

Augustus chuckled. "It is overwhelming for me, too, at times, but you get used to it. And you will find strength and skills you never knew you possessed. Now I must inform Tiberius of this development, so please hold off telling anyone until I get a courier to him on Rhodes. I doubt he'll be too upset, though, since he didn't have the stomach for politics anyway—"

"I can't do it."

Augustus wasn't used to being told no, so I kind of feared what his reaction would be. He still wore a shadow of his previous smile, but his eyes narrowed. "This is a great honor I am giving to you."

"I know that, and I appreciate it. Really. But...I can't rule an empire."

"I will teach you."

I shook my head. "I'm sure you could. But what I'm saying is that it wouldn't be *right*. Silanus saw himself as a god whose rightful place was to rule empires simply because he had magic. Well I believe that having magic makes me no better or dangerous than any other person. What matters is what I do with it. And to be honest, I have even less stomach for politics than Tiberius."

Augustus frowned. "You don't seem to understand that your life is over, Natta Magus. Your fame will not allow you to go back to your humble shop on the Aventine. This is the only way."

I heard the implied threat in his words, which only solidified the decision I had made over the last few days.

"No," I said, "there's another."

"Exile!" Vitulus growled. He stood in the front room of my Aventine shop with his fists on his hips. It was the middle of the night, so I had a couple of candles burning on the table. The yellow light created shadows on his face that made him look all the more angry.

I had packed the last of the spell components I planned to take with me. I'd have to leave most of them behind, which gave me a twinge of regret. But Augustus had given me enough money to not only travel comfortably, but replenish my components whenever I needed them. His gift—or bribe?—was generous for a traveler...though not generous enough for me to potentially raise my own army to come back to Rome. I still shook my head at that; I'd turned down his offer of "co-Princeps" and yet he still thought I might come back to take it all for myself someday. I supposed you didn't get to Augustus's position without a healthy dose of irrational paranoia.

"It's not exile," I said, stuffing components into my satchel. "It was my idea."

"But once again you saved Rome from annihilation," Vitulus said, his face growing red with anger. "You should be given triumphs, not run out of the city." He stared at me grimly. "You *should* be Caesar."

"Come on, Vitulus. Can you see me as a Caesar?"

He stared at me for several moments and then barked a laugh. He sat down slowly at the table, wincing from the wounds he'd sustained during his battles with the Dea Tacitas on the Capitoline. "It would've been entertaining see Capito have to grovel before you."

I grinned. "Yeah, that would've been fun." I put my components bag down on the table and sat down across from him, just as I had when we had met two years ago. "Augustus is right. I can't stay in Rome. Sooner or later some-one—whether Roman or one of Rome's enemies—will get it into their head that I'm too dangerous to let live. I don't want to look over my shoulder every time I leave my shop."

"You could hire bodyguards," Vitulus said quietly. "You could move into a larger, more secure home."

"And do what, sit in that secure home all day surrounded by bodyguards? Because I would no longer be able to walk the streets a free man and use my magic to help people like I used to. Augustus would constantly wonder if I'm trying to usurp his legitimacy or something. You might as well throw me back in the Tullianum. It's better that I become just another anonymous traveler on the famous Roman highways."

Vitulus raised an eyebrow. "Anonymous? You're a foot taller than everyone and you wear a cap from the future."

"Yeah," I conceded. "Not much I can do about my height, but I'll have to think of something for my cap." After two years in the ancient world, my originally black Wolverines baseball cap was now more of a gray-brown and fraying on the bill. In my home time I would've replaced it long ago with another enchanted cap, but my options were pretty limited here. Enchanting a focus item was something I didn't know much about. I supposed that was one more thing I needed to figure out.

He nodded slowly. "Where will you go?"

"Egypt," I said quietly. "If Silanus or Helva survived Invidia pulling them into the underworld, then they might have escaped through the Ptolemy tombs." Vitulus looked up at me with narrow eyes, so I said, "Yeah, it's a long shot, but I've got nothing better to do. I'm just really sick of people sacrificing themselves for my so-called destiny. Lares, Helva, Brianna. Hell, even William sacrificed himself in his own twisted, mad way. If there's anything I can do to help Helva, or even Silanus, then I have to try."

"To fulfill your destiny?" Vitulus asked.

I shrugged. "I don't know. I've been so obsessed with figuring out what my 'destiny' is over the last year. But maybe it's not something I have to figure out. Maybe it just happens while I live my life."

He stared into his hands. "I could go with you—"

"No," I said firmly, "don't even think about it. Your duty is here, to your family and your country." I softened my voice a bit and said, "But I appreciate the offer. Tell Claudia and little Lucius that I will miss them terribly. The three of you are family to me and always will be." My voice only cracked a little bit.

I was saved from a complete breakdown by a soft knocking at my door.

"Besides," I said, standing up, "I have a couple of tagalongs to keep me company."

I opened the door to find Cana and Paetus loaded down with their backpacks and satchels. Paetus was thin-lipped, but looked more resolved than I'd ever seen him. He'd begged me to come along so that he could chronicle my travels, though I suspected he really wanted to get out of town since he was afraid Augustus might suspect he helped me escape the Tullianum. And Cana was more eager to learn magic and test her skills than any student I'd met in my old university job in Detroit. She was going to learn with or without me, so I figured she'd be less dangerous to the world if I taught her the right way to do things.

I'd been all prepared to travel on my own. But truthfully, I was glad for the company.

Paetus hurried inside while Cana studied my doorframe. "No wonder all the crowds are gone today," she said. "You increased the power of your turning wards. I can't wait to do that."

"Very good, *leerling*," I said, using the same Dutch word for "apprentice" that William once called me. "Anyone who knocks on my door, without first using the key spell I taught you, now gets about a block away before they realize they were turned back. It's only temporary, though, and it'll dissipate in a few days. That would be a nasty surprise for the new tenants. Paetus, you don't have to write down every word I say..."

Paetus had taken out a clay tablet and was furiously scribbling down my words into the soft clay with a bone stylus. "This is history, Natta Magus, and I mean to record it all. Perhaps your future, Detroit self will one day read about your own past adventures, and I will be the author who transcribed them. I could be another Homer!"

I didn't want to get into a discussion about how that was impossible due to alternate and divergent timelines—or the fact that I'd been keeping my *own* journals for the last two years—so I just smiled and nodded. I would do that a lot with him in the months ahead.

I picked up my satchels and glanced around my shop one last time. I was leaving a lot behind, and I'd already told Tanith and Balnor they could take whatever they wanted before the shop's owner threw everything away. My gaze stopped on the statue of Lares next to the door. Her hazy glow was gone, but I picked up the cherubic statue anyway and shoved it into one of my satchels.

I then looked at my team and said, "Ready?"

Cana and Paetus nodded eagerly, while Vitulus stared at the floor with a grim face and clenched teeth. I led the way out the door and up the steps to the dark street in front of my shop.

I stopped in the darkness, turned, and gave a surprised Vitulus an enveloping embrace. He sighed and returned the embrace.

"Farewell, buddy," I said.

"Farewell, Natta Magus. You will be in our prayers."

"Thanks." I hugged him a few moments longer before breaking away.

I turned to Cana and Paetus, and said, "Let's go see the world." Then I began striding down the alley as they fell in beside me.

I had no idea what lay down the path ahead of me, but I was determined to be the man that all my lost friends thought I was. My destiny would just have to catch up.

*Read WOUNDED MAGUS, book three in the Journals of Natta Magus series.*

# AFTERWORD

Thanks for giving *Shadow Magus* a read. If you enjoyed it and have the time, please leave a review, I'd appreciate it.

If you're ready for more adventures in the Journals of Natta Magus, continue with the next novel *Wounded Magus*.

Check my website (https://robsteinerauthor.com) for a full list of my novels.

If you'd like a quick note when I release something new, please sign up for my newsletter on my website. For social media fans, you can find me on Twitter, Facebook, Goodreads, and BookBub.

# Acknowledgments

Many thanks to Edmund R. Schubert at *Orson Scott Card's Intergalactic Medicine Show*. He got this book rolling when he bought two Natta Magus short stories, which convinced me this character might just carry a novel.

Thanks to the two guys whom I consider my core publishing team: David Drazul and Tom Edwards. David for his nit-pickin' editing (and I mean that in the best possible way) and Tom for another outstanding cover.

And as always, thank you Sarah and Amelia for your support, encouragement, and big hugs on the rough days.

# PRAISE FOR *THE CHOSEN QUEEN*

"Arthurian legend has long been a deep well from which myriad retellings have been drawn. Davey's first entry in her Pendragon Prophecies series adds to this body by centering Igraine, Arthur's mother . . . The focus on the roles of women—Igraine and her sister Elaine, Lady of the Lake, Vivian—and the futures promised by Igraine's daughters Morgan and Morgause—may remind Arthurian fans of Marion Zimmer Bradley's Mists of Avalon, though the world here is more grounded in its detail and interpersonal relationships. A great opening chapter for a series providing a refreshing twist on a classic story."

*—Booklist*

"Attending to gaps in the Arthurian legends with care, Sam Davey's captivating fantasy novel *The Chosen Queen* delves into the dangerous web of politics, religion, and magic that led to the birth of King Arthur . . . Elegant and intricate, the novel fills a recent void for feminist fantasy audiences, fleshing out Igraine beyond her traditional role as a mere vessel for Arthur's birth and refreshing the timeless atmosphere of Tintagel with everyday details . . . The compelling historical fantasy novel *The Chosen Queen* breathes life into an overlooked figure of Arthurian legend, giving her dimension and personality."

*—Foreword Reviews*

"[A] welcome and refreshing retelling of the story of Igraine, mother of King Arthur, in her own voice . . . Complex characters who engage in behavior that is sometimes honorable and sometimes atrocious for many different reasons, and a swift unfolding of events that could be viewed as either inevitable or purposeful, drive this powerful story forward. Highly recommended for all Arthuriana fans wishing to explore or newly imagine the prequel days to the ascendancy of King Arthur through the compelling voice of one remarkable woman."

**—The Historical Novel Society**

"The pain and strength of Igraine, Duchess of Cornwall and mother of the legendary King Arthur, shines vividly in these pages. Her richly drawn character is entirely relatable—across more than a thousand years. Hers is a story of a woman rising to stark challenges and refusing to be a puppet to others. It is a story heartbreakingly relevant to the present . . . a story that deserves to be told and is, masterfully, in *The Chosen Queen*."

**—Sophie Perinot, author of *Medici's Daughter* and co-author of *Ribbons of Scarlet***

"In the tradition of Marion Zimmer Bradley, Sam Davey brings to life the tale of King Arthur's conception from a female perspective. Igraine, a character previously little acknowledged, emerges as the titular 'Chosen Queen,' determined not to become a pawn in the political machinations of the Lady of the Lake, Merlin, and Uther Pendragon."

**—Judith G. Benz, PhD, teaching professor of German and University of Notre Dame's Medieval Institute Fellow**